Gladly BEYOND

A BROTHERS *MALEDETTI* ROMANCE

NICHOLE VAN

Fiorenza Publishing

Gladly Beyond © 2016 by Nichole Van Valkenburgh
Cover design © Nichole Van Valkenburgh
Interior design © Nichole Van Valkenburgh

Published by Fiorenza Publishing
Print Edition v1.0

ISBN: 978-0-9968936-0-2

In memory of the original Clare,
for late-night fingernail painting and cans of Dr. Pepper.
I was so blessed to have a *nonna* like you.

And to Dave,
for carrying my fear on your *own* back
and holding my hand through the dark.

THE BATTLE OF CASCINA—BASTIANO DA SANGALLO (COPIED FROM THE ORIGINAL CARTOON BY MICHELANGELO BUONAROTTI)

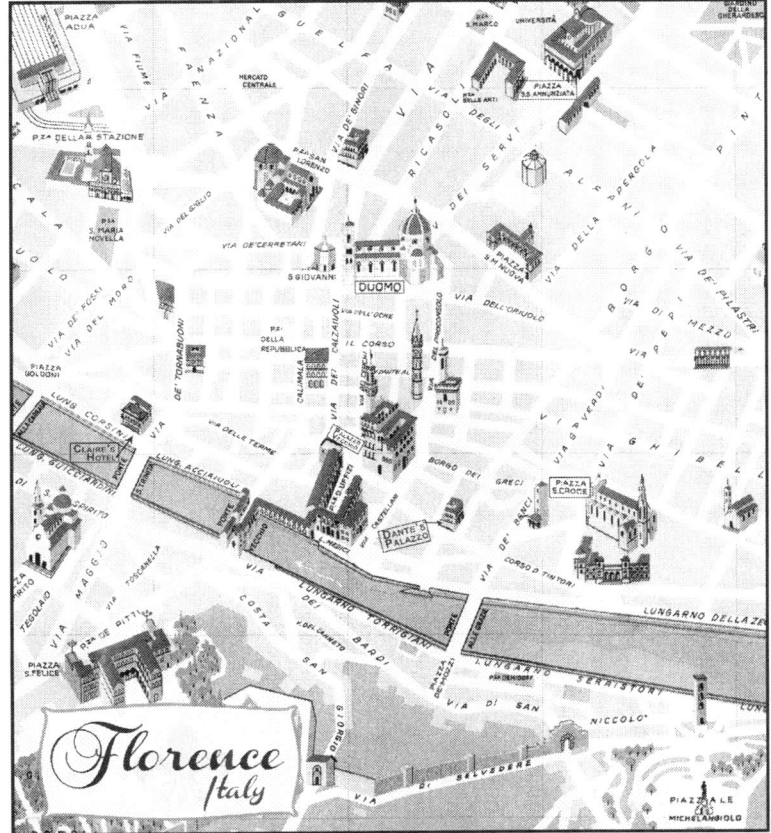

somewhere i have never travelled,gladly beyond
any experience,your eyes have their silence:

—*e. e. cummings*

How like a winter hath my absence been from thee . . .
What freezings have I felt, what dark days seen . . .

—*William Shakespeare*

PROLOGUE

When the gods wish to punish us, they answer our prayers.
—OSCAR WILDE—

History would call him *il Conte del Maldetto*—the Damned Earl.
His descendants would call him 'that damned idiot.'

For his part, Giovanni D'Angelo simply called himself desperate:

Desperate to preserve his family.

Desperate to win at any cost.

Desperate enough to seek a forbidden solution.

On a dark moonless night in 1294 A.D., Giovanni slipped through the eastern gate of San Gimignano, past the gurgling *fonti* and into the woods beyond. Silently making his way to the camp of the *zingari*—the gypsies.

Giovanni begged the old gypsy woman—*la zingara*—to grant his request: the gift of Sight. To see, hear, feel what had been . . . what would come. An unholy boon from her pagan gods.

"Knowledge. It is double-edged." The *zingara* tried to explain in her broken Italian, firelight skimming her face. "You are sure?"

"*Sì.*" He nodded, eager and bright-eyed.

Giovanni did not understand her words. Not then.

The wrinkled *zingara* took her payment and performed the required ritual. Made the necessary sacrifice. Bestowed her gift on Giovanni and his heirs . . . forever.

Giovanni was reborn. Like birds on the wind, whisperings reached his ears. Tales of what his enemies had done, fleeting glimpses of the future.

With his newfound talents, Giovanni saved his family, outmaneuvered his opponents, crushed his rivals.

But all too soon, whispering evolved into vivid immersion. Giovanni constantly pivoted round, tracking invisible things—the past and future swirling about him.

The voices destroyed him in the end.

Not the sights nor the feelings.

No.

It was the never-ending noise.

Giovanni threw himself off the church bell tower at the age of forty-one. Raving mad.

Twenty-five years later, his son was found swinging from the southern city gate, foam and blood dripping from his mouth.

A generation after that, his grandson strapped himself to the front of a newly-invented cannon and lit the fuse.

And so it went. Relentless.

The gift passed from first-born son to first-born son. Each D'Angelo heir dying, usually by his own hand, before his thirty-fifth year. The gypsy's gift splintering the mind.

The family tried to remove the gift from their bloodline, but later *zingari* knew nothing of the original power used—the secret lost to history.

It continued for seven hundred years. Until a more modern age arrived.

Another first-born D'Angelo sired a child.

But in the very instant of conception—that breathless moment when life combines and sparks anew—the unforeseen happened.

Life infused . . . not once.

But twice.

And then . . . split in half again.

Fracturing. Shattering.

Forever altering what had been.

CLAIRE RAYTHORN

I've always thought Italian cities are like guys I knew in college:

Rome—the hot frat boy I was dying to go out with (and I did, and it was awesome). But, turns out, *everyone* dated Rome.

Naples—Rome's frat house roommate. The guy on no sleep and his tenth can of Red Bull. No one messed with him cause he knew people who knew people . . . catch my drift . . .

Venice—the dreamily gorgeous philosophy major. Brilliantly eccentric but exotic enough that no one quite knew what to make of him.

Milan—the second-year MBA student who was big on power-ties and power-lunches. Basically, the organized guy who held everyone else together.

And then there was Florence.

Firenze, to those who knew him.

Quiet and unassuming. When we first met, I wondered what all the fuss was about.

But Firenze . . . he was a subtle seducer. If I asked, he could talk for hours about art and history. But, generally, Firenze simply listened. Peaceful. Steady. Ready to shoulder my sorrows.

Firenze is the guy I never got out of my system.

Truth.

I took a sip of my hotel coffee and studied the huge Piazza della Signoria around me.

Classic Firenze.

Stately buildings squished around the perimeter, arched green shutters pushed open, looking out like so many eyes. Across from me, golden April sunlight cheerily danced across the ancient stone of the town hall—the Palazzo Vecchio. (Thirteenth century. Crenelated clock tower.)

Though still early, people filled the piazza. Retired couples nose-deep in Frommers. Rowdy school kids waiting in line for the Uffizi museum. African street vendors offering selfie-sticks for purchase. A line of Japanese tourists cut through, their guide holding a red umbrella aloft like a war banner.

My Grandma Adelaide had loved this city to distraction.

I did too.

In my mind's eye, I could still see Grammy giggling with excitement over being in Florence for the first time. I had been fourteen then, convinced I would have her with me forever.

Grandmas are stodgy and old, she would say. *Grammys are awards. Guess which one I am?*

I blinked, biting hard on my bottom lip.

Why is death like this? It's not enough to face loss once.

No. You have to bury your loved one over and over. Confront each place where she still feels so vibrantly *alive.*

I hadn't known to mentally prepare myself for this pain before leaving my hotel today. To anticipate the pounding waves of raw grief. Grammy's death was still new, and I was a novice to this form of sorrow. I had yet to learn its valleys and cliffs, its ebb and flow . . .

I had simply thought to enjoy a leisurely stroll through downtown

Florence, become reacquainted with my long-time-no-see boyfriend city. Let Firenze soothe away my nerves before my hopefully career-resuscitating meeting in an hour.

But, of course, I couldn't escape my problems so easily.

Instead of comfort, Florence had ripped the Band-Aid off my heartache.

I stared at the Palazzo Vecchio, memories swamping me. Grammy had marched over to its massive front doors and pretended to swoon in front of Michelangelo's *David*. (Replica. Victorian.) And then she had snagged some poor guy to take a photo of us both, waving our arms like idiots. Looking as if we could embrace the whole world.

It was a talisman, that photo. I took a copy of it with me everywhere. A reminder that, at one point, I had been thoroughly loved just as I was.

Something I needed, now more than ever. What with the harassing texts at all hours and that scathing, mega-viral video. All due to Pierce, my former fiancé, who I was going to see this morning for the first time since becoming spectacularly *dis*-engaged.

For the record, Grammy had never liked Pierce.

I drained the last of my coffee and tossed the empty cup in a nearby garbage can. Checked the time on my phone. Just under an hour before my potentially life altering meeting.

Suddenly, my neck prickled with awareness. That jungle-sense of being invisibly watched. My nerves flared to high alert.

Please. Not today. Not now.

Carefully, I turned in a circle. Looking for the tell-tale glare of a camera lens aimed my way. People talking and pointing.

What I saw instead was a wrinkled gypsy woman, staring intently. Ragged loose skirt, head scarf, wooden cane. Completely anachronistic.

We locked eyes. Her dark gaze drilled me, wispy strands of gray hair escaping to flutter in the slight wind.

My breath hitched. I instinctively wrapped a firm hand around my purse, pulling it tight against my body. I had seen too many tourists robbed over the years.

"It begins again," the gypsy called in heavily accented English. She regarded me with unnerving directness.

I blinked.

"It will repeat." She smiled, maniacal and toothless. "*Ripetere.*"

What?!

The gypsy lady winked and waved a gnarled hand my way. Before I could react, she turned and hobbled off, swallowed up by a group of Indian tourists.

Okay.

That was . . . weird.

Somewhere on the scale between 'Beware the Ides of March' and a movie trailer for *Borat.*

I stood, frozen. Still clutching my bag across my chest. I thawed my spine enough to scan the people around me, half expecting another gypsy to make a grab for my purse.

Nothing.

I swallowed. Told the pulse in my throat to settle down.

My parents—Lisabet and my step-dad, John-Baptista—are flamboyant installation artists and former stars of their own reality TV show on IFC. (Canceled after one season. Producers said they were too 'nutty.' I repeat: My parents were deemed *too* crazy for reality TV.)

Basically, *weird* and *out-there* have always been par for the course in my life. So an old gypsy lady yelling nonsense at me in the middle of Florence?

Usually, I would just file that under 'quirky.'

But given the hell of the last six months, it was hard to brush things off anymore.

Courage isn't a lack of fear, Grammy had always said. *It's hefting Fear onto your back and trudging forward into the dark.*

I was *so* tired of Fear.

I would *live* my life.

To that end, I lifted my chin and walked farther into the sun-drenched piazza. One more scan for gypsies. Seeing nothing unusual, I pulled out my phone. Framed my face. And took a selfie.

Me. The Palazzo Vecchio. Michelangelo's *David.*

Just to be clear, I'm not usually into selfies. I find them a bit fratgirl-narcissistic.

Grammy, on the other hand, had *loved* them. I've decided selfies move from vain to awesome once you're over fifty.

Today, selfies in our boyfriend-city felt like a fitting homage to my grandmother.

Some people build memorials or start charitable foundations to commemorate a loved one.

I take selfies.

Phone in hand, I walked across the Piazza della Signoria and onto Via dei Cerchi heading toward the Duomo. The medieval streets closed in, buildings rising four and five stories above me.

I paused now and again to take a selfie. The act of taking photos calming me. Allowing me to leash my grief (Grammy), my anxiety (weird gypsy ladies) and my nerves (code-red-critical meeting).

Which was good. I would need deep reserves of serenity today. I had to keep my cool during this meeting. Remain professional no matter how much Pierce taunted me.

Only the combination of a career meltdown and impending financial disaster could force me to deal with my former fiancé in any capacity. But this meeting could result in a job—an extremely well-paying, career-re-suscitating job.

I kept walking, moving through the narrow, pedestrian-only streets, a tight hand on my phone and my purse. Heaven knew, I couldn't afford to replace either if they were stolen.

I've always been poor and struggling. Famous parents do not equal moneyed parents—infamous parents even less so. Mine are both and, therefore, eternally one foot ahead of bankruptcy (or behind, depending on the year).

I work as a fine art appraiser and authenticator. Out of grad school, I got a job with Whitman Auction Services, met Pierce Whitman and finally felt like things were on track. I was the appraisal wonder-kid, building a strong professional reputation.

But six months ago, Grammy died of cancer.

It happened so fast. She was with me one week and then gone the next. Cancer does that sometimes. *Devastated* doesn't begin to describe the blackness of my grief.

I had lived with Grammy through most of high school and college, as my parents didn't have the time or money to deal with me. Grammy's arthritis made housework difficult, so I did the cooking and cleaning. We thrifted and budgeted and laughed and somehow made it on her small pension.

Grammy taught me the art of rich-slumming—you know, shopping sales and outlets, cultivating style over expensive couture . . . basically, maintaining a facade of having cash. It's critical in my line of work. Rich clients prefer to work with stylish peers, not charity cases.

But after Grammy died and Pierce . . . did what he did . . . money evaporated right along with my professional credibility.

The meeting this morning was my hail-Mary pass. The last-minute buzzer basket. I was pinned to the mat and about to be counted down-and-out.

I paused, trying to think of another cheesy sports metaphor.

Basically, I needed this job or I was benched.

Reaching the edge of the Piazza del Duomo, I spent a moment drinking in the enormous white-marble cathedral and its distinctive red dome. (Renaissance. Victorian facade.) It never failed to impress. I took a few more selfies and kept walking.

Ten minutes later, I arrived in the Piazza della Santissima Annuziata, stopping short of the palazzo that was the location of my potentially life altering meeting.

The piazza was all charming Firenze, with overhanging arched loggias running the length of the buildings on three sides. A fountain and small gated monument decorated the middle.

I'm one of those people who would rather be a half hour early than two minutes late. But there is such a thing as *too early* and that currently described me.

In an attempt to calm my nerves while I waited, I flipped into my phone's camera roll and opened my first selfie of the day.

Me, across the street from my hotel. Standing on the bridge Ponte Santa Trinitá with the Ponte Vecchio and its precariously clinging medieval houses behind me.

I stared at the photo. Surprised.

And then gave a much-needed smile.

A man stood smack in the middle of my selfie.

The best part? He was dressed like Mr. Darcy from *Pride and Prejudice*. Completely legit.

Top hat, olive-green tail coat, fawn-colored breeches, waistcoat, snowy cravat, tasseled knee-high boots, gloved hands holding a polished walking stick.

His hat sat low, shadowing his face and eyes. I got the impression of dark hair, long nose and full lips.

Okay. Score one for awesome randomness.

Was there some sort of Jane Austen festival going on today?

Or was this a little gift from Grammy?

No one would have appreciated a guy dressed up like something from BBC central casting more than her.

I chuckled and sent a mental *thank you* heavenward. I had desperately needed this boost.

What is it about guys in Regency era costume? It's like insta-toe-curling hotness.

I'm not going to lie; I spent a solid thirty seconds staring at those tight breeches. Because *da-yum*.

And whywhywhy hadn't I seen him when I first took the picture?

I would have taken a second, third and, let's face it, fourth photo.

And then walked across the street and asked if I could take a selfie snuggled up close. Would he smell as good as he looked?

This mysterious Mr. Darcy felt . . . electric. Thrilling.

Which was too bad.

I had sworn off thrilling and exciting men many years ago.

And in the last six months, I had given up the steady, boring ones too.

Cold sober. That was me.

No men.

Not just a temporary boy*cott*, as Grammy would have called it. Nope.

You have a man*agement crisis.* I could hear her laugh. *Time to become officially* eman*cipated. Write yourself a proclamation, sweetheart.*

I had vowed to never trust men again, especially after Pierce—

I swallowed. I still had twenty minutes before scurrying down that rabbit hole. No need to jump into it voluntarily beforehand.

I gave Mr. Darcy one last longing look (and maybe even blew him a kiss . . . from Grammy, of course, not me.)

And then swiped to the next photo.

Stared.

Swiped to the next.

The next.

And the next.

Breathe. Just breathe.

He was *there*.

Mr. Darcy.

In Every. Single. Photo.

Walking toward me along a medieval street, sun streaming behind.

Standing in the middle of Piazza della Signoria, tourists eddying around him.

Paused beside a boutique storefront, head angled my way.

Resting a shoulder into the white marble facade of the Duomo, hand on his walking stick.

It was this *zing* with each image. Something about the man seemed . . . monumental.

As if he could *see* me. As if he knew me, to my very inner self.

My hands shook, heartbeat pounding in my ears.

How had I not noticed someone following me?

I whirled around, scanning the piazza—the hum of passing tourists, the roar of a motorcycle, the occasional voice yelling in staccato Italian.

No historical romance novel models in sight.

I closed my eyes.

Breathe. Calm down. Reason your way through this.

I was simply paranoid. Trauma does that to you. Turns you into someone who sees danger in the innocuous. First an old gypsy lady yelling bizarre things. Now a costume-inclined man with a fetish for photo bombing.

Weird, sure. But hardly threatening, per se.

Besides, what idiot would stalk someone in plain sight dressed like a Regency era nobleman? No one, right? That was nutty even by my skewed standards.

Most likely, Mr. Darcy had just been heading my direction and thought it amusing to pop into my photos.

The reality? This meeting was too critical for me to lose focus; I *needed* this job.

If Mr. Darcy had an issue with me, he could take a number and get in line.

DANTE D'ANGELO

I recognized her instantly.

In my defense, Claire Raythorn was kinda hard to miss, paused beside the arched loggia across the piazza. I nudged my motorcycle into the square, eyes on her.

She stood with long-limbed confidence, staring at her phone. Immaculate in a pencil skirt, ruffled pale-blue blouse and heeled boots. Blond hair gleaming-straight past her shoulders despite the frizz-inducing Tuscan humidity.

Even at a distance, she was striking. Unique. Drawing a man's eye.

And, let's face it, I was male enough to look long and hard.

As I watched, she waved and blew a kiss at her phone. Gave a girly-gushy smile.

Huh? Was she on a video call?

Wait—no. She wasn't talking and now she was tapping her phone.

Claire stared at her screen. Then her shoulders sank and she whirled around. Her relaxed body language instantly morphing into panicky and afraid.

Right.

They didn't call her Batty Ray Psycho for nothing.

I guided my bike around the fountain and across the piazza, keeping an eye on Claire ahead of me.

Of course I've seen that video. You know, the one where Claire walks in on Pierce Whitman with another woman. Granted, I think anyone with an internet connection has seen it.

The video is hilarious in an *America's Funniest Home Videos* sorta way—you wince and know you should look away but laugh instead.

It starts with Claire stomping through the door, swaying drunk, head swiveling as she takes in the clothes scattered, the tangled bodies on the couch . . .

You can practically *see* the moment where she loses it. An almost audible *snap*.

She goes full-banshee on Pierce and the other woman. Screaming. Hysterical.

Claire throws random things from her purse at them—lipstick, notebook, pens . . . tampons.

Pierce and the woman shriek in terror. That's nearly the funniest part—the pair of them squealing like teenage girls over flying tampons. The hashtag #tamponsofrage trended for a while.

But then Claire tosses her purse aside and starts pulling bottles from a wine fridge just inside the door. Winds up her arm.

"No!" Pierce shouts.

The first bottle smashes spectacularly, painting the wall in brilliant, dripping red. Three more follow. Pierce ducking under each one, yelling to stop.

Claire—sobbing, out of control.

"Look!" she screams, wildly waving her arms at the wine-soaked room. "It's smashed and bleeding. Just like my achy breaky HEART!"

Forever branding herself as Batty Ray Psycho. Though #bitchyraypsycho also made the rounds on social media.

Branwell and Tennyson laughed so hard they cried, playing the video over and over for a solid week.

Brothers. What you gonna do?

The take-away here? No matter how attractive, no self-respecting guy would get involved with Batty Ray Psycho.

As a D'Angelo, my life was already two Froot Loops shy of a bowl-full of crazy. Literally.

I had no interest in Claire Raythorn and her cargo-hold's worth of baggage.

So I forced myself to look away from her and focused on parking my bike next to a miniature Fiat.

But all too soon, my gaze swung back to Claire. Almost unbidden. Like rubbernecking at the scene of a car accident.

She had stopped her panicky twirling and had moved down the piazza a bit. Now she stood in front of a Baroque-era palazzo, gazing up at the Tuscan-orange building with its pedimented windows and carved marble corbels. The building that was my destination.

Of course. She was attending the same meeting.

Branwell had suggested she and Pierce might be in the running for this job too. Heaven knew, the poor woman probably needed it as badly as I did.

With a toss of her head, she threw her shoulders back, as if steeling herself.

She had guts, I would give her that.

It was only as she stepped forward and pressed the call button that it all clicked. That I *finally* noticed.

Stupid typical guy . . . I had been too busy checking her out and cataloging the crazy to analyze *why* she drew my eye. But now it was so obvious—

I couldn't *see* her.

Not. A. Damn. Thing.

Chills goosebumped my arms and back.

I blinked. Squinted.

She was *blank*. Absolutely and completely capital-B *Blank*.

All the air punched from my lungs. My heart went from zero to sixty.

I instantly whirled my head around the square, mentally noting other people: three university students, a pair of tourists, a black-habited nun with groceries—

Shadows. Movement. Normal.

I could *see* them just fine.

But when I came back to Claire . . .

Niente. Nulla. Nothing.

She was empty air.

What. The. Hell.

Claire pushed the palazzo door open, disappearing inside.

With shaking hands, I shrugged off my helmet and locked it into the seat of my bike. Pulled my tie out of my shirt and unpegged my suit pants. Grabbed my briefcase.

One thought alone pounding through my skull:

Of all the women on the planet, why couldn't I *see* Claire Raythorn?

3

CLAIRE

I walked into the room exactly four minutes early, politely greeting everyone with a professional smile.

Striding around the large table in the center of the room, I slid into a chair that afforded me a clear view of all exits. (I didn't lie about being paranoid.)

I pointedly ignored ground zero of my paranoia—a.k.a. Mr. Pierce Whitman—seated across the table.

He winked at me from behind his chunky, dark-framed glasses.

Honestly? After everything? *That's* how he chose to greet me? Besides, who *winks* at a female business associate in this day and age?

Stay professional. Calm. Deep breath.

I pretended interest in the mahogany table between us, mentally tracing the contrasting rosewood and satinwood inlay. (Northern Italian. Early nineteenth century. Master craftsman.) Using the moment to tamp down all worry labeled *men*—Pierce, Mr. Darcy stalker—and channeling my concentration into this potentially life altering meeting.

Pierce kept trying to capture my gaze, dipping his head all earnest-like and pleading. He exuded a nerdy, harmless vibe. Brown hair, soulful eyes . . . lots of glasses and bow ties.

The entirety of him shouting he was the safe choice, the prudent one. That had always been his schtik.

A deep voice cleared his throat.

"Can I get you something to drink, Ms. Raythorn? Mr. Whitman?"

This came from the white-haired man seated at the head of the table, Mr. Kenneth Finster-Cline, the billionaire we had come to audition for.

He radiated energy, despite being over seventy years old. He was one of those men who retained a luxurious mane of snowy-white hair well into old age. It complimented his neatly trimmed beard and Frank Sinatra-esque blue eyes.

As is, he *should* have looked like Santa Claus, but instead bore an uncanny resemblance to Colonel Sanders. Combined with his initials (KFC) and drawling Kentucky accent, everyone just called him the Colonel.

The few times we had met, the Colonel seemed grandfatherly, though chatty in the way elderly men can be. I intended to use every charm in the book to make a good impression on him.

"No drink?" The Colonel gestured toward a sideboard laden with bottles, soda and an espresso maker. "Natalia would be happy to fetch whatever you all would like."

Seated to the right of the Colonel, Natalia looked up from her laptop. About my age, Natalia radiated the typical poise and confidence of a beautiful woman well aware she was poised, confident and beautiful.

Pierce kept stealing glances at her. Speculative, inviting sorts of glances. Had I just been too stupid-in-love to notice his behavior before? It was *so* blatantly obvious.

"I'm fine, thank you." I shook my head.

Pierce did the same, flashing a wry grin.

"I understand Claire has been trying to lay off the *vino*." He tilted his head back, aiming his thumb toward his mouth.

Stay classy, Pierce.

I had been up half the night *knowing* the meeting today would be like this. That I would have to bite off my tongue to keep from rising to his cruel baiting.

Professionalbeprofessionalstaycalm . . .

But, of course, Pierce wasn't done. He ratcheted up the posh British accent, moving from his standard condescending into full-blown sardonic.

"You do have an ice princess image to rebuild, after all," he said.

Natalia suppressed a smug smirk.

I chewed on my cheek. *Don't engage.* Any response would only make me look bad. Every word out of my mouth needed to show my calm, *un*-psychotic demeanor.

Sunlight bounced merrily around the room and, like the Colonel, ignored the tension crackling between Pierce and myself.

"That's enough, Mr. Whitman," the Colonel snapped. Okay, so maybe not so ignorant. "Anyone who wants to work for me will remain professional at all times."

Pierce gave a mock-humble wince.

"You show admirable restraint, Ms. Raythorn." The Colonel turned to me. "Bit your tongue off yet?"

"Not quite. This room is lovely." I waved a hand, indicating the opulent space. The wealthy Colonel *would* have a museum-worthy palazzo as his office building.

"Admirable topic change." The Colonel nodded approvingly. "I like a gal who doesn't let emotions rule her head."

"Thank you." I ignored the *gal.* Pick your battles.

Pierce rolled his shoulders—a telling, agitated tic.

The room *was* lovely, with its gilded coffers and molding in colorful geometric designs. (Originally late Renaissance. Victorian remodel.) It was pure PBS Masterpiece Classic elegance, like those lush E. M. Forster period films my sixth nanny, Mrs. Henderson, watched over and over: *A Room with a View, Where Angels Fear to Tread, Howards End* . . . I always called the random women who tended me *nannies*, a rich-slumming euphemism more than a reality. At least Mrs. Henderson hadn't had a parole officer—

"Both Claire and I are here, shall we get started?" Pierce sat forward, clasping his hands, expression carefully neutral, obviously trying to make up lost ground. "I'm eager to begin."

Natalia's perfectly manicured nails clacked as she typed. Pierce eyed her again.

The Colonel leaned back in his chair. "We're waiting for one more expert."

That was news to me.

Drat. More competition.

Pierce shot an eyebrow skyward. "I was under the impression Claire and I had been invited here exclusively. A third opinion is hardly necessary—"

"My game. My rules." The Colonel gestured toward the large double doors. "You don't like my rules, you're welcome to leave."

Which just underscored why everyone called him the Colonel.

Pierce rolled his shoulders again.

"I'm not sure my father is going to approve of this change."

"Boy, I don't give a damn what your daddy has to say—"

Crack.

A tall man strode into the room. Head high. Gaze firm.

Of course.

It had been almost too predictable.

Dante D'Angelo.

The industry hot-shot who used well-oiled charm, and little else, to assess art.

Basically, the one actor this melodrama had been missing.

Dante nodded to us all.

"Welcome, Mr. D'Angelo." The Colonel lifted a hand.

Natalia visibly perked, her body canting toward Dante. I got the distinct impression all her manicured primping had been for Dante D'Angelo's benefit. Granted, I heard that was how *most* women responded to him. The man was definitely a player.

Pierce, on the other hand, bristled like a tomcat spotting competition.

"I apologize for my tardiness." Dante's voice was deep and smooth with an unexpected West Coast American twang. He shut the door behind him.

"Alone, I see," the Colonel said. "Will your twin be joining us?"

Dante shook his head. "Branwell sends his regrets for today."

"That's fine. Have yourself a seat, boy." The Colonel waved at a chair. "I trust you already know Claire Raythorn and Pierce Whitman."

"By reputation. We've never had the privilege of meeting." Dante set down a briefcase, greeting us both with a polite smile and nod.

Dante settled into the chair across the table from me, somehow taking up more than his fair share of oxygen.

He didn't just own the room.

He *saturated* it.

Dante was not classically handsome, per se. His nose was a little too long and his features too strong, though his meticulously man-scaped stubble and dark wavy hair certainly added.

No, he was somehow more than the sum of his looks. He hinted of shadowy, more dangerous things. An apex predator.

He sat back with an attitude that said I-am-literally-larger-than-life.

Which he truly was. So much bigger than I would have expected. You can't get a true sense of size from a photograph. He was tall enough to make even *me* feel dainty, which was saying something.

Given his last name and Mediterranean coloring, I had always assumed the D'Angelo twins were Italian. Hadn't I read somewhere he was an Italian earl?

But Dante's accent was as American as rootbeer and peanut butter. No trace of anything foreign. And the physique in his Armani suit was more hulking Viking than lean Italian. Only genetics could grant a man that kind of bulk.

Natalia certainly made her position evident. She instantly popped over to the sidebar—wiggle-walking in her tight skirt and high stilettos—and snagged a bottle of water.

"We're so glad you made it today, Mr. D'Angelo," she crooned as she *leeeaaned* into his shoulder to set the bottle in front of him, giving everyone at the table a solid understanding of exactly how low her blouse was cut.

Sheesh. Have some self-respect.

Startled, Dante pulled away, shooting her a smooth smile, eyes staying firmly on her face.

"Thanks."

Dante also didn't rubberneck as Natalia wiggled her way back to her seat. Granted, Pierce shot Dante a hostile look and then ogled her backside for the both of them. A deliberately antagonizing display for both Dante and myself.

Not that Dante seemed to care. He glanced at Pierce and the Colonel, studying them for a moment, as if tracing something I couldn't see. Then he swiveled back toward me, settling farther into his chair.

He met my gaze with a tight grin that did not reach his eyes.

It was a very nice smile, full of white hyper-straight teeth. The kind of smile I imagine a tiger gives before eating you for breakfast.

I didn't smile back.

Instead, I pointedly turned my head toward the Colonel. I wasn't being rude; I was just making my position clear.

Right before Grammy's death, I had spent a month authenticating the provenance of a suspected *Madonna and Child* by Gaimbattista Pittoni. (Venetian. Baroque.) The influential owner of the painting wanted to send it to auction at Sotheby's in New York.

I painstakingly researched the provenance, artistic technique, mass spectrometry age analysis . . . the usual routine. I concluded the painting was a genuine early work of Pittoni based on use of line, the unique mixture of Pittoni's azure blue, blah, blah . . .

But the day I returned from burying Grammy, I got a phone call.

For some reason, Sotheby's had decided to get a second opinion— the D'Angelo brothers.

Apparently, Dante and Branwell D'Angelo spent all of ten minutes looking over the Pittoni *Madonna and Child* before declaring it a fraud, created in the late 1960s by a pair of well-known Russian forgers.

Yeah. No discussion of painterly technique. No questions about provenance. No assessment of the oil paint.

Just a quick lookie-loo and *bam*. Here's our 'professional' opinion.

As if.

Sotheby's refused the Pittoni painting. The owner was devastated. I lost a considerable amount of professional credibility.

So I did what any self-respecting woman would do—I found a bar and drowned my sorrows in one mojito too many.

Don't judge.

I managed to drag myself home on the Tube and stumbled into our Kensington flat. Only to find Pierce cuddled up with his father's assistant, Heather. (Literature grad. Slutty. Desperate.)

So yeah. The entire world knows the rest of the story.

Part of me felt that if Dante hadn't negated my appraisal of the Pittoni, I wouldn't have gotten drunk and might have reacted more calmly to walking in on Pierce and Heather.

The rational part of my brain recognized I could hardly blame Dante D'Angelo for Pierce's infidelity and subsequent cruelty in filming and posting that video. From Dante's point of view, he had just been doing his job.

But that didn't stop me from disliking him. I disliked that my pulse rose when he came into the room. Disliked that I wanted to watch him, follow him with my eyes, study him in his natural habitat . . .

Stop!

Not. Attractive.

I refused to be another one of his fangirls.

I dug my fingernails into my palm.

In my peripheral vision, I noted Dante angle his head, keeping his dark eyes firmly fixed on me.

What? Was this part of his alpha posturing?

"Now, we begin." The Colonel placed his hands, palms down, on the table. "I thank you all for being here today. As you can see, I'm an old man—"

"I've always said you only get better with age, Colonel," Pierce said.

"Stuff it, boy. You'll have plenty of time to suck up to me later." The Colonel shot Pierce a warning glance.

Wow. Not much love there. My flame of hope burned brighter.

"As I was saying," the Colonel continued, "I am not getting much younger. Though some might argue, I *am* becoming more eccentric. As you all probably know, I am the sole heir to two old family lines. I have vaults of unknown . . . stuff, I guess I'll call it. I've been meaning for years to hire someone to assess and catalog it. But I want to make sure I hire the right person. I originally signed a contract with Mr. Whitman and Ms. Raythorn of Whitman Auction Services to do just that. However, with the changes in WAS staffing, I pulled out of the project to let things simmer down a bit."

Translation: My mega-viral, mojito-infused rampage gave him cold feet.

"But I'm back in the game." The Colonel cleared his throat. "Or, rather, I have decided it's 'game on.' Which is why you all are here. Despite any personal differences, the three of you are some of the best in the business."

Dante continued to stare at me.

Did I exude man-hating pheromones? I had plenty of reasons to be annoyed with him. But why the reverse?

Or was he like Pierce? Just trying to get under my skin. Rattle me. This meeting was high-stakes for us all.

"It goes like this," the Colonel was saying. "You are each auditioning for the job of curating my collection of art and antiques. This would be a permanent, salaried position based here in Florence, as you have seen from the preliminary paperwork I sent out."

Yeah. My jaw had hit the floor when I saw how much he was offering to pay. It was nearly four times the amount I had been earning with WAS. Being paid an exorbitant salary to curate a billionaire's private art collection while living in my favorite boyfriend-city . . . sheesh, it was every appraiser's dream. Career-saving employment for sure.

I yearned for this job with frightening ferocity.

Dante was still staring at me.

I shot him my firmest *down-boy* look.

He just narrowed his eyes. Unfazed.

Pierce noticed Dante's noticing.

He shot a look back and forth between us, eyes speculative.

Done. With. Men.

4

DANTE

I still couldn't *see* her.

Correction. I obviously could see *Claire* just fine, even with back-lit sun rimming her in golden light.

Close-up, she was shockingly pretty.

The kind of woman a guy slaps a 'trophy' sticker on and fist-bumps his buddies as she walks by.

Not that *I* was that kind of guy . . .

She met my gaze with large, winter-blue eyes. Blond hair framing her face. High cheekbones. Heart-shaped upper lip. Defined chin.

Grace Kelly reborn.

But I couldn't *see* her.

No shadows. No figures. Nothing.

She was absolutely *blank*.

I leaned to the right, casually resting on the carved arm of my chair, getting a different angle. Sometimes backlight could make *seeing* difficult, and she had been at a distance earlier . . .

I narrowed my eyes, trying to force her into focus.

Nothing.

I let out a stuttering breath. Swallowed. Adjusted my tie, loosening it a bit.

This was . . . not good. Unprecedented. I was in uncharted territory.

Claire arched a perfectly manicured eyebrow, coolly meeting my eyes. Every line of her telling me to *Knock. It. Off.*

Fine.

The Colonel opened a folder and shuffled through some papers. As usual, silvery forms gathered behind him. Like a repeating shadow, some clearer than others.

A young man in a pale Edwardian suit.

A grizzled Confederate soldier.

A stern man sporting a Pilgrim's hat.

The typical shapes of who the Colonel had been in lives past.

But in between the figures, the air wavered. Like static noise made visible.

Odd.

Usually, the shadows were clean and methodical.

But at least the Colonel *had* shadows.

Pierce was much the same.

A man in a Nazi uniform.

A primped courtier in a powdered wig and embroidered frock coat.

A Scottish laird in a belted great kilt with a sword in hand.

But that visual static sputtered in and out around the figures.

Again . . . not good.

I shifted my gaze back to Claire.

Still nothing. No shadows. No figures. No static. Just empty sun-filled air behind her.

This had *never* happened before. Strangers were rarely staticky. And *no one* outside of my closest loved ones were blank.

What did this mean? Were things changing? Evolving?

Why couldn't I *see* her?

I resisted scrubbing a hand over my face in frustration. Now I had to talk with Branwell and Tennyson about it.

We all *hated* talking about our GUTs—the Grossly Unusual Talents we got from our father. Yeah, kinda cutesy acronym but we're guys. What else would we call our 'gifts'?

If my GUT was having problems, what did it mean for my brothers? Were things fracturing further for all of us?

Would more and more people start to be blank to me? Or was there something unique about this situation?

I angled further back into my chair, tamping down my twitching anxiety. Or at least relegating it to a bouncing foot and drumming fingers.

There was nothing I could do about Claire's missing shadows right now. I needed to focus on the Colonel. My family was depending on me to nail this meeting.

"Here's how this is going to go down." The Colonel gestured for some papers from Natalia. "There's a work of art I found in my family vaults. Who knows how long it's been there. I can't find any record of it, and I want to know what I have. So, you will each be tasked with individually assessing it."

"Just a regular assessment?" Pierce asked.

"Yep. Starting today, you will have no more than one month to complete the appraisal. You will have all resources at your disposal, as if you were already my employee. I will also pay your salary for that month. At the end of the month—or sooner if you can—you will present me with your findings and the reasons behind them."

"So how will you decide who to hire?" Pierce again.

He was the kid sitting on the front row of class. Hand popping up to answer every question.

I had never liked that guy.

"Well, that depends on several factors." The Colonel ticked off on his fingers. "Am I impressed by your appraisal and expert knowledge? Did you display professional behavior throughout? At the end of the day, I will hire the person who I feel will get the job done."

I nodded, my pulse beating in excitement as I tugged on the arms of my suitcoat. Given the little I understood of the Colonel's family history, there were likely undiscovered gems in his collection.

Branwell and I were perfect fits for the Colonel. Between our industry connections and, uh, GUTs, we would be able to easily assess and organize his collection.

I needed this job. Business had been slow, and I could see the writing on the wall. Either things picked up here or I was going to have to move D'Angelo headquarters to a larger city, like Paris or New York.

I *really* didn't want to move. Florence was home, and my family needed me here. Just the thought of leaving my mom and grandma alone to care for my brothers and their *issues*—

I swallowed. Adjusted my tie again. Not going to happen. This job would be mine.

"So here are the contracts." The Colonel slid a folder down the table to each of us. "Whitman Auction Services has already signed the contract, so you'll find an addendum in yours, Mr. Whitman."

Pierce flipped his folder open, scanned the paper inside. Scowled.

"You've added a Nuisance Clause?" His snooty British accent ratcheted up a notch.

I opened my own folder, rubbing a hand against the back of my neck. Sure enough.

At no time will any job applicant harass, interfere with, hamper and/ or plagiarize the efforts of another job applicant. Evidence of this behavior will result in immediate dismissal.

"I prefer to call it my Sandbox Rule," the Colonel said. "Basically, you all will play nice in my sandbox. Keep your hands and feet to yourself, and no stealing others' toys."

"This is patently ridiculous." Pierce grunted in disgust. "We're all adults here—"

"The jury is still out on that one, son."

"—so there's no need to treat us like children."

"Then don't act like one, and I won't have to," the Colonel said.

I kept my mouth shut, suppressing a grin. Pierce was doing an admirable job of digging his own grave.

"I'm not a babysitter, and I've got no patience for anyone who makes trouble," the Colonel continued. "Any employee of mine will act professionally at all times."

"Seems only fair." Claire leveled a laser-eye look at Pierce. "I, for one, want to be hired on my own merits and abilities, not because I cheated my way to the top."

Claire had one of those silky female voices—urbane and smooth—but threaded with the faintest tang of New England.

I liked it a lot more than I should.

Everyone in the industry had been surprised when Claire became involved with Pierce Whitman. Pierce with his hang-dog, nerdy vibe and Claire with her tall, elegant . . . presence. I remember seeing a photo of them together. Her in high heels, towering a good four inches over him. A supermodel with her accountant boyfriend.

"I assume you are going to tell us about the object we are here to assess?" Pierce asked as we signed the documents. Again, the kid at the front of the class who thought he was so astute but was mostly an annoying kiss-up.

I sat back. Still keeping my mouth shut. I crossed an ankle over my knee, foot bouncing.

"How much do you know about the Battle of Cascina?" the Colonel asked, steepling his fingers.

A thrill chased my spine.

Given how fast Claire's eyebrows went up, she had a similar reaction.

"The actual fourteenth century battle between Florence and Pisa?" Claire paused. "Or Michelangelo's lost masterpiece?"

The Colonel's tight smile said it all.

Madonna mia. Did the old man actually have a lost Michelangelo? My mind spun with possibilities.

The Colonel rolled his hand at Claire. *Go on.*

Eyes wide, she swallowed.

"I'll have to do a little research about the actual battle itself, but early on in his career, Michelangelo was hired to paint a fresco of the Battle of

Cascina on the western wall of the Hall of Five Hundred in the Palazzo Vecchio. The much older Leonardo da Vinci was hired to paint another battle on the wall opposite. Both paintings were to be monumental in scope, around thirty feet long and twenty feet high. It's also the only time the two Renaissance masters worked together on a project."

"Wonderful!" The Colonel's expression seemed nearly parental-proud.

Hmm, was someone already the teacher's pet? And what did that mean for Branwell and I?

"According to history, Michelangelo never actually painted it," Claire continued. "He did complete a full-scale cartoon which hung *in situ* in the Palazzo Vecchio for several years, but he never transferred the drawing from the cartoon to the wall. Of course, that didn't stop other artists from making copies of it. The most notable copy is that of Sangallo, a student of Michelangelo's—"

"Sangallo's drawing is currently owned by the Earl of Leicester, I believe," Pierce said, metaphorical hand up, jumping into the conversation.

Claire nodded. "The original cartoon was lost at some point after Sangallo made his copy. It's unclear what happened to it exactly. Given its massive size and the fragile nature of fresco cartoons—"

I snorted. That was an understatement.

Or maybe I just didn't like being left out of the conversation either.

Every eye turned toward me.

"Sorry. Just agreeing with Claire." I folded my arms feeling my suit-coat pull through my shoulders. "In Italian, the original word is *cartone*, a mix of *carta* meaning paper and the suffix *-one*, which means big." I pronounced *-one*, sounding out each letter, as Italian is wont to do—*OWN-ay*. "So a Renaissance cartoon was just a big paper. Or rather, scores of smaller pieces of paper taped together with a flour and water paste to make an enormous sheet the size of a modern billboard. Not exactly the most stable medium. I can't imagine any significant portion of Michelangelo's original drawing surviving."

Claire shot me an annoyed are-you-done-stealing-my-thunder look.

Got the memo. Clearly not a fan.

The next month promised to be a dog-eat-dog free-for-all between Claire, Pierce and myself. Sandbox Rule or no.

"Let me show you kids what I got."

The Colonel motioned to Natalia, who pulled several large photographs out of another folder and passed them down the table. I leaned forward and snagged one.

It was a photograph of a drawing of Michelangelo's *Battle of Cascina.*

I stared at the image and whistled, pulse thumping.

How do you represent a medieval battle?

Michelangelo's chose to draw the very beginning. The battle occurred on a hot day in July and, according to legend, many of the Florentine mercenaries had been swimming in the River Arno when the horns called them to arms. Michelangelo captured that panicked moment when the naked men scrambled ashore, some struggling to get dressed, while others engaged Pisan forces in the background.

It was a brilliant *tour de force* allowing Michelangelo to showcase his understanding of anatomy with the twisting, turning naked figures. The composition pulsed with energy and movement.

"So this is . . .?" Pierce's voice trailed off.

"Not the original cartoon, I imagine. What are its dimensions?" That was Claire.

I set my photo down on the table. Propped my foot over my knee again.

"The drawing is a single sheet measuring approximately three feet wide by two feet high—"

"Way too small. The original cartoon would have been ten times that size," Claire murmured, head down.

The Colonel nodded.

Pierce pulled out a jewelers loupe and studied his photo. "The detail is amazing, even in the photograph."

"My thoughts exactly." Claire didn't look up.

Pierce. "Is this another unknown copy?"

Claire. "Or an original Michelangelo sketch?"

"We'll need to compare it against Sangallo's drawing—"

"That means contacting the conservator at Holkham Hall in Norfolk."

"Do we still have contacts up there?"

"Probably."

"Uh-mmm." Pierce adjusted the loupe.

I raised an eyebrow, catching the Colonel's gaze. Both of us surprised by the sudden harmony in the Land of Pierce and Claire.

Did they even realize they had slid into an easy, working relationship?

"I'm sure they could email us some scans for comparison," Claire said.

"Exactly." Pierce nodded. "I'll call and get Heather right on it."

He might as well have doused Claire with cold water.

Her head snapped up so hard I winced.

The temperature in the room dropped ten degrees.

Pierce lost his nerdy facade for a brief moment. An ugly smile tugged at his lips.

That last comment of his had been *deliberate*. I tamped down a sudden urge to rearrange his smile with my fist. What an absolute douchebag.

I wasn't a huge fan of Claire Raythorn. But *no one* deserved what Pierce had done to her.

A bright flush crept across Claire's cheeks, and she sucked in her bottom lip, nostrils flaring. Cracks appeared in her composure.

Within her eyes, I caught a glimpse of something so broken, so alone . . . jagged fragments of soul . . .

My heart gave an unwanted lurch.

The Colonel stepped into the tense moment.

"I've already contacted Lord Leicester's estate, and I have an excellent copy of Sangallo's drawing on hand. There is no need to involve any of your staff." He shot a quelling look at Pierce.

Claire cleared her throat. "A mass spectrometry analysis would tell us quite a bit, particularly age. We would only need a tiny amount of material from the edge of document. Is that agreeable to you, Colonel?"

"Of course. As long as you don't damage the sketch. I want to know what I have in my possession."

I nodded my head. Assuming nothing was amiss with Branwell or myself, it shouldn't be too hard to get to the bottom of the mysterious drawing. Our *abilities* being what they were.

Pierce started in about sample collection and scheduling. Apparently he wanted first crack at the drawing. No surprise there.

Branwell and I would consult our GUTs and have an answer in minutes. Then use the rest of the month to build evidence supporting our knowledge. Who was I kidding? We'd have a solid case in less than a week. A month was a ridiculously generous amount of time.

Across from me, Claire shifted. Still no shadows.

Damn. What was up?

And given what was at stake here with the Colonel, now was not the time for my GUT to go on the fritz.

Out of curiosity, I spread my palms on the table top, staring at the family signet ring on my right middle finger. I took a deep breath and centered.

Generally, the images of people's past lives floated involuntarily around them. It was nothing I could control or direct.

But if I concentrated, I could see glimpses of the past life of an object—a directed form of psychometry. In this case, the table before me.

The table blurred around the edges. Like flipping through a slide show, images flickered into view. The darkness of years and years of storage. Servants in uniforms placing flowers on the table. Dinner guests whirling around at hyper speed. First in Edwardian lace, then Victorian hoopskirts, Regency empire waists . . .

Back, back. Farther into the past.

Ah. There it was.

A workshop. A craftsman using a thin chisel to carve sinuous tracks for the inlay. I studied his clothing. Smocked shirt with flap-front knee breeches. Long hair in a queue but unpowdered. Late eighteenth century. Probably French. If Branwell were here, he could tell for sure.

I let my concentration go. The present reality slid back into place, the ghostly shapes melting away.

Hmmm. That had all been normal.

I lifted my head. Claire instantly turned her face away.

Interesting. My little episode had not gone unnoticed. Many assumed it was a small seizure. Which I guess, in certain respects, it was.

She was still shadow-free.

I studied her a minute longer, helpless to look away.

Pale. Delicate. Carved porcelain.

Fragile. The word popped into my head. Which seemed like a lie. Claire was anything but fragile. And yet . . .

A powerful surge of protectiveness swept me. My heart thudded in my ears.

I swallowed.

Why? Why her?

And more importantly, what secrets did her missing shadows hide?

CLAIRE

The Colonel broke up our meeting a little after noon.

The men instantly stood up and started into typical male posturing, each jockeying for position.

Pierce rolled his shoulders and said something schoolyard-pithy to Dante. Dante grunted back, gave a steely alpha warning look and turned away.

At which point, Natalia immediately attached herself to Dante, angling her upper body toward him in subtle invitation. Well . . . make that not-so-subtle, given how far she was leaning.

Sheesh.

The last hour of the meeting had just been housekeeping. Pierce, being Pierce, had demanded to be first to examine the sketch. The Colonel had looked none-too-pleased with Pierce's bossiness, which was just fine by me—let Pierce pour gasoline on his own funeral pyre—but the Colonel relented and gave the first slot to him. Pierce would have all of tomorrow to study the sketch at the Colonel's villa just south of Florence.

I was assigned the day after that, when I would gather the small samples for age analysis and send them off to the University of Florence. Turns out, I was the only one both Pierce and Dante trusted to conduct the sample. They made it amply clear they didn't trust each other.

Dante and Branwell D'Angelo would view the sketch in three days. Surprisingly, Dante had seemed unconcerned about the delay. I would have expected him to be more . . . pushy. Instead, he acted like a guy who had a secret inside-track, unconcerned about the competition.

Obviously, given the unorthodox nature of this job—Contest? Audition? Circus?—juggling access to the sketch was going to be tricky.

For right now, I had a little under forty-eight hours to do some research. I was genuinely excited to assess the piece. Anything linked to Michelangelo Buonarotti would have important historical and artistic significance, not to mention resuscitating my tattered professional career.

I gathered my notes together, eager to get out of the room. I hoped to use the Colonel's Sandbox Rule as an excuse to avoid all further contact with Pierce.

My phone buzzed. Text.

Don't think I have forgotten you. I long to drag my nose along your neck and memorize the smell of your skin.

My adrenaline instantly spiked; my skin crawled.

I closed my eyes. Forced my breathing to slow down.

It was okay. I was okay. They were just words. They only had power if I let them.

I hated this unknown cyber stalker.

After everything went down with Pierce posting that video, the haters had crawled out of the woodwork.

This particular person was tenacious and had been harassing me for months.

That was almost the worst part of the whole video fiasco.

I was the victim in the whole situation. The one who was cheated on, lied to, *man*ipulated.

But after fifty million views, I was known the world over as the psychotic ex-girlfriend Pierce had been fortunate enough to dump before it was too late.

A chip off the old block. Unstable and crazy, just like Lisabet and John-Baptista.

Twenty-eight years of (generally) rock-steady behavior gone in less than forty-eight hours. The masses never want to hear about the straight-laced child of tabloid-fodder parents—the one who keeps their act together despite all odds.

No. People want to watch the train wreck. In detail. Millions of times over.

And then write you nasty emails/texts/tweets and even the occasional snail mail letter just to reiterate what an ugly/stupid/psychotic person they think you are.

I know, I know. Haters gonna hate. But, seriously . . . who cheated on who here?

The bullying had dwindled down to pretty much this one particular texter.

This person always got my phone number, no matter how many times I changed it, blocked them, got a different SIM card . . .

I'd finally called the police over it. Not that they could do much. Come to find out, filing a restraining order against an invisible online harasser is nearly impossible.

I instantly deleted the rude text, firmly telling my shaking hands to settle down.

I was just having this reaction because it had been nearly two weeks since the last text, and I had (maybe) a Mr. Darcy impersonator following me earlier, and I had just spent a solid two hours in the same room as Pierce.

I had let my guard down. That was all.

I was in Florence. Far away from this person.

I clenched my jaw and straightened my shoulders. Lifted fear firmly onto my back, dropped my phone into my purse and headed toward the door.

"Claire." Pierce snagged my arm, turning me back to the room.

I stared at his hand. Pointedly.

He released me and pushed his glasses up his nose. As if *that* were the reason he let go.

"We were great this morning." He tried for a friendly smile, but ended up with something more Cheshire Cat. "Just like old times there—"

"I'm not in the mood for this, Pierce."

"Hold on. I bet I could convince my dad to hire you back. With the right encouragement, of course." He winked.

Oh my word! "As if. I have no desire to talk to you."

I spun around and headed, again, toward the door.

Pierce darted in front, stopping me. "Kidding, Claire. You never could take a joke. Let me take you out to lunch. I promise I'll behave—"

"No."

"You just go from one mistake to another. C'mon, you know I'm the only man for you."

His brown eyes got that hang-dog look, winsome, promising adoration and safety. It's why I had agreed to marry him, once upon a time. Not because I was madly in love with him.

But because I had thought *he* was madly in love with *me*.

The solid, steady man who would never break my heart. The opposite of the bad boy charmers I typically dated.

Wow. Had I learned *that* bitter lesson.

"As the Italians would say, *Ciao*."

I sidestepped. He moved with me.

"I'm good for you. Admit it."

Oh! "You mean I'm still good for *you*. Because you are most decidedly not good for *me*."

"That's not true—"

"Goodbye, Pierce." I walked around him, aiming (once more) for the door.

"C'mon, Claire." His head pivoted with me. "You never gave us a real chance. You just have to trust—"

I froze.

"Trust?!" I whirled on him. "Did that word seriously just come out of your mouth?"

I stomped back over to him, my gaze surely shooting lasers. A smile tugged at his lips, like a small child preening after poking and prodding and *finally* getting a reaction.

I was grateful, for once, that I topped him by about an inch. Add in my heeled boots and towering anger, and I easily gazed down on him. I liked that he had to raise his head to look me in the eye.

I stared into his familiar face and realized I genuinely hated him.

Hated I could pick his laugh out of a crowd.

Hated I knew what he would say seconds before he said it.

Hated that, even now, part of me missed *us*.

Hated that because of his actions, I might never have *us* with someone else.

All because I *had* trusted him. I *had* loved him.

You don't hand a man you don't love the power to destroy you.

Now I knew how thoroughly trust could be shattered. How impossible it was to reassemble.

Humpty-Dumpty and all that.

Never again.

Pierce reached for me. I took a step back.

"Is there a problem here, Mr. Whitman? Ms. Raythorn?" The Colonel appeared at Pierce's side.

Pierce. "No."

Me. "Yes."

The Colonel raised a bushy, white eyebrow. "Seems the lady doesn't appreciate your company, Mr. Whitman. I'd hate to invoke that Sandbox Rule."

His tone implied the opposite.

Pierce thrust out his jaw and, for a split second, I wondered if he would actually argue with the Colonel.

Instead, he nodded at me. "See you later, luv." One final wink.

I barely managed to suppress my eyeroll.

The Colonel's eyes followed Pierce as he walked back to gather his things from the table.

Strike one for pushy men today.

Dante D'Angelo was still chatting with Natalia, saying something that made her giggle.

Not that I noticed or anything.

Swinging back to me, the Colonel smiled. Even at his age, he was still tall. Though all that white hair probably added an inch or two. This was the problem with being tall myself. I always judged others by their height.

"How are you finding your accommodations, Ms. Raythorn?"

"Please, call me Claire."

He nodded, pleased. "Claire then."

"Palazzo Alfieri is lovely," I continued. "Thank you for arranging my hotel."

Typically, clients did not book my housing, but the situation with this contract was unique. The Colonel had insisted on arranging my accommodations. Usually, I just stayed in your average tourist-grade hotel.

But the Colonel had deep pockets and had put me in a luxury suite at Palazzo Alfieri. My hotel room sported carved Baroque ceilings overlooking the Arno, complete with a mixture of sleek modern fixtures and antique touches. The Colonel had arranged a month's stay and included a generous meal stipend, as well as a car and driver at my disposal. All without me having to spend a penny of my salary.

The whole situation was almost too good to be true.

Now if I could only land the job, as well.

"Did the hotel reception inform you of the history of the building?" the Colonel asked.

I smiled politely. "A little. I understand the palazzo housed the British consulate until 2011, at which point it was renovated into a luxury hotel."

I had spent fifteen minutes chatting with the friendly woman behind the desk about it. (Martina. Three grandkids. Likes clubbing.)

"The front desk clerk said the building was named for Vittorio Alfieri, the famous Italian playwright," I continued.

"Yes. I believe he lived the last fifteen years of his life there with his mistress, the Countess of Albany. *She* was quite an interesting figure, I must say."

"The countess?"

"Yes. She was actually Princess Louise of Stolberg-Gedern."

I blinked, not sure if that name was supposed to mean anything to me. Given my profession, my background in history was extensive but hardly encompassing random continental royal families.

The Colonel took pity on me.

"Louise was married to Charles Stuart. You know, Bonnie Prince Charlie . . . the Battle of Culloden—"

"Oh!" My head jerked back. "I'm sorry, Colonel. I've had my head firmly in Italian art and history all day. I wasn't expecting the Scots to make an appearance."

"Completely understandable, darlin'." The southern gentleman coming to the surface. "Charlie's marriage happened well after the Battle of Culloden. Most people don't know about it. Louise was practically young enough to be his granddaughter when they married." He chuckled. "Imagine being married to a man that much older than yourself."

I nodded politely, managed a weak chuckle of my own. From the corner of my eye, I saw Dante leaving the room.

Again, not that I was noticing or anything.

"I just think it's fascinating how interwoven people's lives were in the past," the Colonel continued. "Prince Charlie actually lived his last years in Florence and Rome. Catholics, you know. His younger brother, Henry, was the Dean of the College of Cardinals. Charlie's wife, Louise, left him for Alfieri. She lived for a number of years in the palazzo that is now your hotel. She died just a few years after the end of the Napoleonic wars, around 1824, I believe. I thought you would enjoy staying in a place full of such rich history."

The Colonel stared at me expectantly. Like this little history lesson was supposed to mean something.

It didn't.

Other than to underscore that, yes, the aristocratic world of two hundred years ago had been a much smaller place than many knew. Most anyone who was anyone was related to, or friends with, everyone else in their same social sphere. Like an exclusive high school—jocks, jerks, mean girls, nerds . . . a tight social strata with the rich, popular kids on top.

I smiled. Professional. Friendly.

"Yes. Thank you, Colonel, for everything. Especially for a chance to prove I'm the best fit for this job." I moved to shake his hand. "I look forward to seeing the sketch in-person the day after tomorrow when I take the samples."

He clasped my hand firmly in his and then did that old person thing, placing his free hand over our joined ones. Preventing me from breaking the handshake.

He patted our hands. "I see so much of Adelaide in you. She was a remarkable woman."

I froze. Okaaaaay. How did this man know Grammy?

So far, this conversation had staggered around like a drunken frat boy trying to walk a straight line.

What next?

"Yes. I am often told I look like her. I wasn't aware that you knew my grandmother."

Were she still alive, they would probably be about the same age. But the Colonel was the son of a wealthy Kentucky father and British aristocrat mother. Whereas Grammy had been the daughter of poor Danish immigrants living in Boston. Their paths should have never crossed.

He stared at me, still holding/patting my hand. His palm was surprisingly rough and calloused. The moment stretched well into the range of awkward.

Then, he smiled. "Allow me to take you to dinner sometime. I would love to talk about Adelaide over a *bistecca alla fiorentina*."

Pat, pat, pat.

I had seen the huge Florentine steaks before, thick and barely seared. Sushi was the only thing I ate raw. Beef? Not so much.

And, more importantly, would the Colonel pat my hand the entire night?

You need this job.

"Of course." I kept my expression politely neutral.

"Excellent! Because I won't take *no* for an answer." He beamed at me.

The Colonel was *still* holding my hand.

I managed a weak smile of my own and, gently, extricated my fingers.

Assertive men strike two.

As I clacked down the marble stairs in my boots, I reviewed the odd exchange.

Well, I mostly tried to convince myself that I was just being paranoid and hyper-sensitive and man-hating.

The Colonel was a perfectly nice person, and I was reading things that weren't really there in the subtext of his conversation . . .

So, you're the granddaughter of this woman I knew—and possibly liked—a long time ago, and I've put you up in the house of a woman who married a wealthy man nearly three times her age. Hey, what do you know? Just like you and me!

Here, let me pat your hand one more time . . .

Had the Colonel actually been hitting on me? Or was he just a chatty, perhaps lonely, old man?

Please don't let him be pervy, I pleaded. *I need this job too much.*

I hit the ground floor and took two steps toward the large wooden front door.

How would the next few weeks play out? Like being a contestant on *Survivor*? *The Great Race*?

A voice stopped me.

"Just the person I was waiting for."

I closed my eyes.

Nope. Things were shaping up to be *The Bachelorette*.

Honestly.

Pasting on my polite grin, which truthfully was more of a grimace by this point, I turned around.

"Mr. D'Angelo."

"Dante, please." He stepped out of the shadows at the base of the stairs. A window in the stairwell illuminated half of him. Even that half was huge.

Whereas I looked down on Pierce and was eye-level with the Colonel, I had to look up, up at Dante. At five ten myself, it takes a lot to make me feel short. But he somehow managed it. He had to be at least six four and linebacker-wide. Did he play football in high school?

His dark, wavy hair had been smoothly slicked back when he arrived earlier. But I had watched it creep forward as the morning went along until a section of it came loose, swinging down to kiss his jaw. My fingers itched to brush it back.

Dante was the type of man I had always had a sweet tooth for. Until I learned, oh-so-painfully, how bad for my health they could be.

I could hear Grammy. *Four out of five psychologists recommend avoiding luscious man-candy to maintain proper mental health* . . .

I was the collateral damage of a lifetime of men like him. Pierce was supposed to have been my compromise. The man who didn't make my pulse race but also wouldn't destroy my heart. My savior from all the Dante D'Angelos of the world.

The. Irony.

Dante was staring at me again. A squinty, focused look, just as he had all through the meeting.

What was his problem? Trying to subtly intimidate me without technically violating the Colonel's Sandbox Rule?

"How may I help you?" I asked.

"Just making sure you're okay. I couldn't help but overhear your conversation with the Colonel and Pierce. Things seemed a little tense back there."

"My issues with Mr. Whitman are hardly your concern—"

"Look, I'm just trying to be polite and considerate here."

I sighed. Right. "Thank you. Good day, Mr. D'Angelo—"

"It's Dante, and I was hoping I could talk you into joining me for lunch." His face morphed into a friendly smile. "I have a favorite restaurant off Piazza Santa Croce. Quiet. Delicious traditional Tuscan dishes."

Sheesh. Three meal invitations in less than fifteen minutes had to be some kind of record.

Dante probably thought to sweet talk me into . . . what? Giving him pointers? Not exposing him and Branwell as frauds?

I hesitated too long.

"C'mon. I promise the food will be amazing." His grin widened.

Moving from merely charming into heartbreaking territory.

Granted, I understood stunning smiles were a specialty of men like him. But even knowing this, my heart *still* sped up.

Gah! Why did I *always* have to be attracted to flashy exteriors? I *hated* myself for finding him sexy. I needed to pack every last ounce of that away—

Exactly! Become dismantled, I could hear Grammy chuckle.

Besides, the thought of eating in a public place where anyone could recognize me, take a photo of us together, paste it all over the internet . . .

"Thank you for the invitation. But I don't think the Colonel wants us fraternizing—"

"I don't recall ol' KFC forbidding us from *talking* to each other. Just no throwing sand or stealing toys. I promise to be on my best behavior."

Uh-huh. And the day I believed that . . .

"The less contact we have with each other, the better—"

"There's a lot we could do to help each other."

Ah. There it was.

Did he really want my help? Or did he intend to undermine me? Both?

"Again, the Colonel made it clear we aren't supposed to help each other."

"No, he just said no *plagiarizing*. Talking about the project is hardly plagiarism—"

"You're hair-splitting here."

"If I must."

"I prefer to keep my professional integrity unimpeachable, Mr. D'Angelo—"

"Dante."

"—and I feel that we should work separately. *Buon giorno.*"

I turned to leave. And then paused in front of the wooden doors leading out to the piazza.

They were enormous. Like I'm-here-to-see-the-wizard huge. When open, you could probably drive an Escalade through them. Or at least a carriage and some munchkins. And, like front doors everywhere, they opened inward.

There was no door knob.

I looked to each side of the door, searching for a release button. Something. Anything. Someone had buzzed me in earlier.

It figured that I would be stuck staring at the doors. I swear I could *feel* Dante's amusement tickling my shoulder blades.

"Would you like some help with the *portone?*" he asked.

He pronounced *portone* sharp and staccato, rolling the *r* . . . port-OWN-*ay*. He sounded native.

I turned back to him. "*Portone?*"

"Like *porta* and -*one*. Big door. The door that opens to the outside." He chuckled. A deep smooth sound that rumbled out of his chest.

He stepped around me and threw the deadbolt. Or, at least, what looked like the deadbolt. He spun it one, two, three times. On the fourth round, it caught. With a loud click, he pulled the heavy door ajar. Politely motioned for me to pass through.

Ah.

"*Grazie,*" I said. Agenda or not, he was being courteous. I could at least thank him.

"*Parli italiano?*" he asked as I moved to step out onto the bright piazza.

It would be impolite to not reply. That's what I told myself.

It wasn't that I subconsciously liked every word out of his mouth . . . his very fine, full-lipped mouth.

Nope. I was e*man*cipated.

"Not really," I said. "Just a few tourist phrases. Art words. *Chiaroscuro. Sfumato.* My brain short circuits when it comes to learning a foreign language."

"*Peccato.* I love hearing my native language on the tongue of a gorgeous woman."

I rolled my eyes. *Oy.*

But the teenage girl part of my brain squealed and shook her hands. *He called me gorgeous. Eeeek!*

I was pathetic.

Just walk out the open door, Claire.

Unbidden, I found myself pivoting as I stepped past him. My body a compass helplessly pointing to his north star.

"So you *are* Italian, then?"

"*Sì.*"

"Your English is perfect. I could have sworn you're American."

"Yes."

I popped a hand onto my hip. Shot him a skeptical eyebrow.

"My mom is American from Portland, Oregon." His gaze honey warm. "My dad was Italian from Florence."

"*Was* Italian?"

His smile froze. An emotion flickered. "Yeah. My father passed away when I was a teenager."

"Oh. I'm so sorry. My dad died in a car accident when I was three." The words just popped free. I bit my tongue a second too late.

Why, why, why would I share that tidbit of personal information with Dante D'Angelo of all people? Why would my stupid subconscious leap to confide in him?

His head canted. Interested.

"I'm sorry." Even though he repeated my own words, they hung with genuine sincerity.

I shrugged. "It was a long time ago. I don't have any memories of him. Not like being a teenager."

"Well, it feels like a long time ago for me too. My parents had been separated for years. Though I lived my first ten years in Italy, after that, I grew up mostly in the States with my mom. I just spent summers here with my dad's family."

Wow. I was standing in a doorway, bonding with a (surprisingly nice) playboy over our shared grief. This could not bode well for my emotional state.

I needed to leave. *C'mon feet, start walking.*

But for some reason, my body had stopped listening to me.

"So, do you still live in the States?"

"No. We all live here now. In Florence. My brothers and I took over the family business after college."

"Brothers? You have a brother other than your twin?"

"Branwell is my identical twin, but we're actually triplets. Branwell, Tennyson and myself. We have a younger sister too, Chiara."

I liked how he said her name . . . *key-AH-rah*. Again, trilling the *r*, so it sounded somewhere between an *r* and a *d*.

He braced an arm against the open door. The movement pulled his suit coat tight against his bicep, angling his body toward me. Looming. He looked expensive. Decadent, even.

I could always tell him and Branwell apart in photos. Despite being identical twins, it wasn't hard. Dante had this urbane smoothness about him. Like he had just walked off a Milan runway. His brother, Branwell, was more Free People hobo with a thick beard and homespun vibe. The fun-loving playboy and mountain-man recluse, as the industry gossip labeled them.

Dante was leaning decidedly too close. Probably the Italian in him ignoring my personal space bubble.

I meant to take a step back. Really I did. But then I caught a whiff of his cologne (old school Drakkar Noir . . . classic), and my kneecaps liquefied just as my heart pounded its way up my throat.

Sheesh. Could I *be* more pathetic? Stupidstupidstupid physical attraction.

A wide flashy smile. Some smooth Italian charm. A few bulging biceps . . . and all my hard-won resolve fluttered out the window.

Surely *World's Biggest Idiot* was flashing across my forehead.

"You know—" There went that grin again. I had a feeling women denied him nothing when he smiled like that. "—if you come to lunch with me, you can ask me all the questions you like."

"But would you answer them?"

"Possibly."

"Tempting."

"Mmmmm, so I've been told." He winked, just like Pierce.

My senses plummeted back to reality.

Honestly.

How many times did I have to be sucker-punched before I learned to stay down for good? I was *not* going to let a man ruin my career again.

"Thanks, but I have no more questions to ask." *Finally* my feet listened. I stepped out the door.

"Wait."

His bare hand wrapped around my bare wrist.

And, I swear, the entire universe came to a jarring, hiccupping *stop*.

Sparks. Electricity. *Connection.*

How do you describe that first jolt of contact? When every sensation focuses down, down, down to a single point of touch?

A shocking *ping* of sensation. A zap that chases your spine.

I don't think he actually heard my gasp. But I certainly felt it.

I stared at his hand, heart instantly in my throat. Raised my gaze to his.

Our eyes locked. Fixed. Silence stretched.

He swallowed. Dropped my wrist.

I moved backwards.

One, two, three steps. And then turned, all but running across the piazza.

Trying to wipe the image of his face from my mind.

Eyes wide. Mouth slack.

His expression just as shell-shocked as mine.

6

DANTE

"Something's up with you." It wasn't a question. Branwell folded his arms and sat back.

"What makes you say that?" I asked.

"Womb-mate." Branwell pointed a gloved thumb at his chest. The pun so familiar I didn't even groan. "We *literally* share the same genetic brain, remember?"

Sometimes I hated having an identical twin brother.

We were in Nonna's galley-style kitchen, a floor up from our own apartment, helping prep lunch. Or, rather, I grated fresh *parmigiana reggiano* into a bowl while Branwell watched. Things were easier that way.

Light from the enormous window at one end flooded the room. Nonna's *sugo di pomodoro* bubbled on the stove behind me. The smell of cooking tomato, garlic and basil wafted through the room.

I had already given Branwell a rundown of the meeting earlier in the day: the 'audition' parameters, the Sandbox Rules, the Michelangelo sketch.

"You think the Colonel has an actual unknown Michelangelo?" Branwell asked.

"Hard to say." I glanced at my brother. "It's certainly possible given the provenance of his family vaults."

"And this job?"

"It should be a slam-dunk for us. Pierce is a pretentious jackass, and Claire can be . . . unpredictable. We're the professional, steady ones."

Branwell grunted. "Good. Getting this job would take a lot of pressure off."

"Agreed." I nodded. "The last thing I want to do is move the company to a larger city and leave Mom alone to deal with Tennyson."

And you too, I mentally added.

I had yet to bring up Claire Raythorn's disturbing blankness. Chatting with her in the stairwell had been the same. No shadows. Just her lovely sculpted face and velvet voice. A sense of connection and that shock when I touched her wrist . . .

"How's your GUT been lately?" I tried to lob the question in casually. Like I was changing the topic or something.

But, of course, it detonated like a grenade.

"My GUT?" Branwell's eyebrows snapped to his hairline. "The same."

"No changes?"

"Nope. But you wouldn't ask the question if something hadn't happened. Like I said, something's up with you." Branwell beckoned me with a gloved hand. "Out with it, man."

Even though we technically shared a genome, Branwell was my opposite in many ways—the difference in our 'talents' ensured it.

As usual, he was dressed in jeans and a long-sleeve, homespun-style shirt with embroidered zigzags around the cuffs. Leather gloves encased his hands, the same zigzag embroidery around the wrists. His long hair was knotted in a loose man-bun on top of his head, while his beard currently reached mountain man proportions. All ensuring not a sliver of bare skin showed from his nose down.

In our world, you did what you had to in order to function.

I pretended to assess how much more cheese needed to be grated while thinking how to frame my next question. Branwell and Tennyson's lives were already pressure-cooker tense.

So, you know that supernatural inheritance from our father that isn't too bad for me, but hell on earth for you two . . .

"Has your GUT ever just stopped working?" I finally asked.

"*Magari.*" He snorted. "It never lets up."

That was the truth. Relentless tenacity had always been the strongest feature of our *abilities*.

Every first born D'Angelo male for the last seven hundred years had been cursed with a Grossly Unusual Talent—the ability to see, hear and feel the past and future. It had always been a complicated mix of psychometry, clairvoyance, clairaudience and clairsentience.

But my mother conceived triplets, causing the GUT to fracture, scattering it helter-skelter between us boys.

You'd think the fracturing would be equal or logical or, at the very least, understandable.

You'd be wrong.

Branwell and I—as identical twins who had once been a single egg—shared the past portion. Tennyson got the future GUT all to himself. Lucky him.

My GUT was pretty vanilla, in as much as a paranormal, freak-of-nature talent could be.

Basically, I saw the past in an extremely limited way—I could see shadows of what someone or something had been.

On a daily basis, I saw the silvery shapes of who people had been in previous incarnations. Objects showed me nothing unless I touched them and nudged my GUT. Then, like with the table earlier, I could see things that had happened around the object. I couldn't see entire historical scenes and never heard anything . . . well, almost never.

My GUT was gentle and subtle—vanilla, remember?—not

hampering my day-to-day living. Though there had been two times when it proved more powerful.

My brothers' GUTs were not quite as benign.

The hearing-past was Branwell's portion of the talent. Clairaudience to use the proper lingo. Branwell had a complicated GUT, full of weird rules (that he probably had color-coded and laminated somewhere).

If something inanimate touched his body—bare skin, lips, mouth—Branwell would hear what occurred around the object the last time it changed form in some way.

Through trial and error, we had figured out the object had to be large enough to be felt, liquids and livings things didn't count, the change had to be obviously noticeable . . . (And by *we*, I mean Tennyson and me as kids, and by *trial and error*, I mean we would scream while ripping a piece of paper and then sneak up on Branwell and slap it on his bare neck. We were nothing if not scientifically thorough.)

All of which explained the gloves and embroidery. Branwell altered everything that touched his skin in a sound-proof room.

But, like me, if Branwell touched an object and concentrated, he could sift back through the sound at each point of change. It was tiring and overwhelming—the cacophony of noise, the unexpected situations—but he could do it.

We were two sides of the same coin. I saw the past in a limited way. Branwell heard it. It made art authentication a lucrative business choice.

Tennyson, on the other hand, was future clairsentient (more lingo). He could feel the future emotions of those around him. Or, at least, that was his story and he was sticking to it. Tennyson got all kinds of pissy when we asked too many probing questions about his GUT.

Being around emotion-full people was . . . difficult, so Tennyson lived by himself in the family villa just north of Volterra. We talked on the phone more than anything.

Not that I would bother him with my current GUT problem—

"So what's up?" Branwell asked and then held up a hand. "Wait—do you suppose Nonna has any more of that *pecorino* from Sardegna?"

My twin did have this thing for cheese. Branwell stood, moving for the fridge.

"Let me see." I waved him back down.

I finished with the *parmigiano*, put it away and then dug around the fridge until I found the *pecorino sardo* wrapped in wax paper.

In complete silence, I flaked off several chunks of the white cheese for Branwell, spacing them neatly on a plate. I slid the plate across to him.

He shot me his usual look. A cross between 'thank you' and 'stop treating me like I'm in kindergarten.'

I returned with my typical 'let me help you' blink.

Branwell sighed.

"Okay, go. Tell me what happened." He picked up a piece of cheese and popped it in his mouth. Hyper careful not to alter it in any way before eating it.

"Claire Raythorn has no shadows."

He froze.

"You sure?" he asked around the mouthful of cheese.

"Uh, yeah. I stared at her long and hard during the meeting. I think she was a phone call away from a restraining order by the end."

"No shadows." Branwell pursed his lips, reaching for more *pecorino*. "Is that possible with someone who isn't a relative?"

"I have no idea. She's blank, that's all I know. Granted, the Colonel and Pierce were both a little sputtery too." I cut a wedge of cheese for myself. Salty and tangy. "It makes no sense."

"Weird. So Claire looks like me or Tenn? Empty air behind her?"

"Yep. Not a hint of anything."

For some reason, I couldn't see the past life shadows of those closest to me.

Mom, Branwell and Tennyson were completely blank. Sometimes I would get a flicker from Chiara and Nonna, but they were generally absent too. Aunts, uncles, cousins, close friends . . . I tended to see more, though there was the static with them as well, like I had seen with the Colonel and Pierce.

"How do you feel about her? Claire?" Branwell asked.

I shrugged. "She's pretty. You've seen the photos. Tall. Built like a runway model. Blond. Gorgeous blue eyes—"

"You've always had a thing for tall blonds."

"True."

"So that's . . . relevant, I suppose. Claire seems a little standoff-ish."

"Precisely."

"And then there's the psycho video. She's all ice until she cracks and the crazy sneaks out."

"Something like that."

"Not your type."

"Exactly. Look,"—I waved the cheese knife at him—"I get your subtext and the answer is no. I'm not in *love* with Claire. I barely know her."

Up until now, the family explanation for lacking shadows had been based on available evidence—blank persons were people I loved.

Basically, the more I loved someone, the fewer their shadows. *Love* had been the criteria. We reasoned that people I loved were emotionally too near. It was like holding a pen to the side of your eye. If you were looking straight ahead, the pen was too close to be seen.

But now . . .

I sighed. "Assuming my GUT is not fracturing or changing, we might to have to reassess our assumptions."

"My thoughts exactly." Branwell nodded. "We know one branch of reincarnation theory states that, life after life, you tend to associate with the same souls. You become bound to each other. I'm your brother in this life, but in other lives, I have probably been your father, son or best friend. We know, empirically, that mom and I were vitally important to you in at least one past life."

That was true.

My GUT is generally benign, but if all the stars align just right, it can be powerfully terrifying, sparking a bonafide past life regression. It's only happened twice in my life.

The first occurred when I was a kid. My mom had decided to take us boys to visit an old friend in London.

I was just ten-years-old, so I don't recall where we were exactly.

All I know is this—one minute, I was walking through a perfectly modern British doorway with my mom.

The next—I was rushing into a Victorian bedroom, thrusting a bowl under the chin of a pretty woman just as she vomited bright red blood.

Suddenly, I was thirty-year-old Michael Strickland—London MP—and my sister, Anne, was dying of consumption. A terrified maid hovered nearby, wringing her hands around a handkerchief.

I was fully immersed in the past.

I could smell the metallic blood. I heard Anne's labored breathing as she lay back, trembling hands clutching her cotton nightgown. Felt the cool wet of the washcloth Michael used to wipe her face. Spoke Michael's words of love and support.

I had been at her bedside for nearly a week, tending to her, watching her slowly slip away. So much grief and frustration and loss. The heavy weight of silence filled the room. I focused on Anne's chest, stuttering up and down. Tasted the tears on my upper lip.

I watched, spellbound, as Anne gave one last gasping, rasping breath. Blood bubbled from her mouth. She choked and then lay still.

The agony of that moment . . . I collapsed over her body, weeping . . . ugly, soul-wracking.

I surfaced from the regression into the same room. Only back in the present.

Shocked. Stunned. Sobbing uncontrollably.

I turned to see my mother with a hand over her mouth, tears streaming down her cheeks.

She had experienced everything *with* me. But from Anne's point-of-view. Mom had been Anne. Felt the agonizing pain, the terror of drowning alive. The knowledge that she was leaving her beloved brother alone in the world . . .

Branwell, who had seen us pause, said it was just like a blink. A stutter of only milliseconds.

But for me and Mom, it had been much longer. Minutes. Maybe even half an hour.

The experience was traumatic. It had taken months before I could even talk about it without crying. I clung to my mom, worried that she would die like Anne.

The whole episode was a watershed moment for everyone. Our 'talents' had never affected anyone but us three boys. But now we knew the GUT had fractured so much it could involve outside people.

I had experienced another past life regression with Branwell in college. *That* one . . . well, let's just say I still had nightmares about it.

Fortunately, the regressions implied that most of my past lives had occurred along my mother's Scottish and English heritage, not my father's Italian one.

Which was a relief. I probably had experienced few, if any, past lives in Italy. Which meant the chances of walking down a street with Chiara and suddenly watching her die from a knife through the chest were slim.

It's the little things in life.

But what did this mean for the present situation with Claire?

I looked at Branwell while eating another bite of *pecorino*, pondering.

"Love might still be key." He shrugged. "We've always assumed that love in *this* life was the connecting factor. But what if that's wrong?"

"Meaning?"

"Maybe love in *past* lives affects it too. So if you loved someone in the past, you can't see the shadow of that life, which would result in someone looking sputtery."

"Are you saying I loved Pierce and the Colonel in some past life?" I snorted in disbelief. "Because that seems . . . unlikely."

"They're your past lives, dude, not mine. You must have some freaky stuff in there."

"I don't know—"

"There are two options here." Branwell reached for another slice of cheese. "One, your GUT is going haywire. Or, two, our previous assumptions about how your GUT works are incorrect. Aside from the shadow thing with Claire and the rest, has everything else been normal?"

"Yeah."

I told him about testing the table at the Colonel's.

"Look, Dante, there's no manual for our GUTs." Branwell waved his hand back and forth between us. "We've always been in figure-it-out-as-we-go mode. Up until now, maybe you hadn't met anyone outside friends and family who had been emotionally important to you in other lives. But you probably loved people other than your current relatives and friends in the past."

"It is possible, I'll give you that."

"Possible? No, it's brilliant. For example, if you've known and loved me in *all* your past lives—'cause, let's face it, how could you not?—" He shot me a wink. "—then that could explain my missing shadows."

"Yeah, but Claire is dead air space. Not a trace of a single shadow."

Branwell just grinned—salaciously, I might add—and rolled a gloved hand. *Ergo* . . .

I stared at him. Blinked.

"Are you suggesting Claire Raythorn is *my* woman?" I asked.

"Yep."

"That I have loved her—Batty Ray Psycho, mind you—life after life after life? Loved her so much that I can't see the tiniest trace of a shadow?"

A chill chased my spine—the sensation that my words rang with *truth*.

I shook the feeling away. No way I was getting involved with Batty Ray Psycho.

"Soulmates, brother."

"That seems so improbable . . . I don't even know where to begin."

Branwell laughed, low and wicked.

"I'm not sure I even *believe* in soulmates," I grumbled.

I had never experienced any transcendental, soul-esque connection with any of my past girlfriends. It probably explained why I didn't date much, despite my reputation.

"C'mon, it would be a great story," Branwell said. "Your eyes meet across a crowded room, instant happily-ever-after—"

"That's one-too-many Disney movies talking there."

"No deflecting. Seriously, what's your take on Claire Raythorn? You still haven't answered my question."

I shrugged. "I honestly don't know."

Despite the almost electric shock earlier when I touched her wrist, I wasn't sure she was *that* woman. Physical attraction did not equal emotional attraction.

I preferred women who were more animated and open. Ready to flirt as hard as I did. WYSIWYG women—what-you-see-is-what-you-get.

Which in no way described Claire Raythorn.

I flaked off another bite of cheese. It needed some fruit. I grabbed a pear sitting in a bowl on the table and snagged a paring knife. Branwell's eyes lit up.

In silence, I sliced into the pear. Branwell reached for the knife, intending to cut some for himself. I waved him away.

He sighed. I ignored it.

I sliced the pear into bite-size chunks, being careful to make as little noise as possible. I arranged the pears on Branwell's plate.

"Thank you," he said dryly. "You do realize I am perfectly capable of cutting my own pear."

"Just helping where I can."

And then I winced. That was always the *wrong* thing to say.

"No, you're going all *nonna* and coddling me. Barreling into my space. Treating me like I'm somehow less-than." Branwell gave another hefty sigh and reached for a slice of pear, along with the *pecorino*.

"Branwell—"

"Broken as I am, I wouldn't change myself." He dropped the pecorino/pear chunk in his mouth. "The GUT . . . it's like diabetes, brother. It's manageable."

"You really haven't hung out with Tenn lately, have you?"

"Point taken."

"You live in a cage."

"Don't we all?" With a roll of his eyes, Branwell reached for more cheese and pear. "Besides, you're still deflecting about Claire—"

"Who's deflecting?" Chiara bounced into the room. Our sister was perpetually in a state of bouncy-ness.

"Branwell," I said.

"Dante," he said.

Without missing a beat, Chiara strode over to the stove and stirred the pasta sauce. She had years of practice of ignoring us.

Where Branwell and I took after our mother's Scottish ancestry in build, Chiara was one hundred percent Italian. Petite, dark and constantly in motion.

"I think I'm going to side with Branwell on this one," she said as she turned around. "What's up, Dante?"

"Is something up with Dante?" That came from our mother, Judith.

Mom strolled into the kitchen on Chiara's heels, a white rat on her shoulder. Tall and curvy with vivid blue eyes, it was obvious why our father had fallen so hard for her.

"He's deflecting." Chiara waved a tomato-sauce covered spoon in my direction.

"Dante *is* an expert deflector." Mom stroked the white rat fidgeting on her shoulder.

Mom had sold her veterinary clinic in Portland four years ago and moved to Italy. Given the situation with Tennyson at the time . . . she had been desperately needed. Once here, she had converted part of our rooftop terrace into a makeshift animal hospital for strays. Most she re-homed. But every now and again, she kept one.

Like the white rat, Boney, currently on her shoulder.

I was nearly a hundred percent sure Mom's rat was the reincarnation of Napoleon Bonaparte. Though people always had silvery shadows, animals only occasionally did. And you just can't part with an animal who had once been the Nightmare of Europe.

Boney liked being petted and running on his wheel. But every now and again, he would stand on his hind legs and press a tiny paw to his chest. His entire body coming to attention.

In those moments, the resemblance was uncanny.

"Com'è il sugo?" Nonna waddled into the kitchen, walking over to the tomato sauce. The small space was getting crowded.

My grandma was a truly traditional Italian *nonna*. The ultimate love child of Sophia Loren and Martha Stewart, as Chiara described it.

Nonna cooked and cleaned in a knee-length tight skirt, nylons and heels, her short silver hair always curled and thoroughly sprayed into place. She wore a mink fur coat to do her grocery shopping. In other words—your average, elderly Italian woman.

"Would you like me to cut the bread, Nonna?" I asked, switching to Italian.

"Please."

I slid past Branwell—careful not to brush his skin—and grabbed a bread knife from a magnetic strip on the tiled wall.

"We're not done discussing Claire," he murmured to me. "I won't let you deflect this away."

CLAIRE

"Claire, darling, could you hold on a second?" My mom's breezy voice sailed through the connection.

"Sure. No problem."

Phone to my ear, I stood on the Ponte Vecchio, nestled between overhanging medieval houses and under the arched Vasari Corridor. (Sixteenth century. The Medici's private commuter lane.)

Mom's voice murmured in the background, talking to someone.

Jet lag had caught up with me after the Colonel's meeting. I had returned to my hotel room and crashed. I awoke this morning with a clearer mind and managed to get some preliminary work done—research on Michelangelo's composition in the *Battle of Cascina* and building a list of items to examine. I couldn't really do anything more until I physically examined the sketch.

So now I was rewarding myself with a jaunt through my favorite parts of Florence.

Which led to thinking about Grammy.

Which led to wondering if Grammy *had* known the Colonel.

Which led to calling my mom.

Which might have been a mistake.

"Claire, are you still there?" Mom's voice came back.

"Yeah. I'm here. I just had a quick question for you—"

"No, no, Micky. The gauze needs to be over there, nearer to the light." Mom's voice faded out as she pulled the phone from her ear to talk to someone. Micky, I assumed.

Finally Mom came back to me. "How hard can it be to get gauze wrapped correctly around pink flamingos?"

"Right? Gauze." I gave a strained chuckle. "Look, I just had a question—"

"Oh, good. I have a question for you too. Did I tell you about the installation, darling? The one with the Rockefellers?" Mom had this odd east coast accent that wasn't completely American or British, but something in between. It should have been off-putting, but most people simply considered it bohemian.

"Uhmmm, I think I heard someone mention it—"

"It's going to be brilliant. The music has taken us months to get right."

"Music? But, you guys don't do music—"

"I know, I know. We hired a composer. She's brilliant, but I think your stepfather finds her brilliant in other ways. You know how he is." Mom laughed her brittle laugh. The one that was anything but amused.

Figured John-Baptista would be giving my mom fits.

I had no memory of my real father, Tom, Grammy's son. He had died in a car accident when I was three. Mom remarried JB when I was five. I called him Dad and we got along fine.

Fortunately for me, my mom and Grammy had always had a close relationship, even after my biological father died. Grammy loved people so hard, you had no choice but to love her back.

"Anyway, the music has to be timed with the gauze," Mom continued, "and we just don't have the resources—Micky, Micky! *No!*"

Mom's voice drifted back to that low hum . . . I only caught the occasional word . . . *too high* . . . *more flowy* . . . *not now* . . .

"Mom. Mom!" I tried to pull her attention back.

Mom and her fabric. You can still find postcards of her *Lady Liberty: Mourning* in New York City even though the National Park Service only allowed the black cloth to remain on the statue for twenty-four hours.

I studied the tourists window-shopping along the bridge, gawking at the goldsmith shops. Everyone looking for that special something.

A metaphor for my life.

"Mom!" I said one last time.

"Oh, Claire." She was breathless now. "Are you still there?"

"Yes, but Mom—"

"So you got all that about the Rockefellers, right?"

"About the installation?"

"Yes. The supplier and the media people need to be paid beforehand, and you know how JB is with money. Anyway, I'm sure you still have that inheritance Grammy left you . . ." Her voice trailed into *hint, hint, hint.*

I sighed. There *was* no inheritance from Grammy. Just the house, which I had no intention of selling. Mom never listened to my explanations.

"Mom, how much do you need?"

She named a sum equal to about half my current month's salary from the Colonel.

I needed that money. Grammy's house required repairs and after so many months without employment, I had plenty of credit card bills of my own. But . . .

"I promise I'll pay it all back as soon as the Rockefeller's settle our invoice," Mom said, correctly reading my hesitation.

Right. And the day I believed that . . .

"Promise you'll pay it back?"

"Of course, darling."

The lies we told each other.

"Fine. I'll transfer what I can into your account," I said. Sometimes I hated that I loved my mom.

I just had to get this job with the Colonel. There was no other option.

"Thanks, Claire darling. I love you so much. I need to go—"

"Wait, Mom. Did Grammy know Mr. Finster-Cline?"

"Who?"

"Adelaide. My father's mother. The one you think had lots of money."

An exasperated noise. "Don't be smart with me. I know who Grammy was. Who else did you say?"

"Kenneth Finster-Cline. He's a wealthy art collector I'm working with right now—"

"The Colonel?"

"Yes."

"I haven't seen him in ages. Please tell him I said hi."

My mother *would* know the Colonel. "Okay, I will. But, Mom, he said he knew Grammy and—"

"Does he want another painting?"

"What?"

"The Colonel has purchased a few of my—Micky! Not again!"

The line went dead.

Honestly, how could a five-minute phone conversation so thoroughly summarize my childhood? It was uncanny.

Getting my mother to focus for longer than ten seconds was a lost cause. She was like a gerbil on meth.

I would have to ask the Colonel himself about Grammy, if and when the right moment presented itself. And just hope his answer would make sense and feel normal without a trace of old-man-pervy.

I refused to think about the situation being anything other than above board with the Colonel. Too much of my financial future rested on this job.

Tourists swirled around me on the bridge. I looked up the Arno River toward Piazzale Michelangelo and the cathedral of San Miniato al Monte outlined against impossibly blue sky. My boyfriend-city had produced another stunning red-banner day.

Suddenly, my neck prickled with that all-too-familiar feeling of being watched. I was *so* sick of the sensation.

I casually turned in a circle, pretending to study the jewelry shops. No random old gypsy women. No top-hatted Regency bucks. Nothing unusual.

My phone buzzed.

> *I watched you as you slept last night. Tasted your lips. Never forget—you will be mine in the end.*

My heart rate soared, pulse a snare-drum in my ears.

Ugh.

Bloody hell.

(I learned that little bit of language from my fifth nanny, Mrs. Evans-Sharp. Very British, very proper. Hired her by virtue of her cultured accent alone. She was Mary Poppins-esque until you crossed her. Then her south London roots made a dramatic appearance.)

Stupid online bully. When would this end?

I closed my eyes. Did my normal dose of self-help talk—*breatheyoucandothiscourage*. This online harasser only had the power to upset me if I let him.

Pick up Fear and move on. I could hear Grammy say. *Don't let them win, darling. It should be your* man*tra. Ha!*

Notching my chin upward, I walked into the middle of the Ponte Vecchio and took a selfie. Me and the medieval bridge.

More photos in memory of Grammy.

I would *live* my life.

With a determined smile, I left the Ponte Vecchio and headed down Via Calimala toward the Duomo, taking the occasional selfie.

When I was fourteen, a distant cousin had left Grammy some money. My mom and JB were neck-deep in a project in Miami and done with my teenage angst. Grammy used the money to book a trip to Florence, taking me with her.

Three months in Tuscany.

My passion for Italian art was born in those months. *I* was born.

Could any woman have given her grandchild a greater gift?

I chewed my lip. *Blink, blink, blink.*

We had stayed in a small *pensione* near Santa Croce, visiting museums, wearing holes in our shoes on the flagstone streets and expanding our waistlines with gelato.

When I was with Grammy, I was . . . home. She had always faced hard things head on. I would too. Push worries aside. Engage in normal, everyday activities.

To that end, I popped into a divine-smelling bakery and bought some bread. The sign called it *schiacciata*, though it looked like a thinner focaccia to me, finger-dimpled and slathered in olive oil. In passable English, the cute girl behind the counter said the bread was a Tuscan specialty. (Elena. Crushes on Johnny Depp. Loves Big Macs.)

Tearing off pieces of the hot bread, I walked by the soaring arches of the Loggia del Mercato Nuovo—the *new* market, which was a paltry four hundred years old. Finishing up the bread, I tossed the oil-soaked paper in a nearby trashcan and brushed crumbs from my fingers (and my lips and my shirt and my jeans).

Opposite the market, I paused to take a selfie with the lucky bronze pig, *Il Porcellino.* (Pietro Tacca. Baroque. Modern copy.) Like all good tourists, I dropped a coin in its mouth and rubbed its shiny snout for good luck.

My shoulder-blades tingling the entire time with that feeling of being watched. Selfies and oil-soaked carbs could only push the fear back so far.

I hated this. Hated that I couldn't go anywhere without this paranoia lingering. Hated the stupid texter who was determined to frighten me.

I kept going, walking into the giant Piazza della Republica and took another selfie.

I would show them all.

I flipped to the selfie on my phone and froze. Stared at the photo, heart rate spiking.

He was back—my Mr. Darcy photobomber.

He stood about twenty feet behind, to the left of a brightly-colored retro carousel and facing me. Dressed the same in a cut-away green coat, tight breeches and top hat pulled low.

I whirled around, standing on tiptoe and scanning the busy square.

Nothing.

No bobbing top hat. No one in Regency-era costume.

Why was he doing this? More importantly, *how* was he doing this?

I hesitated and then, steeling my nerves, flipped back through the other selfies I had taken.

My hands visibly trembled by the third one.

Just like the day before. . . there he was. In every single photo.

Standing behind me on the Ponte Vecchio.

Walking toward me on Via Calimala.

Leaning into the *porcellino*, head angled my way.

Never threatening, per se. Just . . . there.

I studied each photo, trying to get a clear look at the guy's face, but that hat was in the way.

Bloody hell. I needed to check my photos more carefully as I took them. I felt like slapping a *moron* sticker on my chest.

Why would some guy dress up like a Regency gentleman and then stalk me through downtown Florence, photo bombing every chance he got? Two days in a row, no less?

It made no sense on any level. Beyond loony and straight into certifiable territory.

Lifting my head, I stood rooted to the spot, studying the bustling piazza around me.

Tourists sat at cafe tables around the perimeter. Kids ran through the center, scattering pigeons. The occasional taxi drove through the enormous arch on the west side. Groups of people moved around me.

No Mr. Darcy.

Now what?

I clenched my teeth. I was in my boyfriend-city, a place I dearly loved. I *refused* to hail a cab and scurry back to my hotel like some frightened mouse. Not going to happen.

Just to prove I would not chicken out, I kept walking. Down the street. Around the cathedral baptistery. And up the Duomo steps.

Almost daring Mr. Darcy to follow me.

I waited in the brief line to get into the cathedral, carefully scanning the piazza below me, looking for my would-be stalker.

Still no top hats, walking sticks or coat tails in sight.

What was up? Why only show himself in my photos?

Behind me, a group of French high schoolers came rushing up the steps and crowded in line, pushing me forward. One boy glanced in my direction and did a double-take, elbowing his neighbor.

I quickly turned my head.

Too late. I heard a mutter of *fou* and then *psycho* before being waved inside the enormous doors. Yet another moment to file under 'Signs Your Life Is a Hot Mess'—a stranger halfway around the world says 'psycho' and you *know* they're referring to you.

Sheesh. Was everyone out to hassle me today?

I quickly moved into the cool interior of the cathedral and wandered down the wide nave, putting space between me and the French school group, losing myself in the crowds of tourists.

For all its lush exterior decoration, the interior of the Duomo is spartan. Mostly whitewashed walls broken by the occasional funerary inscription. What it lacks in ornament, the cathedral makes up in size. Despite being over seven hundred years old, it is still one of largest cathedrals in the world.

Spinning around, I carefully studied the people. The French school group was back at the entrance, security searching their packs.

No tall Mr. Darcys anywhere.

Just to be sure, I framed the vast space in my camera and took a photo. No selfies for now. I immediately flipped to the image.

Whew. Still no Mr. Darcy. Just perfectly normal people.

I breathed out in relief.

Coming inside the cathedral had been a smart move. If he followed me in here, I would notice for sure. There was nowhere to hide in this space.

Nodding at my own cleverness (and feeling somewhat smug), I turned to my left and paused.

A large monument stood above me. I craned my neck to look at it. A mixture of carved stone and fresco, it depicted a man on horseback. One of the many tomb markers.

Painted by Paolo Uccello. Mid-fifteenth century. A fantastic example of his work *in situ*. I couldn't remember much more than that.

I smiled. It was like stumbling on an old friend. I had been unusually drawn to this fresco as a teenager. Dragging Grammy here over and over.

I turned around and, lifting my phone, took a selfie. Me and the Uccello fresco of a random guy.

Still smiling, I swiped to the image. Grammy would appreciate this moment.

Cold washed my body as surely as if I had been doused in ice water.

Impossible.

The phone visibly shook in my hand.

My Regency era photobomber was in *here*.

He leaned against the wall below the fresco, top hat cradled in the crook of his arm, dressed in the same green coat. Dark head slightly bowed, again hiding his face. Casual and yet elegant. As if he had been waiting for me.

Bloody hell!

Frantic, I whirled around, scanning the cathedral, but saw nothing. No man in a tailcoat and tasseled Hessian boots.

He had vanished. Again.

How?!

I looked back at the photo. Shivered.

Feet shuffled behind me. The group of French high school students crowded past, bumping me with their backpacks. A boy said *batty psycho* and laughed. Someone deliberately tangled a foot with mine. I stumbled.

Stupid teenagers.

Gritting my teeth, I pushed (careened) out of their way and tucked my back against one of the enormous support pillars lining the nave. At least no one could creep up on me, costumed stalker or obnoxious teenager. The French group continued on toward the rotunda, thank goodness. Though a few kids kept swiveling back to stare.

I stood on tiptoe, scouring the cathedral.

No Mr. Darcy.

I could still see the Uccello fresco to my right. I lifted my phone and snapped another photo of it. I immediately flipped to the image.

Nothing. Or, rather, no one unusual.

How was he doing this? What *was* his game? Who was he?

And why the Jane Austen costume fetish?

This made no sense.

Hesitantly, I left the security of the stone pillar, eyeing the high schoolers. That sensation of being watched increased, bulls-eye burning between my shoulder blades.

Keeping close to the exterior wall, I made a slow circuit of the building. I paused every now and again to take a photo. No selfies though. I didn't want to put my back to anyone. I carefully looked before snapping each image, studying the results afterward.

Nothing. No stalker in sight.

Those stupid teenagers found me one last time, several passing deliberately close.

"Batty Ray Psycho," someone hissed. More laughter.

I pressed back against the white-washed wall and met their stares. Tucking my shaking hands behind my back.

They pushed their way through a group of Chinese tourists and headed toward the exit. I watched them leave.

With a tight breath, I finally braved walking into the center of the nave. Hands still trembling, I raised my phone. Took another photo. Examined the image. All normal.

But, just to be sure, I turned around. Reversed my camera and framed my own face in the corner. Again, I studied the length of the cathedral behind me.

No Mr. Darcy. Just that wandering group of Chinese tourists.

I snapped the selfie. And then held my position for a few moments more.

Nothing.

No man appeared or disappeared.

I lowered my phone and swiped into my photos.

All the air in the cathedral vanished. My vision darkened at the edges.

Just . . . bloody hell!

How?!

I collapsed onto the floor. One minute, my legs were holding me upright and, the next, they stopped functioning. I sat with a *thump*.

There he was again. About fifteen feet back. Towering over two small Asian women. Hat in his hand. Dark hair sweeping across his brow. Looking *straight* at me.

Clear as day.

I recognized him now.

Despite the Regency clothing. The different hair style. The complete lack of context . . .

Dante D'Angelo.

DANTE

"The Michelangelo sketch is right through here." The Colonel waved Branwell and me through another oversized, pedimented doorway into a well-lit dining room.

We had pulled up the long, cypress-lined drive to the Colonel's villa ten minutes earlier and had been ushered inside. I had caught a glimpse of Claire chatting with Natalia in a side-room. The Colonel said Claire was here to finalize the samples for mass spectrometry analysis.

Claire looked much the same—no shadows. Though I could see the silvery shadows of a Victorian lady and 1950s housewife clinging to Natalia easily enough.

Branwell and I had hashed through the whole weirdness of Claire of the Missing Shadows the day before, even conferencing Tennyson in on a call. There was no consensus. Was she my soulmate and we had been in love life after life? Or was my gift morphing and changing, fracturing in different ways?

I wasn't sure which answer I preferred.

Branwell and I walked across the room, following the Colonel.

The dining room was much like the rest of the villa—opulent and Baroque. Frescoes dotted the ceiling in gilded, recessed panels. An enormous table stood in the center with chairs pushed back from the end nearest the door.

Branwell and I stepped over to the massive table, staring at the paper lying on top of protective white muslin.

I caught my breath. Michelangelo's sinuous lines jumped off the page.

"It's pretty, isn't it, boys?" The Colonel tucked his thumbs into his sport coat and rocked back on his heels.

Branwell and I both nodded.

I had studied Sangallo's copy of Michelangelo's original cartoon the day before. It was excellent, but the Colonel's sketch on the table in front of me . . . it was *detailed*. Subtle. Like fine silk instead of the coarse wool of Sangallo's copy. The lines drawn with that mixture of precision and *joie di vivre* that only the greatest of the great ever mastered.

Surely this had been done by Michelangelo himself. Or, at the very least, a remarkably competent copyist.

"It's beautiful," I said.

"Amazing." Branwell smiled.

The Colonel beamed at us, blue eyes bright, obviously pleased by our reactions.

Branwell bent over the drawing, careful not to touch it.

"Fascinating," he said. "It's different."

I looked at him, eyebrow raised.

"Here and here." He pointed at the drawing with his gloved hands, indicating a figure in the middle and one to the left. "In Sangallo's copy, the pointing man on the far left cuts through the rocks behind. However, he's better framed between rocks in this sketch. Subtle but definitely different."

I nodded. "So assuming Sangallo's drawing is accurate, this sketch probably *isn't* a copy of Michelangelo's original cartoon."

"Exactly."

A bubble of excitement welled up. Was this the real deal? A lost Michelangelo?

Finding a long lost work of a Renaissance master like Michelangelo was almost unheard of. But this sketch . . . I better understood why the Colonel was taking no chances.

"Do you know anything about this damaged edge, Colonel?" I pointed to the playing-card-size chunk missing out of the upper right corner. The edge there was charred, as if the drawing had narrowly escaped being burned.

"No. Can't say that I do. Like I've said, I can't find any family records of where this sketch came from or its background. Claire took samples from both the burned and unburned edge. She said that'll at least tell when the damage occurred. Maybe you boys can develop some theories about it. I like what I'm hearing so far."

Branwell and I shared a look. We would know what had happened to the sketch in about ten minutes. The problem was going to be *proving* what we knew. We would need to scour whatever records the Colonel gave us access to for supporting tidbits.

"Would you mind giving us a little space, Colonel? We're going to study the sketch."

"Naturally." He adjusted a chair and sat down behind us.

Branwell was already bending over the drawing again, pulling a magnifying glass out of his pocket. He scanned the sketch up close.

"It's vellum," he said.

"Really? That's odd."

"Very. They were definitely using paper by Michelangelo's time. Though the vellum may explain why it survived so well. Leather is much stronger stuff."

"Chalk?"

"Appears to be. So no carbon dating possible of the medium, as chalk isn't organic—"

"That's what Claire said yesterday. She's smart, that gal." The Colonel leaned to the side.

I suppressed a sigh. Yep. Someone was definitely the teacher's pet.

Another sweep of the glass. "No silverpoint that I can discern," Branwell murmured.

Mmmmm. That was telling. Nearly all other extant Michelangelo drawings involved silverpoint—using a pencil with a core of silver. It's what gave old master drawings that oxidized, coppery look.

I scanned the lines of the sketch . . . so fluid. It seemed impossible they came from a mere student copy.

Shooting Branwell a you-know-the-drill look, I placed my hand on the table and leaned over the drawing, deliberately allowing my fingers to barely graze the edge of vellum. I didn't need much contact.

We always started with my GUT. For one, I would often see enough to make the call. Second, noises were harder to contextualize. Branwell only stepped in if I was unsure about what I was seeing.

I slowed my breathing and concentrated, pushing with my mind. I knew I wouldn't see Claire or the Colonel. My GUT was strictly about past lives, so I never saw scenes from people still alive.

Images floated around the sketch.

Darkness and long years in storage.

I pushed back farther.

A woman with a close-cropped bob and 1920s flapper dress leaned over the drawing. A man who looked like a younger Colonel stood behind. His grandparents maybe?

And then . . .

Nothing.

I frowned. Shifted my hand to gain more contact. Tried again, pushing out my gift.

Again. Nothing.

It was like a blanket surrounded the sketch. A wall I couldn't break through.

My stomach churned.

What was going on? This had never happened before. Granted, I didn't test objects like this on a daily basis. But I had never encountered something I couldn't see past a certain point.

First weird missing shadows and now blank objects?

I took a deep, steadying breath. There would be plenty of time to freak out about this later. Right now, we had a job to do.

Branwell noted my puzzled frown.

"So what's your GUT telling you?" he asked.

I gave the tiniest shake of my head. Met his eyes. "Hard to say. I'm drawing a blank with this one."

Branwell shot me a concerned look and then cleared his throat, turning back to the Colonel.

"If it's okay with you, Colonel, I'm going to gently touch a corner of the vellum with my bare hands." Branwell's GUT needed more contact than mine. "I don't usually like to touch a work, but sometimes the tactile connection can tell us a lot about the vellum's origins."

That was complete bull, but Branwell was excellent at selling bull. The Colonel just nodded as if it made sense.

Straightening his shoulders, Branwell slowly drew off the glove of his right hand. This was what Branwell hated most—touching something without knowing what he would hear.

Though he *had* heard some amazing things over the years. We called in a favor from a friend at the Louvre once, and Branwell managed to place a finger on the *Mona Lisa*. He heard Da Vinci ask the *signora* to angle her head a little more.

How fascinating to *know* the sound of Leonardo da Vinci's voice.

Sometimes I thought Branwell was a little OCD about his gift. Why did random, unexpected noises cause him so much stress? It was just sound. For only the millionth time, I wondered if something had happened to make him this skittish. I asked him about it at least once a month, but he never gave me a solid answer.

Tentatively, Branwell placed one finger gently on a corner of the vellum, careful not to touch anything else. This would take a few minutes. He had to sort through the voices at each point of change, working his way backward through time, from most recent to oldest. And, unlike me, Branwell wasn't limited to just hearing dead people.

Branwell stood still, eyes closed. Looking a little too much like someone in a magical trance.

I turned back to the Colonel, who was eyeing my brother speculatively.

I deliberately stepped in front, hiding him from view.

"So what are Pierce and Claire saying?" I asked.

The Colonel folded his arm across his chest. "That's the problem, isn't it? I want honest answers from each of you. Not a collaboration on what answer would make me happiest or gain you the most notoriety. No plagiarizing. Sandbox Rule."

I grinned. "Fair enough, I suppose." I leaned back against a nearby chair, more fully blocking my brother. "Though you *have* to know Branwell and I have never been the pandering sort. It's not really our vibe."

"Agreed. You researched the history behind the sketch more?" The Colonel's tone hinted that this was a test question.

"Of course," I said.

Fortunately, I had come prepared for an exam. Teacher's pet or no, I was determined to prove myself the perfect person for this job.

The Colonel waved a hand. *Go on.*

"The Battle of Cascina was fought between Pisa and Florence in July of 1364." I rested my body more firmly against the chair. "The armies met in the shadow of the Abbey of San Savino, which is an old monastery east of Pisa. You can still visit the abbey church today, by the way."

The Colonel nodded, folding his arms across his chest. I took this as a good sign.

"The Florentines won," I continued. "As was typical with Renaissance Florence, the city leaders decided in 1504 to commemorate the victory in painting. Michelangelo was only twenty-nine at the time and one of the most sought-after artists in Italy after the monumental success of his sculpture of *David*. The city leaders jumped at the chance to get him to do the painting. But the money ran out after Michelangelo completed the full-scale cartoon—the one Sangallo copied—but before Michelangelo had a chance to actually transfer the cartoon design to the wall and paint it into wet plaster, creating the finished fresco. By the time city leaders had cash again, Michelangelo was in Rome painting the Sistine Chapel and had forgotten the entire Battle of Cascina project."

The Colonel smiled with approval.

"Excellent, boy. You'll do."

Branwell stirred behind me, clearing his throat. I turned as he pulled his leather glove back onto his hand.

"So what is your GUT telling *you*?" I asked, repeating his same question from earlier.

"I'm not sure, to be honest." Branwell shrugged.

I raised an eyebrow. Branwell met my eyes with a steady gaze.

"We definitely have our work cut out for us." I turned to the Colonel. "This is going to be a fascinating project."

The Colonel beamed, standing up. "Well, I'll leave you boys to it. I need to check and see if Claire needs anything else before sending the samples over to the University of Florence for analysis."

Naturally. Teacher's pet and all.

The Colonel walked out of the room.

I snapped back to my brother. He swung his head, motioning me to bend over the drawing like we were studying it together.

"*Dimmi cos'è successo,*" Branwell said, switching from English to Italian. "What happened? You couldn't get a read on it?"

"No. I went back about a hundred years and then nothing. *Vuoto,*" I said.

"You've never encountered a blank object before, have you?"

"No. But then I hadn't seen a blank stranger before three days ago either."

"Weird."

"Tell me about it. First the thing with Claire. Now this."

"Maybe you were madly in love with this Michelangelo sketch in a past life, too." Branwell smirked. "Wrote it sonnets. Called it your soulmate."

"Sometimes I really hate you."

He laughed. "If it makes you feel better, I didn't get a clear read either. But then when do I ever? You know how it goes. I never get a sense of time. The events could happen minutes or millenia apart, so it's hard to know what's important to provenance and what's just happenstance." He gave his head a subtle shake.

"So what happened?"

"Well, I skimmed past Claire talking to the Colonel while taking samples. From there . . . it was confusing. There was a loud cracking noise with a lot of reverb. It could have been something crashing to the ground or even a gunshot in a tight space. I couldn't tell for sure. Then, I heard a man distinctly say"—here Branwell switched from Italian to English—"'I figure we are even now. You have taken something from me. And now I have taken it from you. Never forget—I always win the game.'"

"*In inglese?*"

"*Sì.* English. Upper-crust British accent with a hint of a brogue. Probably Scottish. Definitely modern. No earlier than late eighteenth century."

I pondered the phrase in my head: *I figure we are even now. You have taken something from me. And now I have taken it from you. Never forget—I always win the game.*

"Intriguing," I said.

"Definitely."

"It implies there was perhaps a conflict over this sketch at some point."

"Agreed. *Some* change to the sketch happened at that point, otherwise I wouldn't have heard what I did. The loud noise certainly didn't clarify things—"

"Not to mention that singed corner."

"Exactly."

"What else?"

Branwell paused, remembering. "After that, the *scratch scratch* of what I assume was chalk on vellum. The pop of a fire. Occasionally, I heard the murmur of voices in the distance, all indistinct, though some of it sounded Italian."

Mmmm. "That's it?"

"Pretty much. You know how it goes. It's not like Michelangelo sat there saying, 'I, Michelangelo Buonarotti, will now create a sketch of the Battle of Cascina.' The actual creation of a work of art is usually limited to breathing and not much more. If someone walks in the room and asks a question *while* the artist is drawing, we've hit pay dirt."

"True. Usually we use our gifts in tandem, but without mine in play this time . . ."

I studied the sketch again. The sinuous lines. The moving forms. It really was remarkable. Was this a true Michelangelo?

"I didn't get a sense of how this happened. Maybe that loud noise was something dropping on it." Branwell moved a hand over the singed corner. Shrugged. "Hopefully the mass spec analysis will clue us in on that."

I grunted. Frowning.

How were we going to figure out this enormous puzzle?

"Don't be glum." Branwell nudged my shoulder with his. A serious breach of his no-contact protocol. He could be so caring sometimes. "We'll get to the bottom of this. It'll just take old-fashioned research."

"I don't excel at that."

"Fortunately, for you, I like to help where I can." Branwell shot me a decidedly dry look. "Take pity on you, as it were."

"*Touché.*"

He chuckled. "Not my fault I actually studied in college. I'll see what I can dig up. Like I said, the mass spec results should be helpful. They will at least give us approximate dates for things."

Branwell and I stayed in the dining room for another two hours, studying the drawing and taking detailed photos. We wrapped up after lunch.

We passed the staircase to the upper floor and were halfway across the grandiose entrance hall when a voice stopped us.

"Mr. D'Angelo!"

As we both answer to that name, Branwell and I spun around.

Claire strode down the stairs, dressed in a light blue suit with just the right amount of curve-hugging tightness. Pale hair wrapped into a loose bun accentuating her clean bone structure. Killer heels and legs, legs, legs.

Yep. She was truly trophy girlfriend material, no doubt about it. That scum Pierce had never deserved her—

I felt more than heard Branwell's grunt of appreciation next to me.

"Claire. Nice to see you today." Though still no shadows.

She stopped in front of me. Chest heaving.

It was a very nice chest. Not that I looked down to notice . . . well, not too much.

I *was* a gentleman.

And then I saw her eyes. Snapping fire. Glaring like I imagine a dragon does before roasting its dinner.

So . . . still more psycho girlfriend than trophy . . .

"May I introduce my brother, Branwell?" I gestured.

She popped her hands onto her hips.

"Nice to meet you." Branwell had never been slow.

Claire barely glanced at him.

"You know, I almost called the police—"

"Police?" That was me.

"—or, at very least, brought this up with the Colonel as I'm sure it violates his Sandbox Rule—"

"Violated? What?" That was Branwell.

"—but I'm a big girl and I like solving my own problems and don't want to be a tattle-tale. So I decided to give you a chance to explain first."

My eyebrows flew upward. "Explain?"

Her hands moved from her hips to folding across her ribcage. "Don't even *think* about pretending not to understand, Mr. D'Angelo—"

"Dante."

"—I know you're going to say it's just all a harmless joke and I'm overreacting. Being *psycho*—"

Branwell let out a full-on guffaw.

Claire and I swiveled our heads in his direction.

"Sorry." He held up a palm. "Continue."

Claire fixed him with that steely stare of hers. He squirmed. It really was remarkably effective now that it was no longer trained on me.

"Do you mind?" she asked him. "Or are you in on this little game too? Despite that man-bun and beard, you *are* his identical twin." She nodded in my direction.

Branwell scrubbed a gloved hand over his beard which he had, at least, trimmed up that morning. It was now more George-Clooney-suave than Hagrid-the-Giant-bushy.

"I'm clueless," he said.

"That I don't doubt." So very dry.

"Right. I'm just going to go examine the paintings I saw in the drawing room over here." Branwell couldn't get out of earshot fast enough.

Figured my own flesh and blood would abandon me.

I turned my attention back to Medusa Claire of the No Shadows. She had added foot-tapping to her anger show.

"Well?" She cocked her head. Expectantly.

I took a step closer to her. "Okay, so let's say I'm a really bad actor and I'm not pretending here, Claire—"

"That's Ms. Raythorn, to you." She stepped back.

"Fine. *Ms. Raythorn.*" I moved closer again. "I honestly have no idea what you're talking about."

"I should call your twin back here. Maybe he'll be more forthcoming." She sidestepped two paces. I swiveled with her.

"Look, just tell me what you're—"

"Is frightening me amusing to you somehow?" She took another step back. "You get your big alpha-male kicks out of intimidation?"

"Excuse me?!"

"What are you trying to accomplish with this whole thing? Are you behind all those harassing texts, too?"

"Claire, please—"

"Ms. Raythorn."

"—I truly, honestly, from the bottom of the soul-you-have-blackened have no idea what you're talking about."

I canted forward, intent on moving closer to her again and then stopped myself. Damn. I was doing that Italian lack-of-personal-space thing where I crowded too close to someone.

Italians, as a general rule, have personal space bubbles that are at least fifty percent smaller than Americans'. I forced my feet to stand still.

"Fine. You want to do this?" She pulled her phone out of her jacket pocket with a flourish. "Let's do this."

She swiped and tapped and then held the screen up to me.

A chill zapped my spine, spiking goosebumps into frantic attention. I gasped.

What the *hell*?!!

Without thinking, I grabbed the phone from her. So much for respecting her bubble.

"Hey—" She reached for it.

I moved it higher, staring at the image.

The interior of the Duomo.

Claire's cute face in the corner.

A man standing behind. Tailcoat, cravat, tasseled boots, top hat in hand—all early nineteenth century. Gazing straight at her.

Me.

Or at least someone who looked a tremendous amount like me.

Madonna mia!

Vaguely, I processed that my hands were shaking. I tried to swallow, but something stuck in my throat.

What was going on here?

"So tell me." Her tone brought to mind tundra and frozen wastelands. "Did you and your sidekick brother decide it would be fun to follow me around and jump into my selfies? And then duck out of view as soon as I turned around?"

Dimly, I noted her questions. "Wait. What?!"

I tore my eyes off her phone. She had her arms crossed again.

"Or have you planted some sort of random phone virus that inserts pictures of you in different positions into my photos?"

She paused. Even *she* could hear how silly that sounded.

"So you're saying this only happens in a selfie? When you're in the picture too? Did you see this guy in any other kind of photo? One without you in it?"

She paused. My shock/panic/surprise finally registering. The toe tapping edged off.

"No. Just selfies."

"Every selfie?"

"Uhmm . . . I don't remember."

I swiped through her photos. Interior shots of the Duomo. I looked at them. Sure enough, no weird BBC costumed extras.

And then . . . *bam*. There he was. Shot after shot. In Piazza della Republica. The Ponte Vecchio. Always dressed in the same Regency-era clothing. Always turned toward her.

"You don't see him except in the photo?"

"*Him?* Don't try to pretend like this isn't you."

"Just answer the question, please."

The toe tapping started up again.

"Fine." Finally she nodded. "I take the photo and you're nowhere to be seen, I swear it. But when I look at the photo on my phone—"

"He's there."

"*You* are there. It's like a magic trick." She narrowed her eyes at me. "Do you practice magic?"

"No. Never got my owl letter from Hogwarts—"

"Ha-ha. Congratulations. You're hilarious—"

"Thank you."

"Not a compliment." She pointed at her phone. "What's your game here, D'Angelo?"

"No game. I'm just trying—"

"And don't go feeding me some line about this being a ghost or something stupid like that."

"A ghost? Possibly."

She snorted and rolled her eyes.

Was this guy a ghost of sorts? I couldn't say I had any other ideas.

The sum of my thoughts consisted of what-the-hell, could-things-get-any-weirder, why-does-Claire-smell-so-good . . .

She noted my pause.

"Take your time. Try to come up with a *logical* explanation." She tossed her head. "You haven't even denied that it's you."

Was this me? A past life me?

The only other times I had ended up in a past life regression, both my mom and Branwell had said I looked completely different. They had too. So what were the chances that this guy would be my doppelganger?

I was honest-to-goodness . . . *flabbergasted*.

There was no other way to describe it.

Was this man the lingering memory of a shared past life making itself known through her photos? An echo of sorts?

What would happen if we went to the Duomo together? Or stood on the Ponte Santa Trinità? Would we experience an actual regression together?

It seemed impossible that every single location I saw here on her phone held emotional significance.

And *was* Claire that significant to me?

My libido gave me an enthusiastic high-five and a hell-yes. She was a beautiful woman, no doubt about it.

But a relationship was so much more than just mere physical attraction. And Claire's stand-offish, toe-tapping routine wasn't exactly appealing.

I flipped back to the image of the mystery stalker inside the Duomo where his face was clear. The resemblance *was* remarkable. Uncanny. No wonder she was freaked out.

Was my GUT actually powerful enough to register in someone else's photos?

What. Was. Up?

I tapped her phone.

"What are you doing?" Claire sounded concerned.

"Emailing this photo to myself."

"Trophy gathering?" She reached for her phone again. I moved back.

"Not a chance."

My phone vibrated in my pocket. Email received.

I swiped into her phone and punched in a number. Two seconds later, my own phone buzzed.

Now I had her phone number and email address.

"Nice." She snatched her phone from me, realizing what I had done. "Trying to complete your stalker image?"

"Claire." I put three fingers under her elbow. Waited for her to raise her pale blue eyes to mine. Threaded every ounce of sincerity I could into my next words. "That man in the photos is *not* me."

Her eyes narrowed. Icy points of crystal blue.

"Ha-ha." Very unamused. "I am so incredibly tired of macho men thinking to intimidate—"

"Claire. Please. Believe me. This is *not* me." I pointed at the screen. "You're more than welcome to go through my phone, tablet, laptop. There might be an explanation—"

"So you *do* have a hunch?" She shook off my fingers.

"An idea, at least. Come to dinner with Branwell and me. Maybe we can talk over some answers . . ."

"Pah-lease!! You stalk and photobomb me—"

"Again, not me."

"—and then expect me to willingly get into a car with you and drive off to, uh, *dinner.*" She air-quoted the word. "How stupid do you think I am?"

Not very, obviously. "What would make you feel safe? I swear, I am honestly just trying to understand this situation too."

"If you have something to say, you can say it right now." *Tap, tap, tap.*

How could I prove our family talents? Though with these photos . . .

I glanced around the entrance hall. "Any explanation is going to be lengthy. If you could just trust me—"

"Trust?! I don't trust you farther than the two inches I could throw you." She laughed. A sharp, *un*amused bark. "You are *so* not dialed into my vibe right now."

Apparently not.

How could this prickly, hostile person possibly be *my* woman?

Had past-life me just had poor taste?

My libido raised its hand again, pointing out that, really, as far as it was concerned, she could totally be my woman . . .

Stupid libido.

But then she sucked her plump bottom lip into her mouth, worrying it between her teeth.

The action achingly familiar. As if part of me had predicted the motion moments before it actually happened.

And something in me *knew.* Understood the action as a sign of her distress.

My heart thumped in my chest. My arms suddenly felt wrong for still being at my side, uselessly *not* holding her in comfort.

"Look. I'm not going to force this issue." I shoved my hands into my pockets to keep from reaching for her. "If you want answers, I might have some. The guy in the photo can't hurt you. It's harmless . . . just unsettling."

"So is it a projection?"

A beat.

"Something like that." I nodded toward the phone in her hand. "You have my number. Call or text if you want to chat."

"As if. I'll be deleting your number the second you leave."

"Claire . . ." All the air deflated from me. "Despite what you may think, I *am* a friend. Call me when you want answers."

With a nod, I spun to go. Paused. Turned back.

Looked at her standing there, phone still in her hand. Eyes pensive. Unguarded. Open.

She tentatively folded her arms again. Hugging herself. Unsure. Somehow seeming so . . . alone.

No. Not just alone.

Lonely.

Something . . . flared.

A rush of recognition. My soul. Hers. Us.

You. I know . . . you.

There was *history* there.

So much history . . .

Blood pounded in my ears.

Without thinking, I took two long strides, barreling my way into her bubble, leaning over her.

I got a heady whiff of Claire in the process. Lavender and a hint of spice.

Madonna mia.

"You're wrong," I whispered into her ear. Sucked in another breath of *her*. "I think you *do* trust me. Instinctively. When you want to know *why* . . . call me."

I pulled back and gave her one last lingering stare. And then turned on my heel and walked through the front door.

I didn't look back.

Say what you want about us D'Angelos—we know how to make an exit.

CLAIRE

I wanted to hate him. Really I did.

I tried to hate him on the drive back into Florence.

As I thanked the driver for dropping me in front my hotel. (Marco. Twin toddlers. Loves soccer.)

As I clomped into my hotel room and threw myself across the bed, kicking off my heels.

But . . .

Just something about the stunned expression on Dante's face when he saw the photos. The pensive way he stared. The heat of him as he loomed over me.

I should have felt threatened or mocked or humiliated. I should have felt . . .

Well . . . any number of normal, *sane* things.

Anything but the sense of concern and shelter I *had* felt.

Sweetie, you are so messed up in that head of yours, I could hear Grammy say.

I closed my eyes. I *was* so messed up. Had the psych eval to prove it.

I had been decidedly freaked out by that final selfie in the Duomo. What possible logical explanation could there be? Nothing made sense.

Why would Dante get his Jane Austen fetish on and then stalk me through downtown Florence? I mean, if you're renting a costume anyway, why not go for Batman or something with an identity-hiding mask? Or, at the very least, a character that's more inherently scary? Freddy Krueger anyone?

And Dante's ghost explanation seemed . . . out-there.

Sheesh. And everyone claimed *I* was psycho . . .

But if this wasn't Dante's doing, who was it? Was Pierce the one behind it all, messing around (I had no idea how), trying to get Dante tossed from the Colonel's contest?

I couldn't land on any one answer.

But it did explain why I hadn't shown the photos to the Colonel yet.

Maybe because, like I said to Dante, I prefer to pull on my big-girl pants and solve my own problems.

Maybe because I wanted to hear Dante's explanation (and, let's be honest, take in his broad shoulders and deep bass voice while doing so—)

Or maybe . . . Dante was right.

I did trust him. Instinctively.

Not that I *trusted* that sense of trust . . . if that made any sense.

I had trusted Pierce too. And the long line of loser boyfriends before him.

My bad judgment knew no bounds when it came to men. They were like crowded checkout lines; I would pick the wrong one every time.

All that to say . . .

I didn't delete Dante's info from my phone. If he broke his promise and contacted me first, *then* I would do something.

I pushed off the bed and strolled over to one of the three enormous windows overlooking the Arno—the setting sun turning the river and buildings and hills beyond into a molten mass. Bathing my hotel suite in golden light.

I opened up the window . . . a warm breeze threaded through the room, bringing with it the rumble of traffic from the street below.

I had to hand it to the Colonel. Despite all the potential weirdness with Grammy and 'hey Bonnie Prince Charlie's child bride lived there,' the hotel room itself was gorgeous.

On the *piano nobile* with soaring Baroque-gilded ceilings, lush drapery and furnishings that were a mix of traditional Versailles and sleek Scandinavian modern. The epitome of tasteful Italian style.

I sighed and leaned out the window. No screens for Italians. Just wide open air.

To be fair, things hadn't been *too* weird with the Colonel throughout the day. He had held my hand too long and used every excuse to touch me. Not creepy touching, mind you. Just a brush on the elbow, a hand at my back. Before Pierce and my stalkers, I would have merely considered his attention grandfatherly. But now . . .

I tossed the thought out of my mind.

He hadn't brought up Grammy again. I had intended to ask him about it, but the right moment never presented itself.

All things considered, I wasn't sure I wanted to invite that level of intimacy into our conversation. What did it really matter in the end? Grammy had never mentioned him, so it probably was nothing.

As for the possible Michelangelo drawing . . .

As an appraiser, you always look first at provenance.

The Colonel claimed there was no family documentation for the sketch. That said, though his father was from Kentucky, the Colonel's mother was British, the only child of the last Earl of Arlington. All of the Colonel's Italian holdings came from that branch of the family. So from a historical perspective, the Earls of Arlington could easily have undiscovered treasures.

Beyond that, it was hard to draw any conclusions until we received the mass spectrometry results. The differences in composition suggested the Colonel's sketch probably *wasn't* a copy of Michelangelo's cartoon for the *Battle of Cascina*.

But was it a bonafide Michelangelo?

I honestly didn't know. The fluidity of the drawing most certainly suggested as much, but the vellum ground and lack of silverpoint were troubling.

I faced the question I had been asking myself for the last two days:

Could the Colonel's sketch be Michelangelo's *modello*? His original model or blueprint for the painting?

In Renaissance Florence, a *modello* was a detailed sketch or model presented for approval to the patron paying for the artwork. Basically, a small-scale illustration of the final work to get the green-light to complete the larger scale cartoon. All the great masters had created *modelli* at times, many of which still survive.

There were no records of a full *modello* ever existing for the *Battle of Cascina* but, for a project that massive and expensive, common sense dictated Michelangelo had probably created one at some point.

Did the Colonel have the only known copy of that *modello*? It would require time to gather evidence, but if it proved true, finding a lost Michelangelo *modello* would be monumental news.

I would need to do a detailed comparison of use of line between the Colonel's sketch and known Michelangelo drawings. But, really, the kicker would be the mass spectrometry analysis. If the dates were later than the 1500s, then no way was the sketch a bonafide Michelangelo. Yet even if that were the case, as a different iteration of Michelangelo's design, the Colonel's *Battle of Cascina* would be important.

Fortunately, I had nearly a month to conduct research. Such time was a luxury I rarely experienced.

I shoved aside the tiny voice whispering that the Colonel might have ulterior motives when it came to me, that I needed to be careful. Finish my job and get the hell out of Dodge, as it were.

Gah. I *hated* this paranoia. This fear. My inability to simply take people at face value.

I continued to stare out the window.

The Arno moved sluggishly before me, swirling underneath the Ponte Santa Trinità. (Sixteenth century. Oldest elliptic arch bridge in the world.) The water eddied outward, dark brown with the sediment of spring run-off. A city bus squealed to a stop at the intersection of the bridge and Lungarno Corsini, waiting patiently between the gigantic statues of *Autumn* and *Summer*. (Giovanni Caccini. Marble. Excellent example of late Renaissance Mannerism.)

Across the river, wisteria sprawled over a private terrace with exuberant abandon, its vines heavy with blue-purple blossoms, a burst of cool color against the warm Tuscan-orange stucco.

Leave it to Firenze to bring on the springtime charm. Though the city was a hardcore flirt any time of year.

I turned back to my room. Even with the sun setting, the rooftop restaurant in the hotel wouldn't open for dinner for several more hours. I had never really understood the Mediterranean habit of eating dinner after nine at night. Why go straight to bed on a full stomach?

So . . . now what?

I studiously ignored the fact that Dante's number and email address were still in my phone.

Not trusting my ability to trust him.

Nope.

I changed out of my suit into skinny jeans and a loose rose-colored silk shirt. Responded to several emails. Wrote to a couple of colleagues.

Ignored three texts from Pierce asking and then pleading and then begging to take me out to dinner.

I think I pulled an eyeball muscle I rolled them so hard.

What was that saying I always mangled?

Fool me once, shame on you, but fool me twice . . .

Yeah.

I watched the sky over Florence move from fiery orange through pale pink and into deep purple-black. Breathed in Italian air, heavy with humidity and the smell of growing things.

Finally, I trudged into the bathroom to tidy my hair for dinner. I pulled it out of the bun, setting the bobby pins down on the marble counter. My hair could be wispy at the best of times.

I paused.

Where had my brush gone?

I looked across the counter, past that talisman photo of me and Grammy in front of the Palazzo Vecchio, beyond the jar of face cream. I had left my brush there earlier in the day, hadn't I? The bathroom wasn't so large as to easily hide a paddle brush.

Nothing.

Frowning, I stepped out into the bedroom.

Ah, *there* it was. Over by the flatscreen TV. Weird.

I grabbed it and went back into the bathroom.

Only to come out two minutes later looking for my small make-up bag. I found it on the floor opposite the bed, pushed neatly up against the wall.

Honestly.

I stared down at the floral little pouch. I was almost one hundred percent certain I hadn't left it there.

Wait . . .

My pulse sped up. I pivoted in a slow circle, eyes inventorying everything.

Had someone been in my room?

Housekeeping *had* come in earlier, as my bed had been made when I returned. Had I left my makeup bag on the covers, and they set it aside when tidying up? It made sense. I sometimes did my makeup while sitting on my bed, and I had been so distracted this morning, I couldn't recall exactly what I had done.

I walked around the room, trying to determine if anything else had been moved. Laptop. Chargers. Credit cards. Jewelry. Right where I left them. Certainly nothing of value had been taken.

I picked up the make-up bag. Hold on. Where was my favorite lipstick?

I dug through the bag, looking for my PH lipstick—the one I special ordered from a boutique in Chelsea. It was one of my rich-slumming splurges.

It's the weirdest stuff, that lipstick. The stick itself is literally green, but it reacts with the PH of your lips and turns them this gorgeous shade of blush pink once you swipe it on. I loved to wear it underneath my favorite lemon berry lipgloss. You know how getting the perfect lip shade goes . . .

I thought I had used it this morning. Hadn't I?

I scanned my purse and then the rest of the room. No lipstick.

Had I just forgotten to pack it?

I sat down on the bed, biting my lower lip, trying to remember. I shook my head.

It was nothing. Just my imagination running wild after a fairly harrowing couple of days. The reappearance of my persistent online hater. The job with the Colonel. Pierce being Pierce. Not to mention my frock-coated, top-hatted photobomber who may or may not be Dante D'Angelo.

I had a lot on my mind. I hadn't been paying attention to where I set things or what I put on exactly. It happened.

Besides, who would take lipstick instead of a laptop? I was a paranoid idiot.

I picked up my makeup bag and walked back into the bathroom, sternly telling my hands to stop shaking as I repinned my hair. After three minutes, I was pretty sure my bun was lopsided thanks to my clumsy fingers.

And, of course, there was no secondary mirror in the bathroom to let me see the back of my own head. *Ugh.* Could just one thing go right today?

Phone to the rescue. I angled my head awkwardly and snapped a photo of the bun. Swiped to the picture.

The world came to a grinding halt.

I'm sure tourists walking along the street below heard my scream.

I was just grateful I caught my phone before it hit the tiled bathroom floor.

I sank to the ground, back pressed against the wall opposite the sink, knees shaking too badly to hold me up.

The photo was so clear. My head with its (lopsided, *drat*) bun.

Dante 'Mr. Darcy' D'Angelo *standing* in the glassed-in shower to my left.

Hatless and coatless now. Wearing only a waistcoat and shirt sleeves. Dark brows drawn down, like he was concerned, worried.

There was definitely no one else physically in the bathroom with me.

I sat trembling on the floor for at least five minutes.

Was someone somehow digitally inserting him into my photos? Like a computer virus?

The bathroom was sleek and modern. No security cameras (obviously). Really no place to hide a machine that could project an image like that. It seemed . . . impossible.

I rested my head against my knees for a while, waiting for my fight-or-flight response to calm down.

Who was doing this? And why?

My right leg started to go numb. What to do? I raised my head and looked at the vanity above me.

Only to have my adrenaline spike again.

Bloody hell!

I moved forward onto knees and snatched the photo of Grammy and me off the vanity mirror.

Impossible.

Just utterly . . .

And, yet . . .

There *he* was. My Regency stalker. Clear as could be.

Standing in the far background of the photo. Top hat, same green coat, boots, walking stick.

Staring at Grammy and me making idiots of ourselves in front of the Palazzo Vecchio.

This was *my* photo. I flipped it over, around. Definitely mine. It had that little crease in the corner from my bathroom mirror in Boston. That glop of mascara at the bottom I'd accidentally splattered on it.

But there he was. In my photo from so long ago. Looking *exactly* the same.

There's no Photoshop to alter an already printed print. And Dante himself would have been a teenager too that many years ago . . .

I swallowed. All of me shaking now.

This made no sense.

But—and here I admitted to myself—Mr. Darcy had probably always been there. It seemed like I remembered seeing him in the photo. I had just never really clued into it, as he was so far in the background.

Was I dealing with the supernatural here? *Was* this guy a ghost? Did I even believe in ghosts?

And, if so, why the creepy resemblance to Dante D'Angelo? And why only in images with me in them too?

With shaking hands, I picked up my phone. I took a photo of my bathroom without me in the shot. Swiped to it.

Just my bathroom.

I angled the phone at my face. Me and the wall behind. No space for anything or anyone else.

I studied the frame and took a selfie.

I closed my eyes. Sucked in a long, stuttering breath.

And then flipped into my photos, looking at the picture I had just taken.

I stared. Breathing hard.

Impossible.

My face on the left. Wide-eyed and apprehensive.

On the right, Dante in his full Jane Austen-esque glory. His head nestled against mine.

Cravat falling across my shoulder. Eyes closed. Nose pressed into my neck.

A contented hint of smile on his face.

How? Why?!

I had no answers for this. It went beyond anything I could explain. I was so clearly alone in this bathroom.

This had to be something supernatural.

Hands still shaking, I took a photo of the picture with Grammy.

I managed to send one text.

This just happened. You're in my Florence photos from fourteen years ago too. You said you have answers.

I attached the photo of Grammy and the ones of Mr. Darcy in my bathroom.

A reply came less than thirty seconds later.

Are you at your hotel?

I hesitated. And then texted back.

Yes. Just tell me what's going on.

I will. I'm on my way.

Wait. You don't know where I am.

Palazzo Alfieri, right? I'll be right there.

What? How do you know where I'm staying?

I overheard you talking with the Colonel about it at the meeting. I'm coming.

I stared down at my phone. Still shaken. Really unsure how to respond.

He knew where I was staying. He had known all week.

I wasn't sure how I felt about that.

I didn't trust him. Or, again, I didn't trust my sense of trust.

Dante sent one more text.

You're safe, Claire. It's nothing that can hurt you, I promise. I'll explain when I get there.

Ugh. Stupid mind-reader.

I instantly called him.

The phone rang and rang.

You've reached Dante D'Angelo. Please leave a message.

Ha raggiunto Dante D'Angelo. Per favore lasci un messaggio.

Grrr.

I tried two more times. Voicemail.

Either he was ignoring me or was already on his way.

Now what?

The last thing I wanted was Dante knocking on my hotel room door.

Still trembling, I pushed myself off the floor of the bathroom and exchanged my lopsided bun for a simple ponytail. I shut my bedroom windows, slid my feet into a pair of heels and then went downstairs. Dante could chat with me there.

Palazzo Alfieri was a small boutique-style hotel, so though the rooms were gorgeous and the rooftop bar swank, the lobby was little more than a glorified entryway and stairwell. Granted, a lovely marble staircase and expansive foyer, but definitely not anything that drifted into *lobby* territory. The 'front desk' was a small office to the right of the stairs.

I glanced in. Good. Matteo was working tonight. (Plays bass guitar in a punk band. Boyfriend. Likes pink.) I waved at him and then retreated back into the 'lobby.'

I sat on a little leather bench next to the stairs, chewing on my lower lip, foot bouncing.

Eyes glued on the large door leading out to the street. The *portone*, I guess I should call it.

Why was my stalker-ghost in that photo from so long ago? Why me? Why Dante?

Crack.

Dante pushed the *portone* open.

That had been fast. Did he live nearby?

He had changed out of the designer suit he had on earlier. Somehow, scruffy jeans, worn boots, an untucked cream button-down and tight-fitting Italian leather jacket suited him more. Even his hair relaxed, falling in dark loose waves on his forehead and around his ears. His bulky shoulders filled the room.

Swoon . . . he was fine.

A younger me would have flirt-flirt-flirted with him. But I was no longer that naive girl.

With pinched lips and folded arms, I stood up and walked into the middle of the entryway.

Dante nodded at Matteo through the office door and then turned his attention to me.

He stopped about two feet too close. So close, the spice of his cologne eddied around me and I had to look up, up into his face. The man really did *not* understand the concept of personal space.

I hadn't processed what color his eyes were. I had just assumed they were brown, given the rest of his Italian vibe. But they weren't. They were a decided hazel . . . golden brown around the pupil morphing to green farther out.

He had very long eyelashes.

He shoved his hands into his jeans pockets, bunching his beefy shoulders.

I took a step back. Firmly told my heart to slow down.

"Claire," he said.

"Mr. D'Angelo."

"Dante. Please." He smiled. White. Toothy. Heartbreaking.

I folded my arms tighter.

"You didn't need to come," I said. "I tried to call—"

"You did?" He pulled his phone from his pocket. "Ah. You did. Sorry. I was driving."

Figured. "Shall we?" I nodded at the bench behind me to the left.

He glanced around me at the bench. And then shook his head.

"This will take too long." He stepped closer again. "You saw the . . . man? . . . in your room. I'd like to start there."

"Do I have a flashing 'stupid' sign above my head?" My eyebrows disappeared into my hairline. "That would be a firm 'hell no' to inviting you into my hotel room. We can talk here."

I gestured at the bench, now at my side, and deliberately stepped back. Again.

Matteo was studying us with careful interest from the hotel office. I appreciated having an audience.

"Look. Like I said earlier today, things are different from what they appear." Once more, Dante stepped right into my personal bubble. "The true scope of this . . . *ghost* requires some explanation."

"Ghost? Seriously?" Another step back.

He shot an agitated hand into his hair. The motion was *not* endearing. Nope.

"Yes. And if we could just go up to your room, I think things might become a little clearer for both of us."

"In my room?"

He moved into my space. "Yeah."

Me. "To see the . . . ghost?"

Him. "Something like that."

I took *another* step backward. "Seriously, Mr. D'Angelo—"

"Dante. Honestly, how many times do I have to ask you to use my name?"

He stepped forward. Again.

Loomed over me. Again.

"*Mister* D'Angelo. Just *stop* right there." I held out two hands. "Personal space bubble." I flapped my arms in a circle around me. "Ever heard of it?"

He froze. "Oh—"

"Sheesh! And you wonder why I'm leery of being alone with you?" I waved a hand back and forth. "Could you *please* maintain a polite four feet of air between us?"

Honest-to-goodness, I swear he blushed. Never thought it possible for a man like Dante D'Angelo. But that slow-spreading burn moving up his cheeks could only be called one thing.

"I-I am really and truly sorry. I didn't even realize." He took a large, *polite* step back. "My Italian self takes over sometimes. Forgive me."

He rubbed a hand over the back of his neck. Grimaced.

Looking uncannily like a bashful five-year-old boy.

Not. Adorable.

I wrapped my hands around my upper arms.

"So let me get this straight." I cocked my head. "You have to be *in* my hotel room in order to explain about the, uh, ghost?"

"Yes."

"Your doppelganger ghost who has been stalking me dressed as Mr. Darcy since the age of fourteen?"

"Exactly."

"Do you ever record yourself and play it back? Just to hear how utterly insane you sound?"

"Sometimes." Total deadpan. "I cackle while I do it. It adds to the ambiance."

A pause.

I wasn't sure if I was horrified or charmed.

Horrified was the safer emotion. I went with that.

"Look," I said. "Just tell me what's going on? Why is this so hard?"

"What will it take?" Dante hit me with a lethal pair of pleading, puppy-dog eyes.

"Excuse me?"

"For you to trust me. What will it take?"

10

DANTE

Claire froze.

"Trust you?" Her icy blue gaze drilled me.

I nodded, reminding my feet to stay put even though they itched to step toward her.

"I don't trust you," she said. "I will never trust you. This isn't about trust."

I *strongly* begged to differ, but I kept that opinion to myself.

"Not let's-be-BFFs-and-paint-each-others'-toenails trust," I said. "Just trust enough to let me into your hotel room. The two of us. Together."

Even by my skewed standards, the photos Claire had texted were freaky. Obviously, something was up with my GUT. But what?

The images from her bathroom seemed more intimate than the ones she showed me earlier. Did that mean anything? This palazzo matched the time period of Claire's Regency-era gentleman. Had an event happened here in the past? Something significant?

I half hoped a regression would occur when I stepped into the foyer. But, so far, nothing. Maybe her hotel room was the correct place.

Granted, I wasn't sure I even wanted a regression to happen. On the other hand, a regression would be irrefutable proof, wouldn't it?

For most people, no amount of simply describing my GUT would be convincing. But if Claire were to *experience* a regression with me? Well. That would speak for itself.

And I would know for sure that Claire had been important to me in past lives.

Claire paused. Truth be told, she was wise to not trust a man who was little more than a stranger. Particularly as I had been showing up in her photos. How to get through to her?

"I mean you no harm. I cannot emphasize that enough. This is important." I pressed my palms together in front of my chest as if praying. "What will it take?" My eyes blazed with sincerity.

Claire kept her arms folded across her chest. Biting that plump bottom lip of hers. Looking far too young and alone.

Finally, she sighed and leaned around me, looking through the open door to my right.

"Matteo," she said to the man behind the reception desk, "do you have any duct tape?"

Ten minutes later, Claire had me trussed up like a Mafia victim.

I tested the tape holding my hands behind my back. They were going nowhere.

It was an uncannily expert job.

"So at what point did you decide to abandon your career as a professional kidnapper?" I asked as she finished taping my legs together above the knees.

"You need to stop talking."

"This gets kinkier by the minute."

She muttered something that sounded suspiciously like, *You wish.*

"If your goal is earning my trust, you're not doing a convincing job of it." She sat back on her heels. Glaring.

"I'm just pointing out that this obviously isn't your first rodeo."

She rolled her eyes. "Cerise, my fourth nanny, was an ex-con—"

"That seems . . . improbable."

"I'm not lying. Cerise did ten years hard time for fraud and being an accessory to kidnapping."

"Nice. I wasn't doubting Cerise's . . . uh, history, per se . . . more the fact she was allowed to add 'child caretaker' to her resume."

"Right? My parents set high standards for my care."

"Obviously."

She ripped off the piece of tape with her teeth. "Anyway, Cerise thought it broadened my horizons to know how to properly restrain someone. She was big on life skills—"

"Wouldn't laundry be more along the line of life skills? Changing the oil in your car? Knowing how to hogtie a victim seems . . ."

"What?"

I shrugged. "Less useful, I guess."

"It's feeling pretty useful right now." She wrapped the tape around my legs one last time.

"And that's your story?"

"Yep."

"Sticking to it?"

"Like stink on a skunk."

"No stories of punking wasted prep school boys?"

"Not tonight."

"Restraining difficult clients?"

"Are you done?"

"Just pointing out what would have been more believable."

"You're impossible."

"Thank you."

She stood up and bit off another section of tape.

"Now what?" I asked.

Without further ado, she slapped the small strip of tape over my mouth.

Shutting me up.

Annnnnnd, now I was going to have to kill her.

She noted my laser death-stare and, then, did the worst thing possible.

She . . . laughed.

The most mischievous sound. Throaty. A little naughty. Completely infectious.

Everything about her changed. Her eyes sparked and crinkled. Her cheeks plumped, revealing a tiny dimple just below her right eye. Open. Fun-loving. Ready to laugh her way through life.

Madonna mia.

It was worth being hogtied just to see her face in that moment. No wonder she didn't laugh much. It was fairly lethal.

"C'mon, big guy." She tucked a hand around my left elbow. "Let's get you upstairs."

Still grinning, she turned me toward the small elevator. She was enjoying this way too much.

I would so make her pay.

Once she untied me. And decided we were friends.

And I earned her undying trust.

Then . . . payback time.

I awkward-shuffled my way past the front desk/office, only able to move my legs from the knees down.

I was pretty sure I looked like a drunk penguin.

Poor Matteo had definitely had an eyeful by this point. He shot me a broad wink. Obviously, he anticipated my evening would be significantly more exciting than I did.

If only he knew . . .

Smiling far too smugly, Claire loaded me into the closet-like elevator and took us up a floor.

"Ya know, this really did work," she said as she helped me waddle down the hallway. "I feel so much safer now."

I mumbled behind my tape.

"What was that?"

I stopped and glared down at her.

She chuckled.

That smile, those lips . . . she was going to be the death of me. A very sweet and pleasant death, mind you. But a death all the same.

She paused in front of her door, pulling a keycard from her jeans pocket.

My adrenaline spiked.

Would a regression happen? And if it did, what would we experience?

Would I only see death and horror? Or did other life experiences merit a regression too?

The other times, I had been caught unawares—tossed into the past before I could process what was happening.

But now . . .

Claire pushed the door open and, holding it with her foot, reached for my elbow, helping me forward.

Across the threshold.

Lights flickered on.

I glimpsed a hallway leading to a larger space with high, gilded ceilings.

And then everything faded.

The world spun. My taped hands and legs released.

Suddenly, I was walking through the doorway.

Same high, gilded ceilings. French paper and carved moldings on the walls. Herringbone wood floor. No furniture.

A young woman sat directly ahead, wrapped in a pool of light from the open window behind her.

At last, I thought. *I have found you, my angel* . . .

11

Doctor Ethan MacLure walked a few steps into the room, staring at the ethereal sight before him.

Feeling like a man deep in his cups, head floating in that odd combination of euphoria and bonhomie.

A woman sat in a simple slat-backed chair, facing away from the window. Brilliant sunlight washed over her, wrapping around the white of her muslin, high-waisted dress and turning her hair into molten honey.

She braced one hand against a large, paper-draped board on an easel, chalk in the other. Sketching. Like a goddess . . . Athena in her bower. All she lacked was an owl of wisdom on her shoulder.

His eyes skimmed the length of her straight nose, rose cheeks that ended at a pointed chin.

Did even heaven itself possess such an angel? How had this creature found her way into this place?

Ethan walked farther into the room. The angel-woman didn't raise her head, her attention absorbed.

An older woman in a mobcap and apron *did* notice him, however. She raked his figure from top to bottom and then returned to her stitching. The angel's chaperone, no doubt.

The noise of the salon drifted through the open door behind him. Voices chattering in a garbled mixture of English, French and Italian. A couple wandered into the room walking past Ethan, perhaps intent on moving through to the room ahead.

He looked back at the woman seated before the window. Aching to know everything about her.

Or, barring that, her name at the very least.

He should wait for an introduction. That was only proper.

But the rules of propriety felt far away here. This was no London drawing room. Not even Edinburgh and home with his mother and sister.

The light enfolded her body, turning her into gold-rimmed curves and valleys. What was it about her that drew him so insistently?

Unbidden, the words flitted through his head again:

At last, I have found you, m'aingeal.

His heart pounded out of his chest. Like a courser, eager to be let loose and given its head.

And still the angel-woman sketched. Ignoring the world around her.

Who was she?

Most high-born visitors to Florence found their way into this house eventually. Even the not-so-high-born ones, like Ethan himself. All and sundry wanted a tale of the elderly Countess of Albany to take home.

The Countess held salons, famed as much for what they did *not* provide, as for what they did.

A footman paused at Ethan's elbow, holding out a tray of small crystal dishes, each sporting a tiny silver spoon nestled against a perfectly round, pale pink ball. With a polite nod, Ethan took a dish from the tray.

Refreshment was part of what the Countess *did* provide. That and scintillating conversation.

However, such was the beginning and end of her hospitality.

Ethan held the dish carefully as he surveyed the room.

It was just like the room behind him and surely the same as the room ahead.

Beautiful architectural creations with carved moldings and soaring vaults. Expensive Venetian wallpaper and polished wood floors. Marble-mantled fireplaces flanking each end.

Not a stick of furniture in sight. No carpets. No drapery. Nothing. The rooms were utterly bare of furnishings of any sort.

The Countess reserved her spartan collection of mis-matched chairs for herself and a few old cronies. Their cackling laughter drifted through the open door.

Visitors had to make do with standing—including chaperones, judging by the woman upright in the corner—ensuring that no one stayed long enough to wear out their welcome.

Except, apparently, the angel in front of the window who had also procured a chair for her comfort while drawing.

Again, who was she?

Still holding his dish, Ethan crossed the room to her. The sunlight curled around her head, threading through the ringlets framing her face. Her hair was more brown than golden, he noted as he drew near, but the light played tricks with its color.

She focused on her work with dogged intent, biting her bottom lip between her teeth in a gesture that surely had vexed more than one governess. Why did that simple act feel so achingly familiar?

"If you mean to offer me the *mattonelle*, I must refuse," she said, setting her chalk down and studying her work. "They are far too dangerous for one of even my skill."

She spoke without raising her head. Her cultured English wrapping through the quiet room.

Confused, Ethan glanced behind him. The other couple in the room were turned away.

"Yes, I am speaking to you," she continued as he turned back. Still without raising her head.

Well.

His heart triple-skipped. He added *flirtatious* and *charming* to her list of angelic attributes.

Hallelujah.

"*Mattonelle?*" he asked, grin tugging at his lips.

She lifted her head (finally) and fixed him with the *bluest* eyes . . . the color of a frozen loch in January. Ethan found himself quite unable to breathe for a moment.

She motioned toward the dish he still held. And then bent back over her work, studying some aspect of it.

Oh.

He glanced down at the dish. The small pink ball appeared frosted on the outside, despite the warm June weather.

"I am just arrived in Florence," he said. "Perhaps you would be so kind as to aid a traveler in a foreign land?"

She raised her head and raked him again with those diamond-blue eyes. And then primly folded her hands in her lap, pressing her lips together.

"Though your appeal has not fallen on deaf ears, I must maintain my neutrality."

"Ah. Like Florence with Napoleon?"

"Precisely. I am merely preserving a long-held tradition. The *mattonelle* are more of an . . . initiation. A rite of passage, if you will, to unite you and your fellow travelers."

He raised a skeptical eyebrow, his grin widening.

"This?" He raised his dish.

"That." She nodded.

He made a production of studying it, lifting the dish into the sunlight, sending shards of prism rainbows across the room.

"It appears quite harmless."

She said nothing in reply.

"Is the danger in its taste?" he asked.

"I would not dream of spoiling the surprise."

She matched his eyebrow. It had a decidedly challenging edge.

Ethan's grin widened. "Well, I canna say I have ever been one to back down from a dare. No self-respecting Scotsman would."

With a salute, he picked up the small silver spoon and dug emphatically into the round ball.

Mattonelle.

Or whatever it was.

But as soon as his spoon jabbed the frosted pink sphere—

The ball shot out of the dish. Bounced loudly against the gilded wainscoting. Thumped twice on the wood floor. Before coming to rest at the lass's feet.

Ethan froze, spoon poised in one hand, dish raised in the other.

The angel-woman laughed. A joyful peal of sound.

"I see," he said, lowering both items.

"Welcome to Florence, sir." She gave him a grin, which could only be described as impish. Infectious.

He added *captivating* to his list.

Smiling himself, Ethan bent and carefully picked up the *matonelle*, placing it back in his dish. It was very cold to the touch.

"*Mattonelle* means tile in Italian," she said. "The Countess finds it amusing to freeze ice cream to the consistency of marble and feed it to the unsuspecting."

"They are quite dangerous."

"Indeed. A Prussian count nearly took out the eye of the Sicilian ambassador last week with a *mattonelle* missile. The Countess only pretended to be horrified. I fear she will start another war with them one day."

Ethan laughed. "She will be known as the Ice Cream Tyrant of Europe."

The angel-woman returned a smile. Utterly charming. "Once they melt sufficiently, they are actually quite delicious. I believe today's *matonelle* are infused with rose petals, as they are finally in season."

Who was this creature? She was obviously familiar with the Countess and these salons.

His heart continued its painful thumping, demanding he *do* something about the emotion scouring his veins.

He swallowed. "I should not be speaking with you. 'Tis not proper."

The angel-woman laughed again. "Ah, yes. We would hate to provide fodder for the scandal sheets, if there *were* such a thing in Florence. Surely tomorrow they would run a scathing report, 'While at the Countess of A's salon, the infamous Lady C was caught in *un*-introduced conversation with the noble Mr. . . .'?" Her voice trailed into a question mark.

"*Doctor* M," Ethan supplied with a grin.

"Oh. Doctor M. Most excellent."

"At your service, Lady C." He bowed.

Their eyes met and held. And held.

A lengthy pause ensued.

A thousand emotions flashing.

Though now a well-educated doctor, Ethan's entrance into this world had been much more humble. Perhaps too humble to fix his attentions on a woman such as this.

But he had clawed and crawled to this point in the world. And he was Scottish to his core; he would never back down from a challenge.

"Well," Ethan nodded. "I fear we must brave the report of nonexistent scandal sheets, Lady C. I find it difficult to readily quit such charming company."

Lady C returned his gaze, delighted and warm, eyes dancing with humor.

With an answering nod, Ethan stepped around her, placing the crystal dish with its dangerous ice cream projectile on the windowsill. There was no where else to set it, other than the floor itself.

He turned around. And then froze, staring at the drawing on the board before him.

Lady C quickly flipped a hanging sheet of paper over her sketch, shooting him a prim look.

The covering sheet of paper was a drawing of Florence from the vantage of Forte Belvedere. Demure. Sedate.

Which in *no way* described what the sketch underneath had been.

Taking a step back to her, he carefully lifted the top paper away, revealing what she had been drawing underneath. A sketch in its beginning stages. But, by Jove, the subject matter of the drawing—

Swirling motion. Sinuous lines. The suggestion of bodies twisted and turned and bent. Naked, *male* bodies.

Which was not *too* scandalous, in and of itself. Florence abounded with naked male figures, starting with Michelangelo's statue of *David* in front of the Palazzo Vecchio which Ethan had passed by the day before.

But it *was* scandalous for a young, unmarried lady to sketch them.

He shot her a questioning eyebrow.

She shrugged.

Ethan was not an expert in art, but he knew some. And, as a physician, he definitely understood human anatomy. It seemed unlikely this work was hers alone.

"Your composition?"

"No. A copy. The *Battle of Cascina* by Michelangelo."

"Ah, yes. I have heard of this." He looked back at her drawing.

"I have just begun the composition. It will take some time to get the shapes right."

"But you do not copy from a physical drawing?"

"No. I copy from memory."

"Impressive. You sell your talents short. 'Tis remarkable how you have captured the lines here and here."

"Thank you. You are too kind."

"Not kind. Honest," he said.

She turned her face up to his. Afternoon light raked the fine bones of her jaw, gleamed across her skin.

Ethan's breath stuck in his throat.

Heaven's above but she was lovely.

But it was somehow more than just the sum of a winsome smile and a pretty face.

I know you, his heart whispered.

Was it that she represented home and hearth and all those things he had left behind?

Something in her eyes, their depths . . . it shot through him, jagged and cleansing.

A sense of familiarity. Of belonging. Of kindred.

Mine.

Despite Ethan's lowly origins, he was well-employed now as the personal physician and aide to the Duke of Blackford, a powerful member of the Scottish peerage. Ethan had transformed himself into a learned, refined gentleman.

A part of him felt that all those years of work and sacrifice and struggle had been for this very moment.

So he could stand on equal terms with this mysterious Lady C and actually contemplate a life with her. Dream of keeping this angel at his side forever.

Lady Caro studied the tall, handsome Scot standing beside her easel. Many, many men passed through the Countess' salon each year. It was easy to blur them all together . . . one hardly different from any other.

But something about Dr. M . . .

Perhaps it was the trace of brogue when he talked. The way his long fingers had clutched the small crystal dish. The curl in his dark hair. The good-natured humor in his brown eyes.

Or maybe it was the sense of careful strength about his large frame— that he could compact all that size and power into the smallest gesture of kindness.

Something in him called to her. A sense of kinship.

You. It's you. At last. I have waited so long . . .

He studied her drawing a minute longer. She was painfully aware the subject matter was decidedly not *de rigueur* for gently-bred ladies. But the composition compelled her. It always had. All those bodies in motion . . . that moment right as the battle engages . . .

"This piece calls to you, m'lady?"

Ah. He read her like a book. How delicious to be . . . read.

Dr. M rested his warm gaze on her, sending a thrum down her spine.

She locked eyes with him, helpless to look away. He was life and absolution and *hosanna.*

She wanted to weep. Of course such a man would arrive too late.

"Yes," she finally said, forcibly turning her head back to her drawing. "I appreciate how Michelangelo captured the moment. How the composition is frozen and yet still pulses with energy."

He looked at the drawing again, studying it. And then turned back to her, no judgment in his eyes.

"I remember reading about the actual Battle of Cascina at university." There went that burr again, tugging at her senses. "It was fought outside Pisa against the walls of an abbey. Didn't Machiavelli say it was the quintessential example of the problem of mercenary armies? It wasn't about winning or losing. It was about keeping the pot of trouble thoroughly stirred. War and politics . . . they were all a game."

"Well, naturally, of course. If a battle was decisive, the *condottieri* would find themselves unemployed."

Dr. M chuckled.

Caro could feel Mary's gaze in the corner, studying them, ever the diligent chaperone. Fortunately, she would say nothing to the Countess. Mary had once been Caro's nursemaid, but now Caro just considered her a dear friend.

"The mercenaries rose to great heights, did they not?" Dr. M let the scene of Florence fall back over the Michelangelo copy. "I thought I saw several monuments to them as I strolled through the Duomo yesterday. Many weren't even Italian."

"Indeed. John Hawkwood is buried there. He was one of the generals involved in the Battle of Cascina itself—" Caro stopped herself. Would he think her a bluestocking and far too educated for a woman?

"Truly? How remarkable." Said without a trace of irony or condescension. "You enjoy history then?"

"Exotic foreign battles, princes and dukes vying for power . . . such things always tempt the imagination."

He smiled again. Wide and charming. Brown eyes dancing.

It made her stomach fluttery.

"Fascinating," he murmured. Leaving her to wonder exactly *what* he found fascinating.

A painful joy cascaded through her chest.

When was the last time a man had actually listened to her? Spoke with her as an equal? Regarded her as something more than just a . . . *thing* to be admired or acquired?

How glorious to be truly *seen*.

"Ah, there you are, Doctor. Lady Caro." A cool, aristocratic voice accosted them.

Both Caro and Dr. M froze.

And then slowly pivoted around to greet the Duke of Blackford, strolling across the room toward them.

The doctor came instantly to attention, giving his grace a deep bow. Caro rose and curtsied.

Blackford nodded, stopping in front of them.

Nearly twenty years older than her own twenty-five years, the Duke still retained his youthful looks, mostly attributed to his shock of thick brown hair. He was not a large man, but he exuded the arrogant confidence of someone who did not understand the meaning of the word *No*.

"Lady Caro, I see you have made the acquaintance of my personal physician, Dr. Ethan MacLure." Blackford gestured to the man at her side.

"Of course," she whispered.

Of course, Dr. M would be in your employ.

Of course, how foolish to think I could keep him for myself.

"Doctor, this is the charming lady I told you about. The Countess of Albany's ward, Lady Caro."

"Of course." Dr. MacLure's *of course* echoed her own.

Caro heard what he did not say:

Of course, I knew she was never for me.

Of course, she is the woman you will marry, your Grace.

She could practically *see* the moment that Dr. MacLure realized. That like-minds and flutter-inducing smiles would never trump money and rank.

Dr. MacLure's eyes shuttered, tucking all that lovely warmth and understanding far away.

She swallowed. Her chest suddenly tight and aching.

A woman such as herself had to make do with the few choices she was given. Caro was quite sure she would marry the Duke of Blackford, whether she truthfully wanted to or not.

"Dr. MacLure and I were discussing Florence and its history," Caro said around the lump in her throat.

"Always an interesting topic." The Duke's smile could politely be called condescending. "The doctor is kind to listen to your meandering musings. Though, I am sure one of the dignitaries circling the salon would be a more valuable source of information for the doctor. We would hate to tax your lovely mind, my lady."

Caro's smile froze. Most days, her smile rivaled the *matonelle* for brittleness.

She caught Dr. MacLure's gaze. *Ah.* A smile just as frozen as hers.

Which was exquisitely wonderful and equally terrible all at once.

She did not need to find a kindred spirit. Not now.

Her decisions were not her own.

"Of course, your Grace." She turned to Blackford. "You are always the soul of consideration."

Caro tentatively wrapped her hand around the arm the Duke offered, allowing him to lead her back toward the main salon.

Dr. MacLure's gaze burning a scorching hole between her shoulder blades.

Every impulse in her body resisting the urge to turn back and bury herself in the arms of a kind Scotsman . . .

12

CLAIRE

I swayed on my feet. Heart pounding. Sweating.

The world righted itself with a lurch.

I was Claire. Claire Raythorn.

Not Caro . . . whoever she had been. Talking to Dr. Ethan MacLure.

I still held Dante's elbow with one hand. My opposite foot propped open the door to the hallway.

It was like waking from a dream. Time felt fluid. Barely a second had passed, but the scene . . . whatever that was. . . had lasted much longer.

What had happened? Was I hallucinating now too?

Except . . . it had felt so real. I had *been* there. The heat of the sun on my back through the window. The teasing grin on Dr. MacLure's lips. The deep burr of his Scottish accent. But Michelangelo's *Battle of Cascina* had made an appearance, which seemed odd.

Did I need to add 'psychotic episodes' to my list of problems? The stress of assessing the Colonel's sketch and my costumed ghost-stalker finally coalescing together into a weird waking dream?

Or had Dante spiked my drink? Wait, he hadn't offered me one—

What. Just. Happened?!

My pulse pounded in my throat.

Shaking my head, I turned to Dante. His hazel eyes pleading above his duct-taped mouth.

He seemed to blend in that moment, becoming Ethan MacLure but still Dante D'Angelo as well.

Like *déjà vu* but somehow . . . more.

Most importantly, his expression said he *knew.*

Let me repeat—

He. Knew.

How—?!

"You experienced that, too." It wasn't a question.

He nodded anyway.

"You *knew* this was going to happen."

He scrunched his forehead. And then shrugged.

"This has happened to you before." Again, not a question.

Yes.

"Did you *make* it happen?"

No.

He looked pointedly down at his mouth, nearly going cross-eyed.

"You'll explain if I remove the tape."

Another nod.

Fine.

I grabbed the tape and pulled.

"Ouch!" Dante bent over slightly.

Huh. What do you know? Duct tape could be used for waxing.

I pulled him the rest of the way into my hotel room, letting the door close behind us. Helped him penguin-walk down the short hallway and into the main room with its king-size bed, large sitting area and desk.

I *tap-tap-tap*ped my foot while Dante continued to wiggle his mouth.

"Sooooo . . . just waiting for an explanation."

He threw a glance over his shoulder, arching to see his hands. "I'm pretty sure my answer will be more interesting if I'm not hogtied."

"I don't think you're in a position to argue that point right now."

He glared at me. Stubborn.

"Did you drug me? Force me to share the same hallucination?" I asked.

"Of course not." His head reared back. "Is that even possible? I don't think people can share the same hallucin—"

"Then what just happened?!"

He twisted again trying to lift his hands. Looking back at them pointedly.

"Please untie me."

"No. Tell me what's going on!"

He waddle-walked three awkward steps to a modern leather and chrome chair. Sat his enormous carcass down with an *oomph*. Leaned back and managed to swing his boots onto the glass-top coffee table.

"By all means, make yourself comfy." My tone as dry as the Sahara.

He shrugged. "I got all night."

He *smiled* then . . . more crocodilian than sheepish.

We engaged in a staring contest for a solid two minutes. He blinked first, shoulders sagging.

"C'mon, Claire. Please."

"I don't trust you."

"Obviously."

"I'm *riiight* on the edge of a serious freak-out. I think seeing your huge body free and prowling my room might be more than I can handle."

"Duly noted."

I wrapped my shaking arms around myself. It had felt *so* real. I had been Caro. Seeing what she saw, feeling what she felt.

Could it have been real? Something . . . supernatural?

"You think it's been Ethan in my photos, not you?" I asked.

"That's my guess."

Even two days ago, I would have sworn such things were impossible. But that was before Dr. Ethan MacLure decided to go on a photobombing selfie spree.

"So was that scene . . . real?"

"Yes." Emphatic.

I should have been better prepared for that response.

Instead, black dots appeared at the edge of my vision, trying to crowd closer. I closed my eyes. Forced my breathing to calm before I completely hyperventilated.

I opened my eyes, focusing on Dante sprawled out on my leather chair. His dark hair had fallen forward, curling around his face.

"So just answer me one thing. Like I asked before, did you know *that*"—I waved my hand—"was going to happen?"

"Not for sure. I suspected."

"Why not just tell me?"

"Would you have believed me?"

A pause.

"Probably not."

"Precisely. I figured showing you would go farther than anything else."

"And it's happened before."

"Yes."

"When? How?"

He sighed. Set his head against the leather seat back. Weary. "Look. It is a long story—"

"I got all night." I threw his words back at him.

He laughed, soft and resigned. "Well, at least, we're both on the same page."

"Who were those people? Lady Caro and Dr. Ethan MacLure?"

"I honestly don't know."

I started pacing the room, Dante's eyes tracking me. My heart drummed against my chest. I swallowed convulsively.

"It was nothing that could hurt you, Claire." His tone gentle. Like he was coaxing a wild animal. "Just a . . . well, a past life regression, if you will."

"Past life regression? Like I was Caro in a previous life?"

He nodded, gaze serious and concerned. "And I was Ethan."

"That I'll believe. Ethan looked just like you." It came out as an accusation. "Why?"

"I don't know why I looked the same. Genetic chance? Generally people don't look alike life-after-life."

"Did Caro look like me?"

"No. She was shorter, rounder face, darker hair. Pretty though."

More pacing.

"So why was there another drawing of Michelangelo's *Battle of Cascina*?"

"I have no idea." Dante studied me.

"It all just seems a little too . . . coincidental."

"Coincidence? Or Fate drawing threads together?"

I paused and fixed him with my sternest don't-think-I'm-stupid look. Dante just stared back, completely unfazed.

I finally turned away, looking out the dark window. The same window Caro had sat in front of, I realized.

Lights flickered across the flowing Arno. Honking rose from the street below, muted.

I shifted my focus to the glass itself and studied the reflection of Dante seated behind me. Hands still bound. Eyes trained on me.

It all seemed so surreal. How could that *regression* have just happened? But I had *been* there.

"It's just impossible to believe." I met his eyes in the reflected glass. "I felt Caro's surprise at meeting Ethan. She had this intense, visceral attraction to him—"

"Yeah. Ethan did the same. It was like a lightning bolt. Soulmate insta-love kinda thing—"

"Well, it won't do him much good. Caro had decided to marry Blackford—"

"Ethan knew the Duke had planned on offering marriage to the Countess of Albany's ward. He just didn't realize that Caro was that woman. His shock in that moment." Dante shook his head. "Poor guy. The Duke had been doggedly pursuing the match, but Ethan wasn't sure why."

I frowned, searching my—or, rather, what I sensed of Caro's—memories. "I'm not sure what her exact origins are."

"The Michelangelo? Did you get any idea of the story there?"

I paused. "No. Caro had just started the drawing. We both know copying old masters is a time-honored way of learning to draw. She drew the *Battle of Cascina* a lot. It was a hobby of hers. I could see the original—the one she copied from—in her mind's eye." I pondered it for a moment. "Could the sketch she copied from be the one in the Colonel's possession, I wonder?"

"Who knows." He shrugged. "Better yet, was the design Sangallo's copy or the Colonel's?"

Mmmm, that was an *excellent* question. I tried to remember, but Caro had thought of it so fleetingly . . .

"I don't know."

I turned back to him. Still reclining on the chair. Still staring straight at me. Through me.

I let out a long, slow breath.

"I'm seriously weirded out right now. How do you know all this? I'm just confused and terrified and—"

"Look." He sat upright, pulling his feet off the coffee table. "I have some answers. Not all, but some. I'm hungry, and I think I saw something about a restaurant on the roof of this hotel. How about you untie me, and we discuss this over a leisurely dinner?"

He leaned forward, eyes pleading. That weird thing happened again, where I saw him as Ethan MacLure. The same teasing grin. Caro had interpreted his smile as kindness, goodness.

Why didn't I do the same with Dante?

My instinct was to trust him. Granted, this was the same instinct that wanted to snuggle up to him on that leather chair, run my hands over his muscled chest and make-out like a giggly teenager.

The same instinct that had considered Pierce a *sensible* choice.

So yeah. Not really going with my gut.

My brain reminded me of Dante's cavalier treatment of my assessment of the Pittoni painting. Of those creepy, awful texts . . .

Ethan MacLure probably wouldn't do those things . . . but Ethan and Dante were not the same person, right?

"I just want answers," I said.

"You'll get them. Please untie me." His eyes plead sincerity.

I wanted to trust him. But—

Dante's leather jacket buzzed.

We both glanced at it.

"Uhmmm, would you mind?" He shot me a beseeching look.

Grimacing, I walked over to him. He rolled onto his left hip, giving me access to his jacket pocket.

"I can't believe I'm doing this." Like I needed to listen to him chat with his woman *de jour*.

I found his phone and pulled it out.

Mom pulsed on the screen.

Seriously. His *mother*?!

I swiped the phone.

"Hello."

I winced. Why, oh why, had I answered the phone for him? I should have just held it up to his ear. *Gah!*

"Dante?" A woman's voice came through the connection. Concerned.

"Th-this is Claire Raythorn. A business associate. Dante is right—"

"Claire. How lovely to hear your voice. I'm Judith D'Angelo, by the way. My boys have told me all about you. How goes the project with the Colonel?"

She sounded so . . . normal. So nice.

Wait—her boys talked about me?

"Uhmm, good. It's . . . It's going good."

"I know Dante and Branwell certainly think highly of your skill and expertise."

They *did*?

"Th-that's a surprise."

Judith laughed. A kind, motherly sound.

"Look. Dante is right here," I said. "Let me put him on—"

"If you don't mind, I'd rather just chat with you. I talk to Dante all the time."

Interesting. "Okay."

"I had no idea Dante was with you. He up and left a half hour ago. I hope he's behaving himself."

I stared down at Dante. Arms behind his back, knees taped together. Smirking at me.

I managed a weak laugh. "I'm doing what I can to keep him in line."

"Excellent. I knew I liked you."

Wow. How could a womanizing hotshot like Dante have such a down-to-earth, no-nonsense mother?

"I called to see if Dante was coming back for dinner," Judith continued. "Nonna was wondering if she should put the pasta down now or wait for him."

"Ummm. . . let me ask."

I pulled the phone away from my ear, tucking it against my body to muffle the sound. Stared down at Dante. "She wants to know if you're coming back for dinner."

"Tell her I won't make it." His grin morphed into total mischief. "You have me tied up at the moment."

Oh! He had *not* just said that.

I glared at him.

He sat back, smirking, giving his head a preening toss. He was trussed up on my chair. Completely at my mercy.

And he *still* had the upper hand.

He gestured toward the phone with his chin. "Go on. No need to be rude to my mom."

I glowered. Raised the phone to my ear. "He's, uh, *indisposed* at the moment—"

Dante grunted. "Tied up, Mom." He raised his voice, sitting forward. "SHE HAS ME *LITERALLY* TIED UP—"

I made a shushing gesture with my hand and moved away from him.

"Did Dante say you guys were tied up?" Judith asked. "No worries. I don't expect him to eat dinner with family every night." What? "I'm sure you two have a lot of work to get through. I won't keep you."

"Thank you?"

"No, thank *you*, Claire. It was lovely chatting. *Ciao.*"

I hung up. That had been . . . illuminating.

I glanced at Dante's phone still in my hand.

The lockscreen blazed bright.

Nobody, not even the rain, has such small hands

The words snagged my breath.

This man! He was determined to blast his way inside my defenses.

I turned back to Dante, still hogtied on my leather chair. Trying to reconcile my phone conversation and the words on his screen with the man I thought I knew.

He shot me a challenging eyebrow.

"*Now* will you untie me?"

DANTE

So, you were going explain to me—in excruciating detail—what happened earlier in my hotel room," Claire said.

We were seated on the restaurant rooftop terrace, facing south. City lights glittered on the Arno below, while floodlights washed Forte Belvedere on the horizon. The restaurant hummed around us, hopping busy.

I had slipped the hostess a twenty euro note, ensuring we were seated at this secluded table nestled against the iron railing. And then had politely returned the phone number she handed me. I was never that kind of guy.

All my attention was on Claire.

She drilled me with pale blue eyes, arms folded across her fluttery silk blouse, legs crossed in those tight skinny jeans of hers. Foot bobbing up and down in a pair of killer pink heels.

Cool. Collected. Seemingly contained.

But I knew better. Seeing Caro through Ethan's eyes . . .

Something had changed.

I now understood when she folded her arms like that, she was holding all the loneliness at bay. That the sharpness of her gaze was pain, not anger.

"Well, are you?" She tilted her head.

Okay, make that *mostly* pain.

I set my phone down on the table and picked up my empty wine glass, twirling the stem. I had never told another person about my GUT. Not a single past girlfriend, guy friend, work associate . . .

No one.

I would have sounded loony. How could I ever prove what I said was true?

But now . . . Claire *had* proof.

And more to the point, so did I.

Claire Raythorn *had* been important to me in past lives. I was sure of it. That wave of emotion—elation, adrenaline, heat—that Ethan had experienced with Caro . . .

I swallowed. Leaned forward across the table. "My family isn't exactly what you would call . . . normal."

"Your mom sounded normal."

"Correction. The *men* in my family are not exactly normal."

"Okay. I'll buy that." Her foot bounced.

Waiters bustled past us, all the restaurant staff in hyper-busy mode. One set a bottle of *frizzante* water on our table with an apologetic look. I gave a *take your time* wave. Claire and I had a lot of ground to cover.

For her part, Claire kept running her eyes over the room, angling her body to see as much as possible. She seemed on high-alert. Ready to jump and run. Did this poor woman ever relax? That protectiveness surged through me again.

I set my glass down and ran a hand over my face. "My father comes from a very old, distinguished Tuscan family—"

"So you actually *are* an earl?"

Ah. She had heard that little bit of gossip. "Technically, yes. I'm allowed to sign letters as the *Conte del Maldetto.*"

"Maldetto is a place? The name of a city?"

"Not exactly. *Maldetto* means damned. Cursed."

"Like a hex or something?"

"Yep."

Claire's foot stilled. "So you're the Cursed Earl?"

"Or the Damned Earl. You can take your pick."

"I'll go with damned." The tiniest hint of humor touched her eyes. "I take it you're going to explain it all."

I sat back and crossed my arms. "Well, family legend states it all started with an off-smelling lamb shank—"

"Seriously?" Her smile warmed a smidge. "A rotten lamb shank?"

"You wanna hear this story or not?"

She waved her hand. *Continue.*

"So it started in the thirteenth century with this nasty lamb shank. My illustrious ancestor, Giovanni D'Angelo, ate it—"

"That's gross."

"Probably." I shrugged. "It was the Middle Ages. Everything was gross. Anyway, Giovanni got sick—"

"Naturally."

"—and missed a town meeting with the *podestà* to resolve disputes. This meant another family was awarded a tower in Giovanni's section of the city—"

"Wait. He owned a section of the city?"

"Italy has always been this loose conglomeration of self-governing city-states. Unlike other European countries, we weren't a united country until the late nineteenth century."

"Yeah, like Germany." She motioned toward me. "Sorry. I keep interrupting."

"Basically, the lamb-shank incident started this whole downward slide. Giovanni found himself out-maneuvered and on the brink of bankruptcy. He had five daughters to dower and marry off. But no sons."

"They always need a son, don't they?"

"Can you blame them?" I spread my hands wide. Claire kicked me under the table. I chuckled.

I kept trying not to stare at her lips as I talked but, let's face it, it was a losing battle. They looked pillowy soft—a perfect swooping heart on top, plump bottom lip. A man could lose himself for hours in those lips.

I gave myself a mental shake. Focus, man.

"Desperate for a solution, Giovanni visited the camp of the local gypsies," I continued, "and asked for the gift of Sight and a son. No one knows how it precisely went down, but he arrived home a changed man—"

"Wait. Your family was cursed by gypsies? Isn't that like every bad historical romance ever written?"

I laughed. "Turns out there's truth in that cliché. Anyway, Giovanni didn't think through what he was asking. As with any fundamental element—like fire or water—knowledge can be a life-giving tool or a destructive curse."

I swallowed. A vivid childhood memory surfacing.

"Dad, why do you keep looking around? There's nothing there." I tugged on his hand, so much bigger than mine. Craned my head way back to look up at him.

"Nothing. È niente, niente, caro . . . Let's go find your mother . . ."

I shook my head.

"So this Giovanni . . . he could see, hear and feel the past and future? All at once?" Claire cocked her head in question.

"That's how I understand it."

"But . . . wouldn't that drive you insane?"

"Smart." I pointed a finger at her. "Giovanni committed suicide . . . threw himself off a church bell tower."

"That's terrible."

"Yeah. The curse fractured his mind. Giovanni had a son before he died, and the son hung himself at the age of thirty. His grandson strapped himself onto a cannon and lit the fuse—"

"Wow. Hence, the title of the Cursed Earl." Claire's eyes widened in alarm.

"Exactly."

She did that thing again with her bottom lip, sucking it into her mouth, biting with her teeth. I tried not to stare. With little success.

Honestly.

Red-blooded male over here. Did this woman even have a clue what she did to me?

"So . . ." I watched her brain work through it. "The gift passed on—"

"We actually call it a GUT."

"GUT?"

"Grossly Unusual Talent."

She snorted. "That's kinda . . . precious."

I winked.

She rolled her eyes.

"So this GUT passed on . . ."

"Every generation, to the first born son only," I said.

"But this GUT destroys the mind eventually."

I nodded.

"When did the suicides stop—" Claire froze, eyes and nose flaring. "Wait." A whisper. "You told me your father died."

She hesitated to make the connection.

"Yeah." I rescued her. "He committed suicide when we were sixteen. It just became too much . . ." My voice trailed off.

"I am so sorry." Her voice a quiet whisper against the hum of the restaurant. She blinked several times and then turned to look out over the twinkling city lights.

My own throat tightened. "Thanks. He was a good man. I still miss him."

A pause. She turned her head back to me.

I continued, "My grandfather committed suicide too—my father's father. Just sailed away from Capri in his private yacht. My *nonna*, his wife, says he could sense the madness creeping in. They found his boat drifting south of Cyprus two months later."

A beat of silence.

"Knowing all this—no offense—but why did your parents decide to have kids?" Claire asked. "I mean, even thirty years ago, there were plenty of ways to prevent a pregnancy."

It was a valid question.

"My father never intended to have children. But then he met my mom. They saw each other across a crowded street cafe in Piazza Santa Croce and the rest, as they say, is history. Crazy in love. They married after dating for just a couple of months, both agreeing that they would never have children. But Mom got pregnant anyway—"

"So every generation, every first born son . . ."

"Yeah."

"You have the title. It therefore follows *you* are the oldest of your brothers. The firstborn son."

Smart. All of her was so damn sexy.

"I am."

Another pause.

"So, assuming I believe this at all—"

"You experienced some of it earlier."

"Right." She uncrossed her legs and leaned forward herself, propping her forearms on the table, clasping her hands together. "Are *you* going mad?"

I grinned. Her eyes narrowed.

"Don't make it so easy to think so," she said.

I laughed.

Would I go mad like every other firstborn D'Angelo for the past seven hundred years?

"I don't know." I answered truthfully. "So far, so good."

She pursed those lethal lips of hers, studying me.

Her hands rested across the table. So close. I wanted to reach over, gather them into mine. I already knew her fingers would be slender and delicate. Her skin soft.

Every part of me was *remembering* her. Remembering *us*.

Madonna mia how I had loved her.

I could sense it. Hovering in the background of my emotions. An understanding I had yet to viscerally *feel*.

But I knew it was there. Waiting. Watching.

At some point, I was going to fall like a stone for Claire Raythorn.

Unfortunately, she remained cool and aloof. Barely even trusting me enough to have dinner, much less anything else.

I was just asking to have my heart shattered.

"How do you know you're not going mad? Wouldn't you be the last to know?" She scanned the restaurant again, still watchful.

"Probably. But, remember, I'm technically the oldest of triplets. Myself and Branwell are identical twins—Tennyson is a fraternal twin."

"Yeah, about the triplets thing. That seems . . . unlikely."

"Not really. Apparently, it's the most common form of natural-occurring triplets. Start with my mother's strong family history of twins and then add in two fraternal twins where one of the eggs splits into identical twins—"

"And you end up with triplets."

"Precisely."

"Soooooo . . ." Her voice trailed off into a string of question marks.

"We are the first multiples born to a D'Angelo. The GUT fractured at our birth."

"Fractured?"

"Changed. Altered. It spread between the three of us. It's like the Law of Conservation of Energy. The power of the family gift is the same. It's just been morphed into different paths, like what you witnessed today, for example."

Her eyes widened. "Changed? How so?"

A waiter took that moment to arrive at our table, breathless from running around.

"*Buonasera. Come posso aiutarvi?* How can I help you?"

Claire swiveled her head away from me.

"*Buonasera,* Tommaso." She shot the waiter a beauty-pageant smile. The kind of smile I would give my left kidney to receive from her. That dimple just under her right eye popped again and her eyes lit up.

I glanced at his name tag. Sure enough. Tommaso.

Younger. Close-cropped hair. Lean face. Strong Tuscan accent to his Italian. Not particularly handsome or memorable.

Tommaso returned Claire's smile. "*Clara!* How glad I am to see you again this evening. I did not notice you here."

His English was passable. What most Italian kids learned in school.

Claire continued to glow up at him.

What gave?

"How is your grandfather?" she asked.

"*Eh, insomma.* He is better and then he is not."

"I'm sorry to hear it——"

"Clara, you have come back." A voice sounded behind me.

I turned as another server stopped at our table. A woman. Short. Plump.

"Rosa, *ciao.*" Claire gave another of those thousand-watt smiles. "I visited the *panificio* you mentioned. You're right. Frederico does make the best *schiacciata* in town."

"*Brava!* I am glad you tried it. You must choose the *fettuccine al cinghiale* for your primo tonight. *Sono buonissime.*"

"I will for sure."

Claire waved a friendly goodbye as Rosa moved on.

"That is true. The *fettuccine al cinghiale* are very good." Tommaso nodded.

"I have no idea what that is, but——"

"Wild boar." I jumped in. I couldn't help it. "Fettucine noodles in a wild boar sauce. It's definitely a regional specialty."

"Oh. Great." Total deadpan at me. No grin. No nothing. "I'll take that." *Big* smile for Tommaso.

It shouldn't have hurt. It really shouldn't have. How could I possibly be jealous of this kid? And yet . . .

"*Perfetto.*" Tommaso wrote on his pad. "And for you, sir?"

We finished ordering. A mixture of *bruschette* for our *antipasto.* Fettucine with wild boar for our first course—the *primo piatto,* which was always pasta. A traditional Florentine steak with potatoes for my *secondo piatto*—Claire choosing fresh fish and roasted vegetables. And then *insalata* . . . salad. Followed by cheese. And then coffee.

Basically, a typical Italian dinner.

And tourists wonder why our meals take over two hours to eat.

All the while, Claire laughed and smiled. Asked Tommaso all sorts of questions about himself, his family, what it was like to live in Florence. Another server waved as he walked by.

She was a totally different Claire. Open. Kind. Friendly.

Not a smidge of ice princess in sight.

Huh.

A Claire who was a lot more like Lady Caro, truth be told. A Claire I would quickly fall madly, completely and utterly in love with.

Careful, man.

She finally sent Tommaso off with one last friendly quip and turned back to me.

"What?" She took a sip of water. "You're staring like I have horns or something."

Not quite but close enough.

"I just saw you smile more in the last five minutes than you have over the past four days with me. What gives?"

Her face froze. She blinked and set her water cup down. She slumped back in her chair. All of that fresh vivacity fading.

Closed Claire returned in force. I would never have known Open Claire even existed. Why lavish such cheerfulness on virtual strangers?

She clenched her fingers on the arm of her chair, scanning the terrace again, as if assuring her safety.

"So how does it work?" She brought her eyes back to mine. "This GUT."

"You're changing the topic."

"I am."

I drummed my fingers on the table.

"Why am I seeing Ethan in my photos?" she asked. "Why not Caro? Are you seeing her?"

Fine. I'd let her direct the conversation. "I don't know. I've taken selfies in this city over the years and never seen Caro. I'm guessing that it's something to do with the power of my GUT, pulling the echo of me—Ethan—from the past. It's my GUT after all."

A pause.

"Okay. That makes sense in a freakishly supernatural sorta way, I suppose. So how does the regression thing work?"

I continued to tap the tabletop with my fingers. "Generally, my gift is fairly weak and benign. But under certain circumstances it is so powerful, it draws in other people. The Law of Conservation of Energy, remember? These past life regressions only happen when three criteria are met."

I stopped drumming and ticked off the points.

"One, I have to be in the exact place where the event occurred. Two, I have to be with the other person who is significant in the event. Three, the event has to have some strong emotional resonance."

She nodded her head. Processing. "Got it. So something about the meeting with Caro and Ethan was significant."

"Right."

"And this has happened before? This past-life regression?"

"Just twice. Once with my mother. Once with Branwell."

She was going to ask it. The moment inevitable. "What happened?"

I paused. I *really* didn't like talking about the two other, more traumatic, past life regressions I had experienced. But, if she were to experience any more with me—and, let's face it, I intended to pursue Caro and Ethan's story with her—Claire needed to know what could potentially occur.

"The first regression happened when I was ten . . ."

I told her about Michael Strickland and watching Anne die of tuberculosis. The terror of feeling Michael's grief at her death.

Claire listened, attentive and interested.

"Wow. What a horrid thing for a child to have to deal with."

"Yeah. Part of me was terrified to go anywhere new after that. I was always on edge."

"What was the second incident? The one with Branwell?"

I sucked in a long breath.

This was the one I dreaded the most. I didn't *have* to tell her.

I leaned my forearms on the table, hanging my head forward.

She noticed my pause. "You don't . . . you don't have to talk about it."

I told myself she deserved to know if we continued to pursue this.

But the truth was much simpler.

I *wanted* to bare myself to her. To kick aside my walls and invite her into my soul.

"I know." I raised my head. "But I want you to know."

I met Claire's eyes and then thought the better of it, moving my gaze to a point just beyond her head.

"We were twenty-two and on vacation in Scotland," I said softly. "Just Branwell and me. Tennyson had opted to stay behind with his girlfriend. We were hiking the Highlands, on the edge of Loch Lomond National Park. We topped a ridge and dropped into a small glen. And just like earlier this evening, the world spun and lurched.

"Suddenly I was Dougall MacDonald, a knight in the service of Robert the Bruce. We had been retreating from the English only to find ourselves trapped in a deadly battle in the hills above Tyndrum. I was immersed in a bloodbath."

Claire gasped, soft and quiet, but I heard her all the same. Met her gaze. Surely my eyes were haunted, shadowed.

"Can you even imagine the true horror of a medieval battlefield?" I asked. "We romanticize it far too much. The screams of the dying. The sound of a sword cutting through steel and flesh. The stench. Blood and piss and smoke. It was ghastly even to Dougall, and he was born to it. He . . . me . . . I had been fighting for hours. My horse was staggering beneath me. My sword arm so tired. Dougall was a big man, like me, but even so, he . . . I was at the end of my strength. I watched a man be disemboweled in front of me, one of my men-at-arms. I swung my broadsword and took off the attacker's head. Or at least enough of it."

I shuddered. "The feel of my sword cutting through bone. The shower of blood . . . by that point, two more attackers were on me. As I swung again and again, I looked up and saw Malcolm. He was my best friend, the man who always had my back. My sister's husband. The person I loved most in the world. We had survived so much together. Somehow I knew, even though he looked totally different, that Malcolm was Branwell.

"Two men came at him. One took out his horse, while the other grabbed him off. I screamed and urged my own horse forward. I had to get to him—" My voice choked. I swallowed convulsively. "I didn't. I watched those men run him through with a spear, impaling him. I screamed again and again, fighting like a madman. I met Malcolm's eyes across the battlefield, watched the life in them flicker and then fade. I howled and fought, tears blinding me. Something stabbed me in the side. The chest. But all I could see was Malcolm dying."

I paused, staring down at my hands. I rubbed my face. As if I could erase the memory so easily.

"We came out of the regression, still standing in the same glen," I continued. "I was sobbing. Part of me hugely relieved that Branwell was alive, that it was the twenty-first century and not the fourteenth. But another part of me still screamed in agony over Malcolm's death. I had felt everything in that moment. Every iota of Dougall's anguish and horror.

"Branwell grabbed and held me. Both of us bawling." I raised my head. "Branwell had experienced it all from Malcolm's point-of-view, of course. The battle. Dying impaled on a spear, watching Dougall frantically trying to reach him . . ." I took a sip of water. "*That* is why these regressions can be . . . worrisome."

A massive understatement.

"But something like that could have happened this evening," Claire frowned and tucked a wisp of hair behind her ear.

"Perhaps. But I needed *you* to understand, Claire." My eyes begged hers. "No, that's not entirely true. *I* needed to understand. To make sure the man in your photos was a past life self and not my GUT fracturing further. I'm truly sorry if you feel I played you in any way."

"No. I suppose I don't." Claire bounced her foot, pink heels bobbing. "I would probably have done the same thing in your shoes."

She did have a strong sense of fairness, bless her.

"Thank you." I breathed out with a smile.

Our antipasto arrived. The *bruschette* were delicious. But I wasn't letting up on Claire. Not yet.

"Now tell me something about yourself," I said. "This has all been about me so far. I want to know about *you*."

Claire snorted. "Log on to YouTube. Or, better yet, google 'Batty Ray Psycho'—"

"You know that's not what I meant. C'mon, Claire." I nudged her feet under the table. "Why not answer my question?"

"Dante—"

"You called me Dante. That's a good start."

She gave a small shake of her head. "Why go there, Dante? You have a terrible reputation with women. I saw that hostess slip you her number."

Of course. "Did you see me hand it back?"

"You did?"

I nodded. "You're welcome to frisk me if you want." I wiggled my eyebrows.

She rolled her eyes and shifted in her chair. "See. Comments like *that* hurt your cause—"

"It's called *flirting*, Claire. It's fun. Try it. You might like it."

She hit me with a truck-stopping glower.

"Why? So I can be another of your discarded conquests?"

"What have I done to earn your distrust? We didn't meet until four days ago."

"Your reputation *does* proceed you."

"I think you're wrong about me." I stared at her, leaning forward.

She stared right back. Seeming icy and contained.

But I had seen Open Claire . . .

Did Claire understand the challenge she presented? The medieval, cave-man part of me saw her as a fortress. Something to be scaled. Put under siege. How did that old song by Sting go? *Let me set the battlements on fire . . .*

No way was I letting this woman go without a fight.

"Are you seriously telling me your reputation is exaggerated?" she asked. "That you're *misunderstood?*" The word dripped sarcasm.

Yep. That pretty much summed it up.

"You, of all people, should know better than to believe industry gossip, or what you read on social media. I don't date around, Claire. I'm not that kind of guy. I just have a playboy kinda look and people make assumptions. But I do like flirting with *you.*"

"Well, I'm not in a good place right now. Psycho, remember?" She pointed a thumb at her chest.

"You're not psycho, Claire."

She blinked too rapidly and turned her head away, looking out over the dark cityscape.

"I want to get to know you." I angled my head, getting her to turn back to me. "Whatever little tidbits of yourself you are willing to share, I'll take."

Silence.

It stretched on too long.

Finally, she reached across the table and tapped my phone.

"Nobody, not even the rain, has such small hands," she whispered. "E. E. Cummings. *Somewhere I have never traveled.*"

All the air punched out of my lungs.

The quote on my lockscreen. The last line of my favorite poem.

No one recognized that line. *No one.*

The fact that she recognized it . . . that barest glimpse into her soul . . . that she reflected the part of myself the world rarely saw.

I stared into her blue eyes. An ache creeping down my spine toward my heart.

Claire leaned forward. "Why?"

Why that poem? Why on my lockscreen?

I paused. Would I tell her the whole truth?

Could I tell her anything less?

"I want that kind of love." I answered. "The kind that renders 'death and forever with each breathing.'"

Yes. It seemed I *would* tell the whole truth.

She sat back. Eyes pensive.

"Why?" I lobbed the question back.

Only different subtext: *Why that poem? Why do you like it?*

Would she be honest with me? Give me this tiny taste of her.

A beat.

"Because it's comforting to know someone found a love like that." She bit that plump bottom lip again. "That others have been 'somewhere I have never traveled.' I hope to visit that place myself someday."

Ah.

I recited slowly. "Love . . . the breaking of your soul—"

"—upon my lips," she finished. Another Cummings poem.
I nearly forgot how to breathe. This woman—
She shattered and healed all at once.
Illuminated places deep within I hadn't known existed.
"Oh, Claire." Voice hoarse.
I closed my eyes. Opened them. Reached for her hands.
She pulled back. Shutting me out.

CLAIRE

Dante stared, letting his hands rest on the table. His gaze . . . it cut me.

Seeing that poem on his lockscreen . . . it had been a sliver of Dante D'Angelo's soul that I hadn't wanted to know. It was easier to think of him as a handsome playboy—gorgeous packaging around an empty box.

Because if that pretty packaging proved to be full of amazing treasures . . . I would fall for this man so hard, I don't know that I could ever recover.

With one last look, Dante sat back. Swallowed. Adam's apple bobbing up and down.

His eyes told me that this conversation wasn't over. That he would be patient. Bide his time. Wait to make his next move.

I wasn't sure how I felt about that.

He had shed his leather jacket. His cream button-down hugged his broad chest, and he had rolled the sleeves up his forearm, revealing tan, muscular forearms. His dark hair fell forward, lapping his jaw and wrapping over his shirt collar. He sat with a restless energy. As if he would jump up at any moment, call for his sword and horse, and ride off to slay the dragon.

Every woman in the place had already checked him out at least ten times. Not that I blamed them. One woman at the bar slightly behind him kept staring at his back. Waiting. Probably hoping he would leave the restaurant alone.

Part of me exulted that he chose to be here. With me. That he had returned the hostess' phone number. (I thought he had but wanted to be sure. Pathetic, I know.)

But most of me was tired of the game. Of that prickly sense of being watched. Of worrying that someone was videoing us together and would post it online. Terrified of trusting.

A quote from Hemingway kept a steady thrum in my mind:

The world breaks everyone, and afterward, many are strong at the broken places.

Grammy would say that from time to time.

Heaven knew I had a hell of a scar right along the part of my psyche labeled *Men* and *Trust*.

I wasn't sure I believed Hemingway.

At what point is the scar tissue too deep? When do you become too broken to ever heal? How many times can your heart be shattered before collapsing altogether?

I had no intention of finding out.

Dante let out a slow breath and sat back, folding his arms over his chest. Bulging his biceps in the process. The moody restaurant lighting painting his face in a captivating terrain of sharp edges and deep shadows.

Stupid man with all his stupid hotness (and even stupider kindness) trying to worm his way behind my walls.

"So how does it work? Your GUT?" I asked.

A pause.

"Claire, I want you to know everything about me, but it should be a two-way street—"

"Dante . . ." I instantly hated the whiny breathy-ness of my voice. "Please. Don't push."

This was as open as I was going to be. As open as I *could* be, right now.

He sighed. But nodded. Dark eyes understanding.

I listened as Dante explained how his GUT worked, the silvery shadows he saw trailing after people, the ability to concentrate and see events moving around an object. Tommaso brought our *fettuccine al cinghiale* as Dante finished talking.

"If you can see things that happened around an object, why don't you use your GUT to solve crimes?" I asked. It was a logical question.

"It doesn't work like that. Even when I scan an object, I can only see people who are dead. So I could maybe solve cold cases where all the relevant parties are no longer living, but that doesn't really help police, per se."

I thought that over for a moment. "Okay, so how do you see people's past lives?" I asked. "Do they just follow them around?"

"Yeah. Tommaso over there"—he gestured with his chin—"was a World War II soldier, a Victorian farmer, a seventeenth century peasant, a medieval peasant. Most people are just peasants."

"What about Rosa?" I nodded toward the other server two tables over.

Dante looked at her. "A factory worker. A midwife. A mercenary foot soldier—"

"Soldier? As a woman?"

"Gender can be somewhat fluid, I've noticed. Most people stay the same gender life-after-life, but for a few it can change."

"Interesting."

"I've become extremely adept over the years at using clothing to determine someone's history."

That did make sense, I supposed. "I'm assuming you used your GUT with the Colonel's Michelangelo sketch. What did you see?"

"Wouldn't I be breaking the Colonel's Sandbox Rule if I told you?" He chuckled around a mouthful of pasta. "No plagiarizing, remember?"

Seriously?

"I think having a 'grossly unusual talent' is an automatic violation," I countered, twirling fettuccine onto my fork.

"I didn't see anything significant with the sketch. It was blank."

I paused, pasta halfway to my mouth. "Blank? Does that happen often?"

"Never. It's never happened before. I'm wondering if it has something to do with Caro and Ethan maybe. Who knows."

"Hmmm. Interesting. So tell me about your brothers."

Tommaso brought our *secondo piatti* while Dante explained about Branwell and his ability to hear the past.

"So I assume Branwell 'listened' to the Colonel's Michelangelo sketch?" I asked around a mouthful of divine seabass. "Or was it silent for him too?"

"No, it had sound. Nothing too helpful, but Branwell did overhear a man with a slight Scottish brogue say." Dante frowned, trying to remember the exact words. "'I figure we are even now. You have taken something from me. And now I have taken it from you. Never forget—I always win the game.'"

I shivered. I'm sure my eyebrows drew down into a neat 'V.'

"That's fascinating. Branwell was sure it was a Scottish brogue?"

He shrugged. "Just like I specialize in clothing, Branwell is an expert with accents. If he said it was Scottish, it probably was. Upper-class, he specified."

We exchanged a that's-quite-intriguing look.

Dante moved on, talking about Tennyson, sitting back as our *insalate* arrived. He described how Tennyson feels the future. I got the sense that Dante was glossing over the reality of Tennyson's situation, but obviously some secrets weren't his to tell.

Tommaso brought out the cheese and coffee. Dante ordered some *tiramisù* too, saying the American in him could never resist dessert.

I sipped my coffee. "Do you see your own past lives when you look in the mirror?"

"No. It doesn't work that way." Dante took a healthy bite of gooey *tiramisù*. "I usually don't see anything that pertains to my own past." He nudged the plate toward me, indicating I should take a bite.

I shot him an eyebrow, but grabbed my teaspoon anyway. I was American, after all.

"Okay. But do you see Malcolm clinging to Branwell?" I reached across the table and snagged a bite of *tiramisù*. Mmmm, the dessert was incredible. "Do you see Caro clinging to me?"

Dante smiled indulgently, obviously appreciating my reaction. "I don't see silvery shadows of those I love."

"So love is the key?"

"Exactly. Basically, the more I love someone, the fewer their shadows."

Huh. That was interesting. I took another bite of *tiramisù*.

"So you see some of Branwell's past lives, but not all of them?"

"Not exactly. Branwell is entirely blank. No shadows at all."

"Right. Because he's your brother—"

"Womb-mate, he would say."

I groaned. "That's a terrible pun."

"Tell me about it. Anyway, Tennyson and my mom are the same. Chiara and my *nonna* are nearly blank too." He scooped up some marscarpone.

"Because you love them."

"Yeah. The farther away from me emotionally someone is, usually the more plentiful their shadows."

"You didn't answer my question." I put my spoon down and sat back before I ate his entire dessert. "Do you see Caro's shadow behind me? Was I a peasant most of the time like everyone else?"

For some reason, the question troubled him. Dante set his own fork down. Drummed his fingers for a second.

"You're blank," he finally said. "Like Branwell or my mom. Just . . . nothing."

It took a second for his words to sink in.

And then every hair on my body stood on end, chased by a bone-rattling shiver. My alarm level went from *danger* to *high alert*.

"Are you . . . are you saying you l-love me?"

A loooong pause.

"No." His dark eyes drowned in mine. "I don't love you."

My heart . . . *sank.*

Really? How could that possibly be disappointing?

"But you just said—"

He ran a hand over his face. "I don't know what's going on here, Claire. This is completely new ground for me too. Maybe we loved each other in past lives—"

"Yeah, but you said I'm blank. Nothing, right?"

"Empty air."

I was shaking now, two deep breaths away from a hyperventilating panic attack.

"You believe we *have* been in l-love . . . in the past."

It wasn't a question.

He leaned farther across the table. Reached out and took my hand in his. Swallowing up my smaller fingers in his huge palm. Warm. Comforting. I could feel the scrape of callouses as he rubbed my hand.

"It's the only explanation that makes sense."

"Like soulmates?"

"Something like that. Life after life, we've found each other. The connection so powerful it even spills over into your photos."

I stared at our joined hands. A surge of energy flowed through the connection. An aching sense of *rightness.* Of *us.*

I had been here with him before. We had done this countless times. An eternity of memories just out of reach.

Part of me wanted to close my hand around his. Hold on.

But . . .

"I don't love you. Not yet," he continued. "But think about it, Claire. I know I feel a sense of connection with you. You *have* to feel it too. We have a lot in common. Our shared profession and love of art. The same taste in random mid-century American poets. I'm betting you like offbeat art house films and moody folk rock just as much as I do too."

Curse him. I did.

My five-year-old self wanted to stuff my fingers in my ears and chant *la-la-la-la—*

But he wasn't done. "Not to mention, I think you're stunningly attractive. Can you honestly tell me you're not interested in me? Because I absolutely am interested in you."

My throat closed, my heartbeat clawing to escape. Choking me.

I wasn't ready for this. Not him. Not now.

I twisted my hand out of his. Gave a weak laugh. "Wow. Talk about a good line—"

"Claire. Please. You know I'm not just playing you—"

"Dante, I can't—"

I stood up. He rose with me.

"Don't be like this." He barged right into my personal space. Even in three-inch heels, I still had to look up at him. "I don't know what happened between Ethan and Caro. I don't know about all those other lives. But there's something here. I want to give it a chance."

Wordlessly, I shook my head. It was too much. Too soon. I could barely trust the man enough to be semi-alone with him. Anything more was going too far.

"I can't . . . I'm not in a good place right now." I stepped away from the heat of his body and snagged my purse off the chair back.

"Claire—"

"Thanks for dinner—"

"Wait for me, at least. Let me pay and walk you down to your room—"

"No. It's better like this."

"Claire." His gaze entreating.

I could feel every eye in the restaurant on us. *Was* someone videoing us?

My heart pounded. Sweat teased the back of my neck.

Calm. Polite. Don't make a scene. Just get away—

"Good night, Mr. D'Angelo."

And like Lady Caro, I strode off without looking back. Dante's gaze burning a scorching hole in my head.

CLAIRE

My phone buzzed me awake the next morning. I rolled over in bed and snagged it off the nightstand.

I lay next to you again last night. Breathed in your skin. Dragged my lips along your neck.

My heart tried to escape out of my chest, adrenaline spiking through my veins.

Ugh! This online bully.

I dropped the phone on my covers and rubbed a hand over my face. And then spent a solid fifteen minutes chanting my mental, self-help litany . . . *theywantyoutobeafraiddontgiveintoit . . . courageyoucandothis . . .*

Though, really, I simply wanted to scream a loud chorus of *whyme-whymewhyme* and crawl back under the bedspread. But I knew from experience (and hundreds of hours of therapy) that it wouldn't help.

All I could do was go on with my life.

I understood only too well how people could live in a war zone. You just got used to the terror, adopted a fatalistic attitude and moved on.

What would be, would be.

For now, I would just do what I always did. Ignore the anonymous text, load Fear onto my back and get on with my day.

Silver lining, though.

After the events of yesterday, I felt reasonably sure Dante was not my online harasser. There was no logical explanation for Ethan's appearance in my photos or for the 'scene' Dante and I had experienced together.

Correction. My emotions or heart or intuition or whatever was *sure* it wasn't him.

That part of me wanted to trust, trust, trust. Wrap him up in a bear hug, bury my face in his broad chest and dream of unicorns and rainbows and happily-ever-afters.

The thinking, *sane* part of me knew my intuition had the stability of a sorority pledge after twenty rounds of beer pong. Not to be trusted to walk a straight line into the kitchen, much less be handed the keys to my life.

So . . . not sure where that left me, actually.

Dante's remarks about love had really freaked me. Honestly, you can't just drop a four-letter word like that into a normal conversation. Or even the weird conversation we *had* been having.

It had felt like a huge step simply to eat dinner with him. The idea of anything more . . .

Love.

My heart rate spiked just thinking about it.

I snorted, draping a hand over my eyes.

Yeah. Maybe with another ten years of therapy I *might* reach a place where I could trust in love and a romantic relationship.

I mean, I wanted it. Who doesn't want capital-L love?

But . . .

I might shift it to my back, but Fear was still the crippling burden I carried.

Wasn't that how the old Sarah McLachlan song went? *There's nothing I'd like better than to fall, but I fear . . .*

Yep. Pretty much summed it up.

And despite the similarities between Dante and I—that sense of finding a kindred spirit with the same tastes and likes—I was pretty sure we did *not* share a love of random '90s fem rock.

I had too much self-healing to do before being functional in a romantic relationship again.

After another twenty minutes of pep-talking, I crawled out of bed and into the shower. And then blow-dried my hair completely down, hiding my neck.

Passive-aggressive? Probably.

I brushed on a little make-up, wishing I had my PH lipstick. I was sure I'd return home to Boston and find it sitting on the bathroom counter. In the meantime, I just had to wear my favorite lemon berry lipgloss sans color.

Moving around my hotel room caused my brain to churn over the events that had happened in this same space two hundred years ago.

Who had Lady Caro been?

I booted my laptop and did a basic google search for her but pulled up nothing. Granted, trying to find a woman named Lady Caro who lived in Florence, Italy, after the fall of Napoleon was difficult.

I did find plenty of information about Louise, the Countess of Albany, the woman who was Caro's guardian. Louise had indeed been married to Bonnie Prince Charlie, just as the Colonel had mentioned. Louise had gone on to separate from Charlie and had lived most of her life with Vittorio Alfieri in this palazzo. She had died in 1824, which meant that the scene Dante and I experienced had happened after Napoleon left Florence in 1814 but before Louise's death.

That was all the information I could deduce.

I was still puzzled over the appearance of the *Battle of Cascina* in Caro's drawing. It seemed such a strange coincidence. Was it Fate, like Dante said, pulling past threads together?

I finally opened my research folder and added a separate page of notes, trying to organize my thoughts:

1. The Colonel's sketch of the Battle of Cascina doesn't match any known copies of Michelangelo's cartoon. Is the Colonel's sketch

Michelangelo's original modello for the cartoon? Or, at least, a copy of the modello?

2. Lady Caro (who was the ward of the Louise, Countess of Albany, who was the wife of Bonnie Prince Charlie) liked to copy the *Battle of Cascina* from another source. Was she imitating Sangallo's copy or the alternate version of the Colonel's? And, if the latter, what was her original source and where was it located?

3. The words that Branwell heard in English around the Colonel's sketch imply that there might be a connection with Caro and Ethan: *I figure we are even now. You have taken something from me. And now I have taken it from you. Never forget—I always win the game.*

I studied my list for a moment, but couldn't think of anything else to add. I would just have to wait for the mass spectrometry results. Having dates on things would tell me a lot.

I spent the rest of my morning responding to email and did more research on the Michelangelo, starting a meticulous comparison of line between the Colonel's sketch and known Michelangelo drawings. The similarities were compelling.

In the middle of it all, the Colonel called, inviting me to have dinner with him the next night. I was pretty sure he hadn't extended similar invitations to Dante or Pierce.

His dinner invitation filled me with mixed emotions—elation that I was perhaps winning the contest, but also worry that the Colonel had *Intentions* where I was concerned . . .

But as I needed this job more than anything else . . .

I said yes.

The sun climbed higher, flooding my room with light. And then my rumbling stomach reminded me I had missed breakfast and, if I didn't get a move on, would miss lunch too.

I snagged my purse, wrapped a scarf around my neck and waved to Martina behind the reception desk as I strode out the *portone*.

A blast of sun and noise greeted me as I stepped onto the side-walk—cars and motorbikes buzzing across the Ponte Santa Trinità and down Lungarno Corsini. I was immediately engulfed in the smell of diesel fumes and cigarette smoke—the scent of Europe.

Tourists waited for the stoplight, crowding around the base of Caccini's enormous statue of *Summer* across the street. White tennis shoes on the Americans; brown loafers for the Germans; black dress shoes for the Japanese. I swear you can identify nationality by footwear alone.

Pigeons cooed and fluttered around the statue, only to scatter toward me as two school kids startled them.

And then I saw *him*.

Straddling a gleaming chrome BMW motorcycle. Right in front of me.

Of course. He *would* be a motorcycle man.

That same tailored leather jacket and battered jeans. A tight gray t-shirt underneath. Expensive oversized sunglasses.

My heart lurched. Stupid, excitable thing that it was.

Dante saw me. And smiled.

The world went slo-mo.

His grin, spreading like honey. The wind in his dark hair as he lifted a leg and swung off the bike. The shake of his head as he tipped the sunglasses off his face and pocketed them. The swagger in his shoulders as he walked over to me.

All exaggerated and slow. Movie-trailer perfect.

My heart was jumping up-and-down, clapping like a crazed idiot. There had to be a better way to get my cardio.

Then all too predictably, Fear came stomping along, trampling the stomach butterflies. I swallowed.

"There you are." Dante shoved his hands into his jeans' pockets. "Martina said you hadn't left, but I was beginning to wonder if you'd ever come out."

He stopped in front of me. So tall he blocked the sun. Or was it just because he was, once again, in my bubble.

The pigeons on the sidewalk shuffled and moved around him.

"You could have just texted."

"Yeah, I could have. But I did promise not to contact you via phone, and I don't want to be accused of breaking any Sandbox Rules."

A pause.

And then we both spoke at once.

"I'm sorry I freaked out last night—"

"I'm sorry I freaked you out last night—"

"Jinx." Again, both of us speaking together.

He chuckled.

"I *am* sorry things came out like they did." He loomed over me, expression contrite. "So I'm here to apologize. If you're going to trust me, I need to be as trustworthy as possible."

I shot him a skeptical eyebrow.

His smile widened, crinkling his eyes.

"Well, all that and my mom insisted I invite you to lunch," he continued. "I figured you would find it harder to say 'No' if I showed up in person."

"Your mom?"

"Yeah."

"Your mom said you had to invite me to lunch? That seems . . ."

"What?"

"You just don't strike me as a mommy's boy."

"I *am* Italian, remember? We're *all* momma's boys."

"Half-Italian."

He shrugged. "When it comes to Judith or my *nonna*, I'm entirely Italian. One hundred and ten percent. They tell me to jump; I ask how high."

Right.

"As much fun as a cozy lunch with you and your *mother* sounds—"

"*Uffa!*" He rubbed the back of his neck. "Branwell, Chiara and my grandmother will be there too. C'mon. You'll enjoy it. Trust me."

Trust? *That's* what I just couldn't bring myself to do.

He read my hesitation.

"Claire. Hey." He bent his head. Got even more in my space.

"Personal bubble." I waved my hands, causing several pigeons to scoot around.

Though it was half-hearted at best.

Both my waving and the pigeons' scooting.

Dante sighed. Took a small step back. "You clearly have a lot of wrong impressions of me. How's about you toss those aside and start fresh?"

If only life were that easy. "Dante, like I said last night, I'm not in a good place. I'm not interested in dating anyone right now. And then you dropped that L-word—"

"I understand, and I'm sorry my explanation came out like that. Let's back up. Why don't we start with being friends?" He held out a hand to me. "Please. Just consider me a neighborly guy-friend."

I would say about sixty-percent of me wanted to shake his hand and agree. Another seventy-percent wanted to run fast and far. A solid fifteen-percent wanted to wrap myself around him like static cling. The remaining five percent wondered if Dante was always like a bull in a china shop when it came to women.

Or something like that.

Math had never been my strongest subject.

"Please." He smiled and that fifteen percent edged up to seventeen. "Or if not friend-friends, will you at least entertain the *possibility* of becoming friends?"

"I think the Colonel will have a problem with us being on friendly terms." I chewed on my cheek.

Dante shoved his hands into his jean pockets. "The Sandbox Rule just says no plagiarizing, nothing about friends."

"Yeah, but I'd hate for us both to get tossed—"

"Not going to happen, 'cause that would leave the Colonel with Pierce. And we *both* know Pierce is only here because the Colonel was contractually obligated to invite him. You can't think the Colonel actually *wants* to hire Pierce?"

Okay. That was a valid point.

"Fine." I nodded. "I'll *consider* the possibility that we could become friends at some point, but if the Colonel has an issue with it, I'm ratting you out."

He chuckled, warm and rumbly. "Great. Let's go."

"Wait—I didn't agree to—" I started.

But Dante had turned toward his bike and then froze. Staring at the sidewalk.

No. Not the sidewalk. A pigeon *on* the sidewalk.

The poor thing hopped on one foot, its other foot bent at an unnatural angle.

Dante tracked it, like a hunter.

Uhmm . . . okay . . .

He backed the bird up against the wall of the palazzo. Crouching, he slowly reached for it.

But this was a street-wise pigeon. It hopped frantically away, flapping its wings and fluttering across the street to settle next to the statue of *Summer* holding her cornucopia of fruit.

Grimacing, Dante pivoted around, following the bird with his eyes.

I grabbed his arm.

"Whoa there, tiger. It's just a pigeon."

"No, it's not."

"Uhmmm." I swung my head. Studied it. It cocked its little pigeon head at me. Batted its beady eyes. "Yep. Pretty sure it is."

"I mean, yes, it is a pigeon, but I think it was a nun in a former life."

What? "You see past lives of animals too?"

"Occasionally." His head swiveled, waiting for a break in traffic to cross the street. "Only when they were once people."

"What will you do once you catch it—"

Dante darted out in front of an orange city bus, barely making it across the street in time.

The bus zipped past, and I saw him hunched over, trying to catch the poor pigeon . . . nun . . . whatever. It had fluttered down from the statue and Dante had it up against the large stone railing.

The stoplight went red and I threaded my way across the street to join him.

He made a sudden quick jab and then straightened, face triumphant. He raised the struggling pigeon in his large hands, showing me his catch.

"There has to be an easier way to get lunch," I called as I stepped around the last car and joined him on the sidewalk. "Besides, I'm fairly positive eating a pigeon who used to be nun is some form of cannibalism."

That little comment caused two tourists to take a hasty step back from me. (White Adidas. Americans. Wusses.)

Fortunately, Dante had the pigeon cradled against his chest by that point, stroking its feathers and making soothing noises. Stupid lucky nun . . . I supposed he didn't intend to eat it/her after all. He had walked around the base of the statue onto the bridge and was leaning back into the stone, facing the Ponte Vecchio up river.

He raised his head as I drew near. Eyes drilling into me.

The world suddenly lurched. The smell of auto exhaust and cigarette smoke fading into horse manure and dust.

Dante's body morphed. A long skirt clung to my legs.

Please, please be there, I thought. *I am quite desperate to see you.*

16

Caro hurried around the base of the statue and onto the Ponte Santa Trinità, Mary following discreetly behind.

Hallelujah.

He had waited for her.

Dr. MacLure—*Ethan*, she shyly whispered in her mind—leaned against the stone, ostensibly checking the time on his pocket watch. His beaver top hat shadowed his eyes, longer curls escaping, lapping his ears and rolling over the high collar of his dark coat.

Her heart thumped—painful, aching, yearning.

What an impossible dream.

His head snapped up, face lighting as he saw her.

"Dr. MacLure, what a surprise." Caro curtsied.

A wry smile tugged his lips. He bowed, tipping his hat. "My lady."

Caro always sighed internally when someone called her a lady. She wasn't . . . not precisely.

But her mother had, technically, been granted the title of duchess. And her great-uncle was powerful enough that, if he decreed she be called Lady Caro as befitted the daughter of a duchess, then so be it.

Lady Caro she was.

"Imagine meeting you here," Caro said. "And after all your fine talk of us not seeing each other until . . . summer."

"Indeed, Lady Caro. But I should always hope to see you in summer." He winked and glanced up at the statue beside them—Summer with her bountiful cornucopia.

Caro risked a peek behind her. Yes, she was safe. The large statue blocked the front of the Countess' palazzo, hiding Caro from its view. Mary stood slightly behind her, ensuring propriety.

Nothing improper or scandalous.

Just two friends who had happened upon each other. Utterly accidental.

And, yet, it seemed the most clandestine assignation. Each stolen moment with him precious.

"Did you enjoy the book I recommended?" Ethan leaned forward. Perhaps a little *too* close, that flutter scattering through her stomach again.

The scent of wool and clean soap swirled around her. She could *feel* the heat of his warm body. Or maybe the heat was all her own . . .

"Yes. Mrs. Radcliffe's stories always curdle my blood. They are quite scandalous."

He gave a soft laugh. "Says the shocking young lady who sketches unclad Michelangelo drawings—"

"Hush, Doctor. You shall set me to blushing." Caro pressed a gloved hand to her cheek.

"Are you pleased with the final sketch?"

She sighed, thinking about the hour she had spent that morning, tweaking the shadows one last time. "I believe so. I wish to perfect the shading more, but—"

"But at some point, you must declare the work finished."

"Precisely."

A long moment passed. Standing near him felt like basking in the glow of the warmest sun. Summer indeed.

She hoarded the tiniest revelation about him. Like a child on the beach, gathering prized seashells. Putting them up to her ear, listening to what they told her of him.

She knew that he missed Scotland in autumn, when reds and golds threaded into the green hills. That he loved swimming but not being wet; disliked traveling but loved the seeing of new places; hated sickness but found joy in doctoring the ill. He discussed history and science for hours but tired of current politics after five minutes. He loved his mother and sister with fierce passion yet felt guilt over his desire to live better than their humble hearth. He dressed like a gentleman and usually sounded like one too, but the more he spoke of home, the more adorably Scottish his vowels became.

She discovered he had a middle name—Charles, named for the absent king—when he had lent her a handkerchief, the initials ECM lovingly embroidered in the corner by his sister. Caro kept the handkerchief, and it may or may not be currently resting underneath her pillow.

Sunlight off the river reflected in his eyes. She had thought his eyes to be simple brown, but over the past few weeks, she had realized they were nothing so monolithic.

Flecked with gold and green and gray darting in and out of rich chocolate.

Plaid eyes.

Looking like she imagined Scottish heather and gorse to be.

How was she to ever live without him? But Blackford and the Countess had spoken; Caro had no say in the end.

The very thought made her throat burn with unshed tears.

Ethan stared at Caro. Willing himself to look away.

Any moment now.

But . . .

"I merely wished to thank you for the recommendation of the book." She gave that tentative smile. The one that only he saw.

Shy. Uncertain. Longing.

"It is, as always, my pleasure." He clasped his hands behind his back, telling them sternly not to reach for her.

"You understand my likes and dislikes so well. It is as if you read my mind," she said.

"Yes."

"It is similar to that sonnet by Shakespeare—"

"'Let me not to the marriage of true minds admit impediments . . .'"

Her smile broadened.

His breath caught.

"Precisely," she whispered.

"You had not been thinking of a different sonnet? Shall I compare thee to a *summer's* day, perhaps?" He darted another glance at the statue looming above them.

She laughed. Breathy and carefree. Heartbreaking.

The soft late afternoon light caught her hair, kissing it with golden light. She called to mind the beach on a calm day. Colors of sand and endless blue water. Calm. Welcoming.

It was as if they had always known each other. His entire existence hurtling toward *her* and *this* and *now*.

He adored the flare in her eyes as she spoke of art. How hours passed in just minutes, their wit like a racket ball in play, pinging back and forth. Every little facet of her a revelation. Something shiny and new to be hoarded and relived in the long hours between *her*. He saw the loneliness she soothed through her drawing. Understood the fire within her for a life that was more than her current course.

He knew her soul. It was the twin of his own. Forged in the same furnace.

Heaven help him. He was utterly in love.

It shattered through him, a crashing wave, scouring every other emotion away.

Love. *An ever-fixed mark*, as Shakespeare described it, *that looks on tempests and is never shaken.*

A gentle breeze caught a tendril of hair escaping her bonnet, twining it around her slender neck.

Yes. He understood the emotion now.

Humbling in its force. Dragging him to his knees before her.

Leaving him ragged and gutted and so very *new*.

She risked much being seen with him on the street like this, even with Mary chaperoning her steps.

Blackford had offered for Caro. Or, rather, had negotiated a betrothal settlement with the Countess. Ethan wasn't sure if Caro had even been granted the formal opportunity to decline the offer.

But it wasn't surprising, really. Blackford always got what he wanted, in the end. When he set about to collect something, he did. Like the purchase of a rare Raphael that Ethan had helped negotiate last week, along with a pair of Etruscan urns.

Like Lady Caro herself. The rarest prize of all.

Given her parentage, she was so far above Ethan's own meek origins. She would never be his. He knew that . . .

Love alters not with his brief hours and weeks . . .

If he were wise, he would turn away. Never look back. So much rode on his shoulders. Blackford owned him. His mother and sister relied on him.

Ah, but when it came to matters of the heart, wisdom had never been his *forté*.

"Caro, dear, there you are." A voice called.

Ethan just managed to avoid startling as the Countess of Albany strode across the street to them, a maid in tow. Though gray-haired and stout, the Countess retained a strong sense of command.

"Lady Albany." He doffed his hat and bowed precisely.

"Doctor." She nodded in his direction. And then studied her ward.

Ethan swallowed. The woman's sharp eyes missed nothing. Would she report this 'meeting' to Blackford?

Caro turned and fixed the duchess with a brittle smile. "My lady, I stumbled upon Dr. MacLure as I was leaving the palazzo. Was that not fortunate?"

"Fortunate, indeed." The Countess' dry, dry tone said she clearly understood this situation. "Well, now that you are here, Doctor, you might be so good as to escort us up the street to the Cascine. We must take the air and the park is the closest place."

Interesting. What was her game? Why throw him and Caro together?

Ethan clicked his heels together. "I should be honored, my lady."

He offered each lady his arm. Polite. Respectful.

"Thank you, Doctor. You are always so kind." Caro beamed as she wrapped her gloved hand around his elbow. Each finger searing, branding despite the layers of cloth separating them. "I do believe you were telling me of your friend—John, was it not? You said he likes to fly hawks every Tuesday morning. Is that not most odd, my lady?"

The Countess harrumphed as she took his opposite arm.

Ethan glanced down in surprise at Caro, who merely winked up at him as they strolled off the bridge, tightening the grip on his elbow.

Heaven help him indeed . . .

17

DANTE

I reeled, still clutching the fluttering pigeon to my chest. A *motorino* buzzed by my elbow, brakes squealing, jarring me back to the twenty-first century.

Claire gasped in front of me, standing just as Caro had, sunlight raking her. Shimmery blond hair wrapping around her face. Blue eyes drops of molten sky.

"Wow." Claire massaged her temple. "That was . . . unexpected." She reached out and braced a hand against the base of the statue to her right. Blinking as if trying to clear her head. Absorbing the shift back into our reality.

"Agreed." I nodded, adjusting the pigeon.

I glanced down at it, seeing the silvery shadow of a nun clinging beyond. An old habit . . . probably mid-seventeenth century.

I looked back up at Claire, still shaking her head.

Ethan's emotions lingered, sliding from me oh-so-slowly. Love. Devotion. Admiration. I saw in her what he did. That spark of life. The mixture of kindness and spunk.

Let me not to the marriage of true minds admit impediments . . .

But Ethan knew Caro far better than I knew Claire.

In his memories of that brief regression, I saw they had been meeting like that for weeks. Coded meaning in their dialogue leading to seemingly accidental encounters where they talked and laughed.

The Countess and Blackford hammered out betrothal papers behind it all. Ethan had been privy to some of their discussions. He knew more of Caro's story . . .

All the while, poor Ethan falling hopelessly in love with a woman destined to be his employer's bride.

"I thought you said only a scene of emotional turmoil caused a regression." Claire shook her head. "That seemed almost . . . banal."

"It probably did seem unimportant from Caro's point-of-view. But, remember, the scenes just need to have emotional resonance for *my* past lives—"

"You're saying this is all about you?"

I chuckled. "Something like that. For Ethan, that brief conversation on the bridge was the moment he realized he loved Caro."

"Poor Ethan." Claire's gaze seemed haunted.

"Yeah. It pretty much shattered him, madly in love with someone he could never have."

Not that I thought for a second Ethan's situation would parallel Claire and I, thank goodness.

Abruptly, Claire's eyes flared to life. "The Michelangelo! Caro saw it clearly in her head this time. It's definitely the same composition as the Colonel's drawing."

Excitement chased down my arms. "Really?"

"For sure. She thought about the shading she had worked on that morning, and it was identical—"

"Could the drawing she is copying from be the exact same *sketch*, I wonder? The exact thing the Colonel has?"

Claire's eyes glazed as she searched her memory. "I don't know. My visual of the sketch she is copying from seems like it was done partially in silverpoint, not chalk. Not to mention it is undamaged."

"It doesn't have a charred corner like the Colonel's?"

"Exactly. Without the mass spectrometry analysis, it's hard to make any definitive decisions about the Colonel's drawing."

"When will we get those results, by the way?"

"Hopefully any day now."

"Interesting." I shifted the pigeon squirming in my hands. "Regardless of the specifics, this is all far too coincidental to not be related somehow."

"Agreed. I just wonder how either sketch would come to be in the Colonel's vaults."

"Who knows. Maybe the sketches were sold at some point?"

"Possibly. Though what about the weird thing Branwell heard?"

"That voice in a brogue saying, 'You have taken something from me. And now I have taken it from you.'"

"Was that Ethan talking, referring to the sketch in some way? I mean, if this is all about *you*, as you say, then the sketch has to be important to Ethan, not just Caro."

Smart. "This whole thing just gets more interesting."

I startled as a large bus swooshed by us. Both Claire and I took a quick step back from the road.

"So many emotions from Caro." Claire chewed on that plump bottom lip of hers, that haunted look returning. "She is convinced she has to marry Blackford. Don't get me wrong—she adores Ethan, but nothing can happen there. The Countess determines her life."

"Well, with Caro's parentage, she can definitely aim to marry a duke."

"You saw that? Caro didn't think of it again specifically. Just something about her mother being a duchess and her great-uncle having power . . . I wish I could direct her thoughts." Claire paused, waiting.

I cocked an eyebrow at her.

"Well?" She matched my eyebrow with one of her own. "Who are her parents? Aren't you going to tell me?"

I grinned, stretching out the tension.

Claire folded her arms, willing to wait me out.

"Caro is the granddaughter of the Pretender. Of Bonnie Prince Charlie," I said.

"Seriously?" Claire cocked her head. Blinked. "But . . . wait. The Countess was married to Charlie, but I'm pretty sure the Countess isn't her grandmother. Caro never thinks of Louise in those terms. Just as her guardian."

"Yeah, I'm with you. I'm not sure what Caro's exact relationship with the Countess is. Ethan just thought about how far above him socially Caro is, as the granddaughter of Prince Charlie. He didn't ponder how it had come about. We'll probably have to do some research."

"It explains why Blackford would marry her."

"Yes. And according to Ethan's memories, Blackford's very eager to . . . acquire her. That's the word Ethan used. Kinda odd. Blackford likes to collect things, including people apparently."

"Poor Caro."

"Yeah, they're both in a bad fix. And what was up with that parting shot she gave: *Your friend—John, was it not? You said he likes to fly hawks every Tuesday morning.* Ethan was puzzled by that."

"Yes. Caro saw the place in her mind's eye as she said it." Claire wrinkled her forehead and then snapped her fingers. "It's that monument by Uccello in the Duomo. The one of the equestrian."

"More of their hey-imagine-seeing-you-here meetings."

"Probably."

The pigeon squirmed again. The good sister trying to make her escape.

Claire gestured with her chin. "So a nun, huh?"

"Yeah. Habit and everything." I motioned for us to cross the street back to my motorcycle.

"What did a nun do to end up reincarnated as a pigeon?"

"No idea. I just see shadows. I'm not judge and jury."

Claire glanced up the road, waiting for a break in traffic. "I mean, was she rude to her Mother Superior?"

I grinned. "Broke her vow of silence?"

"Exactly. I bet she was sneaking into monks' cells at night. I've heard about those tunnels linking monasteries and abbeys."

I laughed. The stoplight changed and we crossed the road. I juggled the pigeon in one hand while unlocking my bike seat with the other.

Claire suddenly shoved my arm. Score one for uninitiated physical contact. I turned a questioning glance her way.

"Oooooh. I bet she was a floozy-nun." Totally serious.

I laughed, embarrassingly too loud. "Floozy-nun? Of all the possibilities out there, you go with floozy-nun?"

"Yep."

"Not fallen sister?" I angled the poor pigeon closer to my face. "Doesn't this look like Our Lady of the Night to you?"

She smiled at me. That bright, shiny smile I adored. Dimple popping. Whoa.

I forgot how to breathe.

"Sister Floozy?" she suggested.

I just shook my head as if disgusted. Claire was flirting with me. The last thing I wanted to do was call her attention to it.

I opened the bike seat and handed her a helmet. Dug around for a second and then shook out a paper bag. I gently stuffed Sister Floozy into the bag head first, carefully folding the top of the bag over several times.

Holding the bagged pigeon with one hand, I texted my mom with the other.

On our way.

Pocketing my phone, I pulled a second helmet from the seat and tucked it under my arm.

"I'm going to have to ask you to hold Sister Floozy on the drive to our palazzo."

Claire froze, her smile instantly fading. *Uffa.* And we had been making such progress, she and I.

"Uhm, I'm good. Just text me the address. I'll walk." She tried to hand the helmet back to me.

I shook my head. "Claire—"

"I-I'm not comfortable riding on that bike with you."

"What? I'm a perfectly safe driver—"

"Your driving isn't the issue. The bike just seems a little . . . intimate."

Well, duh.

That was *entirely* the point of bringing my motorcycle.

"I promise to behave." I crossed my heart with the bagged bird.

Claire eyed the bike. And then me. Shook her head. "I'm good walking—"

"Can't. It's too late." I handed her the pigeon bag as I buckled my helmet and slid on my sunglasses.

"What? It's not too late." She gave the pigeon back to me.

"Nonna put down the pasta."

She crinkled her brow, adorably confused. "That makes no sense."

"It makes perfect sense. It means that in less than fifteen minutes, the pasta will be hot and steaming on the table. And if there is one thing I have learned, nothing upsets an Italian grandmother more than letting pasta sit for even a minute after it's ready. C'mon."

She popped her free hand onto her hip. Stubborn, as usual.

"Porca miseria, cara." I threw an arm up, being my most Italian self.

"Did you just swear at me in Italian?"

I stared at her. Appalled. "Swear at you? Like some temperamental teenager? Hardly." I shook my head and exchanged Sister Floozy for her helmet and began buckling it on her head. "What kind of person do you think I am, babe?"

She glared daggers at me. "Don't call me babe. It's Claire."

"Fine. Claire."

I turned away from her and straddled my bike, hiding my smile.

Ha! Finally. No more *Ms. Raythorn's* for me. Victory was sweet.

I looked over my shoulder at her as I kicked the stand up.

Claire rigidly standing. Holding the squirming paper bag, helmet pulled low on her head. Biting her lower lip.

Unsure. Anxious. Utterly adorable.

Mine.

Emotion flooded me. Liquid fire.

You, my love. Always and ever, only you.

I swallowed. But it was no use. My heart was firmly lodged in my throat.

Damn.

I was falling so hard and fast for this woman.

Just breathe.

I straightened my shoulders.

"Sister Floozy is getting antsy," I said. "And you so don't want to see Nonna upset over her pasta getting mushy."

"Mushy?" Claire tossed her head. "Isn't *cold* the word you were looking for there?"

"Nope. You're in Italy, *cara mia*. We eat our pasta *al dente* and not a smidge more well-done than that."

I'm pretty sure she growled, "It's Claire." But it didn't sound like her heart was in it.

With a frustrated sigh, she straddled the bike behind me, wrapping one arm around my waist, the other holding Sister Floozy carefully.

Oh man.

I took a deep breath as I started the bike, closing my eyes briefly. The feel of her pressed up against me from waist to shoulder. Every point of contact sizzling, smoking fire.

My entire body had just gone from zero to sixty faster than my bike.

"Hold on." I said over my shoulder. She tightened her free hand around my waist as I waited to edge out into traffic.

One more steadying breath. Maybe she had been wise to resist riding with me . . .

But I wanted Claire's trust more than anything else.

There was so much . . . *possibility* between us. I could see it. Glimmering in the distance, drawing nearer. An eternity of love and devotion and *together*. My heart pounded at the thought.

I was all-in with Claire. Determined to prove myself *worthy* of her trust.

Though that didn't stop the Italian in me from taking more than one corner a little faster than strictly necessary. Just to force her to hold on that much tighter.

Shameless, you say?

Why, yes. Yes, I am.

18

CLAIRE

I'm not going to lie.

I've always had a thing for guys with motorcycles.

That heady rush of g-forces as the bike accelerates, the wind tugging at your clothing, the shameless excuse to cuddle close to the man driving.

So, let's just say there was something oddly magical about riding through the narrow medieval streets of Florence clutching a hot Italian-American playboy with one hand and a wounded pigeon who used to be a naughty nun in the other.

Okay, so maybe the nun part was more offbeat than magical . . . but you get the idea.

I may have leaned into Dante more than was strictly necessary.

He was just so . . . big. Solid and strong. I could feel his abs flexing under my hand with each turn.

I may have even relaxed into him for a minute. Indulged in a fantasy where I wasn't damaged and shattered and fear-ridden. Where I could simply take a man like Dante at face value and not doubt his every action.

And then I remembered who I was and who *he* was and how that was extremely unlikely.

This last regression had been more . . . powerful.

Ethan may have been madly in love with Caro, but she wasn't far behind. She teetered on a precipice, where the tiniest motion would send her tumbling down a waterfall of love and adoration.

Part of me wanted to shake her. Rattle her cage. Force her to clearly *see* the heartache and pain waiting just past the signpost for Love. Caro was so unbearably innocent.

But just as I wanted to unnerve *her*, Caro's trust and adoration of Ethan jarred *me*.

Had I ever been that . . . free? I couldn't remember a time in my life where I hadn't viscerally understood the cutting force of love.

And yet Caro, whose life had been neither easy nor kind, possessed a heart much more open than my own.

Her emotions still swamped me—blurring the line between Dante and Ethan.

When I leaned into Dante on his bike, was I Claire, eager to be close to the hot twenty-first century playboy?

Or was I Caro, hungry for a stolen moment with her nineteenth century Scottish gentleman?

I honestly couldn't tell you.

Basically . . . these regressions were royally messing with me, and I couldn't see myself willingly participating in any more of them.

I *had* to know my emotions were my own.

We zoomed along the Arno and then darted back into the rabbit warren of narrow streets around Piazza Santa Croce. It took us less than five minutes to arrive at a palazzo.

An enormous double-doored *portone* stood flush with the narrow street, *D'Angelo Enterprises* etched into a brass plaque next to it. Again, the doors were big enough for a full-size SUV to pass through. Dante pulled what looked like a garage door opener from his pocket, and the huge *portone* swung inward.

The doors opened into a wide arched corridor running the depth of the building, leading into a small courtyard beyond. Several cars were parked there, nestled in between lemon trees in enormous terracotta pots.

Dante nudged the motorcycle through to the courtyard, parking it between a battered Jeep Wrangler and a gleaming Mercedes E350. A mini Cooper, BMW sedan and vintage VW bus rounded out the cars.

We unbuckled our helmets, and Dante led the way back into the arched passageway, unlocking another large door. He took Sister Floozy and then gestured for me to walk through.

I stepped into a stairwell, paved in old flagstones with an aged dark railing, smooth plastered walls and ancient exposed ceiling beams. No later than the sixteenth century, I'd say. Were they original?

Dante climbed the stairs ahead of me, Sister Floozy squirming in her bag.

"So how old is this palazzo?" I asked.

"Around four hundred years. Been in the D'Angelo family the entire time."

Wow.

"It seems . . ." My voice trailed off.

"Old and yet not?"

"Yeah."

"My brothers and I are big on modernization without losing the sense of antiquity."

We arrived at a landing with two steps up to another huge wooden door on the left. Dante unlocked it with a long skeleton key that seemed more movie-prop than an actual functioning tool.

The interior opened into a vestibule with soaring gilded ceilings. Dante walked through a set of double doors on the right.

I followed him into a large room which, again, had a coffered ceiling and even fresco-painted walls. All clearly dating from the mid-seventeenth century. An eclectic mix of modern and vintage furniture dotted the space, including an enormous flatscreen TV against one wall.

"My apartment that I share with Branwell." Dante gestured as he set down Sister Floozy on a side table. "My *nonna*'s apartment is directly above us. Mom and Chiara are on the top floor."

He pulled off his jacket and tossed it over the back of a chair, leaving him in just a tight gray t-shirt and jeans.

I slowly turned around. The room felt historic and yet fresh all at once.

Modern chrome lighting nestled into the coffers; crystal sconces dotted the walls. Sleek mid-century modern chairs mixed easily with sculpted Parisian couches. That effortless blend of modern and vintage that Italy pulled off with such flair.

"I assume it meets with your approval?"

I nodded. "Not quite your typical bachelor pad."

"We finished up an extensive remodel about two years ago. Hopefully it will hold for a while. That's the thing with these old *palazzi*." Dante shrugged. "It seems like you finish one restoration just to start on another."

He picked up the paper bag with Sister Floozy and motioned for us to head back out into the stairwell. We climbed a further flight of the twisting stairs to another huge door, this one slightly ajar. Voices floated out.

The door swung open just as Dante reached for the handle. A tiny dark-haired young woman strode out, a huge bowl of pasta in her arms.

"Dante! You made it. *Dammi un bacio*." She presented him with her right cheek.

Smiling, Dante bent down and pressed his right cheek against hers, kissing the air next to her ear. He repeated the action on the other side, left cheek to left cheek. That typical Italian greeting I had seen repeated countless times on the street.

Why had he never tried that with me? I mean, the man *was* Italian, right?

I wasn't sure if I was relieved or jealous.

Honestly, could I be any more of an emotional mess when it came to Dante D'Angelo?

"Watcha got there?" She looked pointedly at the bag where Sister Floozy squirmed.

"Pigeon. Nun." Dante held the bag up.

She nodded. As if that explained everything. Which, I suppose, it sorta did.

"Hi. You must be Claire," she said, turning to me.

"Yes. Claire, my sister, Chiara."

Chiara shot me a bright smile. "Nice to finally meet you. I would hug you or something, but as you can see . . ." Chiara lifted the pasta. Penne with a hint of red sauce. It smelled divine. "Love your name, by the way. We're name-twinners."

"Twinners?"

"Yep. Claire and Chiara. Same name. Different languages."

I blinked. "Really? Chiara sounds so . . . modern."

She shrugged, jostling the pasta she was holding. "*Beh*, Chiara is super traditional. Ya know, like St. Clare of Assisi. *Santa Chiara di Assisi.* Anyway, we're ready. I'm sure Nonna could use some help." She nodded her chin back through the open door behind her.

Chiara turned for the stairs, heading up.

Dante rotated with her. "Wait, are we eating outside—"

"*La pasta é pronta.*" An elderly lady walked out of the door, carrying a basket of bread. Housecoat, blouse, wool skirt, nylons . . . gray hair meticulously styled. She balanced effortlessly in—

Yep. She was wearing heels.

She presented her cheek to Dante who dutifully exchanged kisses with her, just as he had with Chiara.

"*Nonna, questa é la mia amica, Clara.*" He gestured my way, introducing me, I assumed.

"Hi. Nice to meet you," I said.

"*Ciao, tesora.* Nice to meet you too." Though heavily accented, her English was understandable. "*Dante, dai. Fa bel tempo. Mangiamo sù.*" She moved past us and up the stairs.

"The weather's good, so I guess we're eating on the upstairs terrace. Let's see if there's anything else to take up."

Dante walked into a long hallway with doors evenly spaced along it. The door on the right led to another grand sitting room. He walked through the door on the left.

I followed and found myself in a narrow galley-style kitchen. Stove, sink, fridge and small counter on the left. Tall, paned window straight ahead. A narrow table pushed up against the tiled wall on the right.

Two men filled the space. Branwell was seated at the table, back to the window, a bowl of pasta in front of him, gloved hands on the table. Another man leaned back against the counter perpendicular to him, arms crossed.

"Tenn!" Dante grabbed the unknown man in a crushing hug, thumping his back with one hand, still carefully holding Sister Floozy in the other. "Saw your Jeep downstairs. You didn't mention you were coming into town today."

Ah. The elusive third brother. Tennyson.

Tennyson returned his brother's embrace and then looked past Dante at me, a wry smile on his lips.

"Claire, I presume?"

All three brothers turned their attention my way.

Seeing them together highlighted the similarities between Dante and Branwell. They were identical twins after all. Large men with strong faces that would be called handsome or attractive.

Tennyson, however, could only be described as beautiful. Weird, I know, to call a guy that, but sometimes there's just no other word.

Carelessly styled dark hair worn moderately short, a face that defined the word chiseled, startlingly blue eyes. Several inches shorter than his brothers and clean-shaven, he clearly favored his father's Italian heritage—more soccer wiry than football bulked. He sported casual shorts and a black t-shirt which clung to his lean frame.

He was the kind of guy you wanted to stare at. Too pretty for everyday use, but nice eye-candy for an afternoon.

"Hi. You must be Tennyson." I took a step forward and offered him my palm.

His smile broadened. He shifted past Dante and took my hand. But instead of shaking it, he leaned in and pressed his right cheek against mine, kissing the air near my ear. He repeated the action on the left side.

"When in Italy . . ." he said.

I looked into his eyes as he pulled back, expecting a teasing warmth.

Instead, I saw mocking brittleness. As if all the world had let him down and only bravado held him together. He settled back against the counter.

"How long are you here?" Dante tightened his grip on the paper bag while reaching for a bowl of grated parmesan cheese. He seemed to be doing everything possible to make the question appear casual, but something about the tense set of his shoulders told me it wasn't.

"*Si trovi sempre quelle belle, no?*" Tennyson leaned forward and picked up a large bowl of mixed greens from the table.

Dante frowned. Branwell chuckled.

"Tenn just called you pretty," Branwell said to me with a wink. He motioned Dante to lower the cheese so he could scoop a spoonful onto his pasta. Dante shot a frown at his twin.

"Seriously, Tenn. How long are you here?" Dante angled the cheese toward Branwell.

Tennyson shrugged. "Until I can't handle it anymore. Same as always."

He moved around Dante, the salad bowl cradled in one arm.

It was only when he started walking that I noticed his left leg. Or, rather, the jointed prosthetic which *was* his left leg.

He noticed my noticing.

"Afghanistan," was all he said as he walked out the door, slapping the frame with his free hand.

Dante's eyes followed his brother. Pensive. As if Tennyson were an ache he didn't know how to soothe.

"Better hurry." Branwell stirred the cheese into his penne. "Pasta's getting mushy."

Dante glanced back at him. Nodded.

"Claire, would you mind grabbing the *oliere*?" He motioned toward a cruet of oil and vinegar still on the table.

I followed him out the door and up the stairs, Sister Floozy in her bag still wiggling in his hand.

"Is Branwell not eating with us?" I asked as we passed another landing and continued up another floor.

He shook his head. "Bran hears the last moment of alteration with food as he eats. Pasta, obviously, constantly changes as you scoop it up. He says eating pasta at a table with everyone talking is like listening to a TV show being played randomly, multiple times at once with sentences overlapping and repeating. So he'll eat in the quiet of the kitchen and then bring the *secondo* up with him."

"There will be a *secondo* too?"

"There's always a *secondo*." He chuckled as he pushed open a door at the top of the stairs.

I stepped out onto an enormous rooftop terrace. The roofs of Florence stretched in a sea of orange terracotta, defunct chimneys and TV antennas. The enormous dome of the Duomo rising above them all.

Oranges and lemons in huge planters dotted the terrace. A large wisteria vine curled around and over a stone pergola, sweet-smelling purple blossoms hanging like clusters of grapes.

Under the pergola, a table was set for lunch. Chiara and Nonna were scooting things around, making room for the pasta and bread. Another woman, who I could only assume was Dante's mother, placed napkins on the pasta bowls with a . . . why, yes, . . . a white rat perched on her shoulder.

"Here you are." She looked at us and smiled.

"Hi. I'm Claire." I took a step toward her, holding out my hand.

"Judith." She shook my hand with a firm grip.

Maybe in her late fifties, Judith radiated warmth and kindness. Tall and curvy, she had curly, shoulder-length hair and the same deep blue eyes as Tennyson. The rat scampered around her shoulders.

Judith arched an eyebrow at the bag Dante still carried. "You brought me a present?"

"A pigeon with a hurt leg."

"And?"

"Nun."

Like Chiara, she nodded, as if that explained everything.

He gave his mother the bowl of cheese and took the cruet from me, handing it to her as well.

He motioned for me to follow him around a row of lemon trees to the opposite side of the terrace where a large room sat. I could hear squawks and meows and snuffles coming from inside.

Dante opened the door and I walked into an animal hospital. Cats, birds, rodents and even a dog or two sat in comfortable cages lining one wall. All of them sporting bandages of some kind. The room smelled of fur, antiseptic and sawdust. He absently scratched the head of a cat through the bars of the cage as he passed.

"My mom was a veterinarian before she retired." Dante lifted a clean, empty cage off the shelf, setting it on a metal table in the middle of the room. "She treats injured animals and then releases them back into the wild, in the case of birds, and finds homes for the others."

"You bring her animals often?"

"Sometimes. I seem to be drawn to ones who used to be people."

"Makes sense, I suppose."

Gently, he opened the bag and set Sister Floozy into the cage. The pigeon hopped around, looking at me with weary eyes. "Mom will deal with her leg after lunch."

I looked around the room. "So all these animals were people in a past life?"

"Some. The cat there was a pirate."

"Please tell me his shadow has an eye patch."

Dante chuckled. "Nope. Just scraggly hair and missing teeth." He stepped too close to me and motioned for us to leave.

The cat meowed as I passed by. I tried to feel sorry for it, but a scurvy pirate? It didn't take much imagination to understand the things a pirate had done to end up reincarnated as a cat.

Dante led me out of the room, carefully shutting the door behind him.

Two minutes later, I was seated next to Dante at the table under the wisteria vine, eating some of the best pasta of my life. How could simple penne, tomatoes and parmesan cheese taste so good?

Conversation bounced around the table. Dante talked about our project with the Colonel. Judith asked questions, the rat still perched on her shoulder, twitching its nose at the pasta. Tennyson ate mostly in silence, but I got the impression his eyes missed nothing.

Chiara was the life of the table. She focused all her energy on you when she spoke, asking and answering questions. Laughing too loud at my lame attempts at humor. *Darling*. It was the only word I could think of to describe her. She was just this darling bundle of life.

She worked as a researcher of sorts. "I'm the person you come to when you have a historical question no one else can answer—I do everything from genealogy to dramaturgy."

It all felt casual and normal, but I could sense an undercurrent. A lingering tension.

Somehow Tennyson being here was meaningful. I definitely got the impression he didn't join the family often.

Judith asked him questions about the family villa near Volterra where he lived. Dante mentioned a hiking trip they were planning to Mont Blanc at the end of summer.

Everyone drawing Tennyson into the conversation and, yet, tiptoeing around him at the same time. As if he were a bomb that needed to be handled with care.

I wasn't sure if I should be confused or just sorry for him.

When I was about halfway through my bowl of pasta, Tennyson lifted his head and fixed me with a look. As if he knew what I was feeling or thinking . . . which, I supposed he did. Maybe. Dante hadn't been too clear on how Tennyson's gift worked.

Sheesh. And I thought Caro's emotions were messing with me. How would it be to constantly feel the emotions of people around you?

Tennyson raised an eyebrow as if to say, *Welcome to my hell.*

Not wanting to contribute to his emotional overload . . . or whatever he experienced, I turned to Judith and asked the question I had been wondering about.

"So why Dante, Branwell and Tennyson as names for triplets?" I stabbed more penne. "They seem a little—"

"Random." That was Dante.

"Unrelated." Tennyson.

"Adorable." Chiara winked.

The brothers groaned.

"There *was* a method in my madness." Judith chuckled, petting the rat on her shoulder.

"Mom has this thing for Victorian British writers." Tennyson gave a weak smile.

"I would say artists, more than writers specifically," Dante said.

"I do love poetry," Judith agreed.

That explained a lot about Dante's interests, I supposed.

I glanced at Tennyson. "So you were all named for Victorian British artists?"

"Yep." Dante turned to me. "See if you can guess."

I raised my eyebrow at the challenge.

"Well, the first one is easy. You're named for Alfred, Lord Tennyson." I waved my fork at Tennyson across the table.

He nodded.

"And British Victorian . . ." I turned to Dante. Raked his *fine* form up and down. He took a bite of pasta, smirking. "So *not* named for Dante Alighieri, the thirteenth century Florentine poet—"

"Which would have made a lot of sense," Chiara said.

"Agreed." Judith sighed.

I ran my brain through Victorian artists . . .

"Hah!" I crowed. "Dante Gabriel Rossetti. Pre-Raphaelite poet and painter."

"She's good." Tennyson saluted me with his fork.

"One more." Dante returned my perusing look, running his eyes over me. "Branwell."

Mmmm, that was more difficult. I searched my brain but was coming up blank.

"Does it help to know my middle name is Bronte?" Chiara offered.

"No giving hints." Dante shot her a stern look.

Bronte . . . three sisters—Charlotte, Emily, Anne—all writers. But they had a brother . . .

"Branwell Bronte." I snapped my fingers. "The ne'er-do-well artist and poet brother of the Bronte sisters."

"Who's saying I'm a ne'er-do-well?" Branwell asked, crossing the terrace.

Branwell carried a large platter of heavenly-smelling roasted chicken and potatoes in his gloved hands which he set on the table.

Everyone passed their dirty pasta bowls to Nonna, who placed them on a side table.

And then we all dug into the *secondo*. Lemon-herb chicken and garlicky, oven-roasted potatoes. It was all so good, I couldn't help but eat until I was stuffed.

This was the problem with Italian food, I had decided. You didn't need to eat it all, but it was so delicious, you couldn't help yourself.

Branwell joined us this time, placing an already dished plate on the table with pieces of chicken cut up. He then proceeded to eat with chopsticks, careful not to alter the food before it hit his mouth. Which made sense, once I thought about it. A fork would pierce the chicken, altering it at that moment, making it difficult for him to follow our conversation. Chopsticks just lifted.

The conversation continued to ping around the table, some in English, some in Italian. The brothers ribbed Chiara about a new boy-interest. Apparently she had terrible luck with men. Obviously, our names weren't the only thing we shared.

Judith asked supportive questions and laughed at their jokes. Nonna teased and scolded. Through it all, I clearly saw the web of love and support that bound them all together.

Part of me felt incredibly uncomfortable. I was an intruder on an intimate family moment. I didn't belong and wanted to make my excuses and leave.

Another part kept swallowing a large lump in my throat.

Did Dante even remotely understand how blessed he was to have all these people in his life? A mother, grandmother and sister who clearly doted on him? Brothers who loved and supported him?

When had I ever had the privilege of even *seeing* a family like this?

It felt almost sacred somehow. A moment of shining hope. That such a family was actually possible.

I thought about the last time I had a meal together with both my parents. Gosh. How long ago had that been? Three years? Four?

We had met at a restaurant in downtown Boston. JB had been forty-five minutes late due to traffic (so he said), but both Mom and I knew it was more likely because of his assistant, Jennifer. My parents' marriage could politely be described as unconventional. They tolerate each other's serial philandering and stay together as more of a business arrangement than anything else.

On this night, my mom refused to start dinner until JB got there, unloading her irritation on my ears and a full bottle of Chianti. Then JB arrived, and I listened to them snipe back and forth for the next hour—neither one asking me any questions beyond wondering (to each other mostly) why I had chosen the tuna instead of the salmon—JB ordering a bottle of some California white for himself.

I wisely chose not to drink. Someone sober had to drive those two back home.

But seeing the D'Angelos together . . . I swallowed back that lump again. An odd mixture of longing to be part of it all and anxiety that they would expect me to be.

I was so messed.

I caught Tennyson studying me. Was I being impolite again, not controlling my emotions better around him?

Which emotion he probably felt . . . *oy*.

We finished up the *secondo* and moved on to the *insalata*. Everyone piled mixed greens on their plate and dressed it with olive oil and syrupy balsamic vinegar from the cruet I had carried up.

Dante was recounting our little regression on the bridge, including what we had found out about the Michelangelo sketch and Caro's history.

"So, wait. She was literally Prince Charlie's granddaughter?" Chiara asked.

Dante nodded. "That's Ethan's understanding."

"Legitimate granddaughter? Did Prince Charlie have any legitimate children?" Chiara asked.

"I have no idea. We haven't had time to research it yet."

"How unsettling to just have a regression in the middle of the street like that." Judith lifted a small piece of bread to the rat on her shoulder. He grabbed it with his little paws and politely nibbled.

I gave a nervous laugh. "They definitely catch you . . . unawares."

The rat fixed his eyes on me. Angled his head. And then stood at attention, placing a paw over his ribcage.

It was . . .

"Uncanny, isn't it?" Branwell motioned toward the rat.

"He looks just like—" Did I dare say it?

"Napoleon." Chiara finished my thought.

"Yes."

I whirled on Dante.

"Boney's shadow has the bicorne hat and everything." He shrugged.

I looked at the rat, who had gone back to nibbling bread. "Well. I suppose there are worse things to be reincarnated as."

Judith smiled and rubbed Boney's head with her fingers. "Yes. He makes an excellent rat."

I laughed.

"So back to this regression," Dante said. "Caro gave another coded message at the end of the conversation. Something about their friend John who likes to fly hawks on Tuesday mornings."

Dante shifted, stretching an arm across the back of my chair. Totally moving into my bubble. Again.

I froze, not sure how I felt about that level of familiarity. He clearly hadn't even noticed what he had done. As if drawing near me was somehow completely natural for him. Dumb Italians and their lack of personal space.

"John who likes to fly hawks?" Chiara asked.

"Didn't you say Caro saw a monument in her mind?" Dante turned to me. Or rather just leaned about three inches. The heat of his body lapped my side.

Emancipated-Claire wanted me to scoot my chair out, say a few polite *thank yous* and get the hell out of here.

Senti*mdash*tal-Claire was begging me to lean about five inches in the opposite direction, snug myself firmly into his shoulder and stay until he kicked me out.

It's just Caro's lingering emotions, I reminded myself. That sense of security I felt around Dante.

Without Caro's trust thrumming through me, I would have *runrunrun* by now. Even as it was, panic was winning out.

My mind finally caught up with his question. "Yeah. I did—or rather, Caro did. It was one of the monuments with the knight on a horse. The one by Uccello—"

"Of course!" Chiara snapped her fingers. "The monument to John Hawkwood."

"Chiara, your knowledge of Florentine history is encyclopedic." Tennyson's tone so very dry. "You're a living Wikipedia page."

"*Grazie.*"

"I'm not entirely sure that was a compliment." Tennyson sat back.

"Don't care. Hawkwood was one of the generals of the Battle of Cascina actually."

"Again. Encyclopedic."

Chiara stuck out her tongue at him. Tennyson folded his arms in reply.

"Interesting coincidence," Dante said.

"Is it?" Chiara asked. "You said Caro knew John Hawkwood was part of the battle featured in the Michelangelo. It's no stretch to know about his funerary monument in the Duomo."

"Hawkwood was so celebrated for his feats in saving Florence, they buried him in the Duomo?" I asked.

"*Eh.* Not really." Chiara waved her hand in a big, Italian way. "I'm pretty sure he was a general for Pisa during the Battle of Cascina, but Florence later won him over and then used his celebrity to lure other *condottieri*. It was all a game for them."

Dante leaned even closer; his ribcage brushed my shoulder. Spicy male and heat and *him*. My heart sped up.

My emotions were a volatile cocktail of excitement and panic.

The *panic* portion was all mine. Fear was a bird of prey digging its claws into me.

The excitement . . . I wasn't so sure. Caro's emotions again?

Curse these stupid regressions, messing with me like this.

It was all I could do to remain glued to my seat.

I knew it was weird to be struggling with this. But sometimes you just react and there's no logical explanation. It's just how you feel.

"Didn't Ethan say something like that during our first regression?" Dante asked. "That the wars of the *Trecento*—sorry, the thirteenth century—were all a game?"

I reminded my lungs to breathe and nodded. "Yeah."

Dante finally sat back a bit but didn't remove his arm from my chair.

I locked eyes with Tennyson across the table. His blue gaze was all too knowing.

Yep. Not sure what was worse. The fact that the poor guy had to deal with all my emotions (and, quite frankly, Caro's too) before I did or that he *knew* how I felt.

"Two minutes," Tennyson said.

Everyone turned toward him.

"Claire's going to be upset in about two minutes. No offense." He shot me an apologetic grin. "Just figured I should give fair warning."

Heads looked back at me.

"Uhmmm, thank you?"

"Think nothing of it."

"Any idea what causes this anger?"

"Not really. But logic says I should lay my money on Dante."

"Hey, why you throwing me under the bus? I thought you had my back," Dante said.

"I do. Which is why I'm giving you a friendly warning."

Tennyson and Dante stared at each other.

A beat.

"So back to our conversation. Let me research all the players for you. I have some time right now, and I know you guys are busy with the Colonel's stuff." Chiara pulled out her phone, typing as she spoke. "So

Caro Stuart—for lack of a better last name—Ethan MacLure, Countess Louise of Albany and the Duke of Blackford. I'll see what I can find."

"Thanks, Sis. That would be great. Now Claire and I just need to figure out how the Michelangelo fits into it all too."

Chiara continued entering notes on her phone. "Mmmm, good point. Seems too coincidental. I'd be incredibly surprised if there isn't some link between Caro and the Colonel's sketch."

"Yeah." Branwell kicked back in his chair. "Especially given the brogue I heard."

"Was it Scottish?" I asked.

"Definitely." Branwell's voice confident. "It was faint but there."

"Assuming the Colonel has one of Caro's drawings in his possession, the question is which one? Caro's own sketch or the one she is copying from?" Dante tapped his hand still resting along the back of my chair.

"The mass spectrometry should sort that out pretty fast," I said.

"Maybe," Branwell shrugged.

"Agreed." Dante inched even closer. "Unfortunately, no amount of studying the Colonel's sketch or reviewing mass spectrometry will tell us the *exact* history. The best source of information is the most obvious."

I looked at him, raising an eyebrow.

"Based on everything we know, I think Claire and I should visit the Duomo." Dante winked at me. "Another regression could give us all the information we need."

My lungs tightened, cutting off my air supply.

Yep. Tennyson was right.

Two minutes on the nose.

DANTE

Claire froze. And then jumped to her feet, walking away from the table and around some of my mom's potted lemons.

I shot daggers at Tennyson.

"No one ever listens to my warnings." He nudged my foot under the table, nodding his head toward Claire. "Go talk with her. If it makes you feel any better, she doesn't stay upset for long."

I leaned forward, mouth open.

"No." He kicked me again. "Don't even ask it. Her emotions are her own. I'm not spilling how she feels about you."

"What good is having a brother who can feel others' emotions then?" I half-laughed.

A beat.

Tennyson's eyes got that weary too-knowing look. The one full of shadows and things unspoken.

"Not much, Dante." He sat back on a sigh. "Really not much at all."

Damn.

I held his gaze for a moment, dragging all my love for him to the surface, letting it flood me.

Feel *that*.

I stood, tossing my napkin on the table.

Tennyson used to tattle on us as kids, saying Branwell and I were *throwing* mean emotions at him.

We always denied it, but he was totally right. We did. Anger, jealousy, scorn, disdain . . . I'm sure he got every nasty emotion possible from us over the years.

Love, acceptance, devotion. *Those* were the emotions I channeled when around Tennyson nowadays. He had lost so much more than just a leg in Afghanistan, not to mention the events afterward—

I stopped myself right there.

Better to think about Tennyson when he wasn't around to *feel* all my thinking.

I rounded the corner. Claire stood at the iron railing on the edge of the terrace, hands hugging her arms, looking out toward the Duomo.

Fitting.

Clouds were moving in. A breeze ruffled her hair.

I *wanted* to wrap my arms around her waist from behind, snug her tight against my chest and just hold her until the tension passed. Let her soak up my strength.

Instead, I joined her at the railing, gripping the iron tight to keep my hands and feet still.

Silence.

"Let's go over my problems with chasing a possible regression in the Duomo, shall we?" She spoke without looking in my direction.

Score one for honesty. I had to give her that.

I would always know where I stood with Claire.

"First, despite your hedging on the Sandbox Rule, we're definitely drifting into trouble territory here—"

"Regressions aren't plagiarism, Claire." I moved to lean against the railing, angling my body toward hers. The need to study her winning out.

"No, having the occasional lunch or dinner together isn't plagiarism." She brushed a strand of hair out of her mouth. "Actively pursuing a joint answer to the Colonel's sketch is. It's like sharing exam answers or copying homework."

"No. That's cheating. Not plagiarism."

"Wow. Splitting a *very* fine hair there."

"If I have to."

"You should have been a lawyer." She rolled her eyes. Her knuckles were white, gripping her upper arms.

"How would the Colonel *ever* find out about this?" I relaxed an elbow into the railing. "On the outside, we're just colleagues visiting a completely unrelated Uccello monument in the Duomo."

"Well, I'm having dinner with the Colonel tomorrow night, and he's going to ask how things are going—"

"So don't volunteer to tell him. I know I won't."

"And that makes it okay?"

"Claire, we have a unique way of finding an answer to the provenance of the Colonel's sketch that would be impossible with any other methodology."

"Yes, which also means it will be impossible to prove too—"

"Possibly. But we don't know that right now."

"Look, Dante, I get your point. But any information we *might* find will be useless when I get tossed off the project and lose this job."

"Maybe. But aren't some answers worth the risk?"

She sucked in that succulent bottom lip again.

And then very slowly turned her head my way. Gave me a definite you-must-be-nuts look.

"Dante, I don't have the *luxury* of a loving family and an already successful business and . . . and people who care. I have *me*." She tapped her chest. Emphatic. "That's it. That's all I have. Just psycho me, a mountain of baggage and the pathetic *hope* that I might get this job."

My heart constricted, so fast, so painful . . .

"*You* might be willing to toss this job aside, but I *need* it. It's all I have—" Her voice broke.

"Claire, *cara*—" I took a step forward.

She instantly put out two palms, stopping me. Shook her head. Blinked back the shimmer in her eyes.

"No. There's too much at stake for me here."

We engaged in a staring contest. Her brilliant blue eyes pulling me under.

"Okay." I relaxed back. "Glad we got that out of the way. Now tell me the truth."

All of me *knew* her. Knew to listen to what she wasn't saying.

"Excuse me?"

"This isn't about the job or the Colonel. It's an excuse but not your real reason. You and I both know it."

She let out a breath of air. Her shoulders sagged. A balloon deflating. She turned back to the railing, staring over Florence.

"I don't like you very much right now," she finally said.

"I can accept that. How's about you tell me the truth?"

A pause. I could practically see her mind churning through possible responses.

"I don't like the regressions," was the one she landed on.

Okay. Better. Closer.

"Why?"

Another pause.

She shrugged. "You say only scenes of emotional significance cause a regression. Logic dictates that, at some point, we'll have a regression that is more traumatic."

"Possibly. But, so far, they've been harmless, and the historian in you has to find them fascinating," I countered. "That still isn't the real reason for your hesitation."

She didn't disagree.

C'mon, Claire. Talk to me.

"Will they continue to be so . . . tame?" She ignored my last comment.

I considered pushing her harder for the real answer, but I let it go for now.

"It's hard to say. I will venture, however, that if a regression *were* to happen in the Duomo, it probably won't be anything horrid. A scene of violence there would still be talked about."

Claire continued to stare across the rooftops. Face impassive.

"Please, Claire?" I scooted forward, getting more of me in her line of vision. "This matters. Partly because of the Michelangelo, but mostly due to Caro and Ethan themselves. I want to know their story. *Our* story."

She said nothing, staring over the city. The breeze tangled her hair, dragging it across her face. Traffic noise drifted up from below.

"Meet me at the Duomo. Tomorrow. C'mon," I pleaded.

She didn't relax.

"I'll think about it," she finally said.

"Promise?"

"Promise. I'll text you when I decide."

"Okay. I'll wait for your text."

She didn't know it, but we hadn't finished this conversation. I would discover her real reasons.

But . . . baby steps. This was a marathon, not a sprint.

When she was ready to talk, I would be waiting.

20

CLAIRE

It always brightens my day to see you here, darlin'."

I whirled upright as the Colonel strode into the room, a chipper spring in his step and a pile of papers in his hand. He stopped next to me, placing the papers on the table.

I was back at his villa this morning, going over the Michelangelo sketch with a fine tooth comb. Searching for anything that hinted toward Caro. Hoping I could find the answers I needed without involving Dante.

I was so torn. The information from a regression could be key to solving the Michelangelo mystery. But was the information worth the emotional upheaval? I didn't want any more of Caro's adoration of Ethan seeping through my walls.

Dante himself wasn't much help with that. After lunch yesterday, he and his brothers had cheerfully kicked us women out of the kitchen so they could do the dishes. And true to his word, he hadn't texted or harassed me in any way. Respecting my space.

The man was practically a caricature of perfect boyfriend material. Either that or I was so jaded I couldn't see straight—

Yeah. I needed to stop.

The Colonel leaned a little too close. What was it with men ignoring my bubble?

"I couldn't stay away. It's so compelling." I gestured toward the drawing on the table.

I gave the Colonel my cheery smile and angled back. Walking the line between keeping my distance without offending him.

He reached for my hand and did that dual hand-clasp thing of his again. Blue eyes intent on mine. "It is indeed."

He didn't break eye contact with me or release my hand as he spoke. Clouding what exactly he meant.

Okay. Awkward.

My smile morphed from cheery to strained.

"It really is, isn't it?" I pretended to miss his innuendo and took a casual step backward toward the table, forcing the Colonel to drop my hand. "The lines are fluid and confident."

I leaned over the sketch, effectively keeping all of me out of the Colonel's easy reach.

If I did get this job, how would it be working for the Colonel long term? He was decidedly, uh, hands-on.

Which I suppose would have been marginally alright if I saw him behaving similarly with anyone else, but he seemed to reserve it for me and me alone.

Other than the physical contact thing and odd occasional flirting, the Colonel was fine. Your typical warm, charming Southern gentleman.

Sigh.

"You'll be happy to know these just arrived." He tapped the stack of papers he had set on the table.

I looked at the papers. "The mass spectrometry results! So soon!"

I practically pounced on them.

The Colonel laughed, a delighted sound. "Gotta love a gal who finds such joy in numbers."

I smiled, ignored the sub-text in that comment and sank into one of the high-backed dining room chairs, studying the results.

Instead of leaving me to it, the Colonel sat down (too close) as well. Staring at me the entire time.

I told myself it was old-man, lack-of-social-cues weird. Not stalker-creepy.

I focused on the chemical age analysis results.

Ten minutes later I had some fascinating answers but more questions.

The vellum dated to the mid-sixteenth century, plus or minus fifty years. Michelangelo drew the original cartoon around 1504, placing the vellum just inside the right time period.

Which was *hooray*-good.

The charred edge dated to 1800, again plus or minus fifty years.

Which was also good.

It was like puzzle pieces slotting into place.

So based on the assumption the sketch was related to the drawings in Caro's possession, these results pointed toward the Colonel's copy being the *original* source Caro used, not her own drawing.

Had Caro been copying from the original Michelangelo *modello?* Everything certainly hinted in that direction.

Though in the mental glimpse I got of the drawing from Caro, it seemed like the original was done in silverpoint, not chalk like the sketch in the Colonel's possession. But, honestly, how accurate was a fleeting glimpse in another woman's mind from two hundred years ago?

My heart sped up in excitement. As the granddaughter of Bonnie Prince Charlie, the family provenance could certainly have an unknown Michelangelo. How it landed in the Colonel's vaults . . . I had no idea. The Colonel's maternal relatives, the Earls of Arlington, must have purchased it at some point afterward.

Obviously, the drawing sustained some damage—the charred edge—around Caro's lifetime. In her memories, neither sketch had any damage so far.

So when, why and how did the charring occur?

Was it when Ethan said those odd words about taking something back and winning the game? Was that how the drawing became connected to Dante? Up until now, the drawings had all been attached to Caro, who was one solid step removed from Ethan and Dante's past lives.

The problem? Regressions were the *only* way I would get answers to these questions.

Damn.

"You're completely buried in those papers," the Colonel drawled at my elbow.

Right.

"The results are . . . compelling," I replied.

"So do you have any thoughts as to the origin of my sketch?" He bent over the arm of his chair, moving even more into my bubble. He fixed me with his pale blue eyes.

I resisted the urge to lean away. Swallowed.

"Not . . . specifically. The vellum is the right date for the sketch to be a genuine Michelangelo."

"Excellent."

"Yes. It's definitely exciting news. But we'll need to do more research to know for sure."

The Colonel just nodded, finally turning his head to look at the drawing on the table. Face impassive. It was hard to get a read on him.

"I look forward to seeing your official assessment," he finally said.

"Thank you."

Silence hung.

The Colonel turned back to me. "I understand you had dinner earlier this week with Dante D'Angelo."

I only barely managed to keep a suspicious panic off my face.

"Yes." I let out a calming breath, but inside I was a mass of *bloodyhell* and *thisismyworstnightmarecometolife*. "He invited me and I found it hard to say no."

Sorry, Dante.

The Colonel gave a tight smile. "Dante can be like that, I've heard. Determined and persuasive."

Wait—how did the Colonel *know* Dante and I had dinner together?

"Did you have a good time?" the Colonel asked, expression neutral.

When in doubt, grab the bull by the horns. "We didn't discuss the project, if that's your concern, Colonel. It was just a friendly, get-to-know-each-other kinda thing—"

"I trust you, darlin'. I just wanted to make sure Dante behaved himself. I don't want those boys causing you any trouble now."

He reached over and patted my hand.

How was I supposed to read this territorial concern?

"About our *own* dinner tonight . . ." the Colonel began.

"Yes?" My eyes widened.

"I have a small business matter to attend to in London. It should only take a couple of days. Would you be okay if we postponed dinner until the weekend?"

Please! "Of course. Let me just check my calendar."

I pulled out my phone and made a production of looking at my blank, blank, blank appointment schedule.

"I should be good any night later this week."

My phone buzzed.

Please smile when you see me today. I want to imagine your hungry lips on mine.

My heart sank about twelve feet. My pulse hammered.

Ugh. My stalker.

Talk about terrible timing. Could I *please* go just five minutes without something creepy happening?

This person was just trying to get in my head. I knew that. They weren't here. They wouldn't see me today.

I was okay. Deep breath. Slow my heart rate down . . .

"—I'll have Natalia contact you with the arrangements," the Colonel was saying. He paused. "Is everything okay? Your face just went three shades whiter."

I set my phone in my lap.

"I'm fine. Just . . ." I shook my head. "It-it's nothing."

The Colonel looked skeptical. And then leaned over the arm of his chair again. He reached out and snagged my hands, doing his signature hand-clasp thing again, trapping my right hand between two of his.

"Your grandmother was a good friend—"

"Adelaide?"

"Mmm, yes. We met in Boston when we were both young and foolish. She was an incredible woman, and I love seeing so much of her in you."

I stared at him, really not sure where this conversation was going.

"My point"—another hand pat—"is that you should consider me a friend too. I have your best interests at heart. If you find yourself in need of anything—anything at all—please don't hesitate to call on me." One more pat *and* a finger wag. "Got it?"

I nodded. "Uhm, yes. Got it."

"That's a good girl."

I managed a weak smile.

He gave my hand one last pat for good measure before releasing it. He stood and, with a wave, walked out the door.

I breathed a sigh of relief and stared sightlessly into the dining room.

Did I take the Colonel at face value and assume he had grandfatherly feelings toward me based on his past . . . whatever with Grammy? Or was more going on here?

Mostly I hated that life had taught me to question the motives of a seemingly kind and, perhaps, lonely old man who was just trying to make a wise hiring decision.

Though . . .

How did the Colonel find out I had dinner with Dante? Was he tracking us? Spying?

But it wasn't like Dante and I had been particularly circumspect. The hotel staff could have casually mentioned it when Natalia called to settle my bill (or something) and then she mentioned it to the Colonel.

But, if so, why bring it up under the guise of 'just making sure the boys are behaving'? Like it was his job to protect me?

Worse, was my friendship with Dante putting my chance of getting this job in jeopardy? Would the Colonel be having a similar conversation with Dante?

Or was this territorial behavior reserved for just me?

Ugh.

And thinking of Dante . . .

And what to do about the regressions?

They came with risks. Being seen with Dante. More emotional confusion. The possibility of witnessing something tragic.

But—

I needed this job. Which meant I needed to know the true history of the Colonel's sketch. One more regression could give me that information.

What to do?

The answer was obvious.

I sighed and pulled out my phone.

> *Okay, I'll meet you at the Duomo.*

Awesome. Could you come right before lunch?
In about two hours?

> *Yeah. I'll be there.*

My heart sped up, but I had a hard time labeling the emotion. Was I excited to see Dante? Or just nervous about the regression? Both?

I tried to concentrate on the mass spec results, but it was a lost cause. My mind was too full of *Dante* and *Duomo* and *what will happen?* I gathered my things together.

"Claire! There you are!"

An all too familiar voice accosted me as I headed out the front door.

Figured. Pierce was never too far away. He had probably rushed over the second he heard the mass spec results were in.

I briefly considered stomping out the *portone*. But Pierce would hound me until he got his way.

"Pierce."

His glasses were a little askew and his tie loose. Not sure if that meant he was frazzled or if he had formed a cozier relationship with Natalia.

Either way, I was out.

"How are things?" He gave me his hang-dog brown eyes. "I feel like you're avoiding me."

"I *am* avoiding you. What do you want, Pierce?"

"Nothing much. How's the project going?"

"Fine."

"I miss you like crazy. I want you to come back and work—"

"Never going to happen."

"Hey, no need to get all defensive—"

"I'm not defensive. I'm standing here having a calm conversation. I'm assuming you stopped me for a more rational reason—"

"Fine." He rolled his shoulders, obviously agitated. "I hear you're hanging out with the D'Angelos nowadays. Well, specifically Dante . . ."

A chill crept down my spine.

Silence.

"How do you know that, Pierce?" My eyes narrowed.

"A little birdy told me." He shrugged, like it was casual knowledge. But his body language was a little too smug.

"Not buying that. Have you been following me? Did you tell the Colonel?"

"Whoa." He held out two hands. "No need to attack the messenger. And for the record, maybe the Colonel told *me*. Ever consider that?"

Lovely. "Your point?"

"I just want to make sure you're careful around D'Angelo. I've heard stories—"

Pot. Kettle. Black.

Did he *listen* to the words coming out of his mouth?

"What stories, Pierce? And don't think I missed the irony of you warning me about *other* men treating me poorly—"

"Why are you always so down on me?" His voice heated. "I said I was sorry. Heather meant nothing to me—"

Like *that* was supposed to make me feel better. Why had I never seen how wacko he was?

"I'm not having this conversation again. Goodbye, Pierce."

I turned and pulled the *portone* open. Thank goodness the Colonel had a car and driver waiting for me.

But Pierce wasn't done.

"I know all about D'Angelo. Stuff's weird with him." Pierce nipped at my heels as I took the front stairs down to the car. The driver opened the back door for me.

"Let me guess," Pierce continued. "You and D'Angelo hope to convince the Colonel that what he has is fake, don't you? Then you two can buy it and make a killing on the black market. Disappear a Michelangelo into some sheik's private collection, never to be seen again."

I reached the car. Pierce grabbed my arm before I could get in.

"Don't trust him, Claire. Not D'Angelo—"

I wrenched my arm out of his hold and stepped into the back seat. I refused to look at Pierce as the car pulled away, though I could see him shaking his head.

My entire body vibrated. Anger seemed too tame a word to describe my emotions. It was this volatile cocktail of outrage and fury and hurt.

I had the driver drop me in Piazza Santa Croce. I needed to cool off before meeting Dante. Take the edge off my anxiety.

I stood in the large piazza, sucking in deep breaths of city air, determined to re-center myself. Let my boyfriend, Firenze, charm me out of my mood.

The Cathedral of Santa Croce stood regal at the far end of the enormous square. (Medieval Gothic construction. Victorian facade.) It is to the Duomo what Westminster Abbey is to St. Paul's Cathedral in London. The former cathedral being the flashy showpiece. The latter housing the dead and most of the history of the city.

Pretty much everyone who was anyone in Florence was buried in Santa Croce. Michelangelo, Galileo, Machiavelli . . . even Alfieri and Louise, the Countess of Albany herself. You literally walked on the shoulders of giants visiting the place.

Very few people were buried in the Duomo. Which made the whole John Hawkwood memorial thing more notable.

I spent a few minutes browsing the kitchy tourist vendor booths crowding the edges of the piazza, sifting through my thorny thoughts. I was pretending interest in a Duomo snow globe, when I got that prickly sensation of being watched.

Not again.

Rolling my eyes, I spun in a slow circle, studying the large piazza, hating the way my heart sped up.

Was someone watching me?

I thought through the possibilities.

Was Pierce following me?

That seemed unlikely, as I had just left him at the Colonel's villa.

Had the Colonel hired someone to spy on me?

That was a viable scenario, but again, why? To catch me breaking his Sandbox Rule? Again, I couldn't logically think of a reason *why* the Colonel would do that.

Was my online harasser stalking me in real life?

Possible. But though ugly, the texts in no way indicated my online harasser knew where I was.

Soooo . . . what?

Was it all just in my head? A phantom sense created by my anxiety?

I couldn't say.

I carefully searched my surroundings. That bristly tingle along my spine wouldn't go away.

Wait? Had I seen that man sitting on the cathedral steps before? Was *he* the one following me?

I studied him for a second. Dark hair. Nondescript coat. I couldn't tell—

The man suddenly stood, head angled in my direction. I took an involuntary step backward, breath hitching.

The man smiled. I *finally* noticed the woman walking up to him.

I stared as he kissed her and tucked an arm around her waist, strolling away from me.

I clenched my jaw and closed my eyes.

I needed to get a grip.

Stop. Enough.

I swallowed and determined to ignore my flight-or-fight response.

To that end, I moved to another street booth and contemplated buying a statue of *David* apron—for no other reason than to make the wearer look like a chiseled, naked man. I chatted with the booth owner (Ottavio. Not married. Shameless flirt.) and gradually the sense of being watched receded.

Progress.

Slowly, I threaded my way through the narrow streets to the Piazza del Duomo. I was a little early, but I didn't mind waiting for Dante.

I stood in the tourist line and passed through the guards inspecting bags. The interior of the Duomo soared ahead and above me. Most cathedrals are cool and somewhat damp on the interior . . . the lingering mustiness of history, I suppose.

But Santa Maria del Fiore—the Duomo's formal name—bucks that trend. It's cooler, yes, but the white-washed walls and contrasting, unpainted greenish-gray stone accents give the entire building a fresh, alive feeling.

I wandered up the left side aisle toward the monument to John Hawkwood.

And there he was.

Dante.

Leaning against one of the central stone pillars, one foot propped up. Jeans and a white button-down, untucked, cuffed to his elbows and open at the throat. He was studying his phone, dark hair flopping onto his forehead, perma-scruff neatly man-scaped.

My heart did this crazy triple-skip thing and my feet wanted to run-runrun to him.

Stupid, stupid emotions. Always getting me in trouble.

Not this time. I was street-wise. Not going to happen.

Besides . . .

Twice now I had stumbled into a regression. I still wasn't a hundred percent sure I wanted to do this again. I dreaded absorbing more of Caro's affection for Ethan. I found the entire situation . . . terrifying.

Just because my soul had loved Dante's soul in a past life, it didn't automatically follow that I had to fall for him in this life too, right? It was already bad enough that emotional-me in the here and now felt pulled toward him. Add in Caro's emotions from the past . . .

So yeah . . . I was just trying to avoid another spectacular soul-crushing guy-tastrophe.

But . . .

For one tiny moment, I allowed my heart to . . . hope. To want.

To see the situation the way my naive self of several years ago would have.

He hadn't noticed me, head bent over his phone. It was touching he was here early, ready and waiting. Like this mattered to him. Like *I* mattered.

It would be so easy to fall for him. Give in. Let go.

Que sera, sera . . . isn't that how the song went? What will be, will be?

The mere thought of giving in to my emotions for Dante . . .

My hands started to sweat. My lungs constricted, sucking all the air out of the building.

Of course, he chose that moment to lift his head and see me.

Oh!

That first jolt of eye contact. The way his entire face lit.

Like sunrise. Revelation.

He pushed off the pillar, pocketing his phone, muscles flexing and moving under his shirt. Dark eyes locked with mine.

I was in such trouble. Even without any further goosing from Caro.

He walked up to me. I tensed. Waiting for the tell-tale swirling of a regression.

But he came nearer. And nearer.

He stopped his usual two feet too close. I craned my neck up to meet his eyes.

Nothing happened.

"You okay?" He cocked his head. "You look like you're about to visit the dentist for a root canal . . . I promise I'm not that bad."

I laughed. *Relax. You can do this.*

"Sorry. I guess I expected a regression to happen."

He shoved his hands into his jeans. Leaned even closer. Involuntarily, my head moved an equal amount away.

"Yeah. Who knows if Ethan and Caro met here in the end. And even if they did, it may not have been significant."

Now what?

"Did the Colonel send you the mass spec results?" I asked.

"He did." Dante's face brightened. "I was just looking at them on my phone."

We talked for a few minutes about the results. His conclusions were the same as mine.

Dante unconsciously crowded closer as we chatted. I half-heartedly backed up.

It was this fun game we played.

I told him the Colonel knew about our extra-curricular activities.

"So did the Colonel say anything to you about our dinner together the other night?" I asked.

"Yeah. He called earlier and we chatted." Dante scrubbed a hand through his hair. "But it felt less like a warning about violating the Sand-box Rule and more of a friendly hurt-her-and-I'll-hurt-you kinda thing."

A pause.

"That's weird," I finally said.

"It was weird."

My shoulders sagged. I'm pretty sure I sighed.

Dante bumped my shoulder with his. Yeah. He was totally in my bubble.

"If it makes you feel any better, the Colonel came off as more paren-tal-protective than alpha-territorial," he said.

It didn't make me feel any better.

"I told him we were meeting here today," Dante continued.

"You did? Why?" My eyes grew three sizes.

"Preemptive strike, I suppose. If we're up front and honest, then it's harder for the Colonel to later accuse us of rule breaking."

That made a sort of twisted sense.

"Did the Colonel say we shouldn't be talking to each other or meet-ing like this?"

"No. He just seemed . . . concerned. Told me he would be watching to make sure I *behave*. His exact word."

"Again, that's—

"Weird, I know."

I pursed my mouth, trying to shove worrying thoughts about the Colonel away.

Dante was still standing too close. Big and warm and so very male.

"What do you think about John Hawkwood's monument?" I asked.

I used the question as an excuse to walk around him and down twenty feet to the enormous fresco on the wall.

Effectively changing the topic and putting some much needed space between us.

Granted, the fresco really *was* an excellent example of Paolo Uccello's work from the mid-1400s. Hawkwood was staged on an enormous pedestal, seated in profile on his horse. The entire thing painted with a strong *trompe l'oeil* effect to make it look like a carved stone statue instead of merely a painting.

"It's nice." Dante came to stand beside me. So close our shoulders all but pressed against each other.

Figured.

Part of me wanted to draw a circle diagram for him explaining how personal space bubbles worked.

But . . . he smelled so good. Shower-fresh with just a hint of that cologne.

I held my ground.

"I always want to touch things like this," he continued. "Skim through past scenes to see the original artist."

I swung my head to look at him. "You've done that?"

"A time or two. A friend of the family let me set a finger on Michelangelo's *David* once. He was a *remarkably* unattractive man. Michelangelo, that is."

"Really?"

"Really and truly. Huge nose and matted, dark hair. I don't think he ever bathed."

"Wasn't that just a sixteenth century thing?"

"Possibly, but I caught a glimpse of Raphael once too. Now there was a sophisticated, urbane *artista*."

We studied the fresco in silence for a moment, necks arched to look at it.

"Still no regression."

"Yeah."

"Now what?" I asked.

"No idea." He rubbed the back of his neck.

"Should we wander?"

"Sure."

And so we did. Up the rest of the nave to the center of the cathedral—Brunelleschi's enormous dome covered in a monumental fresco by Vasari. Dante maintaining a too-close distance the entire time.

Still nothing.

"How's Sister Floozy?" I asked.

"Good. Settling in. Mom set her leg and said she'll be fine in a week or two."

"And Boney?"

"Bossy. He has definite opinions about everything."

"Some people never change."

"True. Though it's cute in rodent form."

"Context truly is everything."

We strolled along the center aisle, past the chairs set up for Mass but roped off to deter the tired tourists looking for a place to sit.

I stopped and circled around, thinking. And then pulled out my phone.

"Okay, so when I saw Ethan in here . . ." I scrolled to the relevant photos. "The first one was over there." I pointed to a spot just below the fresco. "But he's not looking at me. See?"

I tilted the phone for Dante. He leaned over my shoulder, pressing his chest against my upper arm.

I ignored the sizzling sensation of his touch. Or, rather, tried super-duper hard to ignore it.

"But we were over there and no regression happened," I continued.

Dante reached over my shoulder and swiped to the next photo. The one of Ethan staring straight at me.

"In this one, he was about right . . ." Dante studied the photo and then looked at the cathedral around us. "There." He pointed to a spot twenty feet in front of us.

"Shall we?" He held out a hand to me.

I pocketed my phone. And, with a deep breath, took Dante's hand.

Strong, warm fingers wrapped around mine. What was it about *us* that made me want to melt into him? This aching sense of familiarity. Rest my head against his shoulder and never pull away?

He led me forward.

Darkness blurred my vision.

This situation is so utterly impossible, I thought. *How shall we ever come to a resolution?*

21

We risk too much meeting like this." Caro pulled her shawl tighter around her shoulders, keeping her face impassive and neutral.

She *wanted* to throw her fists to the sky and rage about injustice and helplessness.

Instead, she calmly checked that Mary was following close at her heels.

Propriety was paramount.

All and sundry had to see Ethan walking at her side as a mere coincidence. A chance encounter.

Nothing more.

"I know. Yet, I canna help myself." His low murmur shivered through her.

Just the *sound* of his voice . . .

Ethan tipped his hat to an acquaintance as they strolled up the nave.

Proper. Polite. His simple wool coat clean and well pressed. Cravat neatly tied.

He was the handsomest man of her acquaintance.

This was the fourth time they had met in the Duomo. Not to mention the chance encounters in Piazza Santa Croce, near the Palazzo Vecchio, at the Countess' salons . . .

All very proper and yet entirely not.

Caro walked at his side. Not touching, of course. Taking his arm without the Countess present would be deemed . . . inappropriate, given the difference in their rank.

But all of her longed for it. Yearned to claim him as her own.

Caro closed her eyes, trying to stem the ache spreading out from her heart.

She had fallen in love with him. A Scottish physician with not much more than his manners and education to recommend him, a mother and sister under his care.

Why did everything about him have to feel so . . . right? As if Ethan were a part of her very soul. And if they were cut off from each other, everything that was Caro would wither. Like a rose denied sunlight.

She had spent her life as a blank canvas. An empty space for other men to draw their hopes and dreams upon. She had learned long ago the safety of being deemed . . . vacant.

But now . . . there was something so incredibly painful in being *seen*. Known.

Which was why she risked these meetings. She was helpless to stay away. Despite her all-but-announced betrothal to the Duke of Blackford.

"I fear Lady Albany knows," Caro said.

She felt more than saw Ethan's sudden tensing.

"How so?"

"She told me a decidedly long story about a 'friend' who found herself in love with a—well, she used the word *unsuitable*—gentleman, but the lady was betrothed to a wealthy earl."

Ethan shot her a decidedly grim look.

"I know, I know. Spare me your dark expressions." Caro managed a weak smile. "The Countess continued saying that the lady married her splendid earl and then went on to conduct an affair with the *unsuitable* suitor for the next ten years."

Ethan let out a harsh breath.

"My thoughts exactly," Caro murmured.

"Did she say this woman was herself?"

Caro laughed, low and breathy.

"I think her meaning was well taken. Will you be offended if I say I am no adulteress? Unlike others, I would feel honor in my marriage vows. I am dreadfully bourgeois in that way."

"Heavens! What sort of a man do you take me for? Offended? Exactly the opposite. I admire anyone who holds true to a sacred vow. Particularly you, *m'aingeal*."

"Hush. Others might hear."

A pause.

"I would shout it from the rooftops, were I at liberty to do so."

His warm breath brushed her ear, indicating how far he had leaned. The heat of him lapped her, causing her breath to hitch.

"Say the word, my love," he continued. "I can leave Blackford's service. He does not own me—"

"Perhaps not. But you do *owe* him. He saved you from poverty, paid for your education. And then there is the matter of your mother and sister."

"I can send for them. We live in enlightened times. Surely Blackford would exact no revenge."

"Are you so sure?"

Another beat of silence.

"He is the consummate collector, Ethan," she continued. "He wants the rare and unusual. The brilliant Scottish lad plucked from poverty and transformed like Pygmalion. The granddaughter of the last Pretender, no matter my illegitimacy. The Michelangelo *modello* that is the dowry my great-uncle left me—"

"You misjudge Blackford, I think. He is weak and spoiled. If we left, he would soon find something else to amuse himself."

"Perhaps. But he has seemed terribly insistent on the point of me marrying him—"

"Bah!" Ethan turned his head away. "It is all just a game to him. A fanciful sport to pass away the *ennui* of his privileged life. I do not mean to offend you, my love, but he does not see the beauty of your soul as I—"

"Be that as it may, he has been putting pressure on Lady Albany, who in turn has been pressuring me."

"Patience, *mo chridhe*. If we are but patient—"

"My betrothal to him is all but secured. I fear time is not on our side." Caro fought to keep her face calm. Serene to all those eyes in the Duomo looking at them.

"We will stall," Ethan murmured.

"How is it to be done?"

"I shall think of a way. Remember what I have said? *Love alters not with his brief hours and weeks.* I shall remain true, love."

Caro sighed, low and harsh. Most unladylike. "You omit the next line, I fear. *Love alters not with his brief hours and weeks/ But bears it out even to the edge of doom*—"

"We are *not* doomed. We shall find a way—"

"Ah, Lady Caro. How remarkable to find you here."

Caro startled at the voice at her elbow.

It was like the devil himself had summoned him.

Only a lifetime of practice enabled her to keep her expression calm and pleasant as she turned around.

Blackford stood before her.

Immaculately dressed in fawn breeches, tight blue coat and shining boots. His shock of brown hair carefully styled. Hat tucked under one arm, leaning on a walking stick with the other. A calculating look in his eye.

"Your Grace." She curtsied. "I was just asking Dr. MacLure after you."

Ethan bowed politely to his employer.

This was an unmitigated disaster.

Ostensibly Blackford's physician, Ethan acted more the part of secretary and traveling companion than anything. Blackford's health was ever excellent.

Ethan had been charged earlier in the day to visit the Duke's banker in Florence.

Would Blackford remember he had sent Ethan on that errand? The Duke could be difficult to read at times. Warm and welcoming one minute. Cold and remote the next.

Caro was doing an excellent job of deflecting any concern.

"I had considered asking Dr. MacLure to see me home, but as you are now here, your Grace, perhaps you would be so kind?"

"I should be honored, Lady Caro." Blackford offered her his arm. "I dislike the idea of you tarrying in less *suitable* company."

Caro wrapped her gloved hand around Blackford's elbow, head lowered.

Blackford caught and held Ethan's gaze over her head. Eyes intent. Icy. Cold.

An electric shiver chased through Ethan's limbs.

Blackford knew. The man absolutely knew. *How* hardly mattered at this point.

Blackford rolled his shoulders. A slight hint of Scotland had crept into the Duke's speech as well. Ethan knew him well enough to understand both as a sign of his agitation.

Ethan and Caro should have been infinitely more careful.

But now . . .

Blackford was spoiled. He liked to get his own way. And when he set his sights on something . . .

Ethan didn't stand a chance.

What was to be done? What *could* be done?

Love alters not . . . even to the edge of doom . . .

Caro glanced in his direction. "Doctor. I bid you good day."

Politely, Ethan tipped his hat.

She shot him a forlorn look, so full of resignation—

Blackford tugged her back to his side.

Ethan watched them stroll down the wide nave, Caro's maid, Mary, politely at their heels.

His future walking away . . .

DANTE

I surfaced out of the regression with a deep breath, still holding Claire's hand. It felt so right in mine. Not too small. Fine-boned. Like I had already spent a lifetime holding it.

Had I?

Uffa. Poor Ethan.

I ran my free palm down my face.

Claire tugged her hand out of mine, wrapping her fingers around her upper arms. A now-familiar indication of her tension.

I stared at her. Haunted pale blue eyes. Blond hair tucked behind one ear. She was sucking that bottom lip in again.

Ethan's emotions roiled through me. Claire . . . Caro . . . they blurred. Which was okay, I supposed. She was the same person after all.

How many lifetimes had I longed for her? How many had we actually experienced together?

"Hey. You okay?" I touched her arm.

"Yeah." She nodded, swallowing, refusing to meet my gaze.

She was *so* not okay.

A large group of Japanese tourists jostled past us. Followed by a rowdy bunch of Italian school kids.

This was not the place to have any sort of serious conversation.

"C'mon. Let's go back to my apartment. We can chat there."

I half expected her to protest, given her track record. But she didn't. Progress.

She followed me out of the Duomo and down Via del Proconsolo. We dodged speeding taxis and bicycles and an endless stream of tourists until I led us into the quiet of my apartment. Branwell was out with a client.

I could hear my mom and *nonna* upstairs, chatting as Nonna made lunch. She cooked pasta sauce from scratch every day. Italian to her core, that was my grandmother.

I led Claire into the large *salotto* with its collection of comfy chairs and overstuffed couches. She kicked off her shoes and curled up in the corner of a couch near one of the huge floor-to-ceiling windows, setting her phone on the cushion next to her. Exuberant Tuscan sun lapped at her face.

"Can I get you anything to drink?" I asked.

"I'm good."

I pulled up an ottoman, facing her with my elbows on my knees, almost touching her but not quite. I'm sure I was closer than she wanted me to be. But given that I ached to sit next to her on the couch and pull her into my arms, I figured this was a decent compromise.

"So . . . want to talk about it?"

A long pause.

"Maybe." She pulled a fringed pillow onto her lap, running its tassels through her fingers. We both stared at her hands. "Caro was really conflicted. She adores Ethan . . . like, a lot . . . but she fears what Blackford will do. And Ethan feels beholden to him, it seems."

"Yeah. Blackford paid for his education and was basically a big brother to Ethan for years. But what Caro said was true. Blackford is the consummate collector."

"Caro feels he's after the Michelangelo as much as her—"

"Which isn't that a nice confirmation of what we already suspected?"

"Yes. They all thought it was the original *modello* for the *Battle of Cascina.*"

"She said it was her . . . dowry?"

"Caro had a brief flashback memory of meeting with an older gentleman who was her great-uncle . . . her father's brother. Henry Stuart, I'm guessing. He was dressed in the red holy robes of a cardinal—"

I nodded. "Henry was a cardinal in Rome. The Stuarts all being Catholic, of course."

"Precisely. Anyway, Henry gave Caro the Michelangelo *modello* as a dowry."

"That would be some provenance, wouldn't it? A lost Michelangelo *modello* actually owned by the Scottish Pretenders."

"It makes sense, though," she said. "The Stuart court attracted a lot of aristocrat sympathizers. The *modello* could easily have been a gift from an admirer at some point. Something infinitely collectible, even then."

"And then it passed on to Caro—"

"And from her to the Colonel somehow."

"Once we prove this, the Colonel will be ecstatic." The more we talked, the more I pulsed with energy.

What was the rest of the story?

When and how was the Michelangelo damaged?

Did Blackford relent? Did Ethan and Caro elope? Or did Caro marry Blackford, torturing Ethan every day for the rest of his life . . . forcing him to constantly interact with the one thing he could never have?

And, if so, what did that mean for Claire and myself?

I knew the best way to find out.

"So let's keep going, shall we? Now that we've figured out how it works."

Claire furrowed her brow at me. "What?"

"Your photos." I pointed at the phone sitting next to her on the couch. "Ethan shows up in selfies where a regression might happen—"

"But we didn't have a regression next to the Hawkwood memorial."

"True, but Ethan wasn't looking at you there, either. Maybe they only happen in places where he actually makes eye contact."

Still frowning, she grabbed her phone and swiped to her photos.

Almost helpless to stop myself, I moved off the ottoman and onto the couch with her. Sitting as close as I dared, looking over her shoulder. Noting the wispy lock of hair trailing down the side of her neck. Longing to brush it aside and press my lips there instead. I breathed her in.

"See what I mean." I pointed at the photo of Ethan on the Ponte Santa Trinità. He stared straight at her. You could see his eyes glinting from under the shadow of his hat.

The images from her hotel room were the same. Close. Intimate.

I studied the picture of Ethan with his nose buried against Claire's neck.

Madonna mia, how I longed to do the same.

But in the other images of Ethan, he was looking away. Not quite *at* her.

"So . . . what are you suggesting, Dante?" She turned her head and fixed me with her icy eyes. Pointedly glanced at my body so close to hers.

Right. I was in her bubble.

I sat back.

"We connect with our inner teenage girl," I said. "Go on a selfie rampage across the city. Me and you."

That got me a hint of a smile.

"Hunting for places that might spark a regression?"

"You're quick."

"Dante, I'm not sure—"

"No. You started that sentence wrong. What you meant to say was 'Dante I enjoy spending time with you and would love to solve the mystery of what happened to Caro and Ethan.' Try that."

She sighed. A deep, bone-weary sad sound.

Not good.

"I don't know, Dante. The Colonel is already being weird about us spending time together."

"True. But he hasn't said we can't, either. And so far we haven't technically broken any of his Sandbox Rules."

A pause.

"Claire?"

She stared away from me. Shook her head.

Again, not good.

"The regressions make me nervous. What if we stumble into something truly tragic?"

"We haven't yet."

"That's not a guarantee we won't. Besides, Caro is just so . . . naive. So trusting of Ethan and his motives—"

"She *should* be trusting of Ethan and his motives. He's one hundred percent committed to her."

"My heart hurts for her. Her life is so narrow and controlled. She wants this little slice of happiness with a longing that just . . ." Claire rubbed a fist over her sternum. "It aches. I ache for her. A huge part of me is afraid to pursue the story. What if it ends unhappily-ever-after?"

"It might. But it also might end joyful. This isn't some random story about two people, Claire. This is *our* story. Something that literally happened to our souls two hundred years ago. And there is a potential Michelangelo thrown into the mix, a drawing that we have been hired to assess."

Claire chewed on her bottom lip some more.

I knew her. I don't know how, but I just did.

"You're like my sister playing darts here. Throwing bolts randomly at the board, hoping something will stick." I leaned forward, getting my face (and most of my upper body) in her space. Personal bubble be damned. "Why don't you tell me the real reason you don't want to at least *try* to answer this mystery?"

I expected to read irritation or frustration or even outright anger in her eyes.

Fear was what I got. Terror.

What—?!

She jerked her head away and pushed past me, standing and walking over to the window. Hands hugging her arms again.

I understood that ache she had referred to. It thrummed through my chest. Pulsing. My throat tight.

"Talk to me, Claire." Voice pleading. "I promise to respect your decision, but please give me the consideration of being honest. You don't like these regressions. I get it. But why? Give me the real reason."

Silence hung in the room.

Her shoulders slumped.

"I ha-hate . . ." She started. Gave an audible swallow. "I-I hate that I can't separate Caro's emotions from my own."

Huh. "I'm not sure I follow you—"

Claire made a somewhat exasperated noise and threw out her arms. It was *almost* an Italian gesture. It just needed to be about fifty percent bigger. She turned around.

"Caro is completely in love with Ethan. Like head-over-heels, to-the-moon-and-back in love. She would do anything for him. She loves him enough to sacrifice every personal happiness."

I was clearly missing something.

"Good. Ethan feels the same way."

Claire shifted her weight onto one leg. Glowered.

"You and me"—she swept her arm out and in—"are not Ethan and Caro. Not precisely, at least."

A beat.

"Yes."

Another pause.

"You're going to make me spell it out, aren't you?" She placed a hand on her hip.

"Claire, I swear I'm not being intentionally difficult here—"

"The more time I spend as Caro, the more I absorb her emotions for Ethan, the harder it is for me to remain emotionally distant with *you!*"

My head reared back. Surely confusion plastered my face.

"So . . . don't." I shrugged. "Don't remain emotionally distant." I stood and walked over to her. "I don't want you to. I most certainly haven't. Why is this a problem?"

She sucked her bottom lip in so fast, so hard. She crossed her arms and turned back to the window.

That ache spread again. Something was wrong.

"Why do you dislike the idea of being with me? Why is that bad?"

Nothing.

"It's a long story."

"I have nothing but time."

Silence hung. Taut. Strained.

Finally, her shoulders sagged.

"Kendall Sharp was my first real boyfriend." She didn't look at me. Still faced the window. "He taught me that a guy will say, 'You're beautiful,' to your face and then tell all his friends what a dog you are. He dumped me at high school graduation because stupid Kelly Shumaker told Tiffany Lamb that she liked him."

"Claire—"

She held out a silencing hand.

"Alexei was a poet with the face of Apollo. I was naive and stupid and adored him to distraction. He broke up with me after we spent a weekend with his parents. Turns out he just wanted to convince his mom he was straight."

I wisely held my peace.

"There were a few others but I dated Tayson for three years. Tattoos. Motorcycle. We had one of those toxic on-again, off-again relationships. I was so determined to make *us* work. He lied and lied and then lied again. He text-dumped me after taking two hundred dollars from my purse."

I closed my eyes. If I *ever* met any of these men—

"Milos was my Tayson rebound," she continued. Voice low and monotone. "Charming. Suave. Bad boy handsome. He was . . . remarkably awful, always playing this passive-aggressive game of 'prove you love me.' I had to tell him everything I was doing, every second of the day—who I was with, where I was going . . . He finally dumped me because I wasn't being attentive enough.

"Which lead to Pierce. See, he was supposed to be my safe choice. The nice, down-to-earth guy who wasn't exciting like the others, but also wouldn't betray me and break my heart. The whole world knows how *that* played out—"

Her voice broke. She let out a stuttering breath.

I stayed silent.

"Like I told you over dinner earlier this week, I'm not in a good place right now, Dante. You asked why I smile at waiters and receptionists and everyone else. The answer is simple. I can accept their casual friendliness because I'm not hovering on the brink of something . . . *more* . . . with them. And, in return, they don't expect anything more from *me*."

"I see that. I do. You give others so much—"

"No, you don't get it. I talk to strangers not because I have something to give, but because I know what it means to have nothing. How vast loneliness can be."

Oh, *cara mia*—

"Claire." I tugged on her elbow, turning her toward me. She kept her head down, staring at my chin. I dipped my head, forcing her to meet my eyes.

Yeah, I was totally done respecting her bubble.

I stared hard at her. "I am not Kendall or Alexei or Tayson or Milos. I am most *certainly* not Pierce Whitman. Part of me is glad they were all jerks—"

She stiffened and instantly turned away.

I rotated her back. Lifted her chin with my fingers. Forced her eyes back to mine.

"You didn't let me finish. I *am* glad they were all jerks. Not because they hurt you. No, for hurting you I would happily pummel them all senseless. But because their loss is *my* fortune. You are here. With me."

She swallowed. I could feel the motion of her throat moving up and down under my fingers.

"Dante . . . I . . ."

"Yes?"

She sighed. A sad, deflating sound.

"Come here." I tugged her closer. Wrapped my arms around her.

Predictably, she stiffened.

"Calm down. It's okay. I'm not going to do anything more than give you a much needed hug."

I held her gently. Not crushing or eager or insistent. Just comfortingly.

Buried my nose in her hair. Lavender and something a little spicier. My eyes closed.

Madonna mia.

She felt like heaven in my arms. I wanted *me* and *her* and *us* and I wanted it *rightnow.*

She relaxed somewhat and even tentatively placed her hands around my waist. Not tight or anything. But it was a capitulation of sorts.

"You have a terrible reputation." Her voice was muffled against my chest.

"It's completely unfounded. I've never been a player."

"I find that *so* hard to believe." She pulled back, nose adorably wrinkled.

"It's true. I've already told you." I willed her to believe the truth of my words. "People just make assumptions. I don't bother to correct them. I actually don't date much. I'm a mama's boy, remember?"

She looked doubtful, moving her arms from my waist and folding them across her stomach. I kept my hands around her back. I had no intention of letting her go.

"Claire, up to this point in your life, you have associated with boys. I know about your parents—"

She snorted. "The whole world knows about my parents."

"Exactly. Forgive me for speaking ill of them, but their relationship isn't normal."

"An understatement."

"Their marriage most certainly isn't a healthy standard to emulate. Then, you've had the misfortune to date a serious string of losers—"

"Again, an understatement."

"—who seem more like narcissistic douchebags than actual men. I can understand why you are leery of me."

"It's not just you, Dante. It's men, in general."

"Gotcha. You're afraid."

She lowered her eyes to my chest.

"Isn't there an old Sarah McLachlan song about this? Fearing love?"

Her eyes widened and she bit her lip. Nodded.

"I get it. You're terrified the past will repeat itself. That you'll give your heart to me body and soul, like Caro to Ethan, and then watch it be crushed."

Two huge tears spilled down her cheeks. That was all the answer I needed.

I bent lower. Whispered in her ear.

"I. Am. *Not*. Those. Boys."

She hiccupped. A gulping stuttery sound.

"I am not cut out of that same mold," I continued. "If nothing else, do you honestly think Judith and Nonna would have raised a jerk? Look at how I act toward the women in my life. Respect. Love."

"B-but—"

"No. Throw out everything you've heard about me. I know I've done that with you."

"Trust you to bring up my *psycho* reputation." She gasped, pushing half-heartedly against my chest. I held her firm.

"I don't care what others say about you. I observe what you are. What being around you tells me about Claire."

"Dante . . ."

I pulled her closer, keeping my head close to hers.

"Take me as I am, Claire. As *you* know me. Have I lied to you?"

She shook her head.

"Have I been anything other than up front and honest?"

Again, a head shake.

"Have I belittled you or made you feel stupid and small?"

Another shake.

"I have never, in my life, met anyone like you, Claire. I am desperate to give *us* a chance."

I could feel her pulse, the tense hammering of her heart. But I kept going.

With this woman, I would never give up.

"I hunger to know *everything* about you: favorite food, music, vacation, bad holiday memory. I want to make you laugh so hard you snort. I want to hold you when you cry over a sappy movie. I want to buy you ugly Christmas sweaters and kiss you every New Year's Eve. I want to experience every milestone life has to offer from this point onward with *you* at my side."

I hugged her tighter and tighter as I whispered until she was cuddled firmly against my chest again. Her arms trapped between our bodies.

"So h-help me, if you say that f-four-letter L-word . . ." she stuttered.

I laughed. Soft and low.

"Don't worry. This isn't a marriage proposal, *cara mia*. Consider it more like fair-warning. A statement of intent."

She sniffled. And then the seemingly impossible happened.

She *snuggled* closer.

It wasn't much of a motion, really. Just a small tucking in of her elbows. A pressing of her face into my shoulder.

But that tiny capitulation . . .

Her loneliness engulfed me. She had such a generous heart. So much to give. I knew it. Had known it.

And life had kicked her down, over and over. Beating every last ounce of trust in basic human goodness out of her.

"I want to thrash every idiot who has convinced you to stop reaching for happiness. Made you doubt the beauty and joy life holds for you, Claire."

Her shoulders shook. I could feel her tears through my shirt.

I gathered her closer, threading a hand into her hair.

"Trust me," I pleaded. "At some point, you're going to have to get back into the game. You and me, babe. We would be amazing together. But, before that can happen, you need to let me in. Just make a little Dante-sized hole in the walls around your heart. You're welcome to seal it right back up once I'm inside. But, please, let it happen."

I held her, letting her cry her fill on my chest.

Cathartic. Cleansing.

After a while, she pulled back, rubbing a hand over the large wet spot on my shirt. "Sorry—"

"Never apologize for that, Claire." I cupped her cheek. "I will always be there for you."

She bit her trembling lip. I was pretty sure I would have given about anything to kiss her right then. But this conversation wasn't about me. And I refused to do anything that might damage the fragile trust we had established.

"I probably look terrible," she sniffled.

I cocked my head, studying her. "Somewhat. You get all splotchy when you cry—"

She pushed against my chest, a soft smile making an appearance. "Not winning brownie points here. You're supposed to make me feel better about myself—"

"Yes. But I promised you honesty too."

A pause.

"Thank you," she said, wiping underneath her eyes.

"You're welcome. You going to *try* to trust me now?"

She shrugged. "It's a lot to absorb. Trust is really . . . uhm, hard. I want to trust you. And, you're right, on a certain level, I intuitively do. But getting my heart and my head on the same page is difficult. Let me think about it. I'm a work in progress."

"Aren't we all, *cara mia?*"

I waited. Expecting her to correct me with a firm, 'It's Claire.'

She shrugged instead.

"C'mon, Romeo." She snagged my hand. "Let's go see what Nonna cooked up for lunch. It smells divine."

CLAIRE

My cell phone rang just as I closed my laptop for the day. After lunch with Dante and his family, I had returned to my hotel. With the mass spectrometry results officially in, I had even more work to do. If the Colonel's sketch was the original *modello* for Michelangelo's *Battle of Cascina* like we suspected, I needed to build an airtight case.

The sun sank over the Arno, spilling red-gold light through my room.

I glanced at the caller ID.

Sigh.

"Hey, Mom." I managed to keep my voice upbeat.

"They were madly in love, you know." My mom's voice blasted into my ear. She must be holding it against her shoulder while she painted. Typical.

"Lucy and Desi?"

"No."

"Brangelina?"

"No, no—"

"I give up."

"—Adelaide and the Colonel."

Oh! Right.

Mom probably needed to up her ADD meds.

"Completely in love, though Adelaide never talked about it. Your father—"

"Tom?"

"Yeah, Tom. He found some love letters Adelaide had stashed in a shoe box. All from the Colonel, going on and on about Grammy being—what did he call her?—his divine goddess."

I sat down on my bed, staring sightlessly at the window in front of me, the last gasp of sunset raking my face.

Grammy had never mentioned an old flame to me. She always told stories of my grandpa, who had been her childhood sweetheart. But never anyone else.

I was having a hard time wrapping my head around there *being* anyone else in Grammy's life.

"Did Grammy ever say what happened to them?"

"Mmmm . . . no. Like I said, she never talked about it." Mom's voice pulled away a bit. Muffled. Reaching for a different brush. "Though there was this one time . . ."

Her words wandered away.

"Mom?"

" . . . so I was pretty sure Adelaide dumped him—"

"Mom!"

"What?"

"You're drifting. Stay with me."

A pause. The sound of something being put down.

Wow. She never did that.

"I'm sorry, dear." Mom's voice was much clearer. "I was just saying that Adelaide loved your grandpa to pieces. Tom always talked about how in-love his parents were. Before they married, Adelaide and your grandpa dated some, but then he left for a job in Pittsburgh, and she stayed in Boston doing something secretarial, I think—"

"Grammy did pride herself on her stenography."

"Very true. So she could have dated the Colonel then. But even if she did, it didn't last. She married your grandpa as soon as he returned to Boston. I remember asking Adelaide about your grandpa and all she would say was, 'When something is right, it's right. You just have to trust.'"

That sounded like Grammy.

"Though could you imagine our lives if she *had* stayed with the Colonel?" Mom continued. "Things would have been a lot easier after Tom's death, that's for sure. The Colonel would have stepped in to help us out."

Of course. My mom *would* focus on the Colonel's wealth.

Had Grammy broken the Colonel's heart? Dumped him for my grandpa?

"Anyway, you had asked about the Colonel and Adelaide. I just wanted to tell you what I know."

"Thanks, Mom. How are the flamingos going?"

"Fabulous! Micky is a genius with cloth . . ."

Mom drifted in and out for the next ten minutes, babbling about flamingo placement and budget problems and the ephemeral nature of performance art.

I paid attention, making appropriate responses when needed.

Seriously? I can't believe she said that.

Of course, I can wait longer for the money.

Yes, Warhol completely destroyed the concept of art . . .

Basically, the usual conversation with my mother.

I hung up with Mom after promising to call in a couple of days.

But my mind was on that phrase from Grammy.

When something is right, it's right. You just have to trust.

Didn't that pretty much sum up where I was with Dante?

Lunch earlier had been . . . amazing.

Weird, I know, to describe a casual luncheon with a guy and his family like that, but *amazing* was the only word that came to mind.

Judith laughing with her children, despite Tennyson's return to Volterra. Branwell and Chiara teasing Dante about his closet-love of modern poetry, which he shamelessly defended. Dante, in turn, ribbing Branwell about his non-existent love-life. Nonna chiding everyone in Italian and piling more pasta in my bowl. Boney the Rat scampering down the table, stealing bits from my plate.

Everyone easily accepting my presence. Love wrapping through and around them like gauzy tendrils. Every part of me longed to just let go, to be swept away in the lovely emotion of *belonging*.

Panic skittered along my nerves when I thought about it.

How could I want something so badly and, yet, be so terrified of it at the same time?

That damn Fear again.

My head was messed.

I plugged my headphones into my phone and swiped to my music. Dug up that old Sarah McLachlan song.

Fear. Appropriately titled, I supposed.

I kinda love/hated that Dante knew it too. Curse him and his wall-busting . . . awesomeness.

The words hummed through me . . .

But I fear, I have nothing to give, I have so much to lose here in this empty place . . .

Truth.

My heart pounded as the song ended.

The next track on the album came on.

Sarah's answer to *Fear* . . .

All the fear has left me now, I'm not frightened anymore . . . I won't fear love . . . I won't fear love . . .

I sat back against the bed pillows, twirling my phone in my hand. Brushing tears away.

The sun had firmly set by then. Lights twinkled across the Arno, the soaring steeple of Santo Spirito gleaming above the rest.

When something is right, it's right. You just have to trust.

Had Grammy done that? Walked away from the Colonel and

regretted it because she hadn't trusted? Or was my grandfather the true love of her life?

Why the Colonel's interest in me? *Was* it interest? Or just normal human politeness to the granddaughter of an old flame?

And *why* did I always have to second guess people's actions?!

Anger washed me. Suddenly, I hated all this . . . *fear*.

How *dare* they!

How dare those awful men in my past destroy my sense of trust! Defraud me of a future with a guy like Dante D'Angelo.

My eyes stung. *Blink, blink, blink.*

I deserved better than this emotional . . . half-life. I deserved to *live*.

And *just like that—*

I was done.

Something snapped.

If I was ever going to get over my fears, I needed to let go. I intellectually had known that.

But in that moment, I viscerally *felt* it.

I *had* to trust Dante.

Yes, the panic was still there, hovering at the edges, waiting to pounce.

But my desire to move beyond the trauma of my past was greater. I swallowed back the anxiety.

I won't fear love . . .

I would hate myself forever if I walked away from Dante right now. Big scary L-word or not . . .

Clenching my jaw, I swiped to the camera on my phone. Framed my face. Took a selfie.

I looked at the picture.

My head nestled into the pillows on my bed, staring determinedly at the camera.

And there *he* was too.

Dante as Ethan, tucked up against me. His cheek pressed into mine, nose slightly turned toward my face . . . a smile on his lips. As if he were about to kiss me.

It was a photo of such intimacy, such adoration . . .

I could practically feel Caro hovering in the background of my mind, whispering, begging me to trust this man as she did.

My past-life self—my soul—had loved this man. Perhaps even spent life after life with him.

How could I not at least give Dante a chance?

Longing flooded. I wanted to *know* him. Understand him. To sink down, down, down into . . . *us*.

I comprehended, as I never had before—

Trust is a decision. A commitment. An act of faith.

Sometimes you just have to step off the cliff, fight the panic and *believe* that you will land okay.

I won't fear love . . .

I opened my text messages. Attached the photo I had just taken.

I trust you. I really do.

His reply came almost instantly.

Thanks, Claire. I won't let you down, babe. ;)

> *Choosing to ignore the word 'babe.'*
> *How's about you invite me to lunch tomorrow and we hit the city afterwards?*

Selfie rampage?

> *Yep.*
> *Start practicing your frat-girl, pouty-lip face.*

DANTE

There he is."

I leaned over Claire's shoulder as she pointed to the background of the selfie she had just taken.

Sure enough. Ethan stood at the base of the *David* in front of the Palazzo Vecchio, shoulder casually leaning into the enormous pedestal, head turned to his right.

"That's the same place he was in the old photo with me and Grammy," Claire continued.

"He doesn't seem to be looking at you this time," I said.

"Yeah. So probably no regression there."

I pressed my chest into her back, ostensibly to get a closer look at the photo, ignoring the tourists swirling around us in the enormous Piazza della Signoria.

Breathing in the scent of her . . . lavender and herbs. Claire fit against me like a glove. Like my entire body had been made just to hold her.

She didn't make a comment about her space bubble or pull away. *That* was the most significant part. She didn't relax into me either, but I was no longer a pariah.

"Now what?" Claire turned her head toward me, her nose practically touching my bent cheek. I felt her exhale . . . a puff of air blowing across my face.

Madonna mia.

You know how it goes. When you like someone . . . really, really like someone . . . the slightest touch burns. Every point of contact—no matter how small—sizzles with heat and electricity.

Claire was a live wire.

I took a step back before I did something to break her fragile trust.

Her text the night before had floored me. Honestly, I thought it would take a lot longer for her to reach this point. I had been prepared to wait her out, for as long as it took.

So even though every last part of me wanted to gather her in my arms and bury my face in her hair and let us be . . . *us*, I held myself firmly back.

"What about this?" Claire turned away from me and aimed another selfie at the Loggia dei Lanzi to the right of the Palazzo Vecchio. Snapped a photo.

I maneuvered to her side as she swiped to the image, pressing into her upper arm before I thought the better of it. I couldn't seem to stop myself. I was stupid-crazy for her.

We both studied the image. The extravagant loggia, tourists sitting on the steps up to it. The tops of ancient sculptures underneath it.

"No Ethan." She lifted her head. "Where should we go next?"

Claire scanned the piazza, which meant I saw the incoming text message before she did.

> *I see you. I hate that big, dark-haired idiot standing so close. Like he wants to eat you up. When will you stop being such a slut?*

I hissed. Claire looked back to her phone, saw the text and froze. I felt, more than heard, her swallow. She shot me a glance and then turned, stuffing her phone in her jeans pocket.

Or, at least, tried to. Her hand was trembling too badly to get the phone to fit.

"Hey, hey—"

I took her phone from her, shoving it into my own pocket. Grabbed her shoulders and spun her around. She was white as marble, the fear in her eyes shouting at me.

"It-it's nothing. Just nothing." Shaking her head, over and over.

"It's not nothing. Who is it? Who's texting you crap like that?"

She was frozen, nostrils flaring wide.

"Talk to me. Who is it? Pierce?"

She finally stirred.

"No, no," she said. "I doubt Pierce could be this focused. It's just some cyber stalker." She did her signature lip-bite thing, blue eyes staring at my shirt. Chest heaving. "So many came out of the woodwork after that video. I've changed my phone number. I block every text . . . nothing seems to deter them. It's really no big deal."

Was she freaking kidding me? She was seconds from a full-blown panic attack.

"Forgive me, but this *is* a big deal. I don't like the thought of anyone harassing you—"

Without thinking, I gathered her into my arms. Crushing her to me . . . as if my arms alone could keep the world away. She trembled, hands trapped against my chest. I rubbed her back.

"It's okay. I'm here. You're safe with me. I will pulverize anyone who tries to get to you . . ."

I was babbling like . . . well, like a big idiot.

"How can they be here?" Claire shook her head, voice muffled against my shoulder. "They're not supposed to actually *be* here. That was the only thing keeping me sane. Assuming they were far away and couldn't harm me. But if they're actually here, watching us—"

"No one's going to hurt you, babe. Not with me around."

She leaned against me. Upright. Stiff.

And then . . . little by little, she relaxed.

First her head. Then her shoulders. Her knees followed.

Finally (hallelujah) actually cuddling her weight into mine . . .

Unconsciously, my arms tightened.

She moved her hands and wrapped them around my waist. Tentatively to start, but then holding on with a fierce grip. Fisting her hands into my t-shirt in the middle of my back, pressing herself that much closer. Holding me as tight as I was holding her.

I closed my eyes. All the air in my body swooshed out.

My throat constricted. That she would trust me enough to let me hold her like this . . . to accept my support . . .

Even more, to return it.

I slid one hand firmly into her hair, the other bracketed her ribcage.

Damn if she didn't feel perfect in my arms. Tall enough that I didn't have to hunch to hold her. Just the right amount of curve.

Finally, I did what I longed to do—I buried my nose in the hair next to her ear, drawing Claire-scented air back into my lungs. Drowning in her.

It was like every last piece of me had been made for just this. To hold Claire Raythorn. To be her rock in the storm. To destroy anyone and everyone who tried to hurt her.

I had *never* felt like this before.

I wanted to describe it as *possessive* . . . but possessiveness implied a sense of jealousy, a distrustful greediness. And that wasn't it.

No . . . the word I kept landing on was *bramare*.

A yearning. An ache. Hunger. To want something with such fierceness . . .

Ho bramato per noi.

I longed for us. Craved it.

And so I held her, a motionless island in the bustling crowd.

"They're just words." Her shaking subsided. "Words can only hurt me if I allow them to."

"Has this person threatened you physically?"

"No. They just say creepy, nasty things."

"Have you talked to the police about this?"

She nodded. "Because the texts have never been physically threatening, there's nothing they can do. And even if they *were* threatening, tracking down a cyber stalker is almost impossible."

I hated the truth in her words. Her helplessness.

The crap this woman had been through . . .

"Damn cyber bullies."

"I know. I just need to not let it affect me."

"It's hard not to."

"But it's what they want. Whoever is sending these *wants* me to be afraid." She pushed away from me. I instantly let her go. "And I refuse."

She jutted her chin, defiant. "My fifth nanny, Mrs. Evans-Sharp, always told me to keep a stiff upper lip—"

"Your *fifth* nanny?"

"She was very British—"

"I was more focused on the number five and the word *nanny* rather than her nationality. You had five nannies?"

"Well, I prefer the term *nanny* over random-person-who-was-poorly-paid-to-keep-me-out-of-my-parents'-hair."

"Wait—was this the same nanny who taught you how to truss a kidnap victim?"

"Still smarting over that, are you?"

"Just trying to understand the colorful assortment of people who raised you."

She gave a small laugh. It didn't quite touch her eyes, but it was a nudge in the right direction.

"You have *no* idea." She paused. Lifted her gaze to mine. Those eyes so impossibly blue. "Thank you. Just . . . thank you."

I knew what she meant.

Thank you for listening. Thank you for fighting this with me.

"Here. Turn this way." I walked around her, pulling out my own phone. She swiveled with me, until her back was to the far left end of the piazza where it led into Via dei Magazzini.

"What?"

I framed her in my phone camera. "I don't think it matters who takes the photo."

"True. I just have to be in it."

And bonus—I would have images of her.

"You are fabulous. A tigress. *Rawr.*"

She sank a hand on her hip. "Seriously?"

"You're not roaring."

She smiled, broad and genuine, that dimple on her upper cheek popping. Sunlight tangled in her blond hair.

I took the photo.

"Wait." I reframed the image. "Let me get one with the background this time. You distracted me."

That got me a second smile. I snapped another photo.

I swiped to the image and studied it. Claire came around, pressing into *my* arm, mimicking my posture from earlier. I tried (unsuccessfully) to contain a silly-happy grin.

"There." Claire pointed at the image. "He's way back there, right at the entrance to that street."

Sure enough. There was Ethan, top hat popping above tourist's heads near Via dei Magazzini.

I glanced at her, still pressed against my side.

"You're in my bubble," I said.

She lifted her head. Studied our bodies. And then . . . grinned. Shy. Sweet.

"So I am." Completely unrepentant.

I'm pretty sure my eyes went lovestruck glazed.

I slid my phone into my pocket and gave her own phone back. She tucked it away.

I nodded my head toward the opposite end of the huge piazza.

"Shall we?" I held out my hand to her.

She stared at it. "You're pushing your luck."

"I know."

A beat. And then she gave me a welcoming smile and slid her hand into mine. Fine-boned. Soft and warm.

I laced our fingers together.

She was going to be *very* lucky if she got that hand back anytime soon.

A group of rowdy teenagers, chattering in German, swarmed around us. Claire pressed closer to me. One of the teens did a double and then a triple-take, staring at her. He nudged a friend who whirled to look at us.

I shot them my hostile, discouraging face. They turned away, but not before I heard something that sounded a lot like 'batty ray psycho.' One of them started to hum *Achy Breaky Heart*.

Claire stiffened.

"So, five nannies?" I asked, determined to distract her. I angled us away from the teens.

She shot me a thankful look. "More like six."

"How much of a hellion were you?"

"Me? Not much. My parents, on the other hand . . ."

"Got it."

The teenagers drifted off, heading away from us. I watched them go, a warning look in my eyes.

"I think there were actually more than just six, but I don't remember anyone before Kristin. She was my first nanny. I was four."

"You liked her?"

"I did. A lot. She was a college student—fine art major, of course. She taught me to read and would cut my peanut butter and honey sandwiches into awesome shapes. Apparently, JB taught her about more than just art, so she was replaced with the elderly Ms. Jones before I started first grade."

I ran my thumb over the back of her hand as we skirted around the Fountain of Neptune with its Mannerist sculptures.

"Ms. Jones liked merlot significantly more than she liked me, so she didn't last long," Claire continued. "Ironically, it was a move from Boston to San Francisco that made her quit, not her drinking problem. Miss Penny was next. My parents were in the middle of this mess with the Getty Museum at the time, so Penny made sure I had a crash course entitled 'How the World Works' which was basically a lecture on not sassing back. Though it came back to bite her when she was let go for being too mouthy. Cerise, my fourth nanny, was the ex-con—"

"How did that happen?"

Claire shrugged as we rounded the enormous statue of Cosimo I on his horse, still heading toward Via dei Magazzini in the far left corner of the piazza.

"I'm not sure. Mom and Dad had recovered from the Getty debacle and were deep in the Statue of Liberty project at that point. I had been living with Grammy in Boston, but they brought me back to New York for some reason. I'm not sure why because my memories are of them frazzled and desperate to have me out from underfoot. I think they just hired the first person who applied for the job."

A huge burst of laughter came from the far end of the piazza. Someone yelled 'psycho' in a German accent. Claire tensed but didn't turn around. My admiration and respect for her had grown ten times larger in the last five minutes. She had more courage—

"Cerise was actually a ton of fun." Claire tightened her grip on my hand. "Her stories were hilarious. She let me stay up late and eat ice cream straight from the carton. She was more like a big sister than a nanny. She was also a huge country music fan—"

Claire paused, wincing.

I held up a staying hand. "I'm not saying a single word."

She shrugged. "Yeah. You can guess what Cerise liked to listen to. Despite our differing taste in music, I loved her to pieces. My parents fired her eventually. Apparently, you shouldn't hire an ex-con and then give her unsupervised access to your art collection—"

"Ah."

"—which led to them hiring Mrs. Evans-Sharp."

"The British nanny?"

"Yeah. Totally Mary Poppins until she got upset. Then she swore like a sailor. She was okay. She left when her eldest daughter married.

"Mrs. Henderson was next. She cried a lot and watched period movies over and over. All those lush Merchant-Ivory films from the late Eighties. My parents finally sacked her. By that point, I was fourteen and old enough to help Grammy with her arthritis. So I just moved in with her."

Claire said everything in a completely matter-of-fact tone. But my heart ached for the lonely, slapdash childhood I could see behind her words.

We neared the entrance to Via dei Magazzini. Though calling it a street was too generous. More like a tight alleyway. From across the piazza, you wouldn't even know the houses led into it. I could still hear the German teenagers yelling at each other.

"Wait." Claire pulled me to a stop and then let go of my hand. "I have an idea."

I lifted my eyebrows.

She darted in front of me. "Does Ethan show up on video, I wonder?"

"*That*, Ms. Raythorn, is a brilliant idea."

I pulled out my phone, framed her in my screen and hit record. "Well?"

I nodded my head, still recording. "You are a bonafide genius."

Claire cocked her head questioningly. But I was focused on the ghostly image of Ethan behind her, walking into Via dei Magazzini.

I stopped recording and showed it to her.

"I *am* a genius." She grabbed my hand again. "Let's follow him."

Claire pulled me out of the bright piazza and into the dim alleyway. Turned around and gestured for me to video again.

Ethan continued to walk away from us, down the dark street.

Claire grinned and hugged my arm when she saw it.

We followed Ethan down the entire length of Via dei Magazzini, heading north toward the Duomo. He turned right onto Via Dante Alighieri and then immediately left onto Via Santa Margherita, leading us deeper and deeper into the narrow medieval alleyways of Florence. Streets that hadn't changed in a thousand years.

Finally, Ethan stopped in front of the ancient Chiesa di Santa Margherita tucked down a tight lane. The tiny church that Dante Alighieri, along with his beloved Beatrice, had frequented in the thirteenth century. Ethan turned to the camera, staring straight at me. Almost beckoning me forward.

"What? What are you seeing?" Claire leaned from side to side in front of me, scanning the narrow road.

I showed her the video.

She darted a look at the church doorway with its dark, aged-wood awning. Studied the place where Ethan stood.

"Could this get ugly?" she asked.

"Possibly."

"I mean, this street might as well be called 'Assassin Alley.'"

"Definitely *mafioso*," I agreed.

"You can practically feel the history bleeding from the walls."

"It only needs someone in a doublet and cloak carrying a stiletto—"

"Yeah. Or an angry nobleman out for blood."

She sucked in a steadying breath. Straightened her shoulders.

"I can do this." Words said low and not intended for my ears, but I listened anyway.

A burst of loud laughter echoed down narrow walls. I looked back and saw the same group of German teens jostling each other as they walked down the cramped street toward us.

One of them noticed Claire and elbowed his friend. The friend's head snapped forward, a hunting dog on the scent.

It didn't take a detective to know they had been following us.

One of them started humming *Achy Breaky Heart*. Another laughed.

All of me tensed, half hoping the teens would get physical. My body itched for a fight—a physical way to combat Claire's demons. She tugged on my arm, giving her head a small shake. *Please don't make a scene.*

The teens came nearer, shoving each other, pinging off the stone walls like bouncy balls.

Grimacing, I wrapped an arm around Claire's waist, pulling her into the alcove of the church door. Twisting us, so her shoulders were to the wood, using my body to shield her from prying eyes behind us.

But as we moved, everything swooped inward.

Day turned to night. Rain sparkled on the pavement.

Please doona be late, Caro-lass. I must see you.

25

E than stared into the darkness.

Light rain pattered against his caped great coat, dripping off the brim of his hat. He slouched against the wooden door of the church behind him, surveying the narrow lane. Though even calling it an alleyway might be too generous.

Did I mention that my friend, Beatrice, was to be married? I think to see her tomorrow evening . . .

Caro's words echoed in his mind. She *had* to have meant this place. The church Dante Alighieri and his beloved Beatrice had frequented before she married another man.

Ethan took a fortifying breath.

Or had Caro meant something entirely different? That she would play Beatrice to his Dante, turning away from him to marry the man her family, such as it was, had chosen?

Please don't let that be our fate . . .

The night shimmered. Dim lantern light flickered down the alleyway from Via del Corso to his right, leaving faint streaks of gold on the wet cobblestones.

One week. It had been one week since Ethan had seen Caro, talked to her.

He pushed against the gloom . . . but a solitary Shakespearean line kept thrumming—

How like a winter hath my absence been from thee . . .

Without Caro, the world felt *less-than*. Bleak. Colorless.

Would she come? She had never risked such a clandestine meeting before . . .

And what would he do if she didn't come?

Footsteps echoed to his left. Ethan pressed back into the sheltering blackness of the doorway. Waiting.

An achingly familiar shadow slipped into the narrow street.

At the last second, Ethan snagged her elbow, dragging her into the door alcove.

She squeaked, whirling on him.

"Hush. 'Tis only me, lass."

"Ethan." His name a benediction. She instantly collapsed against him. Boneless.

He spun her around, tucking deep into the shadows. Protecting her with his body from even the most prying eyes. Not that anyone was out.

She was slight and trembled in his arms. It took Ethan a moment to fully realize . . .

He was *holding* her. His Caro. Snugged firmly against his chest.

Heaven and damnation.

The rain continued on heedless behind him, pattering on the pavement.

"Were you followed?" He whispered against her hair. Paused to breathe her in. Lemon and clean soap.

"No. I waited for Mary to go to sleep and then slipped down the servants' stairs."

"It terrifies me that you risk so much—"

"No more than you," she countered, nestling further in his arms. "Blackford sends you away then? Lady Albany said as much . . ."

"Yes. I am to return to Edinburgh. A Scottish merchant ship leaves Pisa Monday next. His Grace has insisted I be aboard."

"He releases you?"

"No. He will retain my services—"

"But he has not confronted you?"

"Nothing beyond his snubbing at the opera last week."

Ethan gathered her close. She felt fragile. Bird-like. Smaller than she appeared.

As if the force of being *her* somehow amplified the actual space she inhabited, rendering her larger-than-life to the eye.

But in his arms, she became just Caro. Delicate. Soft.

"Lady Albany has given me an ultimatum," she whispered into the dark. "I am to marry Blackford or she will cast me off—"

Ethan hissed through clenched teeth. "Blackford moves in shadows. Pushing us both around like so many chess pieces."

"I am *so* eternally weary of being a pawn for others' ambitions." She sagged her weight against him. Her unwavering trust as humbling as it was overwhelming.

Silence. The rain drummed a soothing rhythm.

"Whatever are we to do, Ethan?" Her voice a whisper of sound against his chest. She wrapped her fingers into his waistcoat. "I hate this feeling of helplessness."

"We are hardly helpless, lass." He pulled back to look down at her face, a suggestion of eyes and mouth in the dim light.

"But Blackford—"

"He is merely a human being. He does not own us. We are not his subjects."

"I cannot bear the thought of losing you, Ethan." Low. Determined. "A life without you—"

"It shallna happen." His voice filled with Scottish heather and gorse. "I canna part from you. *Love alters not . . . even to the edge of doom . . .* remember that, *m'aingeal.*"

"What shall we do?"

"We live in more enlightened times where a man might make his way. I have a cousin in Boston—"

"In America?"

"Precisely. It is a young country, full of possibility. A good place to start anew."

"But how? Surely you would need some capital—"

"My cousin . . . he has a good heart. He will help, though I would be poor until I could establish my practice as a doctor." Ethan tracing the shadowy line of her jaw with his thumb. "A man in that situation would be needing a wife, lass."

Caro sucked in a sharp breath. "But your mother? Your sister? How could we leave them to Blackford's displeasure?"

"Where there is a will, there is a way. I have a small sum set aside for now. Enough to get us to America. It may take time, but I will send for my mother and sister as soon as I gather the funds—"

"No." Caro placed a gloved finger over his lips. "I could not bear it if anything happened to them."

Ethan's heart plummeted.

"You will not away with me then, lass?"

Caro laughed, soft as the rain on the pavement behind them. "You misunderstand me, love. I will go anywhere with you. But I want your entire happiness, and you will not be happy if your mother and sister are left to suffer—"

"They willna suffer." His voice grew husky, deepening his burr. "I will write to an uncle in Glasgow—"

"No need to call upon so many favors. The *modello* is mine—"

"Michelangelo's drawing?"

"Yes. Let us sell it. Use the money to start our life anew."

"I could not ask that of you. It is yours—"

"What does a mere piece of paper matter in comparison to life with an honorable man?"

"Caro—"

"I will do whatever I must to be with you, Ethan."

"But surely there is no need to part with your original. It was a gift from your uncle. What about your most recent copy, the one on the old vellum? Such a fine drawing would command a tidy sum too."

"Perhaps. We will take both and sell them when we arrive in Boston." She pressed a soothing hand to his chest. "You are not hearing me, Ethan. *Nothing* matters more to me than you."

He groaned at her admission, drawing her even closer. "You humble me, lass. I feel inadequate and, yet, somehow *more* for your trust in me."

He skimmed his nose along her cheek, following the line of her jaw down to her mouth.

"You will always be my own." She breathed a puff of air against his lips. "Now and forever."

As surely as if it were noonday, sunshine blazed through him. Brilliantly blinding.

It was more than any man could resist.

His arms pulled her closer. He lowered his head and brushed her lips softly with his. Asking but not taking.

Caro nearly whimpered. Ethan's mouth swept over hers, teasing, pleading—gentle intoxication.

After months of torture, to *finally* be in his arms. To taste the warmth of him.

With a sigh, she raised on her tiptoes, covering the last half inch. Claiming him.

His arms tightened around her waist. A hand moving up her back. His lips devoured.

Every last bone in her body melted into the pavement.

And, yet, she had somehow never felt so jarringly alive.

"My love . . . *mo chridhe.*" Ethan murmured between each kiss. "I *am* truly yours . . ."

She wrapped her hands around his neck, arms trembling.

Did he understand the power of his words?

The illegitimate daughter of a long-dead mother. The grandchild of royal blood, seen only as a pawn to be passed around. Wanted . . . and yet so obviously not.

More *thing* than person.

But with this man . . . that sense of homecoming. Belonging. Of finally finding the other half of herself that she had never understood was missing.

Did he taste her tears?

She kissed him with all the fervor in her heart. Heedless of the rain falling around them.

Ethan pulled back, his lips resting against hers.

"Marry me then, *m'aingeal*?"

"Yes. Most definitely, yes!"

"'Tisn't much of a proposal—"

"It is perfect."

Ethan kissed her again. More than heat and hunger.

His lips were a promise. A beginning. A future.

Caro laughed, happiness bubbling through her. "Oh, my love. All will be well."

"We will find some parish priest to marry us. It will not be much of a wedding, I fear—"

"I do not care. I simply wish to be with you, my love. We will run away, sell what we can, send for your mother and sister and see ourselves settled in Boston. We will make a new life for ourselves, far from those who would use us as puppets—"

"When? When shall we leave? Our time is short."

Caro rested her head against his chest. "Saturday evening. Lady Albany throws her annual musicale—"

"Heavens! Surely not with actual seating?"

"Lady Albany *owns* chairs. She simply chooses not to use them."

"Blackford will attend."

"Yes, which means it will be hours before anyone notices my absence."

"And I will be packed off on my way to Pisa."

A beat.

"I will wait for you outside Lady Albany's palazzo—"

"No, Ethan, it is far too dangerous. With so many guests coming and going . . . you will be seen."

"Caro, I must ensure your safety."

"If I am noticed around the palazzo, others will assume I am assisting Lady Albany with her guests."

"But—"

"I can meet you. I came tonight, did I not?"

His shoulders slumped in agreement. "Where then?"

She thought for a moment. "We should meet where we gathered for the Duke's picnic two weeks ago. The old monastery outside the city gates. You can wait for me there without being seen."

Another long pause.

"Very well. It is agreed." He nodded. "Can you make your way?"

"Yes. I will be there waiting, my love."

"I fear Blackford will not release his claim so easily."

Caro wrapped her arms around his neck. "He does not truly care for me. As I have said, I am little more than a prize to be won. He will let us go."

"I trust your intuition." Ethan pecked her lips.

On a happy sigh, Caro raised on tiptoe and demanded another kiss, giving herself over to the moment. The thrill of his closeness, the power in his arms surrounding her.

Love. Happiness. *Him.*

At last . . . at long last, she was . . . home.

CLAIRE

I blinked, reeling at the sudden bright sunlight, the blare of modern noise.

The world righted itself. This odd warping of reality, where I literally stretched and became taller. Not quite so short in comparison to Dante. My body morphing back into Claire.

But Caro's emotions clung, thrumming through me.

Dante sheltered me against the wooden door of the church, hiding me from the street with his body. An exact mirror of our positions in the past, my hands on his chest, his arms around my waist. His heart pounded underneath my palms.

At least, I think it was *his* heart I felt.

I made the *enormous* mistake of lifting my eyes to his.

Chocolatey warm with flecks of green. Plaid eyes like Ethan. Intense . . . no, *intent*. His gaze flicked to my mouth.

The whistles and jeers of the teenagers passing behind his back faded. Everything receded.

"*Madonna mia*, what you do to me," Dante whispered, head dipping down.

He slanted forward, pulling me even more firmly against him.

My blood pressure spiked.

No. Too soon!

Reflexively, I pulled back. Not that I had more than three inches of room to go.

"I'm not Caro, Ethan . . . I mean, Dante . . ." I winced, shutting my mouth with a click. I pushed against his chest.

Dante instantly froze. Lifted his hands off and took a small step back. Giving me space but keeping his enormous body between me and the street. Shielding. Protecting.

I instantly felt the loss of him. His warmth. Security. Most of me wanted to pull him back into my arms.

But that accursed *fear* . . .

He stared. Eyes purposeful.

The air between us crackled, saturated with energy.

"I know *exactly* who you are, Claire Raythorn." His deep bass vibrated through me. "You're thinking I'm channeling Ethan right now. That my emotions are lingering from him, transferring from Caro to Claire."

Damn him and his mind-reading.

Dante canted forward. Respectful. Careful not to crowd me. But fierce. Focused. His eyes locked with mine.

"That. Is. *Not.* True." Words low. Vehement.

I sucked in a stuttering breath.

"I'm sorry, Dante," I whispered. "It's a big step to go from saying, 'Hey, I'm going to trust you,' to 'Let's get the party started—'"

"I do love Pink." He chuckled, a low rumble of air thrumming through us both. "Please don't apologize, *cara mia*. I want to move at your pace."

I reached for him then, palms outstretched. Helpless not to. Almost pleading.

With a quick smile, Dante's arms swept around me, pulling me to him. Gentle. Kind.

He drew in a deep breath, his nose burrowed into the hair above my ear.

My arms wrapped around his shoulders, reveling in the sheer size and power of him. But tension threaded my limbs. My heart a wild bird.

How could I want something so badly and yet be so afraid at the same time?

"Is this okay? Me holding you?" he asked, a soft breath of air.

Okay? It was heaven.

I nodded. Wordless.

He lifted his hand to cup the opposite side of my head, cradling my cheek against his. Tender.

"Good. Then I will just hold you. Breathe you in. When you're ready for more, you'll let me know."

He nuzzled that space between my neck and earlobe, gently brushing his lips against my skin. Goosebumps skittered down my spine.

I forced my body to relax. To bring him that much closer. I could still sense panic fluttering around my edges, like a tiger waiting to pounce.

I swallowed. I could do this.

I could open up, just a little bit.

Caro had loved this man . . . her emotions still swirled through me. The joy of finally claiming what she yearned for most.

I ached to be her . . . to simply *be*. To know I held his heart, without doubt, without worry.

Dante sighed. A deep, contented sound. "I adore you. *You*. Claire. The person you are in this life." The man really did read minds. "I love how you bite your lower lip when you're emotional, just like you are right now."

I nudged my lip out of my mouth.

"I love the dimple that pops below your right eye when you give a genuine smile, like a punctuation mark on your upper cheek. I admire how you face adversity with your chin lifted and jaw defiant—"

I sucked my lower lip back between my teeth. Who was I kidding?

This man was determined to reduce my walls to rubble.

I needed this. I needed him. I had made my decision to trust and, dammit, I was going to run with it.

I shifted and wrapped a hand around the back of his head, holding him close.

"Mmmm," he breathed into my hair.

And nothing more.

Dante just . . . held me, true to his word.

My nose buried in his neck, my cheek pressed against his shoulder. Held me until our heartbeats slowed. Until I relaxed entirely against him, the warmth of his huge body surrounding me. Draining all panic, that fight-or-flight reflex.

He was incredible cuddly.

My hungry soul lapped up his comfort. When had previous boy-friends simply held me without expecting more in return? Had any ever offered me a place of refuge? Seeing me not as a thing to be possessed and used, but a friend to be treasured and respected?

Maybe I was more Caro than I realized . . .

Peace washed through me. An ache for this amazing man who would always be my own personal battering ram. Destroying anything that tried to hurt me, sheltering me.

Who knows how long we would have stood there, huddled against the door . . .

"Excuse me? Is this the church of Dante and Beatrice?" A very American voice asked behind us.

Sigh.

Dante pulled back, giving me a wry smile. And then turned to the elderly couple staring at us, tourist map in one hand, half-eaten gelato in the other.

Dante charmed them, introducing himself, asking questions.

The man was smooth. That I could never deny.

Oiled snake charm—a more bitter me would have called it.

But I took him at face value now. He was just a genuinely nice guy. Kind. A bit of a romantic at heart.

He gave them a solid run-down on the history of the church. (Early eleventh century. Standard Roman basilica construction. One of the oldest churches in Florence.) And then made several excellent recommendations for dinner. Smiling. Looking utterly delectable in his tight t-shirt and battered jeans.

Dante wrapped his fingers around mine as we waved goodbye to them. (Jane and Bob. Des Moines. Ten grandkids. Love bingo.)

Hand-in-hand, we strolled up Via del Corso toward Piazza della Republica. I found myself leaning into him as we walked. The comfortable closeness of good friends or long-time lovers.

We were neither and yet . . .

The crowds swirled around us. That ever-present prickly sensation of being watched skittered down my spine.

Would that feeling just *stop* already? I was so done with the paranoia. So tired of resisting the urge to constantly look over my shoulder.

I snuggled closer to Dante, squeezing his hand, wrapping my free hand around his elbow.

He looked surprised, clearly not expecting me to initiate any kind of physical closeness. But being near him felt so warm and safe—

The entirety of Ethan and Caro's conversation finally caught up to me.

"Wait!" I pulled Dante to a stop. "The vellum!"

"That's right." He pulled me out of the stream of foot traffic, against a stuccoed wall. "The Colonel's copy of the sketch—"

"—probably *isn't* the original Michelangelo," I finished.

"That's a serious shame. The poor Colonel."

"Yeah." I pursed my lips and sighed. "It *was* too good to be true. Caro distinctly described the original as being on paper. And, again, in her mind's eye, the *modello* was done in silverpoint. Not chalk."

"And Ethan described Caro's drawing as being on old vellum. But why?"

I pondered it. "I got the impression that the vellum came from her great-uncle."

"Henry Stuart? The Catholic cardinal?"

"Yeah. I just got a sense that he had given it to her to use for her sketching."

"Right." Dante nodded. "As a cardinal in the Vatican, finding old pieces of vellum probably wouldn't be difficult."

"Exactly. And even back then, copying a Michelangelo onto antique vellum would have been vintagey-fun."

We moved back onto the street, holding hands again.

"So now what?" I asked. "We still don't know how the damage was done to the Colonel's drawing."

"Yeah. And despite Caro's words, I still wonder about the exact origins of the Colonel's sketch."

"Do you know where Ethan and Caro were going to meet?" I asked, snuggling my shoulder into his side again. "I saw the place in Caro's mind, but I didn't recognize it. Just tall walls overgrown with ivy and lots of trees."

"I got a sense of a cloister and a tower from Ethan. A large building set on a hill outside of Florence proper. I'm pretty sure it was San Miniato al Monte—"

"The ancient church above Piazzale Michelangelo?"

"Exactly. It's part of an old monastery complex."

We skirted around a bunch of milling Indian tourists, summery in their bright saris.

"So, uhm, are we going to go?" I asked.

"Show up there, take some video and see if Ethan makes an appearance?"

"Yeah."

He stopped, looking down at me. "I'm game if you are. I know the regressions worry you."

I shrugged. "They do, but nothing bad has happened so far. Apparently, not every regression involves death and mayhem. Besides, I want to hear Ethan say those words that Branwell overheard."

"You're so sure that it was Ethan?"

"Who else could it be?"

He lifted a shoulder. "Who knows. There's no guarantee those words even happened in Ethan's lifetime."

"True, but we do know the charred damage occurred around then."

"Well, regardless, I'm all in." Dante pulled me closer. "I'm desperate to know where that Michelangelo ended up."

"And I want to see Ethan and Caro get their happily-ever-after."

"Speaking of which . . ."

Dante stopped in front of a *gelateria*, dragging me inside.

I stared at glittering row after row of mounded, shiny gelato. Fruit and chocolate and candy on top announcing the flavor if you didn't understand the Italian written on small tags stuck into each tray.

He wrapped his arms around me from behind, pulled me back against his chest and rested his chin on my shoulder. Like he was helplessly unable to control the impulse to touch me, to have me as close as possible.

I can't say I disliked it.

We contemplated the wealth of ice cream before us.

My phone buzzed and I pulled it out of my pocket out of sheer Pavlovian habit.

> *Whore. How dare you allow that ape to touch you. You will never belong to him. Only me.*

I would have dropped my phone if Dante hadn't wrapped his hand around mine. Staring at the screen over my shoulder. A low hiss streamed from his lips.

"I officially hate this person." His voice growled in my ear. "Hate that they're spying on us."

He instantly let go of me and moved to stand in the *gelateria* doorway, looking out onto the busy pedestrian street. Head moving back and forth, scanning for . . . who? Neither of us knew what this online stalker person looked like.

I walked over to the door and peeked around his arm, trying to stop my hands from shaking.

"Does anyone look familiar?" he asked.

Tourists leisurely walked past. The occasional harried Italian office worker threading through.

Nothing and no one out of the ordinary.

"No."

"*Uffa.*"

We contemplated the street a little longer.

Still nothing odd.

"You shouldn't have to put up with this, Claire." Dante turned back to me. Wrapped me up in a hug and pulled me all the way inside the *gelateria.*

"I know," I whispered, relaxing my head into his remarkably solid chest. "I want them to go away so badly. I'm so tired of being afraid—"

Dante's arms tightened. "I don't like the thought of you staying alone in your hotel with someone like this roaming around. I would never forgive myself if something happened."

I stilled. Was I in real danger?

It was hard to say.

Had my cyber stalker upgraded to a real-life stalker? Though bullying and creepy, this person had never actually physically manifested himself, always careful to walk the line between verbal harassment and tangible threat. Close but never enough to force the authorities to take the texts seriously.

What to do?

I sagged into Dante. Weary. Rubbing a hand over his stomach. Also surprisingly solid. How often did the man work out?

He ran his palm up my spine, soothing me.

"I decided months ago I wasn't going to allow fear to control my life," I said. "The best way to thwart a cyber terrorist is to just go about your life."

"I don't disagree, but I still worry—"

"Let's assess this rationally." I pulled back enough to look at him. "My hotel has twenty-four hour security, and I know the staff. They watch out for me."

"But you're not always there."

"Agreed. The Colonel sends a car when I have to visit the villa and that's perfectly safe."

Dante brushed hair from my face, tucking it behind my ear. "Would you agree to allow me to accompany you when you roam the city? I would feel even better if you were staying in my palazzo—"

"With you and Branwell?" My expression surely skeptical.

"No. Nonna would box my ears. But I'm sure you could stay with my mom and Chiara. The palazzo has an excellent security system."

"I'm sure it does, but I don't think there's any need to go to such extremes. I'll just be a little more careful."

"Like calling me before going anywhere by yourself?"

I didn't have to think. I knew the answer to that one. "Yes. If you're okay with that?"

He snorted. "More than okay, *cara mia*. Like I said, I want to keep you safe."

I smiled and sagged against him. His chest a firm rock propping me up. I siphoned his strength.

He turned me around, so we could both stare at the gelato case.

"Now, Ms. Raythorn, you have a terrible task before you," he said. "You must decide on your three favorite flavors. And before you even ask—no, I'm not sharing mine."

"Not sharing, Mr. D'Angelo?" I twisted my head to look at him, only partially mock-aghast. "I'm not sure I can trust a man who doesn't share his gelato."

"You have it backwards. You absolutely should *not* trust a guy who willingly shares his gourmet gelato with you. Such a man is most definitely *furbo*."

"*Furbo?*"

"Sneaky. Crafty. A man who willingly gives you his gelato either has something wicked planned, or he made a poor flavor selection and is trying to fob it off on you."

"Mmmm, I'm not sure I agree with that logic. I think part of being in a *trusting* relationship is sharing with each other. I plan on sharing with you."

His eyes darkened. Contemplative.

"Fine." Reluctantly. "I'll share too, but only if I get to feed it to you."

I pursed my lips at him. "Are you always right?"

"What?" He tried to look innocent.

"Feed me? That was your wicked plan. You better choose knock-out flavors."

He chuckled and squeezed me hard.

In the end, he won with *tiramisù, cioccolato nero* and *pistacchio*.

I ate every last bite, licking the spoon he held for me.

CLAIRE

"How are your *pappardelle*, darlin'?" The Colonel asked me from across the table.

"Delicious." I pasted on my bright smile. "Thanks again for the invitation."

I was finally having that long-promised dinner with the Colonel. He had pushed it off for several days, which had been fine by me.

I had been busy completing my detailed comparison between the Colonel's sketch and known Michelangelo drawings. Upon close inspection, I had found compelling differences in crosshatching and stroke length. Even without the regressions, I was confident I would have realized the Colonel's sketch was not a bonafide Michelangelo.

Dante and I talked about the Colonel's project but were careful not to plagiarize from each other (Sandbox Rule). Between our schedules and some seriously rainy weather, we hadn't had a chance to continue tracking Ethan and Caro.

Which meant we hung out together in our spare time and talked and laughed about non-work related stuff. Among other things, I had learned that Dante adored fem rock (go figure), hated talking politics (Italian *and* American), and secretly enjoyed watching *The Bachelor* with Chiara and Nonna. The man was a study in opposites.

But tonight I was with the Colonel.

We were at some restaurant south of Florence, buried in the Chianti region. It was a high-end, family-run affair nestled into one end of an ancient castle-like villa.

The Colonel and I sat in front of a crackling fireplace under a frescoed ceiling, rain pattering against the dark windows. Italian buildings seemed to be a solid ten degrees cooler inside than out. Which must be heaven during hot summers but not-so-much for the rest of the year. I found myself dressing for the indoor temperatures more than the outside. The fire definitely helped.

The *pappardelle* were delicious, coated in what the waiter called a *salsa rosa*, which I realized was a tomato ragu with a healthy dollop of heavy cream . . . leaving it a definite pink color.

The Colonel dabbed at his mouth. He was in fine form tonight.

Wild white hair tamed as much as it could be. Dressed like he was ready for a swinging 1960s cocktail party. Which, I guess, he probably figured this was something of that sort. His diamond cuff-links sparkled in the firelight. I kept waiting for him to pop a fedora on his head.

He was on his third glass of Chianti red, and we weren't even through our *primo*. Would he be snoring under the table by the time we hit the *insalata*?

If I didn't know better, I would almost say he was nervous. But what was there to be nervous about?

"Pierce Whitman met with me today to give his preliminary assessment of the drawing." The Colonel took another bite of pasta.

My head snapped up. "So soon?"

"He seemed confident enough to not need extra time. Wanted to beat you all to the punch, he said."

Ah. Now we came to it.

"And?" I had to ask, though I had a strong hunch I knew where Pierce would land.

"He provided me with a thirty-page analysis, showing point-by-point why he firmly believes my sketch to be a genuine sixteenth-century drawing. He's eighty-percent certain it's an original Michelangelo *modello*. He wants another week to examine it further before making a more definite call."

Solemn. Careful. Seemingly meticulous. That was Pierce.

"I see," I said.

Needing to settle my thinking, I took a reserved sip of my own wine, hating how my lipstick stained the rim of my glass. Why did I have to leave my PH lipstick at home? It didn't rub off or leave sticky residue on cups. I discreetly rubbed at the mark with my thumb.

"So, at this point, where do you stand, darlin'?" The Colonel sat back, studying me. "I haven't got a hint of anything from you or those D'Angelo boys. Do *you* think I have the real deal?"

Drat. I had only just begun to build a case for the drawing being done by Caro. I didn't want to tip too much of my hand.

That said, I knew from experience, clients didn't like suddenly finding out a prize possession wasn't what they expected.

Given that Caro was most likely the artist behind the Colonel's sketch, not Michelangelo himself, I needed to start planting the idea. She deserved no less.

So what to say?

"That's a good question, Colonel. To be honest, I'm not sure. There are several factors that don't jive for me—"

"Such as?"

Here we go. "The vellum dates correctly, but it's a decidedly odd medium for a Renaissance drawing. Most old masters used paper by that point. The lack of silverpoint is puzzling. Michelangelo preferred silver lead for his sketches—"

"What is your gut telling you?"

Gut? Ironic that.

"It could easily be a later copy on old vellum," I said.

"But my sketch clearly wasn't copied from Sangallo, from the original cartoon."

"Exactly. Which means even if it *is* a later copy, it is still extremely significant. It implies that, at one point, there was another version of the *Battle of Cascina* that might be original to Michelangelo."

He studied me in silence, reaching again for his wineglass.

"You have a theory, I'm betting." Eyes canny. "I want to hear it."

Talk about putting me on the spot.

"If I were to give you an opinion right now"—deep breath—"I would say it is a later copy of a Michelangelo original."

"How much later?"

I pretended to think about it for a moment. "Perhaps early nineteenth century."

"That late?"

"Yes."

"Why? What makes you think that?" He gazed over the rim of his wine glass. Expectant.

I cleared my throat. Folded my hands in my lap as primly as possible.

"Too many things don't add up. The fact that the charring on the edge occurred then. Additionally, something about the way the chalk skims onto the vellum implies a later time period."

That last part was all bluff, bluff, bluff. But I needed something to go on until I could build a stronger case.

"I stand to lose a lot of money here."

"I am well aware of that."

"Are you sure you're not just being contrary to get back at Pierce?" the Colonel asked. "I know you've been running around with Dante D'Angelo behind my back. You guys concocting some plan?"

My blood pressure spiked. Suddenly, I needed a much stiffer drink than just wine.

How to reply to that?

"Things aren't like that, Colonel—"

"I only hire complete professionals to work for me, gal."

"Dante and I have not been trying to undermine Pierce or collude in any assessment. We're just being . . . friends."

"Friends?"

"Yes." I nodded firmly. "You bring up valid concerns, Colonel, but I have to be honest to my training and instincts too. I firmly think the drawing you have is a later copy."

"Do you?"

"Yes. Even more, I believe it was done by a woman. Which, when I gather enough proof, will not be any small thing. A two hundred-year-old copy of a much earlier Michelangelo done in a woman's hand . . . collectors will eat it up."

The Colonel studied me for a long moment.

Pensive. A little threatening even.

I held my ground, matching him look for look.

Somehow, I would prove the history of the sketch. The world needed to hear about Caro.

The Colonel blinked.

And then . . . *smiled*.

Wide, sunny, utterly delighted.

"Brava." He slow-clapped. "*Bravissima!* I knew you would do me proud."

He saluted me with his wine glass.

It was my turn to look surprised, eyebrows disappearing into my hairline.

"I reckoned those D'Angelo boys would figure it out because they always seem to land on their feet," he continued. "But you . . . I wasn't so sure."

I smiled weakly. Without the assistance of Dante's talents, I wasn't sure I would have arrived at the correct conclusion.

But wait—

"You're *pleased* the drawing isn't the real deal?"

The Colonel chuckled.

"Would you care to explain what's going on here, Colonel?"

He sat back in his chair, expression still pleased-as-Punch.

"For years, I've been wanting to find the right person to curate my collection. I need someone brutally honest. A person who won't simply parrot what I *want* to hear, but what is truth. Hence this little 'audition' I arranged. You, m'dear, just passed with flying colors."

"Wait. You've known the provenance of the sketch all along?"

He nodded. "Of course. What good is an audition if I don't know what I have?"

A pause.

"True." I hadn't thought of that.

"I've always known the drawing is a later copy. There's plenty of documentation. I just neglected to show it to you." The Colonel winked and motioned with his wine glass, sloshing the liquid around. "It came into my family around two hundred years ago. Done by a British noble-woman who lived here in Florence . . ."

Caro!

My heart raced. Could I possibly be close to finding out more about her?

"Family lore has it the artist was a ward of Louise, the Countess of Albany," the Colonel continued. "It's the reason I chose to put you in Palazzo Alfieri. Considered it a helpful little hint . . . and damned if you didn't figure it out." He drained the rest of his wine glass in one long gulp. "It doesn't hurt that I've been wanting to get to know you better for quite some time now."

His comment wrenched me back to reality.

I met his gaze. Appraising me.

Almost like I was something he wished to . . . collect.

I paused, wanting to ignore the weird undercurrent. Brush it under the rug, pretend it would go away—

No. Wait. New, fierce, not-afraid Claire didn't let things go.

Why do you have to be so old-man creepy?! she shouted.

"May I ask why you've been interested in knowing me better?" I asked.

Uber-polite. But direct nonetheless.

The Colonel set down his now empty wine glass. Studied me for a moment longer.

His gaze much more *seeing* than I would have expected.

The silence stretched into awkward.

"It's like looking at Adelaide reborn," he finally said. "You could be her—what is the word they use? Doppelganger?"

"You've mentioned more than once that you knew my grandmother."

"Knew her?" He gave a soft laugh, gaze going unfocused. "I breathed her. Lived her. Loved her with every piece of my young, wild heart. I wager she never mentioned me."

Damn.

This conversation had train-wreck written all over it.

What to say?

No, Grammy never did mention you.

I understand she dumped you for my grandpa . . .

I went with, "I can't say that she did. But she did talk to my mother about you, I think."

"Lisabet?"

"Yes."

"Mmmm."

Another one of those long, awkward silences.

"You've been in love, I take it?" he asked.

"Yes." Stupidly so.

"People do crazy things in the name of love."

I didn't understand where this conversation was headed. I just hoped it wasn't the headlights of oncoming traffic.

"I keep her picture, you know. Right here." He tapped the inside pocket on his suit coat. "It helps me remember . . . things. Priorities, I suppose."

Yep. Definitely headlights blaring straight at me.

I needed to get off the highway, as it were. But I asked anyway.

"May I see it?"

He beamed at me. Clearly that was the correct question. He pulled out a photo which, judging by its battered appearance, had been much-cherished. Handed it to me.

It was one of those old, nearly square black-and-white photographs with a white border around it. The kind of thing you pay someone on Etsy to recreate in Photoshop.

This was the real deal.

And there they were. Standing on a beach . . . probably Horseneck, south of Boston. Grammy took me there a lot as a kid.

Grammy in a vintage bathing suit—classic early 1960s style—smiling wildly at the camera. Her arm around a taller man.

My throat tightened. How I missed her!

I traced her face with my eyes. I tried to remember if I had ever seen a photo of Grammy from this period in her life. After her early years but before she married my grandpa.

I didn't think I had.

Her hair whipped out behind her in a long, pale sheet. New England beaches as windy then as they are now.

She did look like me . . . a lot.

Even in black-and-white, I could tell her hair was light blond. The same face shape, the same body. Aside from our eye-color—I remember her eyes being more green than blue—we could have been twin sisters.

No wonder the Colonel fixated on me.

"She was so beautiful," he said. Low and quiet. "Lovely in every way imaginable. I never felt so alive as I did when I was with her."

The Colonel stared at me. Eyes full of some emotion I couldn't quite understand.

"Yes." I swallowed. "That's how it always was with her."

I had always adored the person I was around Grammy. She *made* me into that person. Loved me into it.

I studied the photo.

Grammy seemed so . . . happy. The joy on her face almost contagious. I moved my gaze to the young Colonel. Tall, smiling as well, holding Grammy tight against his side.

His hair had been dark back then. Thick and wavy above his pale eyes.

But something about him . . .

I shifted the photo to get a better look.

The chill started at the base of my neck. Every hair on my body coming rapidly to attention until my lungs felt constricted in a vise.

No! Just . . . no!!

I swallowed, terrified to ask even though my brain had already scrambled ahead to the answer.

"So, the Michelangelo drawing . . . how did it come into your family's possession?"

"An ancestor in my mother's line acquired it. My mother was the last of the Clines, you know."

"The Earls of Arlington? The sketch came from them?"

"Yes. But before they became earls in the English peerage."

I shot him a puzzled look.

"I know, it's confusing to us Americans." He waved a hand. "But the peerage of England is separate from the peerage of Scotland."

"Scotland?" I echoed.

"Precisely, m'dear. My mother's family were dukes in the Scottish peerage before becoming earls in England."

"Dukes?" My voice faint. "Dukes of what?"

"Blackford." He beamed at me. "My mother's family were the Dukes of Blackford."

DANTE

I still can't believe the Colonel is a direct descendant of Blackford."

I held Claire's hand, drawing her up the gazillion stairs leading to San Miniato al Monte. They didn't call it Saint Minias on the Mountain for nothing.

"You and me both. The resemblance is startling." She chuckled. She had been doing that a lot around me the last couple of days. "I turned so white, it freaked him out. He broke out in a sweat and ordered us both a healthy shot of bourbon."

"Kentucky gentleman-ing at its best."

"Truth."

We had been talking over her strange dinner the previous night as we climbed the wide stairs. The sun was sinking over the city, peeking through the cloud cover and bathing the Duomo in light. Though given the clouds on the horizon, the sun wouldn't last long. We were in for more rain.

I pulled Claire in front of me to let a group of rowdy Australians pass. The stairs and threatening weather did not deter tourists, that's for sure.

She pressed back into me from thigh to shoulder, curved and warm. The sudden shock of her body against mine momentarily knocked the air out of me.

Madonna Mia. This woman—

I had given myself a stern lecture before seeing her today. The same lecture I'd been having with myself all week:

Don't push her. Let her set the pace.

Don't initiate physical contact. (Well . . . not too much.)

And whatever you do . . . do not *kiss* her.

No matter how natural the impulse feels.

No matter how many times she bites that lush lower lip of hers.

Do. *Not.* Kiss. Her.

Being with Claire had become a delicious sort of torture.

So instead of holding her against me and drowning in her plump mouth, I let her peel herself off and continue up the stairs.

Though I did keep a tight grasp on her hand.

Did Claire even *notice* the electricity thrumming between us?

"Why did Caro's sketch stay in Blackford's possession?" Claire asked. "That's been bugging me all day."

Focus, man. "Right. I thought they planned on taking it with them to Boston."

"Exactly. So did they sell it in Florence instead and then Blackford bought it back as a memento of Caro? And, if so, where did the original Michelangelo end up?" She shifted her hand and threaded her fingers through mine, almost unconsciously, it seemed. Progress.

"Or did Blackford interrupt their plans, send Ethan off and marry Caro himself?"

"Which, for one, would be sad and, two, still doesn't answer where the original Michelangelo *modello* Caro got from Henry Stuart ended up."

"Or how and when the charred damage to Caro's sketch happened."

"Or who said those words Branwell heard about taking something back." Claire nodded in agreement, puffing as we climbed the steep stairs. "Which is why we're here, I guess."

All of me had wanted to spend the day with Claire exploring San Miniato, despite the unintentional physical torture. But business had called for both of us, delaying our meeting until this evening.

I had insisted on picking her up on my bike, driving up and out of the city, parking with the tour buses in the giant Piazzale Michelangelo. It was the last destination for most people visiting the city. An amazing panorama of the Duomo, the Arno with its distinctive Ponte Vecchio . . . a sea of red tiled roofs.

Little did people realize the view from San Miniato al Monte was higher and just that much better. Perched on a steep hill, the old church and attached monastery were surrounded by an enormous above-ground cemetery, terraced down the mountain.

We continued to climb the stairs, me constantly scanning the crowds around us.

While driving up on my bike, I had noticed a man in the rearview mirror keeping his distance behind us on a smaller *motorino*. The man himself was nondescript in a black leather jacket and jeans. Concerned, I took a deliberately roundabout route up to the *piazzale*. The man had followed us through every twisting turn. But I had lost him right before reaching Piazzale Michelangelo.

Were we being followed? Or was it just random happenstance?

Was Claire's anxiety finally rubbing off on me?

Regardless, I was keeping a diligent lookout. No one would hurt Claire on my watch.

She pulled me to a stop.

"Wait." She darted up three steps. "Let's take some video, shall we? No sense in waiting. It will be dark soon."

I framed her and shot a few seconds of film, studying the background.

"Anything?" Claire came down to me, pressing into my arm. That scent of lavender eddying around me.

I angled my phone screen in her direction, shaking my head.

"No."

Claire stared at the video, the people moving behind her, the two kids leaning in to photobomb, fingers and tongues wagging.

She took in a deep breath. "He offered me the job."

I angled my head as I pocketed my phone, not understanding the *non sequitur*.

She was biting her lip again. "I'm sorry. I know you and Branwell really need the job too—"

"What? The Colonel offered you the job? You won the audition?"

"Yeah."

"Claire—that's fantastic!" Without thinking, I wrapped my arms around her waist and lifted her off the ground. Pulling her into an exuberant hug and spinning her around. "Why didn't you tell me before now?"

She stared into my face, surprise written all over hers.

"W-wait—you're happy for me?" She settled her hands on my shoulders as I, reluctantly, set her down.

I did not, however, let her go.

"Of course, *cara mia*. You totally deserve it."

"But . . . I'm sorta taking this from you—"

"I'm a hack at best. I don't have your keen eye or understanding. Without my . . . talent . . . I would be completely lost. You, on the other hand, are brilliant."

"But you needed this job, too."

That was true. "Branwell and I will figure something out."

"Are you sure?" She looked away, still punishing that poor bottom lip with her teeth.

"Claire, this isn't about you winning and me losing. You *earned* this job."

I tried not to stare at her mouth as I spoke, really I did. What kind of creep stands and stares at a woman's mouth?

But as I still had my arms looped around her waist and her hands were on my shoulders, those lips of hers were less than a foot away.

It was a losing battle.

My own mouth was dry.

"When does the Colonel want you to start?" I asked in a lame attempt to pull my brain away from its chant of, *Kiss her right now, you idiot.*

A pause.

"I haven't told him yes yet."

"Wha—why?" Okay, now she had my full attention.

Her fingers tightened on my shoulders. She gazed past me, staring over the city stretching behind us, the cemetery which angled along both sides of the stairs. "I wanted to make sure . . . I mean—I don't know."

"What?"

She moved her eyes back to mine. "You're really happy for me?"

Her question cut me. She was such an odd combination of confidence and vulnerability.

Had she ever had a cheerleader in her life?

"I will always celebrate your successes." I may have tugged her even an inch closer. "Honestly and truly."

She blinked. And then blinked again. Released a long breath. That bottom lip trembled.

"Thank you. Thank you for being so . . . supportive—"

I leaned into her, brushing my lips softly against her temple. Giving in a little to temptation. "That's what this is all about, *cara*. I'll always be there, cheering you on."

She sagged against me and I could feel her throat working, swallowing back her emotions.

Had she really been so concerned about my reaction? So worried I would be . . . what? Angry? Upset? My heart swelled.

Oh Claire.

She hugged me hard and pulled away. She didn't, however, let go of my right hand.

"Thank you. Just . . . thank you." She smiled. Open. Happy. "I told the Colonel I wanted to think about it. Partially to see how you'd react. But also because of the weirdness with Grammy and, now, Blackford."

I pulled on her hand, starting up the stairs again. I risked a glance behind us. Searching. Observing.

Good. Our motorbike friend hadn't made a reappearance.

"You feel like history is repeating itself?"

"How could you not?"

"There's nothing saying the Colonel is Blackford reincarnated."

"Can you see a life clinging to him from that time period?"

I took a couple steps. "No. The Colonel's shadows have gaps."

"Exactly—"

"But it doesn't necessarily mean anything. Maybe the Colonel was someone else I loved during that life."

"Did Ethan have some affection for Blackford?"

Good question. I sifted through Ethan's emotions. "Some, I suppose. Blackford was a mentor, of sorts. The person who set him on the path to becoming a doctor—"

"So if the Colonel *were* Blackford, you might not see that shadow clinging to him."

A beat.

"That is possible," I agreed.

"And you have to admit the current situation is oddly similar in some ways. First, the Colonel courts my grandmother only to lose her to my grandfather. Then, I show up on the scene, looking way too much like Grammy, and he loses me to you. It's like Blackford with Ethan and Caro all over again."

I couldn't argue the logic of her points. "So suppose the scenario with Blackford *is* repeating itself, it doesn't necessarily mean anything. Do you get a sense of menace from the Colonel?"

"No."

"Is Caro afraid of Blackford?"

A longer pause.

"Not really," she said. "More like concerned and worried. But he doesn't send chills up her spine. Which, I guess, kinda describes how I feel about the Colonel most of the time. Apprehensive of his motives but not skittish."

"So there's your answer."

She stopped, cocked her head.

"About the Colonel. Take the job, Claire."

"You seem eager—"

"I *am* eager. It's completely self-serving. If you take the job, you'll be in Florence for a quite a while."

"Years probably."

"Exactly. I can't think of any better place for you to be than here with me."

She laughed, that dimple beneath her eye popping. "Smooth, Mr. D'Angelo. Very smooth."

"I have my moments."

We finally reached the top of the stairs. San Miniato stood in the center of a wall of buildings, its nearly thousand-year-old marble facade gleaming. Bands of colored marble shining in the last gasp of sun.

Claire turned around, staring at the expansive view. All of Florence stretching for miles before us.

With a sigh, she leaned into me. I took shameless advantage, instantly pulling her in.

Would it always be like this with Claire? An almost helpless need to have her close? The other half I had been missing for so long.

It wasn't obsessive, per se.

Just . . . comforting. Like a hit of dopamine.

My pulse calmed. Breathing slowed. Anxiety melted away. I could conquer anything as long as Claire was at my side.

Did she have similar thoughts?

"Do you think I'll ever stop feeling like someone is following me?" she asked instead. *Not* the direction I had been going. "That tingling sensation of eyeballs staring at your shoulder blades?"

I froze. She did have a point.

I carefully scanned what I could see of our surroundings.

My nervous system moved from dopamine to adrenaline in a heartbeat.

Damn.

She was right. The man from earlier was back. I could see him in my peripheral vision, casually leaning against the stone railing to our left.

No way it was coincidental then.

I didn't recognize him, but he appeared Italian with his dark hair and Euro-trash boots.

Now what? March over and confront him?

Tempting.

How would Claire feel about that? And what if things got ugly?

I turned back around to face the cathedral, Claire pivoting with me. The man stayed in place. Observing.

What was his game?

Claire craned her neck upward, obliviously studying the ancient church.

"Why the eagle on the top, I wonder?" She pointed at the bronze sculpture perched in the center of the peaked roof.

"All of these churches were the project of some guild or another. Florence thrived on business. The guilds had a mission to out-do each other with shows of civic pride—"

"Similar to sponsoring a sports arena today?"

"Exactly. Once the monument was built, they had to pay for its upkeep."

"Like adopting a highway? Only a cathedral?"

"Yep."

Claire chuckled. "We think the world has changed dramatically over the centuries. I mean, obviously it has in some ways. But, generally, what goes around, comes around. If we were to land in Florence around 1300 A.D., I think we would find it a fairly familiar place."

I motioned for Claire to walk across the expansive gravel *terrazzo* extending in front of the church. The sunlight was fading. She passed by our would-be stalker. For his part, he studiously pretended to be enamored of the view.

I followed behind, videoing her progress. Getting some excellent footage of the suspicious man in the process. Though he kept his head averted, denying me a solid shot of his face.

"Anything?" Claire turned around, hands on her hips.

Right. I searched the people behind her for Ethan.

Nothing.

I shook my head, lowering the phone. A Japanese family rambled between me and the man, jabbering at each other. Instantly, the suspicious man stood and walked away, moving behind me.

Uffa.

"Mmmm." Claire pivoted, studying the brown brick wall in front of us. "I'm not sure this is right. Caro distinctly saw a bell-tower and a cloister."

"I think the cloister is behind this wall." I gestured in front of us.

"But the bell tower looks to be on the other side over there." She pointed in the opposite direction.

I followed her finger, grateful for the chance to glance behind me. The man was still walking away from us, aiming for the steps to the above-ground cemetery below the cathedral plaza.

Now what?

Claire moved closer. I twined my fingers through hers.

"Now what?" She unwittingly mimicked my thoughts.

I shrugged. "It doesn't help that parts of the landscape have changed over the years. Ethan saw a lot more trees."

"Yeah. Caro didn't see the cemetery in her mind's eye."

We walked back across the wide terrace, trying to reach the base of the bell tower on the opposite side.

Our mystery man was still wandering the tombs below, gazing back at us every now and again. Inadvertently, I made eye contact with him. His gaze slid past me. Practiced. Giving nothing away.

The man was clearly no amateur.

As if I needed more proof, the silvery shadows clinging to him said it all: a Mussolini-era soldier, a Risorgimento revolutionary, a *condottiero*.

I wasn't sure if that was good or bad. This clearly wasn't some jealous or lovestruck idiot.

No. This was a professional.

A chill chased my spine.

I had a feeling if I launched myself down into the cemetery after him, the man would bolt. Not to mention, running off would leave Claire vulnerable.

I motioned for Claire to walk around the entrance to the cemetery, getting more precious footage of the guy before he melted into the growing shadows.

Still no Ethan either.

Twilight had arrived, bringing more clouds with it. My video became dimmer and dimmer, despite the street lamps popping on.

Our stalker-friend merged with the gloom, disappearing. Was he gone for good? Or just lurking?

I snagged Claire's hand—because, reality check, I intended to hold her hand every possible second—and moved around the church. A stone wall blocked access to the bell tower.

Instead, we followed a narrow road to the left of the church and headed back down toward Piazzale Michelangelo, taking video in every pool of light.

No Ethan.

Just fireflies sparking in and out.

"At what point do we concede defeat?" Claire asked after surveying one last burst of video. "Maybe Caro and Ethan were never here."

"Possibly." I pocketed my phone. "Or maybe their meeting here wasn't momentous. They could have just met and bundled off together."

"Or decided last minute to meet somewhere else."

"That also. We've been freakishly lucky to see as much as we have, honestly."

Tourists were thin on this part of the mountain. We were behind the major attractions and the traffic on busy Viale Galileo was a muffled hum. The lane switchbacked gently downward, winding through a garden.

We walked in comfortable silence for a few heartbeats, holding hands. A couple of raindrops hit my face. Soft. Light. More mist than rain, to be honest.

Just us, a few street lamps illuminating trees and rosebushes, fireflies flitting and the gentle vapor of sporadic rain.

It was movie-worthy romantic—Italy at its clichéd best, almost a parody of itself—but I couldn't relax.

Claire and I were eerily alone. Too alone.

"So what's the plan now?" Claire asked.

"I think we research what we can."

"Yeah. I hate thinking that we may never know what happened to Ethan and Caro. Has Chiara found anything?"

"I'm not sure. We'll need to ask her."

The rain settled in, scattering fireflies into the sheltered darkness.

I chanced a glance behind us.

Did *not* like what I saw there.

"We'll have to discuss this later, *cara mia*." I pulled her closer to me. Steel laced my voice. "Right now, we're heading back to my place."

She looked up, brow furrowing.

"I'm sorry, Claire. Someone is following us. And I am determined to keep you safe."

CLAIRE

We pulled through the double doors of Dante's palazzo fifteen minutes later. Me plastered to his back, arms tight around his waist, both of us a little damp but no worse for wear.

Most of my shaking had stopped by the time we reached the Arno.

Someone *was* following me. Genuinely. In real life. My emotions were this volatile mix of validation and horror.

Dante caught one last glimpse of the man as we sped away from Piazzale Michelangelo. The stalker-guy standing in front of a vendor's kiosk, head swiveling as we zoomed off.

I clung to Dante until he parked the bike and I absolutely had to let go. I craved the safety of his touch.

He led me into the palazzo stairwell, but before starting up the stairs, he dragged me into his arms.

"It's going to be okay." He stroked my back—tender, kind. "We'll find out who he is. Put a tail on *him*. Make all this stop."

I nodded my head, buried in his shoulder. "Do you think it's my online stalker?"

A long pause.

Dante's chest deflated. "I honestly don't know. The man seems to be a professional."

I pulled back, alarm shooting through me.

"Define . . . *professional*. Like a mafia hit man?"

Another pause.

"No. I don't know." A weary shrug. "It just felt like this wasn't his first time shadowing someone."

"Well of course not. He's probably been tailing me from the moment I arrived here. I've felt like I'm being watched from day one."

"But he hasn't done anything, right?"

"Nothing."

"I'm not sure that comforts me. What if he's just waiting for the right opportunity?"

I wrapped my arms around Dante, snuggling closer. "For some reason, I feel like I can cope with this . . . as long as you're here . . ."

I pressed my face into his chest, absorbing the soothing thump of his heart.

This man . . . he undid me. I had been up half the night worrying over how he would react to the Colonel's job offer.

My throat still felt tight over Dante's genuinely enthusiastic support. Before today, Grammy had been my only cheerleader. How I had missed that unconditional support.

I never understood that a romantic relationship could also be a place of safety. That it *should* be a place of safety.

A space of freedom and support. A sheltered cove carved out of acceptance, affection and deep genuine friendship.

Obviously, I needed to reassess everything I thought I knew about love.

Gah. And to think I almost passed this up over fear.

I luxuriated in the warmth of him. I wasn't just *me* anymore. I had become *us*.

I didn't have to fight my battles alone. Together, we would find a solution.

Dante gave me a tight hug and then led me upstairs.

Given the weather, Nonna had set the table in her own dining room. Her apartment was old-school Italian, as Chiara called it. Dante said Nonna refused to let it be renovated and so it remained in all its circa-1960 glory. Every room branched off a long central hallway, each with a discreet purpose: parlor, dining room, kitchen, bedrooms, bathrooms. I easily counted eleven doors stretching down the hall.

The dining room was the second on the left, just past the kitchen.

Dinner was another boisterous family affair with Nonna, Judith, Chiara and Branwell.

Sensing my need for a breather from stress, Dante didn't mention our stalking issue immediately. The problem could wait for an hour or two.

"So I've been researching and researching Caro and Ethan but have yet to find anything concrete," Chiara said as Dante and Branwell cleared pasta bowls off the table. (Penne with pesto . . . I had two helpings.) They had insisted Nonna sit.

"Really?" I perked up, stroking Boney's head as he snuggled into my hand.

Boney the Rat had taken a liking to me. Not surprising, actually. I *had* always attracted troubled men.

"And?" Dante asked, bowls in his palm.

"Nothing much. Caro didn't marry Blackford—that I'm pretty confident about."

"That's a relief," I said.

"Yeah. Blackford married the only child of the Earl of Arlington in 1819 and had several children with her. Queen Victoria awarded the earldom to Blackford after his father-in-law's death."

"They did that?"

"Yeah. It was a way of getting around the whole women-can't-inherit rule. Have the crown award the same title to the daughter's husband and their subsequent children."

"Gotcha. But nothing about Ethan and Caro?"

Chiara shook her head. "Not really. Caro's mother had to have been Charlotte Stuart, Bonnie Prince Charlie's only child by a mistress. Charlotte lived in Florence for several years—nursing her ailing father—before her own early death in 1789. She could have easily had an affair that resulted in Caro during those years. It's hard to know if Prince Charlie knew of Caro's existence."

"But Henry Stuart, Charlie's younger brother and Caro's uncle, knew," I said.

"Yes. That much is obvious from Caro's memories, as you described them," Chiara said. "Henry was the one who gifted her the Michelangelo *modello*. Whether that was at his brother's behest or just out of some feeling of family loyalty, who knows. Obviously, at some point the Countess of Albany was given care of the girl. The Countess died in 1824. I managed to locate a copy of her will. There was no mention of Caro in it."

"But if Caro had eloped against the Countess' wishes, then she might have been cut off," Dante said, handing the stacked dishes to Branwell who left the room for the kitchen next door.

"That was my thought too," Chiara agreed. "From there, I've been scouring ship passenger lists. They aren't thorough for that time period. A lot has been lost over the years—"

"I highly doubt they would have used their real names if they thought Blackford or the Countess would follow them."

"Precisely." Chiara shrugged. "I haven't found a single ship manifest with their names on it."

"And Ethan?" Dante prompted.

"Not too much there, either. I did find record of his time as a student at the University of Edinburgh, as well as his graduation as a doctor of medicine. But beyond that . . . it's hard to say. I found no record of his mother or sister. We would need to visit Scotland and scour parish church records to find out more. Things like birth and death records . . . . marriages."

"I imagine looking for them in the States would be like a needle in a haystack?" Judith asked.

"I did a cursory search of the 1820 and 1830 censuses but didn't pull up anything helpful. Of course, if Ethan and Caro changed their names, then finding them among the over ten million inhabitants of early nineteenth century America is a lost cause."

Branwell brought in the *secondo*. A platter of oven-roasted pork with root vegetables.

We all dug in.

"So this is all a dead end?" I asked.

"I, for one, wouldn't mind a trip to Scotland," Dante said. "We could spend several lovely weeks digging through parish records."

"It would be a place to start," I agreed.

"True," Chiara said. "Though we may never know what happened. Some things are just lost to history."

"If only we had found something tonight," I said around a mouthful of fall-apart, divine pork.

"Yeah, about that. Why did you guys decide it was San Miniato?"

Dante shrugged. "We both saw a bell tower and a cloister on a hill outside town. San Miniato is about it for large, old monasteries on hills outside Florence."

Chiara took a bite. And then waved her hand at her brother. "But what about the Certosa?"

Dante froze, fork halfway to his mouth. He set it down with a *clink*. "You are absolutely right. I had forgotten about the Certosa."

"Certosa?" That was me.

"It's a Cistercian monastery south of town. On a hill," Chiara said.

"With a tower and a cloister. Several, in fact," Dante nodded.

"We'll have to check it out."

"Though, for the record, I still think a trip to Scotland would be fun." Dante winked at me.

The conversation lulled.

Dante and I looked at each other.

It was time to discuss the problem of our unwanted 'friend' earlier.

"So . . . Claire is being stalked," Dante began without any preamble.

"What?!" Judith and Chiara both swiveled their heads toward me.

"It's true."

Dante and I proceeded to catch everyone up to speed. The nasty texts. The sense of being watched. The man tonight.

Branwell had several intelligent questions. Chiara was suitably outraged. Judith calmly absorbed the information. Nonna smiled cheerfully and fetched the *insalata* when we were finished with our *secondo*.

Everyone gathered around as Dante played the video on his phone. The man's face was never completely clear, but we all agreed with Dante's assessment—the man was most likely Italian and gave off a strong vibe of having tailed people before.

Chiara chewed on her inner cheek, thinking.

"I know people," she said, tapping her chin. "Could you send me a copy of the video, Dante?"

He nodded.

"I'll pass it by some friends and see what I can come up with," she continued. "If he is a professional investigator or—"

"Hit man?" I supplied.

She smiled. "That is probably a little less likely, but someone is bound to recognize him if he's part of the industry. I'll get right on it."

Dante shook his head. "Sometimes your taste in friends scares me, Chiara." He tapped his phone, sending his sister the video.

"So now what?" Branwell asked.

"I don't think it wise for Claire to go back to her hotel," Judith said, rubbing Boney's head as he perched on her shoulder.

"Definitely not." Dante.

"Agreed." Branwell.

Chiara perked up, hitting me with her most energetic grin. "Yay! We get to have a sleepover!" She rubbed her hands with glee.

Dante chuckled and muttered, "Hey, that's my line," under his breath. Or maybe I was just mishearing.

"I'll make sure some toiletries are laid out in the guest bedroom." Judith rested her blue eyes on me. "We're more than happy to have you stay, Claire."

An hour later, Dante strolled into his mother's apartment.

I had just gotten the grand tour of Judith and Chiara's gorgeously restored space. Lots of exposed beams and brick coupled with ultra-modern furniture and recessed lighting.

Another successful remodel, I had to say.

I was sitting with Chiara in the living room—*salotto*, she called it—while Judith hunted me down some pajamas. Heaven knew I was at least two of Chiara; nothing in her wardrobe would come close to fitting me. Fortunately, Judith was about my height.

"I want to show you something." Dante peeked into the room, beckoning me to come.

Chiara shot me a skeptical eyebrow as I got up, but I willingly let his enormous hand engulf mine, leading me out of the apartment.

He tugged me up the last flight of stairs to the roof. Like me, Dante hadn't changed his clothes. He was still wearing designer jeans and a tight black t-shirt that hugged his shoulders and upper arms.

A blast of humid air hit me as Dante pushed open the door to the rooftop terrace. The warmth of the day lingered into night, despite the rain drumming on the tiles.

I held back in the shelter of the doorway.

Dante paused, turning back to me. His face all shadows and dark angles. Only his eyes glittered clearly.

"It's pouring." I stated the obvious.

"It is."

Silence.

His thumb brushed over the back of my hand. Soothing. Coaxing.

I could see part of the city scape beyond his shoulder, twinkling lights.

"We'll get wet." Again. Obvious.

"We will." His tone warmer now.

Another pause.

"Will you trust me?" His deep bass thrummed through my sternum. Low. Husky.

I didn't hesitate.

"Yes."

Heaven help me . . . *yes*.

His rumbling chuckle skimmed me.

"C'mon, *cara mia*. I think it's time you danced in the rain."

He tugged me onto the terrace. I instantly grabbed his arm with my free hand, partly because the terracotta tiles looked slippery but mostly to bring myself that much closer to him.

We rounded the table under its wisteria vine and then I stopped.

All of Florence lay before us. Glistening streetlights and gilded raindrops. The Duomo soared above it all, blazing through the misty darkness. Everything reflected on the terrace flagstones, long golden streaks.

It was utterly glorious.

I sighed and relaxed into Dante, lacing my fingers more firmly through his. The rain plastered my hair to my head. I brushed it back and leaned my head on his shoulder. Me drinking in my boyfriend city with the man who just might be my boyfriend.

It was all sorts of poetic.

"Do you think they were happy together?" My voice drifted in the hush.

"Ethan and Caro?"

"Yeah."

He was still caressing my hand with his thumb. "Yes. I think they were deliriously happy."

"Do you think that kind of happiness is actually possible?"

"Yes."

A few more heartbeats.

"I've never experienced it. Have you?"

"Not in this life. Not yet, at least."

"Whenever friends go on and on about how *in love* and perfect their relationships are, I have to roll my eyes. There's this stupid voice in my head that insists they must be lying."

"Such a relationship isn't impossible. My parents' marriage was like that." Another pass of his thumb. "Utterly in love."

"I thought you said they divorced?"

"No. Just separated. And it wasn't due to lack of love. My dad became more unstable the older he got. They were both concerned for our safety. Dad eventually sent us all away. He didn't want to inadvertently hurt anyone. But he always loved my mom and she him. That never changed. It was the great tragedy, I suppose. Sometimes love just isn't enough."

"I hope it was enough for Caro and Ethan."

I could almost feel Caro and Ethan trailing us, the silvery shadow of who we had been. The promise of what we might become.

By now, the rain had soaked us both. Dante's wet hair dripped down his throat. His t-shirt clinging to him like a second skin, bringing every dip and valley of his chest into sharp relief.

Damn but he was a fine specimen of a man.

Inside and out.

From somewhere below, the sound of an accordion and violin drifted up. A traditional Italian folk tune mingling with the soothing *shush shush* of traffic in the rain.

I smiled. "You think of everything, don't you?"

He turned his head . . . a question mark.

"The music." I nodded toward the street.

"Ah, yes. That. Well, we can't dance without music, can we?"

A beat.

"I'm not sure I know how."

"I'll teach you, *cara mia*."

Somehow, we weren't talking about dancing.

He wrapped his free hand around me, pulling me into a traditional dance position. His right hand snugged firmly in the curve of my lower back, left hand holding my right against his shoulder. Our bodies flush.

Slowly, he began to move us in a circle. Junior high slow dance style. Pulling me even closer with each step. The rain pattered softly around us, dripping in romantic gloom . . . the scent of wisteria and lemons and Florence.

"Is this how you dance?" I whispered in his ear. Goosebumps flared across his neck, glinting in the low light.

"With you, *cara*? Always."

He turned me in a circle, hands firm but kind.

He had been true to his promise . . . to let me set the pace for our relationship. To move at my own speed.

So . . . what was I waiting for?

I liked him.

Like-liked him.

Liked him more than I had *ever* liked any other man.

I also knew he like-liked me.

I was so tired of being watched and hunted. Of being prey.

I wanted to be the huntress.

So though I knew I was playing with fire, I pulled our linked hands down and around my back. *Hold me tighter.*

He obliged. The man was anything but dense.

I wrapped both my hands around his head. Nuzzled my nose into the space below his ear. Returning a taste of his own actions.

And then grazed my lips along his neck.

His breath hitched. Sharp. Quick.

I dragged my mouth along his jawline. My destination surely obvious.

He swallowed, adam's apple bobbing. His big frame suddenly shaking.

I brushed my lips over his. Feather soft. Rain chilled.

Dante's reaction was . . . gratifying.

His arms tightened around me justlikethat—

Banded me against him with such fierce strength, I nearly got whiplash. Claiming another, hotter kiss.

And then another. And another.

His mouth a burning brand against mine. Demanding. Hungry.

I melted, arcing into him. Just as Caro had.

My memories blended with hers . . . ours.

He tasted like Ethan. Honey-sweet. Give and take.

Each kiss was a blast of cannon fire against the walls surrounding my heart.

I hated those walls. I was so very tired of them. The sheer effort of maintaining them, patrolling them, always on guard . . .

I wanted Dante to be their keeper now.

Somehow, the rain became . . . cleansing. Purging.

Those walls crumbled in a flash of infinity—

My soul remembered this man. All of him.

More than just cognitive knowing . . . a visceral sense of . . . *us*.

We had been here before. Over and over. Countless times, experiencing this kiss.

Dante kissed me like a man drowning. First ravenous, greedy.

But gradually his kisses morphed. Softer. Savoring. Lingering.

A hand threaded into my hair, turning my head for a better angle. My own arms were around his neck, clutching his head to mine.

Finally he pulled away enough to rest his forehead against mine, heart thumping under my hands. A reflection of my own.

"You're a much better kisser than Caro," he whispered.

I chuckled. Naughty and low. "I should hope so. You certainly top Ethan."

Now it was his turn to laugh. Wicked, full of promise. "Glad to see we have improved on *something* over the last two hundred years."

"Practice does make perfect."

I popped onto my toes, slanting my mouth over his again. Warm. Intoxicating.

Would I ever get enough of this man?

He rumbled deep in his throat. A noise of pure male satisfaction.

After a while, he moved to kiss my jaw, my cheeks, my eyes . . . leaving a final lingering kiss on my bottom lip alone.

"That poor little lip." His breath a puff of air against mine. "You worry it to death."

I laughed. Carefree. Happiness fizzing through my veins.

I was Claire and Caro and a hundred other women all at once.

He was more than Ethan or Dante . . .

He was my soul. The other half I had spent an eternity of lives watching, waiting, longing . . .

Finally. At last.

I was home.

CLAIRE

I'm so happy you have decided to accept my offer, darlin.'" As usual, the Colonel rocked back on his heels, thumbs in his jacket lapels.

Dante and I were on our way to visit the Certosa but, as it was near the Colonel's villa, we had swung by. I wanted to give him word of my acceptance in person. Dante decided to wait with the car, as he could watch me enter and exit the house. It was still raining.

Staying at the D'Angelo palazzo had been . . . delightful.

And not only due to Dante's goodnight kissing skills. Though that *had* been a highpoint . . .

After Dante said goodnight (over and over), Chiara had kept me up late chatting about her latest men troubles. Turned out, she and I had a lot in common when it came to dating losers—Dante excepted, of course.

"Shall we have dinner to celebrate?" The Colonel continued. The Colonel was his cheerful self today. So far nothing weird.

It felt good, accepting the job. The money was necessary. And, even more, this job would go a long way to rebuilding my lost professional cred.

"Sure, Colonel. I would enjoy that. We could discuss my game plan for curating your collection."

And lay down some ground rules about our working relationship.

"It's a date then." The Colonel smacked his hands together.

Annnnd maybe those ground rules couldn't wait.

"Would it be alright if Dante came with me?" I asked. The question giving the Colonel a clear lay of the land, so to speak.

The Colonel paused, both eyebrows shooting upward. "Is that the way the wind is blowin'?"

I nodded. "It is."

He studied me for a moment. Let out a slow breath.

"Well, I suppose it doesn't do any harm to have him along."

"No. I think you'll appreciate his insights. It's like getting us both for the price of one."

The Colonel perked up at that thought.

"Have you considered partnering with any local museums?" I continued.

"I can't say that I know much about any of that stuff. I'm going to leave that to you professionals."

We chatted about pleasantries for a few more minutes and then shook hands. The Colonel doing his signature dual-hand-pat thing which lingered far too long.

Sigh. It was going to be an interesting working relationship, but at least he knew where I stood with anything *more* than a business working situation.

I hoped.

The Colonel and I made arrangements to have dinner the following night.

I stopped by Natalia's office on my way down to sign some paperwork.

"Congratulations, by the way," she said as I added my signature to one more confidentiality agreement. "I know the Colonel has been thrilled to add you to our team."

"Thank you." I set the pen down. "Is that all?"

"Yes, this will do it." Natalia gathered the papers together, scanning through them. "So, have you seen Dante D'Angelo lately?" The question was anything but casual.

A pause.

"He's waiting for me in the car."

Natalia's head snapped up, eyes meeting mine.

"I see." Her tone indicating that, indeed, she did.

She smiled, nice and strained and catty. As polite as could be.

We chatted for a few minutes and I made another appointment with her, as we needed to hash out a plan for working together.

That was going to be fun. I was hoping once she acclimated to Dante being with me, she would lighten up and see me more as a friend than competition.

A girl could dream.

"Oh . . . I think this is yours," Natalia said as I turned to leave.

I stared at her hand.

Or, rather, the lipstick tube in her palm.

"You left it here last week sometime." She noticed my hesitation. "The Colonel picked it up for you and asked me to make sure you got it back."

I took it gingerly from her. "Thanks."

I smiled, forced, on my way out the door, tapping the lipstick tube against my thigh.

My favorite PH lipstick, green before you put it on, perfect when worn under lemon berry lipgloss.

I had a routine. Part house make-up, part purse make-up.

I was about a hundred percent positive I had never taken the lipstick to the Colonel's. This lipstick stayed with my house make-up kit. It never ended up in my purse. At least, not intentionally. I most certainly hadn't taken it *out* of my purse.

Had it really been the Colonel who had 'found' it and given it to Natalia? Or was she going rogue? Was this part of some convoluted plot to come between me and Dante?

And why steal my lipstick and nothing else? That was just . . . weird.

And why, why, why couldn't things stay normal with the Colonel and his people for longer than just a few hours?

DANTE

I had talked Claire off the cliff by the time we pulled into the dirt field that masqueraded as a parking lot below the Certosa. The enormous medieval walls of the monastery rose sharply in front of us. Looming and imposing. The rain still lingered.

"There is no good reason for Natalia to have had my lipstick. That's all I'm saying."

"Are you even sure it's yours?"

She shot me the *uh, duh* look that all women perfect by the time they're ten. "It's this special PH lipstick you have to order from a high-end boutique in Chelsea. Trust me. It's not some random, over-the-counter Revlon—"

"Got it. So what are you going to do about it?" I pulled into an open parking space.

Silence.

"I don't know." Claire slumped back into her seat. Drummed her fingers on the center console. "I wish you could see shadows around it."

I had tried. It was the first thing I did when she sat back in the car. But . . . nothing.

"I only see dead people." My voice dry.

"Funny. Would Branwell be able to hear anything, do you think?"

"We'll ask him. It's definitely worth a try."

More silence. Rain pattered on the car roof.

"Do you think I'm being paranoid?"

I put the car in park and killed the engine. "You felt like someone might have been in your room last week."

"I brushed it off then . . ."

"Why would the Colonel be in your room stealing your lipstick? That makes no sense either."

"I know, I know." More finger tapping. "I am so tired of not understanding the Colonel's motives."

"Why not ask him?"

She turned to stare at me, eyebrows drawn down into a perplexed V.

"What? It's not a bad idea," I said.

She contemplated a moment longer. "True. I'll just have to think of a way to phrase it that doesn't sound accusatory."

"You'll come up with something."

"If only I didn't need this job so bad."

A beat.

"I am glad you took the job, Claire." I reached down and snagged her fingers with mine, keeping my other hand on the steering wheel.

"Me too." She squeezed my hand. "This whole stalker thing has just thrown me. I simply need to shove my fear under a rock and move on."

"Give yourself a break, Claire. You can't just pretend everything that scares you isn't there . . ."

She snorted. "Clearly you don't understand my *vast* capacity for denial."

I laughed, soft and low. She had a point.

I glanced around us one more time before getting out of the car.

Our stalker friend hadn't made another appearance today. So that was good at least.

The rain persisted, not a torrent but a steady enough drizzle. We dashed up the long drive to the front door of the Certosa. It was tucked in between two imposing medieval walls, one punctuated with open arches rising at an angle.

Honestly, it was like entering a medieval keep. The doors were big enough to fit a tractor-trailer. These ancient monasteries were as much a fortress as anything else. It was probably why I had forgotten about it. It always registered as more *castle* than *church*.

The Certosa didn't take reservations for tours. You simply showed up at the times listed and hoped one of the brothers decided to show you around. Italian tourism at its finest.

Fortunately, we arrived just as a tour group of retirees from York-shire walked up, so the brothers ushered us inside.

We went up a long flight of wide stairs . . . a sort of covered loggia with arches evenly spaced on the right side. The same arches we had seen from the gate below.

Talk about stairs with a view. Each archway framed the Chianti countryside. Lush and green, the hills hung with humidity and freshly-sprung spring. The smell of night-jasmine lingered. The stairs themselves dipped in the middle, evidence of thousands of feet passing before our own.

Claire clutched my hand. I paused, taking a photo of her next to one of the arches.

She looked at it over my shoulder.

"No Ethan."

We reached the top of the stairs and entered into a large piazza-like courtyard. The monastic church stood on one side, its white Baroque facade glistening in the rain. I managed to snap another photo of Claire while two elderly women argued—in their thick Yorkshire burr—over the best way to protect their hair. A scarf over the head won out.

No Ethan.

We darted across to the church piazza with the rest of the group and moved into the dark church itself. I tried to snap a photo along the short nave but got a stern '*No foto, per piacere*' from one of the monks and a hand motion telling me to put my phone away.

Claire grunted next to me and pushed me in front of her. Using my body as a shield, I guessed.

Two seconds later, she handed me her phone.

She looked darling in the corner of the photo. The Baroque interior and organ pipes behind her.

But still no Ethan.

We continued on. Through one reception gallery, and then another. Through a smaller cloister glistening with rain . . .

Still no Ethan.

I had settled on taking constant video, holding my phone low, Claire walking in front of me.

We passed out of the smaller cloister and stopped. A long flight of stairs stretched on both sides of us.

To my right, bright light streamed from doors above opening onto the enormous cloister that made up almost fifty-percent of the monastery.

I aimed my phone to the left. Down the stairs.

Something flickered in my video. Ethan was turning the corner at the bottom of the steps.

At last!

I grabbed Claire's arm, pulling her to a stop against the wall, showing her the video. The rest of the tour group moved past us, climbing the stairs upward.

Claire and I looked at each other for just half a heartbeat.

With a quick glance behind, I snatched her hand and started down the stairs, toward the arched hallway where Ethan had disappeared.

"*Fermatevi!*" A voice called behind us. "Stop. You may not go—"

I ran faster. Claire giggled.

We were two school kids running from the principal, hoping not to get caught.

Footsteps sounded behind us.

Which meant I didn't notice the exact point when the world swirled from day to night.

The point where my laughter melted, morphed, faded . . .
Panic blasted me.
Run. Faster. Ignore the pain—
He canna have her . . .

32

Caro clutched Ethan's hand, racing through the pitch-black ruin, struggling to keep her skirts from tangling in her legs and tripping them both.

They left the long arched hallway and stumbled into a larger room. Pale moonlight poured through windows high on the walls . . .

The refectory.

The old monastery was barren . . . a crumbling ghost. Napoleon had emptied it of monks years ago, leaving an aged couple as 'caretakers.' Without constant attention, however, the Italian countryside had reclaimed the building as its own.

Ethan pulled her down behind one of the enormous, refectory tables, hiding them in the deep shadows of the room.

Ethan swallowed next to her, squeezing her hand in comfort. Caro fought to still her breathing.

Silence. They could not be found.

Well. Not found *again*.

Ethan pulled her against his side, tucking her tight against him with one hand.

He carried a loaded pistol in the other. Even in the murky gloom, she caught a glimpse of its silvery metal.

She felt the puff of his breath against her cheek. The press of his lips on hers.

All will be well, it said.

She trusted him. They hadn't come this far to fail.

The night had gone well.

Up until the point it had fallen apart.

Caro had pleaded a headache an hour into the musicale, readied for bed and then waited for Mary to fall asleep. Slipping back into her clothes, she stole down the servant's stairs with a small bag in one hand and a wooden tube housing the rolled-up Michelangelo *modello* and her vellum copy in the other.

Hiring a hack, she had been dropped at the end of the long lane leading up to the abandoned Certosa. It had been a simple thing to scurry under the gate and make the steep climb to the base of the monastery walls. The bright moon lighting her way.

Full of such hope. Ethan would be there. They would *finally* begin their life together.

But Ethan was *not* there.

Not for one hour. And then two.

Caro sat on her valise, toes numb from the cold ground. Balancing the tube with both drawings on her knees to protect them from the damp. Every night noise—the hoot of an owl, bats fluttering into the eves, things scuttling in the surrounding bushes—causing her to jump.

Finally, she heard horse hooves on the road.

Hallelujah!

But wait! There were too many of them . . . it should just be a pair of horses and a small carriage . . .

She jumped to her feet, pressing herself back into the shadows.

A familiar shape burst from the surrounding bushes, pistol in hand.

"Ethan!" Her voice came out in a horrified whisper.

Something had gone terribly wrong.

The worst part?

She *still* didn't know what had happened.

He had merely grabbed her hand and tugged her into the dark ruin, Caro clutching the wooden tub with her free hand. Halfway across the huge church courtyard, she had heard shouts behind them.

"There they are!"

She had run faster, landing on tiptoe to soften the sound. Through black corridors, across several small cloisters and into the old refectory.

Now crouched behind the table, she gathered close to Ethan, pressing her face into his shoulder to muffle the pounding of her heart. Surely it could be heard at the other end of the room. She set the wooden tube at her side and wrapped her free hand around his waist.

Ethan hissed. Caro instantly loosened her grip, only to realize that her hand was wet. The smell of blood—copper, metallic—assaulted her.

Oh no! No!

"You're hurt." She dared to whisper, a breath of air in his ear.

He shook his head. *'Tis nothing.* Even his gestures had a Scottish burr to them.

Damn the man.

Caro bit her lip. Blinked away her blurring vision.

Everything would be all right. They would wait out whoever was pursuing them and then be on their way.

Footsteps echoed down the hall. Coming nearer. Nearer.

"I know you are here." A cool aristocratic voice echoed through the gloom like cannon-fire.

Blackford.

No—damn *that* man.

"I have merely come to collect that which is rightfully mine." Footsteps moved closer. "My Michelangelo and my bride. That is all I require."

Ethan pulled her tighter against him.

Peeking across his chest, Caro could see dark shadows moving in the room. She heard the click-click of flint on steel. A hiss. Something flickered and then burst into flame. Light filled the room. A torch flitted past her view.

She glanced down, more clearly seeing the red stain spreading from Ethan's waist across his shirt. How badly was he hurt?

Nausea clawed its way up her throat. Stinging.

Caro clenched her jaw.

Boom!

A refectory table across the room crashed to the floor.

"You cannot hide from me," Blackford called.

Boom! Boom! More tables went flying.

Blackford would find them. It was only a matter of time now.

There was no other door, no other way out. She counted three shadows—three men, including Blackford. Given Ethan's wound, they were armed.

Ethan had one pistol. One shot.

Understanding their odds wasn't difficult.

Caro closed her eyes. Made her decision.

Ethan tensed beside her. She shifted, leaned over him.

"I love you," she whispered. "Until the day I die, I will love you. Never forget."

She pressed her lips to his. A benediction. All the anguished yearning and longing in her soul.

"No!" Ethan grabbed at her, voice more a motion than sound.

"Love alters not . . . even to the edge of doom . . ." She breathed into his ear.

"Doona do it, lass—"

Boom! Another crash reverberated.

Caro wrapped a hand around the wooden tube with the Michelangelo drawings. Pushed away from Ethan's grasp and jumped to her feet.

"Stop!" She faced the men, knees trembling, heart pounding. But her resolve was firm.

Blackford whirled to face her. Eyes gleaming in triumph. A polished pistol in *each* hand.

Lovely.

The other two men with Blackford swung their pistols her way, leering openly.

"Enough! Here I am. Here are the sketches." She shook the tube. "Take what you see as yours."

She strode forward. Her only thought to get the men out of this room. Away from Ethan. He was a doctor. He would know better than anyone how to treat his own wound.

She just had to give him a fighting chance.

"Ah. My radiant bride." Blackford gave a mocking bow. "I am charmed you decided to join me this evening."

His tone was anything but. He bristled with outrage.

"Where is the blackguard who would keep you from me?" Blackford practically spat the words.

Dimly, Caro noted that Blackford's hauteur drifted further and further into a Scottish burr. The aristocratic mask slipping.

Caro notched her chin higher, walked a few more steps forward. "He ran the other way. Said he was looking for the back gate. I haven't seen him since."

Lie, lie, lie.

Blackford's gaze said he didn't believe her for one second.

He took three steps, closing the distance between them.

Caro's head whipped back before she heard the loud *crack* of his slap. She only barely managed to keep her grip on the tube.

The pain followed a second later. Her cheek stinging, needle sharp.

"You touch her again, and I *will* kill you." A low voice growled behind her.

Oh, Ethan.

Caro spun around, helpless to resist his gravity, even though it meant putting her back to the other men in the room.

Ethan stood like an avenging angel, pistol unwavering. Hair disheveled. Dirt smudging his cheeks. No cravat or waistcoat and his shirt open at his throat underneath his overcoat. Blood seeping across his stomach from right to left.

Everything ached for him. For them.

Please, she pleaded to whatever saint would listen. *Please grant me a life with this man.*

"Drop your weapon." The loud *snick* of pistols being primed sounded through the room. Caro could feel Blackford pressing closer to her.

Without thinking, she took several steps forward, moving toward Ethan. Blackford lunged to snatch her back. She saw his hand out of the corner of her eye at the last second. She dodged to the side, quickly placing herself closer to Ethan. Out of Blackford's reach.

She whirled to face him, meeting the Duke's eyes.

"Let us go. Here, take the drawings." She angled the wooden tube toward Blackford, almost in supplication. "They are what you truly want. We are nothing to you. Please. If you have an ounce of humanity in you."

Blackford's gaze slid to Ethan's, ignoring her plea.

"Drop your weapon," Blackford repeated, rolling his shoulders.

Ethan held steady.

"If it is me you want, I-I will come with you too." Caro swallowed.

"No!" Ethan barked behind her.

"If I go with you, will you set Ethan free?"

Blackford's lip curled in distaste.

"Ethan?" he sneered. "I do not indulge in another man's bit of muslin."

Ethan hissed.

Caro edged her chin higher. "I am hardly that sort of woman."

"Drop your weapon," Blackford said.

"Let. Us. Go."

The smallest hint of a smile touched Blackford's lips. He shifted his gun six inches to his right.

Aiming it at Caro's head.

The other two men in the room kept their weapons trained on Ethan.

"I repeat." Blackford fixed Ethan with a steely look. "Drop your weapon. I give you to the count of three. One . . ."

"Ethan, do not do it. He bluffs."

"Two . . ."

"He would not hurt me." Caro stared down the barrel of the pistol not ten feet in front of her, eyes wide but determined.

"Thr—"

Ethan's pistol clattered to the ground behind her.

Caro released a breath. Heart clawing its way up her throat.

Blackford smiled then. An unpleasant thing.

"Ah, young love." He snorted. Contempt lacing every line. "So pathetically predictable."

Blackford swung his pistol away from her head.

She saw it move. Flowing through honey. Agonizing precision.

He aimed it past her right shoulder. His finger pressed the trigger.

"Noooooooo!"

Caro jumped to her right, something slamming her in the chest.

An explosion of sound ringing in her ears.

Ethan caught her before she hit the ground. The wooden tube landing gently on her stomach.

"No! Nononono!" He frantically pressed on the wound spreading across her chest, heedless of the fresh gush of blood he felt coursing down his own leg.

"You canna do this to me." His vision blurred. He wiped his tears with a free hand.

She opened her eyes. Blue as the winter sea. Full of such adoration.

"I love you," she mouthed.

"Doona leave me. I *command* you not to leave me."

"Edge . . . of doom." She smiled then. Blinked. "Always love you . . ."

She took one stuttering breath. Another.

Pain shattered through him. Her blood pooling with his.

Her eyes fluttered closed. Her breaths shallow. Labored.

"Well. How touching." Blackford's wry voice sounded above him, edged around with a Scottish burr.

Ethan pressed more firmly on her chest, sobbing gasps wracking. The wooden tube trapped between them, forgotten.

My dearest love, m'aingeal!

"I figure we are even now." Blackford shuffled his booted feet. "You have taken something from me. And now I have taken it from you. Never forget—I always win the game."

Another loud explosion.

Something splintered the wooded tube. Pushed Ethan to the ground. The world went black.

DANTE

I am floundering in a dark sea.

Spinning. Drowning. Upended. Searching.

I have lost her. She is gone.

My soul flickers. Stutters. Stumbles.

I must find light. I must find *her*.

My love, I will protect you. We will be together.

A vise lashes my chest, crushing.

Power scours me in searing waves of black.

I fracture.

Crack.

I am Ahmose.

Egyptian. Born to poverty but risen to fame within Pharaoh's court.

Pharaoh's adviser wants my Sitre for himself. Powerful and ruthless, he will take my love from me.

I stare down the chariot racing toward me. We had hoped to escape. Somehow, someway . . . *he* has found us.

"Run, Sitre!" I scream.

She whirls to stare at me, eyes wild. Black hair billowing behind her.

"Run!"

She does run, spear in hand.

But not away. Sitre *never* runs toward safety.

No!

She dashes straight into the path of the chariot with its pounding horses, throwing herself under their hooves to save me—

No! My love . . . I have lost her . . .

Again. We will try again.

Crack.

I am Gaius.

The cliff is high as I inch closer to it. Surf pounds below.

He grins at me, maniacal, laughing. He swings a knife.

How did *he* find us? How?!

"Aurelia! No!" I scream.

She launches herself at him, knocking the knife away at the last second.

But her momentum is too much.

She snags his hand, pulling him with her as they both sail over the edge of the cliff—

No! My love . . . she is gone . . .

Again. We will try again.

Crack.

I am Wulfric.

Only my sword holds me upright.

Despite all our efforts to hide, he found us.

I stare him down, sighting along the crossbow he holds.

"Run, Sunniva!"

But she does not listen. She never heeds me.

She whirls just as he releases an arrow—

No! My love!

Again.

Crack.

I am Duncan.

How did he find us—

"Elspet! No!—"

Again.

Crack.

Again.

Again.

My soul breaks.

I am sightless and cannot find her.

Beyond. I need to move beyond.

But instead I—

Crack.

CLAIRE

How do you describe the sensation of dying?

The pain. The shock. Inky, suffocating blackness closing in.

That stretching and reaching and hoping toward a light that you're not quite sure is coming. Knowing there is no going back.

The loss of hope and future and *together*.

I hated that I hadn't seen anything past that blackness—

Had Ethan and Caro found each other in whatever stood beyond—

Wait.

I *was* Caro. Dante *was* Ethan.

They hadn't spent eternity together playing harps and dancing through puffy white clouds.

No. They had been reborn and started over again.

It begins. It repeats. Like the gypsy said on that first day in Florence.

Were Dante and I trapped in an eternal cosmic feedback loop? An old-fashioned record player . . . permanently stuck, playing the same snippet of sound over and over?

I was shattered and confused and traumatized and a thousand other emotions.

Dante and I surfaced at the bottom of the stairs, just turning into the long hallway to the refectory. Feet grinding to a halt.

Dazed. Confused.

One of the brothers yelled at us, stomping down the hallway, gesturing wildly. Dante said something in Italian, arm tight around me, dragging me with him . . .

Next I knew, I was sitting on the loggia stairs where we had first entered. Snugged against Dante's chest.

Sobbing my heart out.

Clinging to Dante like the lifeboat he was.

I cried for the life they had never lived. The 'I love yous' never shared. The children never born. All that living cut short—

Dante held me close, drawing my legs across his lap. One hand wrapped around my waist. The other cradling my head against his chest.

Both my arms were around his waist, trying desperately to drag myself closer to him. To somehow *become* him.

Something wet hit my forehead. I drew back.

His eyes molten pools of flecked chocolate.

I pulled my hand from around him and wiped the tears from his cheeks.

"He-he didn't tell her . . . in that moment—" Dante's voice broke.

"Wh-what?" I hiccupped.

"Ethan." He stroked a finger down my cheek. "He did—H-he didn't say 'I love you' before she died—"

Oh!

"But he loved her. He l-loved her so m-much—"

"Oh, Dante. She knew. I know she did."

I cupped his cheek and arched up.

He met me in the middle.

It was grief and need and *hallelujah-I'm-alive-and-with-you*—

I tasted his tears. Reveled in the feel of his mouth on mine. Ached for what had never been. Yearned for what could come.

Love . . . the breaking of your soul upon my lips . . .

Somehow, I was Caro and Claire and an eternity of other women . . . all who had loved this man.

I surrendered entirely to him. To us.

We kissed for an indecently long time.

And then Dante held me. Cradled into his shoulder. Tenderness and security.

Still sitting on those stone steps, worn with the footsteps of countless others before.

Both of us stared through the arched loggia to the countryside beyond. Water dripping on the stretching vineyards and olive orchards, rain tamping down the hanging humidity. Streaks of sunlight broke through here and there on the horizon.

The Yorkshire group murmured as they left through the doorway below the loggia.

Dante's heartbeat thrummed firm and steady under my ear.

I closed my eyes, reveling in the safety of him. How fully I had let him deep inside my walls . . . into my heart.

This man *was* my heart.

"I'm never letting you go." His lips brushed my hair. "Just thought I ought to warn you."

"Good. Cause I'm never leaving."

His arms clutched me tighter.

Anger pulsed behind my grief.

Blackford. He had killed them.

I cuddled closer, wiping my eyes.

"Should we be worried about history repeating itself?" My voice muffled against Dante's chest.

"Yes." Not a trace of hesitation.

I pulled back. Surely my eyes wide.

He brushed hair off my cheek. "As I came out of the regression, I saw more . . ."

"More?"

"Other lives. I saw a similar scenario playing out over and over."

"With Blackford?"

"I can only suppose it was him. His soul. Life after life, a man threatened us—someone we knew who had been hunting us—and, like Caro, you sacrificed yourself to protect me. Every. Single. Time."

A ghastly *zing* shuddered through me.

"A cosmic feedback loop," I whispered.

He nodded. "I-I watched you die so many times—" His voice choked. "You're not allowed to do that ever again, do you understand?" He shook me.

"You . . . you think it will happen again?"

He swallowed. "I don't know for sure. But logic says there's a good chance it will. There is a reason why you have no shadows for me. I have loved you life after life. But has every one ended like this?"

"Who knows." I closed my eyes. "The Colonel . . . everything with him being so weird. But if he *is* Blackford reincarnated—"

"—then his behavior makes a bit more sense in a jealous, possessive sort of way."

"The Colonel is an old man. How could he possibly think that I would be into him in that way?"

"Are you saying that Blackford was rational?"

A beat.

"What should we do? Go to the police, press charges against the Colonel—"

"With what though?" Dante shifted. "His behavior has been bizarre and the whole thing with your lipstick is . . . disconcerting, but it's all circumstantial. He hasn't actually done anything wrong."

"It's only in the context of Caro and Ethan and other past lives that he seems sinister."

"Exactly. We need more proof."

"Agreed, but that will take time," I countered.

"As long as we stay alive, we'll have all the time we need." Dante pushed to his feet, pulling me up with him. He glanced through the loggia to the monastery entrance below.

Froze. Hissed.

"What?" I was instantly at his side.

A dark haired man in a leather jacket stared up at us.

"You—!" Dante barked, pointing a finger.

The man took two quick steps back, and then turned, quickly retreating down the road toward the parking lot.

Dante didn't pause.

He grabbed my hand and ran down the stairs, intent on going after the man.

"Dante! No!" I stumbled after him, my feet clumsy. "Wait!"

I pulled on his hand, forcing him to stop.

He whirled on me.

"Don't!" I said. "We don't know who that man is or what will happen. He could have a gun and be waiting for us around the next corner. We need to be smarter this time."

Dante regarded me, chest heaving. He scrubbed his free hand through his hair.

"You're right." He nodded. Brought my hand up for a kiss. "You're so right."

"From this point on, we're cautious. Unlike other lives, we know what might happen. We can anticipate."

He stared at me but not really. Lost in thought.

"We need to leave. Go undercover, as it were," he finally murmured. "The Colonel has no power over us. This isn't the nineteenth century, after all."

He tugged on my hand, walking again but slowly. Wary. Watchful.

"Exactly," I said. "I cut all ties with him. We go on the lam. How many more years will the Colonel live anyway?"

"Yeah. We just have to wait him out."

"Precisely."

We walked back to the enormous entrance doors. Careful. Calm. Eyes sharp and looking for anything suspicious.

Dante paused before we rounded the wall to the parking lot. Several tourists gave us distrustful looks as he clung to the stone, peering around the corner, meticulously surveying the parked cars.

"He appears to be gone." Dante pulled me forward, always keeping his body between me and the rest of the world.

I didn't breathe until we were snugged into his BMW sedan and pulling onto the highway outside the Certosa.

"Why do I feel like my life just changed forever?" I asked.

Dante snorted. "Because it just did, *cara mia.*"

The rain had started back up, drumming against the car roof.

"How will we live?" I looked back at the Certosa towers receding behind us. "I was planning on the Colonel's job to pay my bills."

"Don't worry about it. I have money put away. We'll be okay. We just have to survive this round."

"It's always a game, isn't it?"

"Yeah. But, this time, *I* intend to win."

DANTE

I couldn't bear the thought of Claire checking out of her hotel. Even that much brought her too close to the Colonel.

My mom and Branwell went over and gathered her things, telling the staff Claire was going on a getaway weekend and would be back in a few days.

Lie and bluff.

Anything to keep her—us—safe.

Branwell, bless him, had listened to objects in Claire's room, trying to find something. But aside from Claire and members of the staff, he didn't hear anything unusual.

Most certainly not the Colonel cackling maniacally about capturing Claire for himself.

Not that any of us expected that. But it would have been convenient.

I had never heard of the Colonel acting as erratically as the man in my fractured visions, but Ethan had never suspected Blackford of such violence either.

Who are we, really, deep down inside? Do we ever even know ourselves?

How soon before the Colonel realized we were on to him? Then what?

Part of me wanted to get my brothers, a few of Tennyson's army friends and march over to the Colonel's and confront him.

How dare he reduce my life to one of fear and hiding?

But I could just see it happening all over again. Me confronting the Colonel. Him drawing a gun from his pocket. Claire showing up, unexpectedly, throwing herself between me and the bullet—

Too raw.

Too vivid. Too soon.

The memory of Ethan watching Blackford's bullet strike Caro through the heart. Knowing instantly that her wound was fatal. Watching her die, life after life—

No. Not this time. Not Claire. Not me.

This life was *mine*.

"Did Branwell hear anything else?" Claire asked as I strode into the large *salotto* of my apartment.

Claire sat on a couch near the windows, rimmed by light from the setting sun. Gold bathed the room. My mom stood by a chair near the doorway. Chiara was in the kitchen, talking to someone on the phone in staccato Italian. Branwell was back in his room; I could hear him moving around.

I crossed over to Claire and handed her the tube of lipstick.

"No. He listened to it long and hard one more time. He just heard the Colonel ask, 'Did you get it?' and then rustling noises. You talking, music playing—"

"The normal sounds of me putting on make-up."

"Yeah. Nothing more."

"Are we sure the Colonel didn't insert a tracking device into the lipstick?" Mom moved around to sit in the chair.

"Pretty sure. But Branwell has a good solution if he did."

Tension stretched thin between us all—rubberbands pulled too tight.

"*Uffa!*" Chiara bounded into the room, wagging her phone in my direction. "That was my guy. You're not going to like this."

"What?" Claire stood and slid her hand into mine. Warm. Soothing.

Chiara grimaced. "He got a match for your stalker. He's a private investigator named Salvatore."

"Just a PI? Nothing more?" I asked.

"Yeah. Apparently a friend of a friend of a friend is cousins with him. I called in about twenty different favors and found out who hired Salvatore to tail you—"

"Let me guess," Claire said.

"Yep. One Kyle Finster-Cline."

"The Colonel," I sighed. "I guess that's solid proof then."

"Can we go to the authorities now?" Claire nestled herself against my side. "Resolve this?"

My sister shook her head. "Hiring a private investigator to trail someone isn't illegal. And, from what we can tell, this Salvatore has played by the book."

"But someone must have broken into my hotel room, despite Branwell not hearing anything. There's no way I left my lipstick at the Colonel's—"

"It's weird. I agree." Chiara tapped her phone against her cheek. "But without any police-reportable proof of a break-in and no harm done, it's going to be hard to build a case. Let me do more digging."

"Be careful." I shot my sister a firm look.

She smiled, imp and mischief. Enjoying this situation far more than she should.

Crack.

We all jumped as the front door opened, every head swiveling toward the doorway into the foyer.

Tennyson walked in.

He scanned the room and landed on me.

"Tenny—" My mom stood and crossed over to him, wrapping him in a huge hug.

His blue eyes met mine. All too knowing.

My mom fussed over Tennyson, who shot me long-suffering looks as if to say, *Look what I go through to help you.*

After everyone said hello, Tennyson nodded at me.

"A word." He jerked his head and walked back into the foyer.

I followed.

He stood in the corner, bending to pick up a small, black duffel bag.

How much did he really see? He only ever talked about emotions, but—

"You want to tell me what's going to happen?" I asked.

"You're going to need this." He swung the bag in my direction. "It's for you and you alone."

"Tenn—"

"Claire can't know you have it. That's extremely important."

My head jerked back. "But why shouldn't she know—"

"I'm not sure. I don't know what is going to happen. I just . . . understood . . . enough to bring you this and tell you what I sensed."

"But how?"

"You know I can feel things for you and Branwell over larger distances. Something about us being womb-buddies." He held up his free hand. *Stop.* "Don't you dare say *womb-mates*; I might have to hurt you."

That made me smile.

"Then . . . thank you." I took the bag from him, placing it behind a console table in the foyer.

He grabbed me, pulling me into a tight bear hug, thumping my back.

"Be safe."

I nodded.

Branwell walked out of his room and up the hallway, tugging on the sleeves of his shirt. He stopped in front of us in the foyer.

Cocked an eyebrow.

Tennyson raked his eyes up-and-down, taking in Branwell. Then turned back to me. "Ya know . . . it really can be uncanny."

"Really and truly." I agreed.

We walked back into the *salotto*. All three of us.

Claire looked up from the couch, darting looks between Branwell and myself.

"Wow. I mean, I know you two are identical, but—"

I gave Branwell a thorough head-to-toe go-over. "He cleans up real good, doesn't he?"

For his part, Branwell just sighed and scrubbed a hand through his hair. An un-gloved hand through hair that now looked identical to my own.

He had shaved his beard down to mere scruff. He was wearing clothes from my closet—designer jeans, cream button-down, corded sports coat. I would probably find small cuts in the clothes where he had altered them to control their sound . . .

To say we looked the same was an understatement. Even I thought he was me . . .

"So what's the plan here?" Tennyson asked. "I feel like I'm always late to the party."

"Well, it should be obvious." Branwell held his hands out, clearly not liking having to abandon his gloves. "I'm Dante. Dante will become Branwell."

Tennyson eyed me. Noting my regular jeans and t-shirt.

"I'm not Branwell yet." I planned to raid his closet tonight

"Yeah. I still need to work my magic." Chiara sank into a chair, curling her feet underneath her. "Dante's hair isn't as long as Branwell's . . . was. But I have a clip-in extension we can fashion into a man bun and, after a week of no shaving, Dante's beard will have filled in enough to be believable."

"Okay . . ." Tennyson paused, obviously waiting for an explanation. "So . . ."

"The plan is simple." I walked over to the couch and sat down next to Claire. Loving how she instantly curled into my side. "Tonight, Mom will put on a blond wig and get into my car with Branwell. Mom is tall enough to pass for Claire and Branwell will be me. They'll head south. Hopefully, if the Colonel still has Salvatore or someone else trailing us, that person will assume Claire and I are going to spend some time together outside of town."

"We should take the lipstick tube with us." Branwell nodded toward Claire. "Just to be on the safe side."

"Agreed." That was Claire.

"For my part," I continued, "I will dress up like Branwell tomorrow morning. Claire will hide herself in the back of Branwell's VW bus, and we'll head west and north, toward Milan and France. Anyone seeing me leave will just assume it's Branwell headed off by himself."

Tennyson nodded. "That's not a bad plan."

"I just hope it works," my mom said, heading for the door.

I chatted with my brothers and sister for a while longer, everyone settling on their part.

I tamped down my anxiety . . .

We would be okay. Somehow, someway . . . this life would be different.

Eventually everyone drifted out of the room, leaving Claire and me alone.

She sighed and twisted, snuggling her body tighter against mine.

I held her close, reveling in her beating heart. The softness of her. The incredible joy of just . . . quietly being.

We would be together. She and I.

She nuzzled my neck. "Thank you." Her voice low.

I pulled back. Tilted my head. My face a question mark.

"Thank you for insisting on . . . *us*." Claire traced my jaw with one finger, leaving a trail of goosebumps. "For not allowing me to stay nestled in my shell. Despite everything right now, these past couple of days have been some of the best of my life."

"Claire . . . *cara mia*." I cupped her face with a hand, ran a thumb over her petal-soft cheek. "I'll always be the one who fights for you, babe."

She smiled then. A small, weak thing. "No matter what happens—"

"Nothing is going to happen, Claire. We're going to live a long and happy life together."

"In hiding?"

"If that's what it takes. It will be okay, *cara mia*."

Her blue eyes searched mine.

"Of course," she finally whispered. But her tones spoke of doubts. Worry.

She swallowed.

"But if something bad does happen, I just wanted to make sure you knew—"

"*Nothing* is going to happen, Claire."

I pulled her head to mine, helpless to resist the lure of her plump lips. I kissed her gently, savoring the pillowy give of her mouth.

Her reaction was gratifying. Her body instantly rising, melting into mine. Hand threading into my hair, refusing to let me pull away.

I loved it when she got possessive.

"You're mine, you know," she murmured between kisses. "Don't forget it."

See? Possessive.

Loved it.

I stubbornly refused to entertain any doubts.

This life was going to be different.

It had to be.

36

CLAIRE

The texts started after the phone calls.

Dante and I were driving again. Or, at least, trying.

We had left Florence about mid-morning, me snuggled in the back of the VW bus. Dante driving in Branwell's bulky homespun clothes. His hair in a pretend man-bun.

Unfortunately, the VW bus turned out to be as unreliable as it was awesome.

Loud, noisy, stinking of diesel . . . An hour into our drive, it had died just off the highway outside Empoli.

Telling me to stay put in the back, Dante buried himself under the hood and managed to get the bus running again.

We were now chugging away, heading generally westward. Though the poor bus sputtered every other minute.

"C'mon, baby." Dante patted its vinyl dash. "You can do it."

According to Branwell, Dante needed a more gentle touch to keep the bus going. Dante felt the bus should have received better maintenance. They went back and forth every five minutes about it on the phone.

I sat in tense silence in the back, hating that the strain of our situation was bleeding into Dante's relationship with his brothers.

Which was why I didn't immediately tell Dante about the voice mail messages.

First . . . the Colonel. Pleasant. Cheery.

Hey darlin'. Haven't heard from you today. I'm still planning on dinner with you and Dante this evening—

His voice scattered chills down my back. Not going to happen.

He left another message an hour later.

Claire, darlin', is everything okay? I called the hotel, and they said you had checked out for a couple of days. Is Dante with you? I'm worried. Please call me.

Right. He was worried I was declining to be his kept trophy-woman. Next up? My mom.

Claire, honey. I just got a frantic call from the Colonel. He says you've disappeared. Are you okay?

Nice. He was now playing my poor mom.

I texted her—short and sweet—letting her know I was fine. Told her to ignore the Colonel. I was suddenly glad she was thousands of miles away and out of the Colonel's immediate reach.

And then, more Colonel.

Claire, why aren't you returning my calls? I'm truly concerned. I desperately need to talk to you. There are so many things I need to say, and I'm worried you're in danger. Please call me.

The man was a good actor, I'd give him that.

But, seriously, how did he know I was in danger unless he was the one putting me there?

Then the harassing texts started. Each creepier than the last.

Where are you headed, Claire?
I know you're with that big ape.
Don't think you can escape me. You will be mine and mine alone.

I finally stopped looking down each time my phone buzzed.

The VW bus struggled valiantly, limping onward. Lurching. Misfiring. Dante coaxing it along to no avail. It finally died just outside Pisa.

In the town of Cascina, to be exact.

Irony, you say? Fate, perhaps?

Indeed it was.

Dante managed to pull off the highway before the car sputtered to a stop, coasting off the road and onto the edge of a corn field.

Cascina was a small, sleepy hamlet. Just as it had been over six hundred years earlier when the famous battle was fought there in the shadow of an abbey. The walls of a church and bell tower loomed up the road. The Arno river rolled sluggishly beyond.

A quick consultation of Google maps clarified what I had already guessed.

I was staring at the walls of the Abbey of San Savino. The very site of the old battle.

I swallowed.

In my research of the Michelangelo drawing, I had read up about the battle. The Pisan and Florentine forces had clashed on the plain between the Arno river and the abbey. Slowly, the Florence mercenaries drove John Hawkwood and his knights back and back, trapping them against the abbey walls. Hawkwood had finally given up the field, retreating inside the abbey sanctuary, leaving many of his Pisan foot-soldiers to the mercy of hostile Florentines.

Only the church remained open to the public. The rest of the abbey had been converted into apartments long ago. Ahead, I could see a small gravel parking lot next to the entrance to the church—several cars and a large tour bus with people milling about.

Dante set his phone down and turned around to look at me.

"Tennyson is coming. He was already on his way when I called. We'll swap this hunk of metal for his Jeep, which should hopefully hold together better. Why my brothers insist on driving these stupid vintage cars—"

He stopped himself. Tapped his fingers on the steering wheel. Let out a steady breath.

I've always thought you can tell so much about a person by how they handle stressful situations. Do they lash out at those around them? Do they yell?

Or do they calmly just do what can be done and let the rest go?

Dante clenched his jaw and then shot me a determined smile.

"Tenn will be here in about an hour," he said.

I nodded. And then motioned toward the bell tower with my chin.

"You realize that's San Savino, right?"

Dante swiveled, peering through the windshield. Grunted.

We both stared out. It was one of those picture-perfect Tuscan days. Blue sky, a light breeze. Temperature a balmy seventy-five degrees.

It was still a little trippy to see Dante in his Branwell get-up. Longer hair, more scruff, less tailored clothes. But I would know him as Dante no matter how he dressed or groomed. There was just something elemental that marked him as *my* man.

Yep. That's how far I had come.

He was mine. And I was going to fight to the death—literally, if necessary—to keep him.

Corn stalks and grapevines rose on either side of us, lining the road to the abbey just ahead. Typical Italian apartment blocks dotted the edges of the fields . . . stuccoed squares of cream, yellow and orange with terracotta roofs. The Italian version of a suburb.

My phone vibrated. Stupid me, I looked.

I will hunt you to the ends of the earth, Claire. Haven't you learned by now?

A pause . . . and then . . .

I ALWAYS win the game.

My adrenaline spiked. I may have actually whimpered.

Dante's head whirled at the sound.

I angled my phone, finally showing him the texts.

He stared at the words and then swore. Impressively and at length.

"I hate us sitting here like damn ducks waiting to be picked off—"

His voice cut off as he glanced in his driver's side mirror. Swore again.

"How did he find us so fast?!"

I looked out the back window just in time to see a dark haired man in a black leather jacket stop his motorbike behind the VW bus.

Salvatore.

"I'm not going to passively sit here." Dante jerked a chin toward the abbey ahead. "Let's at least surround ourselves with other people."

He opened his door at the same time I did, both of us tearing down the street toward the abbey and its touristy church.

"*Fermatevi!*" A male voice shouted.

"Like *hell* I'm stopping," Dante grunted at my side.

Dante reached out a hand as we ran, wrapping mine in his. Sprinting toward the apparent protection of the walls ahead. If nothing else, there was some modicum of safety in numbers. Witnesses.

I might end up dead, but at least my killer wouldn't get away with it, right?

The huge walls of the old abbey loomed larger.

My lungs burned. Feet pounding the pavement. Caro and Ethan had run like this, trying to escape, but it had been futile in the end . . .

No! I mercilessly pushed the thought aside. This wouldn't happen again—

He would *not* win this time.

I risked a glance back. Salvatore was chasing us on foot. I didn't stop to wonder why he hadn't jumped back on his bike.

As we ran, Dante dialed a number, phone to his ear.

"*Pronto? Pronto?!*" he said. "*Ho un'emergenza . . .*"

He rattled away in Italian, voice sharp and edged.

We reached the gravel parking lot, slowing as a large group of Germans exited the abbey churchyard, making their way back to the tour bus.

"The police are on their way." Dante panted, pocketing his phone. "The emergency operator said to wait in front of the church."

Salvatore had reached the parking lot too. Threading our way through the people, we dashed up a long flight of medieval stairs covered in an aged barrel vault. The stairs opened into a small piazza, an ancient church directly ahead.

People milled around the piazza, taking photos. My chest heaved, lungs searing. Was this to be our life then? Hunted? Haunted?

Dante tugged me across the tiny piazza, stopping before the church entrance. I whirled us around and grabbed my own phone from my pocket.

If something was going to go down, I intended to have video evidence.

I trained my phone on the stairs leading up from the parking lot and hit record. Dante wrapped a protective arm around my waist, pulling me tight against him with one hand.

We both tensed. Waiting. Compulsively looking for Salvatore's dark head to pop-up the stairs.

I glanced down at the video I was recording and nearly dropped my phone.

Bloody hell.

I had forgotten to select the rear-facing camera. Instead, I was taking video of myself. And, by extension, the church behind me.

Dante heard my gasp. Glanced down in alarm.

I pointed at the video still recording.

A knight leaned against the stone facade. Literally a knight in shining armor. Breastplate. Broadsword. Helmet raised.

Staring straight at us.

"*Madonna mia!* What the hell next?" Dante asked.

"Who is he?"

"English. Late fourteenth century," Dante said. I stared at him him. "What? I'm an encyclopedia when it comes to historical clothing."

"True." I dared a glance at the wall behind us. No knight. "I'm ignoring the ghost knight." I tapped my phone screen and swiveled the video to front facing. Trying to hold the camera steady despite my shaking fingers.

People were filtering out of the courtyard. In the distance, I could hear the *bee-doo bee-doo* of sirens.

We waited another breath. Two.

No Salvatore.

Where was the man—

"Claire! Woman!"

A voice sailed up the entrance stairs and into the church courtyard where we stood.

An all-too familiar voice.

How did *he* know where I was?!

Dante's arm clenched around me.

Pierce Whitman's brown head popped up the stairs, grin friendly.

"Pierce." My mind whirled, trying to piece the puzzle together. "What are you doing here?"

He stopped at the top of the staircase. Taking me in, obviously videoing. Dante with his arm cuddled protectively around me.

Why was he here?

"I was here doing some research on the battle and saw you guys go tearing past." Pierce kept walking toward us. "It seemed like something was up."

My heart was trying to beat out of my chest.

"Is everything okay with you and D'Angelo?" Pierce paused, eyes narrowing. "I saw the Colonel pull into the car park, by the way. He looked a little frazzled. What gives?"

Wow. And I thought my heart had been beating fast just ten seconds before?

Footsteps sounded on the stairs, echoing up the barrel vault. Involuntarily, I took a step back, still videoing. Dante released my waist and held his arm out, protecting me.

The police sirens sounded closer and closer. *Bee-doo. Bee-doo.* Would they get here in time?

This was *not* happening. Not to us. Not again.

Pierce frowned. "Claire? You've gone white as a ghost. What's up?" He moved toward us.

"Stay back." Dante barked. "Just stay away."

"What the hell?!"

"Claire? That you, darlin'?" The Colonel's voice drifted into the courtyard.

I took another step back, Dante edging in front, shielding me with his body. Always my personal bodyguard.

I peeked around his elbow, ensuring my camera captured any action.

Pierce stared at us both, some unidentifiable emotion on his face.

Bee-doo. Bee-doo.

The Colonel's bushy head popped up the stairs. Salvatore's dark one right behind.

Reflexively, I jumped back.

"Claire!" the Colonel shouted. "Be carefu—"

Too late.

The world swirled around me.

Too late. I fear I am too late.

Please . . . I simply must find him.

Elizabeth stared across the spent battlefield.

The smell of blood and smoke. Scorched earth, tattered banners, bloating horses. Flies swarming in droves. A simmering cauldron of death, festering under the boiling summer sun.

The desolate aftermath of war.

"You mustn't be here, niece. We must retreat." A hand tugged at her elbow.

Elizabeth turned to Uncle Richard at her side. His face haggard. He had already spent hours searching the dead for Hawkwood's fallen.

"Edward isn't among the living or the dead, Uncle. You and I both know Sir Henry. Out of spite, he has hindered those who would look for Edward. 'Tis a sin before God to leave a noble knight like Sir Edward to die like a common pikeman."

She wiped a hand across her eyes and then picked up her skirts, moving to step over another fallen soldier who was not her Edward.

Uncle Richard held her fast. "He is not yours, child. Not Edward. Not now—"

"Silence! I will not hear such th-things. He must still lie upon the battlefield. There is no other place he *could* be—"

Her voice broke as she wrenched her arm out of her uncle's grasp, darting away.

She would find him. Edward.

He was hers. Her heart. Her soul.

No matter what her father and Hawkwood demanded. No matter that she must wed Sir Henry and leave Italy and Edward behind, returning to London.

She would find Edward first. Ensure he was cared for, tended to . . .

The thought of him still lying in this hot sun, wounded . . . surely boiling from the inside out in the heat of his armor . . .

She could bear anything, any future, if somewhere on the planet Edward yet breathed.

Men groaned around her.

"Acqua."

"Please help me, Miss"

"Aiutame, per carità."

Elizabeth wiped her cheeks again and again.

"Elizabeth, come back." Uncle Richard tried to keep up with her.

She ignored them all. And instead called to *him*.

"Edward. Edward Lancey!"

Finally, approaching the tall stone wall of the church, she caught a glimpse of a familiar shield. A torn banner fluttering nearby.

He lay just beyond. A heap of twisted metal, limbs askew at unnatural angles.

Oh, Edward.

On a sob, she sank to her knees, touching his beloved cheek. His face was battered and bleeding. Chest rising in shallow pants. He had managed to tug off his helmet and loosen his breastplate.

She fumbled for the water skin at her waist, pouring a few drops onto his parched lips.

"Edward, my love," she hiccupped. "P-please."

He opened his eyes. Those dark eyes she adored so well.

The agony of his smile . . . the welcome in his gaze.

"Eliza . . . you are here." His voice a thread of sound. "I-I am so glad you have come. Now I can rest in peace."

"No. You will live. Uncle Richard is near. He will send for a pair of Hawkwood's squires. They will see you safely inside the abbey."

She moved to fetch help.

His hand caught hers.

"Stay." No more than a whisper. "I would hear you."

She collapsed next to him, unable to resist.

"Darling, you will be well—"

"No, dearest love." His voice rasped.

"Edward, you will *live*! I cannot—"

"Such a touching scene." A dry voice sounded behind her.

No! Not now!

She whirled to her feet. Swallowed.

"My lord." She curtsied to Sir Henry Marchall. Favored knight to John Hawkwood. Close friend to her father.

The man she was betrothed to marry.

He had changed out of his armor, cleaned himself of the terror of war.

Left Edward to rot in the sun.

Sir Henry was a man of little honor.

"You should not be here, Miss Elizabeth." Sir Henry rolled his shoulders. A well-known sign of his agitation. "I am deeply troubled by your presence."

Elizabeth kept her chin down but her voice betrayed her anger.

"I have been searching for Sir Edward, as you can see. He is wounded and in need of care."

"Yes, indeed. I ken quite clearly what is afoot here." Another shoulder roll.

Her head snapped to attention at the slithering *snick* of a sword being unsheathed.

She eyed the enormous broadsword Sir Henry held with trepidation.

"What mean you, my lord? The battle is finished."

Sir Henry held her gaze for a moment, a smile tugging on his lips.

"I will not be made a fool, Elizabeth. You are mine and mine alone."

The sword raised.

"Noooooooo!" she screamed, hurling herself, chest first, onto Edward.

Something pierced her back. Her breast. Edward heaved, arching upward.

The broadsword pinned them together.

Edward's brown eyes held hers.

"—love you—" she gasped with the last air in her lungs.

One heartbeat.

Two.

And then the black void claimed them both.

DANTE

Not. Again.
    Damn it all to hell.

Never. *Never.* Again.

I surfaced from the regression, shaking. I kept a firm arm out, praying Claire stayed behind me.

My eyes swung between Pierce and the Colonel.

The Colonel. Impassive. Cautious. Drawing near.

Pierce frozen . . . eyes narrowed. Intent.

Back and forth. Surely one of them . .

Pierce rolled his shoulders. Agitated.

And in that simple motion . . . I *knew.*

You! It's been you all this time.

My soul *finally* recognized his.

Pierce swiveled back and forth between Claire and I, swallowing, shoulders rolling again.

A gun appeared in his hand, shaking. The damn idiot was going to shoot us out of nerves alone.

I had been stupidly blind.

Claire moved a little.

"Stay behind me, *cara mia*. Please. We need to break this pattern."

Her phone edged into my peripheral vision, still recording. Good.

Bee-doo. BEE-DOO.

The police sirens drew closer. Even better.

"What just happened? Am I hallucinating?" Pierce almost whimpered. "I've heard the stories about you."

The Colonel approached to my left behind Pierce. Snowy white hair. Icy blue eyes. Apprehensive.

Funny how you don't understand the truth until too late.

Salvatore carefully moved next to the Colonel, coiled and ready to pounce.

"What did you just do to me?" Pierce backed up pivoting enough to take in the Colonel and Salvatore too, shaking his gun.

Not good.

"Calm down, Pierce." I was going for soothing first. "You don't want to hurt us. You don't want to hurt Claire."

His eyes narrowed. He stared at her behind me.

Okay, so maybe mentioning Claire hadn't been my best idea.

"She's mine." He hissed. "You can't have her. She's always been mine—"

"Excuse me?" That was Claire. I could hear the fear in her voice, but she spoke strongly. "I d-don't belong to anyone, least of all you. You threw me away—"

"You were supposed to get jealous," he screamed, waving the pistol. "You were supposed to beg me to take you back—"

"Newsflash, Pierce," she retorted, moving a foot to my side. "That only works in bad, made-for-TV melodramas—"

"How could you take up with big, stupid D'Angelo here?" Pierce sneered, aiming the gun back at me. "I've watched you, Claire. Walking through town, holding hands with him. Hugging him. Staying in his palazzo—"

"Wait—how do you know that?" she asked, coming forward even more.

Stay back, Claire. Stay behind me, I mentally pleaded.

"He had a tracking device placed in your phone, Claire." The Colonel edged cautiously closer. "That's one of the things I've been trying to tell you. Why I kept calling this morning. I hired Salvatore here to help keep you safe—"

"Shut up, old man!"

The gun trembled more violently in Pierce's hands.

The sirens became deafening. *BEE-DOO. BEE-DOO.*

Car tires crunched on the gravel in the parking lot. *Hurry!*

"Let it go, boy." The Colonel said to Pierce. "There are witnesses here. Claire is recording this. You don't want to hurt anyone."

Pierce stared at me. Shot a glance at the Colonel. Fixed on Claire now at my side.

"You don't understand, Colonel. I *do* want to hurt them."

We were frozen. A terrible tableau.

What good was a psychic gift if it couldn't help you save the one you loved?

Knowing who someone had *been* wasn't the same as knowing what they *would* do.

I still believed in free-will. The past didn't determine my future.

I would have given everything to have Tennyson's Sight for just a fraction of a second—

Tennyson. Of course.

Of course!

Duh!

This time *was* different than all the others. This life, thanks to our family gift, I *knew* what had happened. And if things played out like they had, life-after-life, then I understood how this would go down.

And knowing what *could* occur allowed me to make a different decision. Tennyson had prepared me for it.

Everything happened at once.

"I don't do D'Angelo sloppy-seconds," Pierce hissed. "I will *win* this game!"

Pierce's gun tracked, aiming for me.

"No!" Claire cried out, moving involuntarily. Intent on throwing herself between me and danger.

Ready to die to protect.

But I was already in motion. Having anticipated what would happen.

Instead of focusing on Pierce, I concentrated on Claire.

As soon as she shifted, I moved with her. Keeping my body between her and Pierce.

Not allowing her to sacrifice herself for me.

A retort fired just as my body crossed in front of hers.

"Noooooooo!" Claire screamed.

Something hit my chest. Hard. Knocking every last ounce of air from my body.

I slammed to the ground.

CLAIRE

Dante collapsed in a crumpled heap, arms clutching his chest.

"*NOOOO!*" I screamed, dropping my phone. Tears blinded. "No! Dante, my love! My heart—"

"Your *achy breaky heart?*" Pierce's snide voice sounded beside me.

I whirled.

My vision went red. Rage pounded through me.

How dare this man steal my future. Again.

Dimly, I noted Salvatore lunging to take down Pierce.

But I beat him to it.

I swatted the gun out of Pierce's hand, sending it skittering.

I was a thousand-pounds of fury.

And I went full-banshee on his sorry ass.

I kneed Pierce hard in the groin, sending him to the ground. And then I was on top of him.

Jabbing, scratching, biting, pulling.

Sobbing. Hysterical.

Never more grateful in my life for my own size and height and his lack of it.

"You will n-never t-take anything from me AGAIN!" Screaming. Berserk.

I raked my nails across his face. Punched him in the eye.

"GAME. OVER."

Salvatore hauled me off Pierce at that point, pushing me aside. He flipped Pierce and pinned his hands behind his back with ruthless efficiency.

Three police officers ran up the stairs, instantly converging on Salvatore and Pierce, everyone jabbering in Italian at once.

I staggered to Dante, coughing on the ground behind me. He was trying to rise on his hands and knees.

"Dante, honey, babe. You g-gotta stay down . . . s-stay d-down."

I was bawling. Frantic. My hands roaming all over his body.

He was breathing. He was alive.

We could work through anything as long as he stayed alive.

I clutched his shoulders and forced him to lie on his back. He was still coughing, choking.

Feverishly, I ran my hands over his chest.

And then paused.

There was a clear bullet hole smack in the middle of his shirt. Right over his diaphragm.

But no blood.

I pushed his shirt up and then sagged in relief. Collapsing on his chest.

Sobbing in earnest.

"You're okay," I choked. "You're okay. You're okay." I pulled back to glare at him. "But w-why the H-HELL didn't you tell me you were w-wearing a b-bullet-proof vest!"

Dante was *still* coughing.

"T-Tennyson," he managed to choke out. "Tennyson said . . . needed to wear it . . . promise . . . couldn't tell you . . ."

Crying uncontrollably, I buried my face into his neck and held him. Shaking. Shattered.

And so damn relieved we were both still alive.

People had swarmed out of the church and surrounding houses, watching all the excitement.

At some point, one of the Italian emergency responders gently lifted me off Dante.

I clutched Dante's hand to my face as they carefully pulled off his shirt and then the bullet-proof vest. Dante had a nasty red welt smack in the middle of his chest which would likely develop into a terrible bruise.

But no blood.

He had just had the breath knocked out of him.

"*Sto bene, grazie. Sto bene,*" he said over and over to the medics, waving them away.

They helped him to his feet anyway.

"Really, I'm okay," he repeated, shaking out his arms and legs. "See. Just fine."

I didn't wait for the medics to give him a green light.

The second he was upright, I buried my face into his bare shoulder, wrapping my arms around his waist, careful to avoid his bruised chest.

He sagged, clutching me tight.

"Claire. *Love.*" He breathed into my hair. "Are you okay?"

I nodded, refusing to let go.

"I can't believe this is over. We're safe." His lips brushed my hair. "We're safe."

"Why didn't you tell me?" I half-sobbed. "If I had only known you were wearing that vest—"

"Tennyson said you couldn't know. That it was important somehow."

I hiccupped, letting the thought ping around my brain. Branwell's bulkier, looser clothing had hid the vest from me. I never suspected Dante was wearing it.

"If I had known you were wearing the vest . . ."

"Would you have attacked Pierce if you knew I was okay?"

I had to admit the truth. "No. Probably not. I would have been more cautious. I would have held back."

"That hesitation would have made all the difference. And not for the better. Pierce could have easily shot you too."

So close. I had been so close to losing him. Again.

But we were still here. Warm. Alive. The sheer joy of holding his breathing body.

"You kids hurt?" the Colonel's voice asked from behind me. Concerned.

I lifted my face enough to turn and look at him.

His face was simply genuine worry.

"Uhm, hello?! I am *not* okay." Pierce groaned from the ground where he was handcuffed while being treated by a medic. "I'm the one Claire decided to beat up."

"Self-defense if I ever saw it." The Colonel snorted, glancing back at Pierce. "Not to mention attempted murder of D'Angelo here. With Claire's phone as evidence and a courtroom full of witnesses, I have a feeling you are about to become well-acquainted with the Italian judiciary system, Mr. Whitman."

I held Dante as the medics loaded Pierce onto a stretcher, him grumbling the whole time. I rolled my eyes. He had always been a whiner. Though Pierce did have the beginnings of what promised to be a spectacular black eye.

From there, the *carabinieri* demanded Dante and I answer questions. Dante kept an arm around me as he chatted with them in crisp Italian. The Colonel remained at my side the entire time. Supportive.

"What a day this has been." The Colonel turned to me as the police finished their questions. "I am so sorry for this mess, darlin'. I should have said something sooner. I'm sure you're frazzled today, but would you have a few minutes tomorrow to chat? I have questions for you. And I'm betting you have questions for me." He shot a glance at Dante with his arm around me. "I would be honored if you brought Mr. D'Angelo with you."

"Thanks, Colonel." I leaned forward from Dante's arm and gave the Colonel a soft kiss on the cheek. "I would like that. It's a date."

The Colonel smiled, patted my shoulder and walked over to Salvatore, who was waiting for him.

My adrenaline had finally eased somewhat. At least I was no longer shaking.

I glanced up at Dante. He smiled at me, eyes warm.

It was the only warning I got.

A second later, he had whirled me around and pressed my back into the stone wall of the church.

And then he kissed me, lips fevered and branding. Not caring that the piazza was still full of people.

Da-yum but the man could kiss.

"You are never—" *Kiss.* "—ever—" *Kiss.* "—to scare me like that again," he growled.

I took his head in my hands. "Well, you are n-never allowed to *die* on me again. You hear that?"

"I'll probably need a lot of encouragement." Complete deadpan.

"Anything it takes." *Kiss. Kiss.*

"Really? That sounds all sorts of promising." His voice pure honey.

I laugh-choked, pushing at his shoulder. "I'm just so g-glad you're okay . . ."

"I am *so* much better than just okay, *cara mia*."

"Shut up. Too much talking."

I lost myself in the moment. In him. In the knowledge that this wasn't an ending, but a beginning.

A new path.

Somewhere we had never traveled.

A while later, he suddenly chuckled. Pulled back.

"Where did you learn to fight like that?" Humor glinted in those plaid eyes. "It was awesome."

I laughed, tucking my face against his warm skin.

He jostled my shoulder.

"C'mon. Tell me."

I pulled back.

"Cerise, my nanny." I smiled up at him. Bright. Carefree. "Remember? She was big on life skills."

40

CLAIRE

S o that's how it all played out, Colonel." I sat back.
Dante and I were in the Colonel's . . . drawing room, I supposed,
for lack of a better description. The room was too grand to be anything
else. High, vaulted ceiling with scampering putti chasing nymphs painted
in panels. (Baroque. Restored. Lovely.)

I had just finished explaining to him about Ethan and Caro. Dante
had already covered the 'talents' of his family.

At San Savino, the Colonel had experienced the regression with us
as my Uncle Richard. I was still shaking my head over it. I was also pretty
sure the Colonel had been Mary, Caro's former nanny and chaperone.
My soul recognized that sense of *rightness*.

Dante and I had talked it over the night before. Pierce had hiccupping shadows because there had been lives—like the one with

Blackford—where Dante had a complicated love/hate relationship with Pierce's soul. The same with the Colonel. Because the Colonel had been close with me in past lives (so it seemed), there were some lives where Dante had known and cared for him, as well.

For his part, the Colonel had found the entire experience fascinating.

He had already offered to hire Dante and Branwell too, excited to have access to their unique abilities.

Pierce had confessed everything, his face splashed across news outlets world-wide. Someone even leaked the video footage I shot. (Whoops.) His father had flown down from London, appalled and horrified and deeply apologetic.

Not that any of that would keep Pierce out of prison. Attempted homicide is prosecuted just as heavily in Italy as it is in the States.

Before we broke up, Pierce had planted some malware on my phone, allowing him to track me and send nasty texts with ease. He said he just wanted me back, but it was more than that . . . he wanted me cowed and afraid. A sick sort of game.

I cuddled closer to Dante on the sofa, resting my head on his shoulder. I couldn't get close enough to him.

"I want to know how *you* knew about Pierce, Colonel," I said.

It was the old man's turn to look apprehensive.

"I have been concerned about you for some time. Your mother mentioned you were getting terrible texts. I wanted to help, so I hired Salvatore to look into it—"

"B-but why? Why would you want to help a virtual stranger?"

He fixed me with those blue eyes of his.

"You are so much like your grandmother, you know—"

"Yes. I believe we've covered that in past conversations."

"But you"—he took in a deep breath of air—"you also bear a startling resemblance to my *own* mother."

I blinked. Turned to look at Dante.

Yep. He looked just as surprised.

"Adelaide and I fell madly in love," the Colonel continued. "I would have done anything for her. But you have to understand. It was a different era. I was heir to an enormous estate and had painful responsibilities to my family. I couldn't commit to Adelaide at that time. Not like she wanted. We broke off and next I heard, she was married to your grandfather. It wasn't until much, much later that I did the math and realized that Tom's birth was—shall we say?—suspicious."

An icy chill traced my spine. I stared into his eyes.

Eyes that were the *exact* same color as my own.

I covered my mouth with a shaking hand, vision suddenly blurry.

"Are you saying what I think you're saying, Colonel?"

"I am an old man, Claire." He spread his hands wide. "I thought I had no children or grandchildren. No one to pass things on to. I wanted to be sure, you see. So, forgive me. I had housekeeping at the hotel take some hair from your brush. They also took a tube of lipstick—"

"For a DNA sampling?"

He nodded. "I feared you suspected something. But I wanted to be sure. I actually confronted Adelaide about it when you were a teenager—"

"When we were in Florence?"

"Yes. I arranged for both of you to visit—"

"But Grammy always said it was a legacy from a distant cousin . . ."

He fixed me with his blue eyes. Shrugged. "Adelaide and I met. Chatted. I asked to know the truth about your father's parentage. She refused to confirm or deny. She felt your grandfather was Tom's father in every way that mattered. She made me promise to drop it. So I did, for years. But after Adelaide's death . . . well, I wanted to know you so badly . . ."

"You staged this whole audition thing just to meet me?"

"Yes. I was going to tell you that night at dinner, but you seemed so concerned over the portrait of me with Adelaide. Anyway, now you know."

I gasped, trying to keep my crying polite.

I don't know why it meant so much to me. But it did.

I had a . . . grandfather. A living one. Someone tied to Grammy.

It was almost like getting her back.

It took only ten seconds for my crying to go from polite to ugly.

I pushed off the couch and let the Colonel wrap me in his arms.

"I would like to keep you in my life, darlin'. I never got a chance to know my son. He was gone before I even realized he existed. But I would definitely like to get to know my granddaughter. Will you accept a lonely old man as a friend?" The Colonel's eyes were suspiciously bright.

"Y-yes," I hiccupped. "B-but only if I can call you Gramps."

He pulled me to him. Fierce.

"Ah, there's my girl." He tucked me close, smelling of aftershave and peppermint. I lapped up every second of it.

I pulled away from him only after leaving an enormous wet spot on his shoulder.

"Wow." I wiped my thumbs under my eyes. "I've cried more in the last few days . . ."

Dante stood up and hugged me, obviously not wanting to be left out of the loop.

"Would you be willing to stand one more surprise?" the Colonel asked.

I smiled and nodded.

He led us through to the formal dining room. A white sheet spread out on the table.

A familiar drawing on top of it.

"Oh!" I clutched Dante's arm, torn between laughing in glee or staring in astonishment. "You have it. I mean, of course, you have it. But . . ."

"It's beautiful," Dante said.

I stared down at the drawing. A little smaller than Caro's copy.

This one was on paper. Done in a mixture of silverpoint and chalk. Detailed. Shaded. One corner very slightly charred.

Caro had made an excellent copy. But this . . . this breathed the master's hand.

"May I?" Dante gestured toward it.

"Please."

Gently, Dante touched just the very edge of the paper. Eyes glazing with concentration.

"What an amazing talent," the Colonel whispered at my side.

A second later, Dante stood upright. Turned with a smile.

"I've always said Michelangelo was as talented as he was ugly."

I laughed as the Colonel clapped his hands in delight.

"I think this calls for a celebration!"

It did indeed.

EPILOGUE

CLAIRE

I'm still trying to understand how something—which began so empty—ended so full.

Sometimes, you just have to accept the happiness that comes your way.

I arrived in Florence so alone it hurt. A vast well of . . . nothing.

But in the end, I acquired not only a grandfather, but the other half of my heart and his family menagerie.

I had learned one more truth from Grammy:

A soulmate will load your fear on his *own* back and hold your hand through the dark, leading you into the light.

Only those who truly love you have the power to heal you.

The sun was out, cheery and sunnily Italian, threading through the vines overhead as we ate lunch on the rooftop terrace of the D'Angelo palazzo.

We were eating Mexican food—because, hey, Taco Tuesday—and, as Judith eloquently put it, a true American can only go so long without chips and salsa. #Truth.

The Colonel—Gramps—flirted shamelessly with Nonna. Turns out he knew a little Italian himself. Though Dante said it was more sail-or-raunchy than polite.

Given how much Nonna laughed, I don't think she minded.

I was living with Gramps now in his villa. Yes, I was cataloging his enormous art collection along with Dante and Branwell.

But my job was secondary to my role as the Colonel's granddaughter. We laughed, drank bourbon together and cheated shamelessly at poker.

It's a gift . . . when Fate brings two lonely people together.

But, then, my life was full of gifts.

Earlier in the week, I had asked Dante and Gramps to take a pilgrim-age with me to the Palazzo Vecchio in downtown Florence.

I handed my camera to a passing tourist who kindly snapped our picture.

The three of us together. Me in the middle with Dante and Gramps leaning in from each side. All grinning in front of Michelangelo's *David*. Ethan in his top-hatted glory resting against the statue base behind us. A faint smile on his lips.

Dante had the photo framed the next day. It now sat on my night-stand. Next to the picture of me and Grammy in the same place all those years ago.

Today, I relaxed at the lunch table, downing delicious carnitas swim-ming in fresh salsa and avocado. I probably would have fallen sooner for Dante had he wooed me with his amazing culinary skills.

Chiara talked about her latest dating fiasco. (Alessio. Hot. Soccer player.) Judith mentioned Sister Floozy had finally healed enough to fly away. I pinched my lips shut whenever Branwell held his hand for silence. I broke off tiny bits of bread for Boney as he scampered up and down the table. I worried with everyone over Tennyson, still living alone out-side Volterra.

As lunch wound down, I slipped out of my chair to stare over the rooftops of Florence toward the Duomo. Light caught the gleam of tourists' cameras atop Brunelleschi's lantern dome.

"Mmmm, I was wondering where my gorgeous woman had gone off to." Dante slipped his arms around me, pulling me back against his chest. He nuzzled my neck.

I sank into him. Reaching back to run my fingers through his hair.

"I adore you, you know," he whispered into my ear.

Every time I thought about how close to death we had been . . . I would never take a second of my life with this man for granted.

So what was I waiting for?

I turned and wrapped my arms around his neck, standing on tip-toe so I could press my nose against his.

"This is probably way too soon," I began. "And we haven't known each other as Dante and Claire for too long . . . but, I just wanted to say . . ."

"Yes?"

I sucked my bottom lip between my teeth.

"Claire?"

"I love you, Dante," I breathed. "I love you and Ethan and Edward and all the other men you have been to me."

"Darling." He crushed me to him. "I know how you avoid that four letter L-word."

"I know it's too soon, but—"

"I love you, too, *carissima mia. Con tutto il mio cuore*," he murmured against my lips. "I love you with all my heart. To the edge of doom."

"And beyond." I kissed him.

"Gladly."

AUTHOR'S NOTE

As usual, when writing a story set in the past, I have incorporated select aspects of history and then blatantly made up others. Though, be warned, there are (minor) spoilers in here.

First of all, let me express my appreciation for the entire country of Italy—Tuscany in particular and Florence most specifically. Outside of my current home state, I've lived more of my life in Florence than anywhere else in the world. Every time I visit, it feels like coming home. *Firenze, carissima mia, ti voglio un saccone di bene!*

Because of my deep love of all things Tuscan, pretty much every place I discuss and describe in this novel actually exists. The only things I made up are the Colonel's residences and the D'Angelo family palazzo.

Everything else is a real place where you can visit and/or stay:

The Duomo and its exterior baptistry, Santa Croce, the Mercato Nuovo with its bronze *porcellino*, Chiesa di Santa Margherita (Dante Alighieri's ancient church), Piazza della Signoria, Ponte Vecchio, Ponte di

Santa Trinità with its enormous statues, San Miniato al Monte, Piazzale Michelangelo, the Certosa, the abbey church of San Savino in Cascina . . . all of them are decidedly real and lovely places to tour.

This also includes Claire's hotel, Palazzo Alfieri. (Yes, it's actually a high-end luxury hotel in the same building where Vittorio Alfieri and Louise, Countess of Albany lived. It also housed the British Consulate until 2011.) Even the incredible gelateria—Festival del Gelato—where Dante and Claire have some gelato is a genuine place.

As described, Michelangelo Buonarotti was hired to create a monumental fresco of the *Battle of Cascina* in the *Sala delle Cinquecento* in the Palazzo Vecchio. He completed an enormous cartoon of the work (said be around 15 feet high by 25 feet long), which hung in place in the Hall of Five Hundred for several years. The work inspired an entire generation of artists and was copied endlessly, including the most famous by Bastiano da Sangallo (also called Aristotle Sangallo). Sangallo's drawing is currently owned by the Earl of Leicester and on display at Holkham Hall in the U. K. (when not on loan to other museums).

From there, no one is entirely sure what happened to Michelangelo's cartoon. Vasari insists it was destroyed by a jealous rival. Others assert it moved around Florence for a couple of years, losing bits and pieces to souvenir takers, eventually disappearing altogether. There is no record that Michelangelo ever created a *modello* of the work.

Louise, Countess of Albany, was married to Bonnie Prince Charlie (nearly forty years her senior) and lived with her lover, Vittorio Alfieri for most of her adult life. I am indebted to Christopher Hibbert's work, *Florence—The Biography of a City*, for information about Florence during the early nineteenth century. According to Hibbert, Louise did indeed conduct salons without any furniture and served hard *matonelle* ice cream.

As for the Scottish Pretenders, as devout Catholics, they had a long history of involvement in Italy. Prince Charlie's only child, Charlotte, lived the last few years of her life in Florence and Rome tending to her father. Charlotte had three illegitimate children of her own by a French Catholic archbishop (scandalous in the extreme). She left her children with her mother in France to tend to her father in Italy. Charlotte died in Rome in 1789 at just thirty-six years old.

All of the information on medieval *condotierri*, John Hawkwood and the Battle of Cascina is accurate to the best of my knowledge. Hawkwood is a fascinating historical figure, and he does have a large monument in his honor in the Duomo, painted by Paolo Uccello—a propaganda piece intended to lure other prominent mercenaries of the era.

I have created an extensive pinboard on Pinterest with images of everything I talk about in the book. So if you want a visual of anything, pop over there and explore. Just search for NicholeVan.

Other notes, PH lipstick—exactly as Claire describes it—is a real thing. I owe Lyndsie Campbell a huge thank you for gifting some to me.

I have also included a couple of recipes for several of the Italian dishes I describe, including Tuscan lemon-herb chicken and *schiacciata*. So read on.

As with all books, this one couldn't have been written without help and support from those around me. I know I am going to leave someone out with all these thanks. So to that person, know that I totally love you and am so deeply grateful for your help!

To my beta readers—you know who you are—thank you for your helpful ideas and support. And, again, an extra large thank you to Annette Evans and Norma Melzer for their fantastic copy editing skills and insights.

A huge thank you goes to Rebecca Spencer, Lois Brown, Jennifer Jenkins and Amy Beatty for their helpful plot suggestions, revision notes and willingness to let me cry on their shoulders.

And, as usual, this work would not have reached its fruition without the excellent eye of Erin Rodabough. You have a touch of genius, my friend.

Thanks to Andrew, Austenne and Kian for your patience and willingness to eat a ridiculous amount of Italian food while I wrote this book. I'd write about *schiacciata,* and then I'd have to go make some.

And finally, no words can express my love and appreciation for Dave. Thanks for listening to me, no matter how scattered, exasperated or frustrated I am. I also appreciate that you are always up for kissing research and late-night ice cream runs. None of this would be possible without you.

READING GROUP QUESTIONS

Fair warning—these reading group questions contain spoilers.

1. This book had two dissimilar prologues. The prologue that ended up staying and then another one written from Claire's POV. (Flip a page or two to read Claire's version.) Why did the author chose to use the prologue that she did? Do you feel it was the right decision? Which prologue do you prefer and why?

2. Do you agree with Grammy's definition of courage—that it's not a lack of fear, but rather shouldering your fear and walking into the dark anyway? Why or why not?

3. Do you believe in the concept of soulmates? That there is a most-right person out there for you? Why or why not?

4. One of the challenges of this book was world-building Italy for the reader. What aspects of the world-building did you enjoy? Which did you feel went too far or not far enough?

5. Claire desperately wants a relationship with Dante, but she is too afraid and traumatized by past relationships to be able to trust him. Have you ever experienced anything like this in your own life? Not necessarily with love, per se, but something you wanted yet were afraid of at the same time?

6. How does the storyline from 1814 fit into the narrative of the present? How are Claire and Dante similar to Ethan and Caro, and how are they different and why? Did the resolution of Ethan and Caro's story catch you off-guard or did you expect it?

7. Did Pierce's appearance at the end surprise you? Or did you figure out Blackford's reincarnation and the Colonel's presence in the storyline earlier? Did you like the resolution of the book?

8. Several ideas and poems run through the book; 'somewhere i have never travelled' by e.e. cummings and 'Let me not to the marriage of true minds' by William Shakespeare were the most prominent. Why do you feel the author chose these two poems specifically? What similarities do you see between the poems? They are listed below for you to read and discuss.

somewhere i have never travelled,gladly beyond
any experience,your eyes have their silence:
in your most frail gesture are things which enclose me,
or which i cannot touch because they are too near

your slightest look easily will unclose me
though i have closed myself as fingers,
you open always petal by petal myself as Spring opens
(touching skilfully,mysteriously)her first rose

or if your wish be to close me, i and
my life will shut very beautifully ,suddenly,
as when the heart of this flower imagines
the snow carefully everywhere descending;

nothing which we are to perceive in this world equals
the power of your intense fragility:whose texture
compels me with the color of its countries,
rendering death and forever with each breathing

(i do not know what it is about you that closes
and opens;only something in me understands
the voice of your eyes is deeper than all roses)
nobody,not even the rain,has such small hands

—*e. e. cummings*

Let me not to the marriage of true minds
Admit impediments. Love is not love
Which alters when it alteration finds,
Or bends with the remover to remove:
O no; it is an ever-fixed mark,
That looks on tempests, and is never shaken;
It is the star to every wandering bark,
Whose worth's unknown, although his height be taken.
Love's not Time's fool, though rosy lips and cheeks
Within his bending sickle's compass come;
Love alters not with his brief hours and weeks,
But bears it out even to the edge of doom.
    If this be error and upon me proved,
    I never writ, nor no man ever loved.

—*William Shakespeare*

ALTERNATE PROLOGUE: CLAIRE'S POV

S ometimes when writing a book, I end up creating multiple versions of some sections. With *Gladly Beyond*, I went back and forth with the prologue. Should it be from Claire's point of view with a more chatty style? Or did I want a more somber, omniscient tone? After a lot of feedback from reviewers, I opted to keep the more serious prologue as the official one. But here is the chattier version, if you'd like to see Claire's take on the D'Angelo family curse.

I t sounds like the beginning of a lame joke:
      What do a gypsy curse, a man in tight breeches, a lost Michelangelo masterpiece and death have in common?

The answer?

Apparently . . . me.

It all began with a curse.

I know, I know—cursed by gypsies!—it's like every bad historical romance ever written.

But, turns out, there's truth in the cliché.

And, in the gypsies' defense, everyone considered it a 'gift.'

Right up to the point they realized it wasn't.

The gift/curse began with one man—Giovanni D'Angelo.

A medieval Italian nobleman who, after a series of poor business decisions, found himself near bankruptcy. Giovanni faced mounds of debt, five unmarried daughters and one angry wife telling him to *fix this now*.

So he did what any god-fearing Renaissance man would do—he sold his soul to an old gypsy woman.

Okay, so no one knows if Giovanni *literally* sold his soul. But he did visit the camp of the *zingari*—the gypsies—and came away with the gift of Sight. The ability to see, hear and feel the past and the future.

Cool, right?

Eh, not really.

Don't get me wrong. Initially, it was awesome.

With his new talents, Giovanni saved his family, had a son, out-maneuvered his opponents, crushed his rivals. I'm sure it was all stiletto-daggers and velvet-doublets and paid-assassin magnificence.

But the 'gift' grew in strength year by year.

Think about it. If you saw, heard and felt everything that *had* happened and *would* happen in a specific place . . .

It would drive you mad.

They say the voices destroyed Giovanni in the end.

Not the sights or the feelings.

Nope.

It was the never-ending noise.

Giovanni launched himself off the cathedral bell tower at the age of forty-one. Raving mad.

Twenty-five years later, his son was found swinging from the southern city gate, foam and blood dripping from his mouth.

A generation after that, his grandson strapped himself to the front of a newly-invented cannon and lit the fuse.

At which point, the D'Angelo women realized three things:

One, this 'gift' was seriously a curse.

Two, the curse was hereditary, passing on to each first-born son.

And, three—like women have been doing since the dawn of time—they needed to clean up the mess their men had made.

Right.

They didn't have much luck.

Priest blessings and exorcisms proved futile. The *zingari* themselves just shrugged and said the original knowledge was lost to history.

For their part, the D'Angelo men did what men have always done: drowned their woes in wine and war, renamed themselves the Damned Earls—complete with a stylish coat-of-arms—and earned buckets of money before going completely insane.

This dysfunctional dance continued for seven hundred years.

Until a first-born D'Angelo heir said *enough*.

He refused to have children. It was that simple. The curse would die with him.

But then he fell in love. And because he loved, he married.

He and his wife didn't intend to get pregnant. But—spoiler alert—they did.

Shattering everything.

Because nine months later, they became the parents of not one. Not two. But three tiny boys.

My name is Claire Raythorn.

No, I'm not a D'Angelo, though I ended up entangled in their family . . . *issues*.

My own story starts before that—

With me. Utterly alone. Destitute.

Haunted and hunted. Literally.

Desperately determined to put my life back together . . .

RECIPES

SCHIACCIATA—TUSCAN FLAT BREAD

This recipe will make 2-3 cookie sheets of *schiacciata* (skee-ah-CHA-ta). You can halve it if you would like less. But it's so yummy, why would you want to? The dough will keep in the fridge for up 5 days, so make a full recipe and have some now *and* later.

1 c. Warm water
1 t. Honey
2 t. Yeast

2 c. Warm water
1 T. Salt or garlic salt (I opt for the non-traditional garlic salt.)
4 T. Extra-virgin olive oil
6-8 c. White bread flour
Additional olive oil and salt for baking

Proof the yeast in the cup of warm water and honey. Mix with the rest of the ingredients, adding enough flour to make a nice bread dough (just slightly tacky). Knead for five minutes (preferably in a mixer with a dough hook, though you can obvious do this by hand). Let sit for five minutes. Knead for another five minutes until you have a smooth dough.

At this point, you can proof the dough until it doubles in size. Or you can put it in the fridge overnight and let it slow proof. In either case, it will take longer than normal to rise, given the low amount of yeast in this recipe.

Once the dough has doubled in size, punch it down and divide it into 2 or 3 equal size balls. Coat a cookie sheet with 1-2 T. olive oil. Roll each ball out into a thin layer about 1/4" thick (if you can). This can be frustrating, because the dough will be super elastic and will resist being rolled out. I find it best to roll it out on a lightly floured surface and let the dough sit stretched-out for several minutes before transferring it to a cookie sheet for baking. Drizzle the top with another 1-2 T. olive oil.

Let the dough rise until a little puffy. Taking all 10 fingers, press firmly into the top of the dough, pushing all the way down to the pan. Make finger-sized holes every inch or two over the surface. Sprinkle the top with a light dusting of salt or garlic salt (this is optional and go light on it).

Bake @ 400 degrees (preferably convection bake, if you have it) for 12-15 minutes or until golden brown.

Buon appetito!

LEMON-HERB CHICKEN

This chicken recipe is one of my favorites, and something I've eaten more times than I can count in the home of Italians. You can actually find cellophane bundles in the produce section of Tuscany grocery stores that have all the ingredients pre-packaged together (sans chicken, of course.) This is a flexible recipe and can be made with chicken breasts, thighs, quarters, etc. There's no right or wrong here.

1 whole chicken, washed and patted dry

Extra-virgin olive oil

3-4 cloves fresh garlic, peeled and minced

1 lemon, zested and juiced

   (you can also substitute an orange, if you'd like, or even do both)

10-12 leafs fresh sage (or around 1 T. dried), chopped

3-4 sprigs fresh rosemary (or around 1 T. dried), chopped

Mix the minced garlic, lemon zest (but NOT the juice), sage and rosemary together. Add enough olive oil to create a nice paste. Slather the paste all over and even inside the whole chicken. Let marinate overnight or at least for several hours.

Place the chicken on a backing rack in a pan and roast, uncovered, @ 350 degrees for 1-2 hours until a thermometer in the thigh registers 165 degrees. If the chicken gets too brown on top while cooking, cover with tinfoil.

Once done, remove the chicken from the oven and pour the saved lemon juice over the entire chicken. Carve and serve, reserving the lemony pan drippings for drizzling over the chicken.

OTHER BOOKS BY NICHOLE VAN

THE BROTHER'S MALEDETTI

Gladly Beyond (Dante and Claire)
Branwell D'Angelo's (as yet unnamed) story coming in Fall 2016

THE HOUSE OF OAK SERIes

Intertwine
Divine
Clandestine
Refine
An Invisible Heiress (a novella included
in the *Spring in Hyde Park* anthology)

If you haven't yet read *Intertwine*, book one in the House of Oak series, turn the page to read the prologue.

Intertwine
HOUSE OF OAK, BOOK 1

PROLOGUE

The obsession began on June 12, 2008 around 11:23 a.m.

Though secretly Emme Wilde considered it more of a 'spiritual connection' than an actual full-blown neurosis.

Of course, her brother, Marc, her mother and a series of therapists all begged to disagree.

Thankfully her best friend, Jasmine, regularly validated the connection and considered herself to be Emme's guide through this divinely mystical union of predestined souls (her words, not Emme's). Marc asserted that Jasmine was not so much a guide as an incense-addled enabler (again, his words, not Emme's). Emme was just grateful that anyone considered the whole affair normal—even if it was only Jasmine's loose sense of 'normal.'

Jasmine always insisted Emme come with her to estate sales, and this one outside Portland, Oregon proved no exception. Though Jasmine contended *this* particular estate sale would be significant for Emme, rambling on about circles colliding in the vast cosmic ocean creating necessary links between lives—blah, blah. All typical Jasmine-speak.

Emme brushed it off, assuming that Jasmine really just wanted someone to organize the trip: plan the best route to avoid traffic, find a quirky restaurant for lunch, entertain her on the long drive from Seattle.

At the estate sale, Emme roamed through the stifling tents, touching the cool wood of old furniture, the air heavy with that mix of dust, moth balls and disuse that marks aged things. Jasmine predictably disappeared into a corner piled with antique quilts, hunting yet again for that elusive log cabin design with black centers instead of the traditional red.

But Emme drifted deeper, something pulling her farther and farther into the debris of lives past and spent. To the trace of human passing, like fingerprints left in the paint of a pioneer cupboard door. Stark and clear.

Usually Emme would have stopped to listen to the stories around her, the history grad student in her analyzing each detail. Yet that day she didn't. She just wandered, looking for something. Something specific.

If only she could remember what.

Skirting around a low settee in a back corner, Emme first saw the antique trunk. A typical mid-nineteenth century traveling chest, solid with mellow aged wood. It did not call attention to itself. But it stood apart somehow, almost as if the air were a little lighter around it.

She first opened the lid out of curiosity, expecting the trunk to be empty. Instead, she found it full. Carefully shifting old books and papers, Emme found nothing of real interest.

Until she reached the bottom right corner.

There she found a small object tucked inside a brittle cotton handkerchief. Gently unwrapping the aged fabric, she pulled out an oval locket. Untouched and expectant.

Filigree covered the front, its gilt frame still bright and untarnished, as if nearly new.

Emme turned the locket over, feeling its heft in her hand, the metal cool against her palm. It hummed with an almost electric pulse. How long had the locket lain wrapped in the trunk?

Transparent crystal partially covered the back. Under the crystal, two locks of hair were woven into an intricate pattern—one bright and fair, the other a dark chocolate brown. Gilded on top of the crystal, two initials nestled together into a stylized gold symbol.

She touched the initials, trying to make them out. One was clearly an F. But she puzzled over the other for a moment, tracing the design with her eyes. And then she saw it. Emme sucked in a sharp breath. An E. The other initial was an E.

She opened the locket, hearing the small pop of the catch.

A gasp.

Her hands tingled.

A sizzling shock started at the back of her neck and then spread.

Him.

There are moments in life that sear into the soul. Brief glimpses of some larger force. When so many threads collapse into one. Coalesce into a single truth.

Seeing *him* for the first time was one of those moments.

He gazed intently out from within the right side of the locket: blond, blue-eyed, chiseled with a mouth hinting at shared laughter. Emme's historian mind quickly dated his blue-green, high collared jacket and crisp, white shirt and neckcloth to the mid-Regency era, probably around 1812, give or take a year.

Emme continued to look at the man—well, stare actually. His golden hair finger-combed and deliciously disheveled. Broad shoulders angled slightly toward the viewer. Perhaps his face a shade too long and his nose a little too sharp for true beauty. But striking. Handsome even.

Looking expectant, as if he had been waiting for her.

Emme would forever remember the jolt of it.

Surprise and recognition.

She knew him. Had known him.

Somehow, somewhere, in some place.

He felt agonizingly familiar. That phantom part of her she had never realized was lost.

The sensation wasn't quite deja vu.

More like memory.

Like suddenly finding that vital thing you didn't realize had been misplaced. Like coming up, gasping for air, after nearly drowning and seeing the world bright and sparkling and new.

She stood mesmerized by *him* until Jasmine joined her.

"Oooh, you found him." The hushed respect in her voice was remarkable. This was Jasmine after all.

Emme nodded mutely.

"Your circles are so closely intertwined. Amazing."

Jasmine turned the locket in Emme's hand.

"What does this inscription say?" she asked.

Emme hadn't noticed the engraved words on the inside left of the locket case. But now she read them. Her sudden sharp inhalation seared, painfully clenching.

Oh. *Oh!*

The words reverberated through her soul, shattering and profound.

Emme didn't recall much more of that day—Jasmine purchasing the locket or even the little restaurant where they ate lunch. Instead, she only remembered the endless blur of passing trees on the drive home, the inscription echoing over and over:

To E
throughout all time
heart of my soul
your F

Visit www.NicholeVan.com to buy your copy of
Intertwine today and continue the story.

ABOUT THE AUTHOR

Nichole Van is an artist who feels life is too short to only have one obsession. In former lives, she has been a contemporary dancer, pianist, art historian, choreographer, culinary artist and English professor. Though Nichole still prefers the label 'adaptable' more than 'ADD.'

Most notably, however, Nichole is an acclaimed photographer, winning over thirty international accolades for her work, including Portrait of the Year from WPPI in 2007. (Think Oscars for wedding and portrait photographers.) Her unique photography style has been featured in many magazines, including *Rangefinder* and *Professional Photographer*. She is also the creative mind behind the popular websites Flourish Emporium and {life as art} Workshops, which provide resources for photographers.

All that said, Nichole has always been a writer at heart. With an MA in English, she taught technical writing at Brigham Young University for ten years and has written more technical manuals than she can quickly count. She decided in late 2013 to start writing fiction and has loved exploring a new creative process.

Nichole currently lives in Utah with her husband and three crazy children. Though continuing in her career as a photographer, Nichole is also now writing historical romance on the side. She is known as NicholeVan all over the web: Facebook, Instagram, Pinterest, etc. Visit her author website at www.NicholeVan.com to sign up for her newsletter to be notified of new releases. You can see her photographic work at http://photography.nicholeV.com and http://www.nicholeV.com.

If you enjoyed this book, please leave a short review on Amazon. com. Wonderful reviews are the elixir of life for authors. Even better than dark chocolate.

11279542R00224

Printed in Great Britain
by Amazon